THE OTHER SAPPHO

Other books by the author

Look Under the Hawthorn
The Marble Threshing Floor: A Collection of Greek Folk Songs

THE OTHER SAPPHO

A
NOVEL
BY
ELLEN
FRYE

Firebrand
Books
Ithaca, New York

Grateful acknowledgment is made for permission to reprint from the following:

Sappho, A New Translation, translated/edited by Mary Barnard, fragments 24, 55, 60 and 61. Translation copyright © 1958, 1984 by Mary Barnard. Reprinted by permission of the University of California Press.

Sappho and the Greek Lyric Poets, translated by Willis Barnstone, fragments 120, 135 and 144. Translation copyright © 1962, 1967, 1988 by Willis Barnstone. Reprinted by permission of Schocken Books, published by Pantheon Books, a Division of Random House, Inc.

Book and cover design by Betsy Bayley
Illustrations by Ginger Brown
Typesetting by Bets Ltd.

Printed in the United States by McNaughton & Gunn

Library of Congress Cataloging-in-Publication Data

Frye, Ellen, 1940-
    The other Sappho : a novel / by Ellen Frye.
        p.   cm.
    ISBN 0-932379-69-9. — ISBN 0-932379-68-0 (pbk.)
    1. Greece—History—To 146 B.C.—Fiction.   2. Sappho, in fiction, drama, poetry, etc.   I. Title.
    PS3556.R9084   1989
    813'.54—dc20
                                                                                89-23607
                                                                                CIP

For unsung oral poets of Greece, ancient and modern

Acknowledgments

I am grateful to Evfrosyni Tsakami and others who opened my ears to Greek oral poetry during my travels in the 1960s.

I want to thank Claudia Lamperti, Cora Books, Dinny Forbes, Jill Morris, and Sandra Miller for reading and commenting on different stages of the manuscript. Thanks also to Ginger Brown for her artwork, Nancy K. Bereano for her editing, and Marcie Pleasants and Louise Brill for their proofreading. I am especially grateful to members of the Fly-by-Night Writers—Amanda Powell, Athena Andreadis, Patricia Schwartz, and Susan Stinson—for their ongoing warm support and careful criticism.

Prolegomena

This story is history. Not the history found in scholarly books, all carefully annotated, but the other kind, the kind that comes out of people's mouths from memories that have been passed from generation to generation.

I uncovered the story on the island of Lesbos, now called Mytilene, where I went for a holiday last year. I had been reading Mary Barnard's translations of Sappho, and I wanted to visit the birthplace of the tenth muse, as Plato called her. I arrived in Mytilene, not in the summer when all of Greece is resort for European and American holiday-seekers, but in the wintertime when the souvenir stalls are closed and the beaches empty.

Modern Mytilene is not a place where you can easily find the spirit of Sappho. Cars and motorbikes roar up and down the waterfront. On the narrow market street that runs behind the hotels lining the waterfront, fast-food counters are sandwiched between fish stalls and bakeries. The ancient acropolis is buried under a Genovese castle ruin, and the ancient theater, built two centuries after Sappho anyway, is surrounded by a barbed wire fence with an *Hours of Visitation* plaque on the gate. The theater seats are all piled to one side waiting for restoration money.

One morning, when I had had enough of the noise of the city, I decided to hike on a little-used dirt road over the low hills behind Mytilene to the Gulf of Yeras, called Hieras in ancient times. An almost landlocked gulf surrounded by plains of thousand-year-old olive trees, it lies about eight kilometers west of the capital city. I was enjoying the country sounds of my walk—birds singing in the silver-green olive trees and the low clatter of sheep bells in the valley below—when my ears picked out a different set of bells ahead of me. Goats, I said to myself, knowing that their bells are higher pitched than sheep bells. Sure enough, as I rounded the bend, I found myself surrounded by a dozen or more nannies, all black with yellow streaks down their faces and little tufts of beards on their chins. A woman was driving them: you don't often see women herding in Greece. She was neither young nor old, she could have been my age, she could have been twenty years older or younger.

"Good morning," I said.

"Good morning," she replied. "Where are you going?"

"Down to Yeras."

"You are not Greek."

"No, American."

"But you speak Greek."

"I learned it years ago in Athens."

I had had this conversation a hundred times already. Greeks are always astonished that any non-Greek would care to unravel the complexities of their language.

"How do you find our island?"

"It is beautiful," I said. "I came to see the land where Sappho lived." In Greek, it's pronounced *Sap-fo,* with the accent on the last syllable.

"Ah, Sappho," she said.

I love the way every Greek, educated or not, knows the name of Sappho. Many can recite lines of her poetry in ancient Greek.

"There is another Sappho, you know," she said.

This was unusual. All Greeks know about Sappho, but not so many are familiar with the ancient scholarly discourses on "the other Sappho." For readers who have not studied the history of the controversy, the story of two Sapphos arose in the third century B.C.E., three centuries after Sappho flourished, as they say, on the island of Lesbos. Apparently the Alexandrian Greeks were unable to hold in one woman the far-reaching reputation of the greatest poet of the archaic age and her openly erotic sentiments for the young women entrusted to her care for refinement of their skills in the arts. They wanted their Sappho pure.

It was perfectly acceptable for men of this later period to be intellectual and sexual mentors to young boys, but women, except for courtesans, were allowed neither education nor expression of sexuality outside the conjugal bed. So the Alexandrians invented a second Sappho, one the beautiful Sappho, as Socrates called her, and the other an object of contempt and ridicule.

The controversy had been laid to rest, I thought, after the late-nineteenth-century excavations of Hellenistic cemeteries in Egypt, excavations that brought to light thousands of papyrus fragments that had been preserved in coffins—either as reading material for the deceased's journey to the underworld, or as strips of the papier-mâché that shaped the coffins themselves. The famous Oxyrhynchus Papyri. Once the fragments had been painstakingly restored and scholarly consensus reached on whether a missing letter should be a *delta* or a *theta*, it became clear to all the world that most of Sappho's love lyrics were addressed to persons of the female gender. Scholars now agree that there was only one Sappho, and that she was a lover of women.

But my Greek goatherd was speaking.

"You should learn about the other Sappho," she was saying. "Her school was down there on the gulf, right where you are going."

After some confusion—she spoke rapidly and used many Turkish-derived words—I realized she was talking about an entirely different Sappho, a goatherd like herself who had lived in the forest at the side of the gulf in the time of the known Sappho. This other Sappho's real name had been Lykaina—wolf-woman—and she had, according to my informant, taught poetry to young women of humble birth.

"I am taking the goats up to the pasture," she said. "My house is down there. See where the green patch is? Directly across from it is an apple orchard, and a little to the left of that is a downhill path. Take it and you will find my house. My mother is there. Ask her to tell you about the other Sappho."

I went and found the old woman. She was seated on a low stone bench outside the house, spinning with one of those hand spindles I hadn't seen since I'd lived in Greece twenty-five years before. A young woman, her granddaughter I guessed, was kneeling at the side of a stream that ran by the house, beating some clothes on a flat rock. A two-year-old sat in the dirt transforming a pile of stones into a cave. The old woman could have been a hundred, her face was so creased with wrinkles. On the other hand, she might have been no more than sixty. Her eyes were bright, and she spoke clearly. She told me the story of the other Sappho.

After spending several evenings with this strange family—there were no men in the house, and none of the women wore wedding bands—I decided to ask someone from the local archeological society what they thought. I assumed they would dismiss the tale as peasant fancy. But the young woman I talked to, the curator of the Archeological Museum of Lesbos, nodded her head when I told her the story. She told me about an archeological find they had made on the island several years back. Apparently a farmer had been constructing a new pen for his sheep near the Gulf of Yeras (the old stone farm buildings with red-tiled roofs are relentlessly being replaced with concrete and tin). Digging the foundation, the man had come across an ancient cache. For fear of official delay, he hadn't told anyone about it until his building was complete. Then he had brought the coins and potsherds to the local authorities. This was a piece of luck, the curator told me, because often builders who make archeological finds prefer to sell them on the black market. The story of the other Sappho might be true, she said, because fragments of poetry had been deciphered from scraps of papyrus, and at least one of the fragments had mentioned the name *the other Sappho*.

I was very excited and asked if I might be given permission to examine the find. My ancient Greek is rudimentary, but I thought if I could at least make a hand copy of the fragments, I could get a friend at the university to help me. Alas, the curator said, the entire find had been packed away in a crate awaiting money from the government for restoration and cataloging. This had been done before her time as curator, and she had no idea where the crate was stored. There were hundreds of them in the basement of the Archeological Museum and many more at other locations scattered throughout the city.

I decided to write the story of the other Sappho without the archeological verification. It is oral history, after all, and the other Sappho was an oral poet. Her poetry existed only in front of the audience to whom she sang it. When that audience disappeared, her poetry disappeared with it.

For those of you who require scholarly corroboration, I suggest you take a good amount of fellowship money and petition the Greek government to unpack those crates in the basement of the Archeological Museum. For the rest of you, sit back with an amber glass of Greek wine, if you have any, and listen to the story of the other Sappho.

E. F.

*Let me tell you
this: someone in
some future time
will think of us.*

Sappho

LYKAINA'S GREECE · 6TH CENTURY B.C.E.

MACEDONIA

THRACE

PHRYGIA

SAMOTHRACE

HELLESPONT

TROY

AEGEAN SEA

LEMNOS

SCAMANDER RIVER

IDA MT.

ERESOS · LESBOS

MYTILENE

GULF OF HERAS

SCYROS

IONIA

SMYRNA

EUBOEA

BOEOTIA

GULF OF CORINTH

ATTICA

CHIOS

ATHENS

CORINTH

SARONIC SEA

SAMOS

ARCADIA

ARGOS

ARGOLIS

IONIAN SEA

PELOPONNESE

LACONIA

TAYGETUS MTS.

SPARTA

TAENARUS

CRETAN SEA

CRETE

Chapter 1.
The beginning

"Go to Lesbos." The old woman spat. "Sparta's no place for a poet like you. Nothing but old men chanting doggerel for overgrown boys marching off to war. Or bawdy little rhymes for when they come home."

Lykaina raised her dark eyes from the pile of lentils she was picking through and smiled. She looked past the old woman, over the square white houses that marched down the hillside into the city. The midday sun, having swept the narrow paths clear of human traffic, freckled the backs of two gray donkeys who stood patiently under a wild fig tree switching flies with their tails. Occasionally a light breeze struggled across the valley, bringing almost a whiff of salt-sea air. The old woman continued.

"It's too bad you weren't here when Megalostrata was alive. Now *she* could sing. Her voice was as golden as her hair. And her poems—love poems to make you weep! *Aio,* the beauty of it, the pain of it! And then that lecherous Alkman taking all the credit." She spat again. "He didn't fool anyone. The words fell out of his mouth like shit from a donkey's ass, his fingers were always slipping off the kithara strings. Then he'd belch whenever he forgot a line, to cover up. The old fool!"

Lykaina laughed out loud. She loved to listen to the old woman talk about the days of her youth.

"Lesbos. Now there's an island where people know how to enjoy themselves. They eat fine foods and dress in soft linens and braid gold in their hair. They walk up and down the agora singing poetry to each other. Not like these stick soldiers who wrestle and throw javelins and drink horrid black broth for reward. How's a poet to grow on that? Go to Lesbos."

The old woman leaned back on her litter and closed her eyes. Lykaina picked up the bowl of lentils, poured water over them, and set them aside. She threw the stones she'd picked out of them into the street below, where half a dozen scraggly hens fought over them as if they were grain. She moved closer to the old woman and began to rub olive oil into the wrinkled skin of her forearms.

"Well, granny, I'm sure it's a pretty island, but I've heard it lies on the other side of the sea. Why there? Why not some pretty island close by?"

One black eye opened narrowly and closed again.

"Sappho." The name slipped through the dry lips and hung delicately in the air between them. Then both eyes flashed open and drew Lykaina into their intensity. "Sappho. She is goddess of poetry herself. Her words are pure gold. Listen."

She raised herself onto one elbow and sang.

> Stars near the lovely
> moon cover their own
> bright faces
> > when she
> is roundest and lights
> earth with her silver

A cracked tune carried the words like a storm-battered ship might list into port, its hold full of treasure. Lykaina's heart pace quickened, a shiver ran up her back.

"Ah, granny, if there is poetry like that on Lesbos, it would indeed be fine to go and listen."

"Not listen, child. Learn. You are a poet just beginning. Sappho is the tenth muse. You must go to learn from her."

Lykaina bristled.

"I have been singing for many suns' turnings. My grandfather taught me all the songs of my people. Had I not sung them well, you would not have invited me here."

"Smooth the fur on your back, wolfchild. You know the songs of your people, yes. You shape them well and you weave fine melodies around them. Your grandfather taught you how to search out the words of the mountain and put them together to suit mountain ears. But you also have songs in you that your grandfather did not teach you, words that come not from the mountains but from your own heart."

A fly tried to settle on the olive-black mole on the old woman's cheek. Lykaina brushed it away thinking about the words she sometimes sang that seemed to arrive in her mouth from nowhere. The old woman always smiled encouragement, and then more new words would flood out until sometimes she lost the old song entirely. And then felt lost herself.

"Besides, she'll teach you how to write."

Lykaina stopped rubbing and stared.

"Write. What is that?"

The old woman sighed.

"Go into the house and bring me the black leather box that rests behind the hearth. I will show you what is write."

Opened, the box revealed several thick rolls the color of a discarded goat's horn. The old woman unrolled one and held its edges in either hand.

"Here." She nodded with her chin. "The words I just sang are written here."

Lykaina reached out and touched the papyrus. It was not so brittle as a goat's horn, and the inside of it was covered with scratches. Not like the scratches of a tree the goat might have rubbed, these marks marched across the scroll in regular lines. The old woman clucked her tongue.

"You've seen the statue of Lykourgos in the main square. Beneath his feet his words are carved into the stone so that whoever passes is reminded of his laws. If you can read, you do not have to wait for someone who remembers to speak them. And here is written Sappho's poem for anyone to sing. You must learn to write so that your poems can be read and sung by anyone."

Lykaina put both her hands to her head and closed her eyes. These words—*read, write*—made no more sense than the scratchings on the scroll. The old woman rerolled the papyrus and placed it back into the box.

"You will understand when you go." She handed the box to Lykaina and closed her eyes again. "You're not a helot, you know. You were Spartan-born, and you have a right to education. Had you not been born with a twisted foot, you might have grown up in the house next door."

Lykaina almost dropped the precious box.

3

"What do you mean? I'm no Spartan. I was raised in the mountains, you know that."

"By wolves."

"Yes, by wolves at first. But then I had a mother and a father. And grandparents and a brother, too."

"And who do you think your parents were before the wolves? When did you ever see a mountain mother cast out her child to be raised by wolves?"

Lykaina was silent. These words made no more sense than the words about writing.

"It's time you understood yourself, child. We Spartans are a harsh breed. When a baby is born here, there is no rejoicing until it has passed muster before a jury of elders. They poke and they prod, and if the poor babe looks too puny for their taste or doesn't cry lustily enough to suit them, it's off to a ravine in the foothills, leave it to die—not to taint our beautiful race with any form of weakness." She nodded at the misshapen toes peeking out from Lykaina's right sandal. "Clearly your foot made you fail their wretched test. And you proved them wrong by surviving."

Here was a new puzzle. It was true, she didn't look like her mountain family. But although she loved the old woman, she felt no kinship here. The Spartans she passed in the streets made her shudder—sometimes from fear, sometimes from disgust at the arrogance in their stride and their loud voices.

"If I was a Spartan at birth, I deny it now." Her voice carried sparks of anger. "I'm proud of my family, even if they are only goatherds wearing skins. Our poetry is about real life, not just marching songs and hymns praising dead heroes."

"Don't be contrary. I'm tired now. Sing me one of your real-life songs."

Lykaina went inside and brought out her aulos, a long alder tube with a carved wolf's head at one end. She placed her lips over its double-reeded mouthpiece and sent out a haunting melody that turned in on itself. She broke off playing, caught her breath, and sang.

> You mountains of Taygetus, lower yourselves a little
> so I can see milch nannies with their kids,
> so I can hear the bellwether leading the flock,
> so I can smell the cheesehut with the curds,
> so I can feel rocks under my feet.

The old woman fell asleep. Lykaina laid aside her aulos and watched her. As the sun made its way across the blue Laconian sky, she tried to imagine traveling to Lesbos to meet this Sappho. An island on the other side of the sea. How would she get there, fly like a seagull? Even if the old woman were right, even if she'd been Spartan-born, she was a helot now. About as much chance of braiding gold in her hair as throwing a javelin all the way to Mount Olympos. The shadows lengthened across the terrace, and Lykaina fell asleep. She woke with a start to find a pair of small eyes staring at her.

"You were sleeping." The child, hunkered down in front of her, hugged its knees with its arms.

"Yes, Niki, you caught me. Is your mama awake?"

Lykaina opened her arms, and the little girl crawled into them, laying her dark curls on Lykaina's breast.

"She's giving Akis his milk. She sent me out to get you. And you were sleeping. And granny was sleeping. So I watched you both."

"Well, now I'm awake. Let's let granny sleep and go see if your brother's done with his meal."

They went inside together, the child holding Lykaina's hand tightly, and found the mother and son still nursing. Lykaina caught her breath. Every day she watched this ritual, and every day it moved her—the full round breast with the baby attached, the baby fist opening and closing as it sucked, the wide black eyes rolling round to see who had come into the room.

Tall, with a proud bearing, Arete had long black hair wound around her head. The baby let the nipple fall from his mouth and reached out toward his sister. Arete set him down, and he crawled across the mosaic floor. She bent over and gave Niki two small bowls with a handful of broad beans in each.

"Here. Take him out to the courtyard and play with these."

The girl hauled her brother up onto his feet and steadied his way out the door. The women were left in the darkened room together. Lykaina reached out and touched Arete's cheek. Arete's dark eyes drew her in, and she found herself kissing the full red lips, the still-bare breasts pressing softly against her own. Arete pulled away, laughing.

"How is it that I want your kisses all the time?"

"Why does the sight of your breast make my head spin?"

Still laughing, Arete ducked her head and pulled her tunic over her breast.

"Oh, how I love living with you here in the house! How bleak my life was until my husband brought you home. I have much to be grateful to him for."

"Yes," responded Lykaina. "And now that he's done his job, why not divorce him?"

She dropped her eyes. The words had been intended as a joke, but her voice gave her away. Arete stared at her.

"Are you serious?"

Lykaina caught Arete's hand and kissed her palm. She looked Arete in the eye.

5

"I am serious. We are happy, you and I and the old woman and the children. When the war is over, what will happen to that happiness? He will destroy it."

Arete pulled her hand away and shook her head.

"But there's no reason to divorce him. His seed is good. Look at the two children, how perfect their little bodies are. Who would be better?"

Lykaina let her hands dangle at her sides.

"Why not have no husband? Why not just live as we live now, but always, whether there's a war or not."

"But when the war is over, he won't stay here anyway. He prefers to sleep in the barracks with his soldier friends. He'll only come when it is time to make another baby. When he sees I have begun to swell, he won't come at all. I'll hardly see him."

She put her arm around Lykaina's shoulder.

"You are much more to me than he is, you know that. But to divorce him—I could only do that to marry another man who would plant better seed. And I see no one else for that. Come," she said, kissing Lykaina lightly on the cheek, "let's put the lentils on to cook, and I will tell you about my wedding day."

Lips drawn, Lykaina went out into the courtyard. Niki and the baby were sitting in the corner making little piles of their beans. The old woman was still asleep. Lykaina picked up the bowl of soaking lentils and stepped back into the house.

"Well," said Arete, as she poured water from a jug into a large earthen pot, "I told you how I lived with a married woman after I finished my schooling."

Lykaina, her lips still drawn, laid kindling onto the hearth.

"Oh, come, Lykaina, don't pout! You know our traditions. We love women before we marry, then we marry and make babies, and then we love women again. Men are no more to us than the fathers of our children. When I told you this before, you were delighted."

Lykaina blew until the tinder caught the flint spark. She felt her anger melt away as Arete brushed her cheek with a fingertip. She sat back on her heels.

"All right," she sighed. "Tell me about your wedding day, then. After your mentor had taught you how to prepare yourself for baby-making."

"Well," began Arete, "my father had died in a war, my mother from the birth of my baby brother. So it was granny who chose the soldier. He had won the long run two years in a row. She said that I could have someone else if I wanted, but she thought that his seed would be good, that our children would have long limbs and strong hearts. She was right. Look how fast little Niki can run, and she has seen only five summers. And the baby walks already."

Lykaina lifted the pot and hung it over the blaze.

"So it was arranged," Arete continued, tossing a sprig of oregano into the pot. "You haven't seen a wedding here yet. I will take you when my cousin marries next summer. Well, first, I waited for his relatives to come and take me from this house. His three brothers and a cousin carried me away. It was like an abduction, except that my family knew where they were going. When we got to the wrestling floor, his sisters were waiting. They shaved my head and undressed me while my brother undressed my soldier. When we were stripped clean, they rubbed our bodies with oil till we both glistened."

"The wrestling floor?" broke in Lykaina. "You wrestled with your husband on your wedding day?"

"Of course. Everyone does. We say that a man and a woman can learn more about each other in a good wrestling match than in years of marriage. Anyway, when we were both well oiled, everyone stood back and began to shout. We stepped into the ring and touched our foreheads together. I can tell you, I was so scared, you could see my heart beating between my ribs. He was taller than I by a head and a half, and his muscles rolled under his dark skin. But I was the quicker one. I darted in and gave him the first throw. Oh, he was stronger than I was by far, but I kept slithering out of his grasp. He pinned me in the end, but not until after I had given him something to fear. My family was proud of me. His family was too, since it meant our children would be both strong and quick-witted."

Lykaina smiled in amazement. Arete was so soft and round and gentle. It was hard to imagine her wrestling naked with the soldier. And throwing him.

"The men took him off to the mess to eat with the other soldiers," Arete continued, "and his sisters took me away, praising me for my good showing. They led me into a stable. There was a donkey in a stall and a pile of straw on the floor. All the women came—from his family and mine, too. We made a fire and boiled the root of a dog orchid."

Arete blushed and giggled.

"I was shameless! I was supposed to eat only the larger root to be sure I made a boy child, but I pulled the smaller one out of the pot and ate that instead because I wanted a little girl first. My in-laws were shocked, but my own family just laughed. 'She has a mind of her own,' they said, 'you'll have to get used to it.' They gave me the orchid shoot soaked in milk so that I could enjoy my first penetration, as if I needed any help. My lady mentor had taught me all about how to enjoy myself. We drank black wine and sang praises to Aphrodite until the sun went down."

Arete leaned over to sniff the now-bubbling lentils.

"They dressed me in a man's tunic," she continued, "and left me. I waited alone in the dark. My soldier, pushed in by the men, fell sprawling on top of me. He was so nervous, he could hardly find his way out of his clothes, let alone into me. The wine he'd drunk with his comrades had made his rod limp as an earthworm. So I pleasured myself while he rid himself of the contents of his stomach. He was so shamefaced, I promised him I would tell his sisters that he was like a roaring bull."

Arete stood up and pulled Lykaina to her feet.

"Come, let's take a walk while the lentils cook. And you can tell me how it is you never married."

The two women linked arms and passed out through the courtyard. The old woman, awake now, was showing Niki how to string the broad beans on a thread. The baby sat watching.

"We are taking a short walk, granny. You'll watch the children while we're gone? Then we'll eat."

The old woman didn't lift her eyes from the child before her.

"Go. We are busy here without you."

They left the courtyard. Arete let go of Lykaina's arm and stepped ahead of her. A familiar anger flared in Lykaina's chest. Whenever they went out, Arete insisted that they play the roles of Spartan lady and helot slave. Lykaina could not see herself as a slave. She had grown up free in the mountains. She had been brought to the house as singer to entertain the old woman. Keeping her eyes to the ground was not natural. But the one time she had insisted they walk side by side as equals, Arete had been nervous and had looked anxiously at each Spartan they had passed. They had not been able to talk at all. Now Lykaina swallowed her pride and told herself it did not matter how they walked in public so long as they were equals in the house.

"Go on," Arete whispered over her shoulder. "Tell me how you never married. Don't all women marry in your village?"

"They do. They all want to become wives and mothers. It's the only passage into adulthood. Every girl knows that if she doesn't marry, she will be a child for life. She will have no place in village life. But I didn't like the idea at all. I told my father I wanted only to tend goat kids, not human kids."

Lykaina remembered the scowl that had come over her father's face each time she had declared she would never marry.

"When my brother reached his full height," she continued, "the parade of suitors began. My grandfather did not care. If I wanted to live with no man, he said, it was my life, it should be my choice. But my father and my brother saw my marrying as a way to increase our wealth. It is our tradition that the groom bring into the family something of value, something to assure honorable behavior. If he behaves dishonorably, the bride's family expels him, and he forfeits his bridegift."

They walked in silence for a few moments. Then Lykaina continued.

"My first three suitors were old men whose wives had died and who had children almost as old as I was. I told them, no, I would not be mother to another woman's children. Then they found me a young man. His family owned the cheesemaking hut. My father said a family of herders and a family of cheesemakers would make a good alliance."

She smiled to herself, remembering the whey-faced youth who had stood in front of the hut shuffling his feet.

"He came up to our summer pasture to look me over. I dressed myself in rags and danced about, playing my aulos. He laughed, but I could see that he was uneasy. I made up a song about how goats are better company than men. He left making excuses. My father and my brother were furious, but my grandfather only laughed. It was he who had taught me to play the aulos, and he said that anyone who didn't like its music was too stupid for our family."

By now they had reached the edge of the city. Arete dropped back and took Lykaina's arm again.

"What a good joke!" she said, her eyes laughing. "What happened then?"

Lykaina pressed Arete's arm to her side and continued.

"Nothing happened for a long time. I knew that my father and my brother were angry with me, but they said nothing. Then one day a stranger sat at our hearthfire. He had black hair all over his face, and his skin was almost as dark from the sun. He talked goat-talk like any herder. But then, all at once, he looked me in the eye and said, 'I hear you are a musician. Good music makes the milk flow easier,' and I knew why he was there."

"What did you do?" asked Arete breathlessly.

"It was the time of the full moon. We were sitting outside around the firepit. I had been watching a dark cloud move across the mountain. When the cloud passed over the moon, I sprang away from the fire. By the time the ground was yellow with moonlight again, I was crouched on all fours at the edge of the cliff. I howled. I hadn't howled since I was a baby with the wolves. My voice was strong and my howl filled the valley below us. It wound around both mountains and climbed, I think, to the moon herself. My brother sputtered, 'Joke, joke, it is only a joke,' but my groom dropped his cup and began running. I think he didn't stop until he was back safe with his own herd."

"Oh, Lykaina, what a wonderful tale! Did they try again? Or was that when your brother decided to sell you to my husband?"

Lykaina stopped short.

"Sell me to your husband?" She forced the words through her lips. "The soldier heard me singing in the marketplace. He invited me—"

"Oh, Lykaina," Arete said, "I thought you knew. Your brother and my husband met several times before you came. I heard them talking in the outer courtyard. Your brother bragged about how fine your poetry was, how it would be sure to please my grandmother. I remember he said it would be difficult to get you to come, but that he would manage it. The next market day you came."

"How much did the soldier pay for me?" Lykaina carved each word between her teeth. It seemed she was, after all, a slave. Not a musician brought to entertain an old woman, but a houseslave.

"I don't know what bargain they finally struck," said Arete, putting her arm around Lykaina's shoulder. "I heard my husband say, 'How much?' and their voices dropped to a whisper. I heard your brother say, 'The deal is struck.' Then he went away."

She pulled Lykaina closer.

"Please don't fret about it. We don't think of you as our slave, my grandmother and I. Anyway, you are better off here than on the mountain. Eventually you would have had to marry. Here you have my grandmother to sing to and me to love. And we both love you. Forget your brother, let him have the herds. Those are men's things in your village, just as soldiering is man's work here. Come, the lentils must be done by now. Let's go back, and we'll get granny to tell us another story of her youth."

They turned and walked back into the city, Arete stepping ahead of Lykaina as soon as they came to the first houses. They arrived at the inner courtyard in time to hear the end of a tale the old woman was telling the children.

"And that's the way it was, and that's the way it is to this good day."

Arete went quickly into the house, leaving Lykaina standing in front of the old woman's litter.

"You bought me," Lykaina said flatly.

The old woman patted Niki on the head.

"Run, get bowls for everyone, it's time to eat."

Niki jumped up and kissed the old woman loudly before disappearing into the house after her mother. The old woman raised her eyes to meet Lykaina's.

"Sit," she said sharply, "I can't twist my neck forever."

Lykaina sat crosslegged beside the litter.

"The soldier and your brother made the bargain. Your brother wanted your share of the flock if he couldn't get a bridegift for you. The soldier wanted to please me. He hopes to inherit a little orchard I own. Are you angry because you're here?"

Lykaina was silent, her face still clouded.

"Do you sing for me," continued the old woman, "because I command it, or because you have poems that need ears to hear them? Do I tell you stories because I feel sorry for a downtrodden slave, or because I want my past to become part of you? What passed between the soldier and your brother is their affair—it's what men do with each other. Let them. They didn't harm us, they helped us. Without their games, you'd still be singing to mountain goats and I'd be a lonely old woman."

Arete came out into the courtyard carrying the steaming pot. Niki trailed behind her holding four earthen bowls. No one spoke as the lentils were ladled out.

"Games, that's all it is." The old woman picked up her thread again. "Each thought he was beating the other: your brother because he knew the soldier's offer was more than any bridegift you'd have brought, the soldier because he'd sent the young lads in his garrison out to the mountains to steal the goats."

She picked up a spoonful of lentils and blew on them.

"Too hot," she muttered, letting the spoon fall back into the bowl. "Games—that's all any of them know how to play. From the time they leave their mothers, every game they play is mere practice for the biggest game of them all, the game where blood turns the black earth red, where young men die smiling, knowing that all the agony was worth the glorious end. It's all a game." She stirred her lentils and took a mouthful. "Eat and put meat on your bones," she said.

Lykaina chewed her own mouthful and thought about the old woman's words. It was true. She was better off here than on the mountain. She missed the goats and the steep mountain paths and especially her grandfather, yes. But her life here was fuller. She loved the old woman, loved to listen to her talk. And her own songs, she knew, were better here. The old woman seemed to draw out of her phrases she had never sung before.

So why was she angry? If she was a helot, she belonged to the state whether she lived on the mountain or in a Spartan's house. Spartans didn't even live that differently from helots. They all ate the same food, lived in the same rude houses. Only the dogskin hats set the helots apart, that and their perennially downcast eyes.

"Next full moon you'll see the bloodiest game of them all." The old woman interrupted her thoughts. "You've never seen our festival of the Upright Artemis, have you? In the mountains, I know, you still see Artemis as Mistress of the Animals. Even here when I was a girl we knew her as the Virgin Hunter roaming with her nymphs, hunting and dancing and playing. Just after my first blood, I went with my age-mates to a sanctuary in the foothills of your beloved Taygetus range. For three cycles of the moon, we were Artemis' she-bears, wearing only skins. We danced and raced and hunted with our bows and arrows. Every evening we sacrificed small animals to her and sang her praises. At the end of our time there, we sacrificed a black goat we had brought with us and poured its blood over her altar. I learned the meaning of my name there. Theadora—gift of the goddess."

Lykaina looked at her sharply. Theadora. She had never heard the name before. Everyone called her granny, referred to her as the old woman. Just as her grandfather in the mountains was always called the old man. Why was it that old people lost their names as they gained their wrinkles? Were their younger relatives preparing them for the anonymity of death? But the old woman, Theadora, was still talking.

"No more those sacred times for girls. Now Artemis stands upright, in the middle of the city. Next full moon you will see how our young boys present themselves to be flogged before her. Our Spartan Artemis wants human blood now, the kind that runs from the backs of unflinching boys. Her image grows heavy if the strokes are too light. Oh, how we change the gods to match the humans."

The old woman coughed.

"Water," she whispered, and held out her cup. "I talk too much. Why do you need me to tell you about Spartan things? You can see with your own two eyes how our city is a military camp."

Lykaina steadied the water jug while the old woman drank. Theadora lay back on her litter and closed her eyes. Lykaina rubbed her arm gently, watching the wrinkled face relax into sleep. Arete had put both children to bed while the old woman was talking. Now she held out her hand to Lykaina.

"Come with me for another walk. The sun is down, and we can move through the shadows of the city unseen. Let's walk to the river and watch the moon rise."

They left the house and descended the stone steps into the center of the darkening city. The agora, with its merchant stalls closed for the day, was flooded with people enjoying the cool evening air. Spartan matrons walked arm-in-arm. Old men stood in groups discussing the latest exploits of the battlefield. A group of children played an unruly ball game in the center of the main square. A pack of adolescents raced by. Shouts from a noisy game of knucklebone rose from one corner, while at another, a group of youngsters cheered a dogfight.

Lykaina and Arete slipped through the long shadows and walked toward the river Eurotas.

"I dreamed this afternoon," said Arete. "Tell me what you think. I was walking through a field of flowering thyme. The bees were everywhere gathering nectar. I came to a clear stream and took off my tunic to swim.

The field on the other side was full of stones, nothing bloomed there. While I was swimming, the stones suddenly rose up and marched toward me. They fell into the stream and dammed it up. I couldn't get out. When I finally did, the field of thyme was gone. There was nothing but stones."

They walked in silence for a few minutes. When Lykaina spoke, her voice was flat.

"The field of thyme is our love for each other. The stream is Sparta. The stones are your husband and his friends. When he comes home, our love will vanish."

"No!" cried Arete. "It's not true! When the army comes home, he doesn't even stay at the house. You know that. What difference will it make? I will still love you. We will still be together."

Lykaina didn't answer. She didn't want to quarrel with Arete. She wanted the war to last forever, but she knew that it wouldn't. Yesterday she had heard the town crier sing about a mighty battle raging on the Messenian plain. If the Spartans won—and they usually did—the war would be over. The two women stood on the bank of the river and watched the crescent moon on the horizon.

"Hecate rising," remarked Lykaina. "May she shine on us all."

"Hecate is important to you, isn't she?"

"Yes, for my people she is everywhere. She is the far-looking moon. She is guardian of the traveler on the road. She makes the crops grow. She is in every woman's house giving life to the child being born. She is also queen of the underworld. One full moon I will take you to the Black Caves of Phigalia, and we will make an offering to her."

"I like your Hecate. Here she is not so important, she is only a cave-dweller." Arete paused. "The way we Dorians see the gods must seem strange to you. We look to those who dwell on Mount Olympos, and yet all they seem to do is bicker and quarrel and meddle in the affairs of humans."

"Well, your Olympians don't meddle in the affairs of my people. They don't seem to care about us peasants. We look to the goddesses who can help us. Your Artemis may watch men flogging boys, but our Artemis helps us with the hunt. Hecate assists us in childbirth. Apollo, who is he to us? He declares that killing one's mother is no crime, that only the father gives life. That's nonsense. In the mountains, we are the children of our mothers. A man is a stranger in his wife's village."

Arete leaned against Lykaina's shoulder. They watched the river reflect the changing colors of the sky.

"It is not so different here, you know," she said. "Our children rarely see their fathers." She let her breath out in a sigh. "Of course, after they are seven, they don't see their mothers either. I have only two more years before my precious Niki leaves for the training barracks. When she goes. . . ."

Her voice trailed off. Lykaina put her arm around Arete's shoulder. She shuddered at the thought of the gentle Niki becoming one of the street hellions shouting songs and elbowing old people out of the way.

"It's as if your Spartan senate wanted every mother to experience what Demeter felt when her Persephone was stolen away into the underworld," she said quietly, "only you're not allowed to tear your hair and grieve. You're supposed to go and make more babies to replace the ones you lose. I think our Hecate would tell you to take vengeance. Hold back the crops, like Demeter. Let nothing grow. Let no one prosper. Let it be winter year round until your children are returned to you."

"You understand me, Lykaina. My sisters-in-law do not seem to mind their children leaving them. They tell me how proud they are to see them marching to the piper's tune. But I will grieve, I know. I cannot bear to see her go away from me."

The evening sky had deepened from its sunset afterglow to a blue-black. The women finally turned away from the river and made their way back into the city. When they reached the agora, they saw that a crowd had gathered in the middle of the main square. Torches sent black smoke into the sky, and the air was filled with shouting. Children turned cartwheels along the rim of the crowd. Arete tugged at an old man's sleeve.

"What news, old man? What has happened?"

"Victory!" he shouted at her. "Victory again! The Messenians are in flight. The cowards are fleeing. Victory for us! Praise be to Apollo! Long live Sparta!"

Arete's face went white. She stepped back from the crowd and reached her hand out to Lykaina. But Lykaina had already moved away. Arete ran to catch her.

"Don't run from me," she cried breathlessly. "Nothing will change. Everything will be all right, you will see."

Lykaina didn't answer. They walked the rest of the way home in tense silence. As they stepped into the outer courtyard, Lykaina, her face somber, turned to Arete.

"Arete," she said, "come with me to the hills. Come to where we can be free together. We can raise goats and plant barley. We will find a place where there are apple trees, fig trees, whatever you want."

Arete put her finger over Lykaina's lips.

"Don't ask me, Lykaina. I can't do it. I can't go away with you. I have the children to think of. And my grandmother, what about her? Would you just leave her? I don't want him coming here any more than you do, but I can't leave my home and my family. Why can't you understand?"

14

Her voice was pleading. "He won't be here for long. He won't spend much time at all in the house. He'll be in the agora drinking with the other soldiers. He'll sleep most nights in the barracks. Soon enough there'll be another battle to go win."

Lykaina turned away angrily.

"I won't stay here. How can you ask that of me? Am I to listen to him bragging about how many Messenians he ran through with his sword? How many buckets of blood and guts he spilled? And then watch him carry you off to bed—more spoils of war? I'd end up slitting his gullet."

Lykaina walked to the archway of the inner courtyard and looked at the old woman asleep on her litter. Arete came and stood just behind her.

"Come, Lykaina, don't let's waste what little time we have left. Come inside, I'll brew some eucalyptus tea."

"No, no, no!" The words came out in a hoarse, angry whisper. "I won't play pretend with you anymore! You've made your choice, now I will make mine!"

Lykaina jerked herself out of Arete's embrace and ran out of the courtyard and up the smooth stone path. The light was gone now. Above the clusters of houses, the path narrowed, and the stones became sharper. Although her gait was a lope, she didn't miss a step. Her twisted foot had long since learned to take her weight and pass it back quickly to the sturdy leg. She ran out of the city and into the hills. Her breath was steady, her arms pumped wind through her lungs. The late evening air was still warm, although here above the city the breeze from the sea was sharper. Finally she came to a stand of cypress trees and sat down on large flat rock.

She didn't belong here. Only one turning of the seasons had passed since she'd been on her mountain watching newborn kids play tag with each other. Now she was a wretched helot who loved a Spartan woman. The soldier would return from the battlefields. She would be expected to leave the bed of her lover and close her ears to the loathsome sounds of babymaking. She looked at the circles of Sparta spread out before her in darkness. She would not stay. The old woman would not hold her. But where was she to go? Not back to her brother and father who had sold her for a bridegift. Nor to any mountain village where she could either marry or live unwelcome on the edge. There must be somewhere, she thought, somewhere where she could walk freely and sing. The old woman had said, *Go to Lesbos.* She wasn't even sure where that was, only that it was far across the sea.

She shivered as the late evening air dropped its mantle of chill over her shoulders. She stood up and slowly made her way back down into the city. The courtyard was dark when she entered. The pale crescent moon had risen high in the sky, but its light was too faint to penetrate the shadows.

"Come and sit."

Lykaina stared into the dark. Of course the old woman was awake. Probably hadn't missed a thing. She dropped down beside the litter.

"She is right to stay, and you are right to go," said Theadora. "She has her life as a good Spartan woman making babies for the army. She owns this house and three orchards. She has babies she loves. When the state takes them to the children's barracks, she can make some more. If her husband displeases her, she can take another. She can have a woman whenever she wants, to help her in the house and delight her in the bedroom. Would you have her give up all that? For what? To go back to your mountains? The two of you to herd goats?"

Lykaina sat in silence, hugging her knees with her arms.

"And you," Theadora continued, "you have your life as a poet. That's who you are; you can't stop being that by choice. Bring me that black leather box again."

Lykaina fetched the box. Theadora lifted the lid and searched under the scrolls with her gnarled fingers.

"Here it is," she said finally, pulling out a small leather pouch. "This is for you. This will pay your passage to Lesbos. It's from the poet Arion. He was born in Lesbos, but he lives in Corinth now. He is poet for the court of Periander. It was he who gave me the scrolls. He told me about Sappho and her golden voice."

Lykaina took the pouch Theadora handed her and pulled its drawstrings. The coins that fell into her palm were heavy as lead. She stood up and walked to the courtyard doorway where a single moonray fell. She let her fingers trace the figure of a winged horse on one of the coins.

"Yes. Gold. Forbidden here, so don't show it until you're safely in Corinth. Did I tell you about Arion?"

Lykaina shook her head no.

"He stayed here once. He'd gone to Italy to visit Sappho when she was there in exile. And made a lot of money singing. The scoundrels he paid to give him passage back to Corinth decided his fare wasn't enough. They forced him to walk the plank. He persuaded them to let him sing them one farewell song and stretched it out until he could see the shores of Taenarus. Then he jumped overboard with his harp and rode a dolphin to shore. Arete's soldier had gone to the shrine of Poseidon there to burn a sacrifice. He found the poet coughed up on the beach at Marmari Bay and carried him back on his shoulders. Arion stayed with us till he'd rested, and then the soldier's garrison took him to Corinth where they gave a mighty welcome to his would-be murderers. He sent these coins in thanks, although we needed none. His poetry fed us for months. He sends us messages now and then. That's how I know that Sappho is safely back in Lesbos, her exile ended. Go to Lesbos."

It was a command now, a statement of fact. Lykaina turned the coin over and over in her hand. Was it decided then? Was further exile her fate? She took the old woman in her arms and held her tightly. Then she slipped across the courtyard, past the sleeping children, and into the little room at the back of the house. She folded her arms around Arete and lay silently through the night, listening to her own heart beat.

Dawn was sending streaks of red into the eastern sky as Lykaina skirted the hill where the temple of Athena stood in the early morning dew. She nodded to the owl-eyed goddess as she trotted by. Outside the city wall, she passed through wide vineyards and fields of melons where helot men, women, and children were just beginning a long day of sweaty labor. Before her stretched the barren spikes of Taygetus.

Lykaina followed a narrow footpath into a deep gorge, flanked on either side by sheer columns of rock that rose to block out the sunlight. Wet with mist, the still air hung over a streambed full of strangely shaped rocks. No birds sang. No animals rustled through the brush. Only the water danced over the shelves of rock. The path turned, and Lykaina climbed, letting the streambed fall away below her.

The cave was hidden at first by a small crooked willow growing directly out of the flat rock that formed a lintel over the entrance. Inside, Lykaina knelt, laid out her offering of honey and almonds, and lit a small bundle of dried thyme and laurel leaves. Resting back on her heels, she closed her eyes, raised both her arms, and let her voice ring out clear.

"From the three heights of heavens, descend, oh Fates. Am I to journey to a foreign land? Orphaned, am I to be homeless, too? Is the aulos my only father? My only mother a song? Come, Fates, and prophesy me."

Lykaina sat still for a long time. The air in the cave was damp and musty. She listened to the sound of water dripping off a ledge. A rustling sound made her open her eyes. In the dim light at the rear of the cave stood three crones. Black rags clung to their waists, their ruckled breasts were bare. Snakes with flat heads wound round their upper arms. Gray-streaked auburn tresses hung from their skulls.

The light in the cave was dim, but Lykaina could see the three clearly. On the right she recognized Clotho the Spinner, a forked distaff topped with raw sheep's wool in one hand, the other hand twisting a strand of the wool into thread. A half-full spindle hung from the thread, turning and spinning.

"Does not the spindle dance its own dance?"

Next to Clotho, Lachesis the Measurer leaned on a long crooked stick and stared at the whirring spindle.

"How long is your fate when you own it?"

On the left stood Atropos, Cutter of Life's Thread, a sprig of belladonna in her hand.

"When the spindle is full, the thread is cut. But how full is the spindle?"

The smoldering thyme suddenly flared, sending smoke into Lykaina's face. She rubbed her eyes. When she looked again, the three figures had vanished. Their voices continued to echo off the walls of the cave. Lykaina strained her ears to catch the meaning of their words, but the sounds were muted, the words indistinguishable from the sound of water dripping from the ceiling of the cave.

The voices faded and flashes of light began to strike the cave walls, darting from rock to rock like sheet lightning behind the mountains. The sound of horses' hooves filled the cave, at first soft and muffled, then swelling to thunder. The flashing lights outlined a lone horse running free over the hills of Taygetus, a coal-black mare with a gray mane and gray tail, a green stripe down her back. Coming to a cliff, the mare left the ground and rose into the air. The green stripe turned into wings beating the wind. The sounds of the hooves vanished, and Lykaina heard only the rush of the wind and the occasional cry of a hawk.

Now the mare was running again, this time along a pebbled shore. The wind whipped the waves into a frenzy, and the horse staggered each time a wave struck. Just as the largest wave was about to break, the green wings on the mare's back turned into dorsal fins, and she plunged into the sea. Lykaina watched her swim underwater, past ochre-colored rocks covered with spiny black sea urchins, past dark underwater caves out of which schools of bright yellow fish swam, past undulating eelgrass.

At last the mare rose from the sea, folded her fin-wings back into the green stripe, and stood still on a rock ledge. Close by, in a field of olive trees, other mares appeared, some accompanied by their foals. As she joined them, they surrounded her, nuzzled her wet flanks, sniffed her briny sweat. They all began to prance in a circle, lifting their legs high, their hooves barely touching the ground, their manes and tails tossing in the breeze.

The stately dance blurred, and one by one the flashing lights vanished. Lykaina stared at the dim walls of the cave. The bundle of thyme and laurel had become a small pile of gray ash.

The message of the Fates was clear: Leave these mountains, seek a new home.

Chapter 2.
Leaving Sparta behind

The gray donkey stood patiently in the predawn air while Lykaina tightened the girth. Two brightly colored baskets hung on either side of a wooden saddle—one filled with black bread, goat cheese, and olives to eat on the journey, the other with jugs of olive oil and amphorae of wine for barter. A goatshair cloak, folded into a tight bundle, crowned the donkey's backbone. Arete came in from the street carrying two full waterskins.

"Fresh from the hillside spring," she said, as she handed them to Lykaina, "the one where the water is sweetest."

Lykaina took the waterskins and fastened them on either side of the saddle. Arete rested her hand lightly on Lykaina's shoulder.

"You know that I love you," said Arete.

"Yes, I know." Lykaina turned around and faced her. "But you have your life, and I have mine." She took Arete's hand in her own and traced the veins on the back of it with a finger. "I dreamed last night that we were living with a band of other women," she said, "all of us gray and wrinkled and strong and lovely. We each had our own little house, and there was a community vineyard. We picked grapes all day and sang poetry at night. Just before I woke up, you and I were drinking must and singing a grape-harvesting song." She dropped Arete's hand and brushed a tear from Arete's cheek. "Maybe one day that will happen." She pulled her close and felt their two hearts beating.

"Come and sing me a farewell song!" Theadora's command rang through the air. Lykaina kissed Arete quickly, and they stepped into the inner courtyard. Theadora was sitting up straight on her litter, her gray hair falling down to her waist.

"Only once more will I listen to your voice, so make your song long and golden."

Lykaina pulled her aulos from her belt, closed her eyes, and played a single high note that changed color as it stretched out toward the dawn. She paused to catch her breath and began to sing.

> As I leave for foreign lands, granny,
> let me carry you with me,
> carry you in my arms for company.
> As I leave for foreign lands, I promise
> I won't stay away more than a year
> because I can't stand the pain of separation.
> My eyes fill with tears and my heart cries
> when I think about how I leave you, granny.

Theadora lay back on her litter. The first ray of the morning sun broke from the silhouette of the eastern ridges and struck the courtyard tile. Lykaina knelt and embraced the old woman.

"We will meet again," she whispered.

Theadora closed her eyes. Lykaina stood and watched the narrow chest rise and fall in even breaths. She took Arete's hand and led her back to the outer courtyard.

"And you and I will be together again one day," she said. "When you've done with being a proper Spartan woman, we can live as we please."

They embraced, and Arete whispered, "Until you return, then."

Lykaina took the rope bridle in her hand and led the donkey out of the courtyard. The houses of Sparta fell behind her, and she found herself on a hard-packed road that passed through rows of olive trees, their trunks gnarled, their silver-green leaves still wet with dew. Keeping a steady pace, Lykaina stopped only once to look back at the snow-capped peaks of Taygetus. At nightfall she camped on a riverbank and fell asleep listening to a lone nighthawk. In the morning she started her journey again.

When the sun was nearing its zenith that second day, Lykaina rounded a bend in the road and stepped into an uproar. Chickens cackled, mules brayed, and a male voice bellowed, "May the lice of a thousand broody hens come to nest in your hairy armpits, you good-for-nothing donkey's ass!"

The curse was followed by the thwack of wood on flesh and a child's yelp of distress. Lykaina grinned at the sight before her. A string of six mules stood in disarray while a skinny boy pulled frantically at the bridle of the lead mule sitting down in the middle of the road. A grizzled man wearing a patched peddler's cloak was stamping his feet and waving a crooked walking stick over his head. Tipped over with doors ajar, two empty wooden cages had just disgorged a dozen hens, feathers flying to the four winds. The chickens imprisoned in the remaining cages on the standing mules squawked and beat their wings against the bars.

The man dropped his stick, grabbed one hen by its feet, and lunged at another flying past. Lykaina let go of her donkey's bridle and joined in the chase. She captured two hens and the tailfeathers of a third before the rest disappeared over the hill. She helped the peddler push the ruffled creatures back into their cage. With the cage doors secured, the man turned to the boy, still tugging at the sitting mule.

"Let him sit. We'll eat a bite and drink and leave him to bake in the sun." He turned to Lykaina and bowed slightly.

"I thank you for your timely assistance. Will you join us in our repast?"

He disengaged a dirty woven bag from the back of the sitting mule and started toward a small grove of aspen that stood at the edge of a narrow stream. Lykaina pulled a loaf of bread and a chunk of cheese from her basket and followed. The boy untied the rest of the mules, led them down the bank of the stream, and let them drink. The stubborn mule, left alone, heaved itself to its feet and lumbered after him.

"I am Demostratos," the man said as he spread his cloak on the ground, "peddler extraordinaire. I can sell you the air. I can nail horseshoes on a louse. I carry these chickens, or what's left of them, to fill the stewpots of Corinth."

He pulled a skin flask from his bag, unpopped the cork, and drank deeply. Then he handed the flask to Lykaina. She tilted her head and let the water flow down her throat.

"I am Lykaina, on my way to Corinth, too. Might we journey together?"

She broke off a heel of the bread, cut a sliver of cheese, and offered them to him.

"Ah, fresh baked, a luxury. I won't offer you my hardtack. Lykaina, eh? Wolf-woman. By your accent, you are not a Spartan. And you are traveling away from Sparta. Toward the returning victors of battle, but you don't have the look of a soiled dove. You are well packed for a journey, I see, but they allow no immigration into Corinth. So it might seem that Corinth is only a beginning, a port from whence ships set forth on journeys across the sea. Your company is most welcome. The child there is no more companion than the chickens in their cages. You will make the hours of the day pass pleasantly."

The peddler pulled out a handful of black olives and tossed them one by one into his mouth, spitting out the seed of one olive just as another went in.

"But by the cut of your cloak," he continued, "I see that you have just come from Sparta. And not a field worker, either. A baby-minder, then? Or a cooker of that vile black broth that passes for food amongst our ruling race?"

Lykaina furrowed her brow. The man had an uncanny ability to read her past and future.

"I was brought by a soldier to his wife's house," she said, "to sing for his grandmother-in-law and tend his wife's babies. They are Spartans but good women. It is the old woman who has sent me to Corinth to find a ship outbound for Lesbos."

"Ah, I thought I saw an aulos in your belt. You are a singer of songs, a teller of tales. That may get you out of a tight spot on your travels. You're from the mountains, then?"

"Anabretae. My mother is Tragota, daughter of goatherds."

"And your father?"

"Arkteros of deeper Mani."

"Arkteros of the Mani. I was born in the Mani. I know your uncle then. They say you were found in the hills, living amongst the wolves. And that your voice is sweet like wild honey, yet sharp like a boar's tooth."

Lykaina blushed to find so much knowledge of herself in a stranger.

"My mother's father taught me. The old woman in Sparta says I must go to Lesbos to learn from Sappho."

"Ah. From the mountains of Taygetus to the rude houses of the Spartans to luxury-loving Lesbos. Born to journey, ever to search. But tell me, how did you find life with our ruling masters? Were you impressed with their beautiful bodies and empty heads? Do you admire their lust for blood? What do you think of our conquerors?"

Lykaina frowned. She had never heard such contempt in speaking of Spartans. It was true that the old woman pronounced scathing indictments on grown men playing little boys' games. But Lykaina had heard pride in her voice when she admonished Arete's husband to "Come back either with your shield or on it." Arete laughed at the school boys and girls on parade, muscles flexing under their smooth skin, but she had lovingly polished her husband's helmet and greaves.

Her own feelings were confused. In her mountain childhood, she had lived in terror of the marauding Spartan youth who regularly plundered the flocks. On her first day in Sparta, she had been afraid to lift her eyes from the ground for fear of seeing the Many-Headed Monster of the Plains the villagers warned against. But her days with Arete and the old woman had been filled with a caring she had not known since her own granny had died.

"I have not been unhappy in Sparta," she said finally. "My task is to sing songs to an old woman whose opinion of Spartans is often like your own. My life in her house has not been like others who serve the masters. Especially since the men left."

"But now the men are returning, and you are leaving," the peddler remarked. "Is the thought of the conquering hero's footfall in the house a grief to you? Does the promise of invasion of your company of women make life there unbearable?"

Lykaina blushed again. This peddler seemed to know too much. She stood up and brushed the crumbs from her tunic.

"The sun is drifting westward," she said. "It's time we were moving again."

The peddler smiled and stood up, too. They joined the boy on the bank and checked the gear. The peddler hit the lead mule sharply with his stick, and the train began to move out.

They walked until nightfall found them just outside the city of Argos. The peddler led the train to a sheltered spot by a small river where a group of other travelers was tending a string of wild hares spitted over a fire. Most were farmers from the surrounding hills bringing their produce to market. One was a traveler from the north. As a wine flask made its way around the circle, the traveler unfolded his tale of the Spartan victory.

He had seen the final battle with his own eyes. He had watched from a hillside as the two armies had lined up on either side of the plain and marched toward each other. When the first clash of metal on metal had rung out, dust had all but hidden the battling soldiers. For the most part, the traveler had heard rather than seen the melee. For three days they had fought, he told them, each night the soldiers retiring from the field while the helots sorted out the mangled bodies of the dead. On the fourth day the Spartans had entered the fray with a battle cry that resounded for miles. They had broken the Messenians' line and had finally sent them fleeing to the hills. It would be some time before the rascals would try to test their mettle again.

With good food and wine in her belly, Lykaina listened sleepily to the talk. Why were men so fascinated by war? she wondered. Why did detailed descriptions of men hacking limbs off one another provide such entertainment? These men were farmers and herders like her own people. In the village when they killed animals to eat or to appease the gods, they didn't glory in it. But here they devoured the witnessing of gore—how the blood flowed, how life had left a young body. They had no particular admiration of Spartan ways, it was clear. Yet the fascination was there, the thrill of a bloody tale. At length she left the fire and found her donkey by the river. The night air was cold, but she felt warmer curled up in her goatshair cloak than listening to tales of violence by the fire.

In the morning they broke camp. The peddler led Lykaina through the walls of Argos and into the marketplace.

"I won't sell my chickens here. They'll fetch a much better price in Corinth. But I have to replace the ones this good-for-nothing let flap away into the hills."

He struck the boy's shoulder lightly with his stick. The boy yelped and ducked behind one of the mules.

The marketplace was much like the agora at Sparta. Since that first trip to market with her brother, Lykaina had gotten used to the bawling of men and animals. She had learned, from her many trips to the agora in Sparta, to distinguish the cries of different vendors—one tune for melons, another for figs, yet another for lambs ready for slaughter. Here, she found, the same cries made the same distinctions.

She watched the peddler strike a deal with a chicken merchant and helped him transfer six pairs of squawking hens into the lead mule's cages. The chickens secured, the peddler's eyes lit upon a handsome pair of cocks, each in its own reed cage.

"I could take these scraggly specimens off your hands for a sum," he commented casually, and the haggling was renewed with vigor. A different kind of battle, thought Lykaina. Less bloody, but with a desire to win just as strong. In the end, with no wounds to count, each thinks he has outwitted the other. The peddler attached the two extra cages to one of the mules and winked at Lykaina.

"These will bring a fancy price. Corinthians value a good cock fight. The rooster who sired these two is from Rhodes, and Rhodian cocks are the fightingest of the Mediterranean."

They left the market behind and joined other travelers on the road. A brightly painted cart loaded with even more brightly painted women passed them, its donkey trotting under the switch of the young boy driver. A dozen or more urchins ran with baskets of sausages and honeycakes balanced precariously on their heads.

"Taking their greetings to the victors," the peddler remarked. They slowed their pace until they were again alone on the road. As they walked, the peddler talked about his travels in Italy.

"When I was younger, I sold much fancier goods than these rude birds. I traveled from Ionia to Italy, I traded Maltese lap dogs for Milesian wool.

I met your Sappho once—or at least I was under the same roof with her. It was in Sybaris, a city more devoted to luxury than you can ever imagine. You'll see nothing like it, even in Lesbos. It sits in a hollow above the Gulf of Tarentum, and the breeze blowing off the sea is always soft and warm. The men spend their days in idle pursuits. They sleep, they talk, they steam themselves in the most elegant public baths. And they eat, oh, how they eat. The food on their tables is cooked by artists imported from every corner of the Mediterranean, dish after dish of culinary delights. They wash it all down with wines, sweet ones and dry ones and rare ones from Lydia." He sighed. "And all the while they ingurgitate, they feast their eyes on the loveliest of young boys who perform acrobatics and juggle balls and sing the most amazing songs." He winked at Lykaina. "They make the bawdy tunes of your Spartan boys sound like prayers to Hera." He stroked his short beard with one hand and smoothed out the wrinkles of his ragged tunic with the other. "Their young bodies are so lithesome, and their voices are like the voices of gods." He shrugged. "Hard to imagine that in so few years their chins, too, will sprout whiskers and their mouths drop platitudes."

He slapped the lead mule who was leaning toward a fig branch that hung over the road.

"One night, your friend Sappho was persuaded by my host to make a brief appearance with her daughter. She was the only woman there who was not a lady of the night. Respectable women, I'm afraid, are housebound in Italy. But our host prevailed upon that sweet young woman to regale us with a poem. Her voice was like that of a nightingale, her face radiant. She seemed to be singing only for that glorious infant in her arms. The rest of us might well have been eavesdropping. 'I have a little daughter,' she sang, and she sang it as if that little tyke were a goddess. She called her a golden flower. I can't remember all of the poem—something about how she wouldn't trade the child for all of Lydia, or even Lesbos. And we all knew how she longed to be reunited with her land of birth."

He closed his eyes, lost in reverie. Then he looked at Lykaina and frowned.

"You wouldn't like it there, you know. You'd have to marry, like Sappho, to retain the armor of presumed virtue. Not that her marriage was all bad. The man was rich and spent most of his time in trade. We all do what we must to survive."

The peddler fell silent. Lykaina pondered the idea of living in a land where women couldn't walk freely. She had heard there were many places where women weren't allowed outside the house, even during the day. They lived in special rooms, it was said, eating only with each other and with the children. How could Sappho have lived in such a place? How could she compose poetry if she never breathed fresh air? Her thoughts were interrupted by the muffled sound of tramping.

"The victors return," commented the peddler. "We'd best get these animals off the road. Ourselves, too, if we don't want to become a carpet for their glorious feet."

They pulled the mules up a bank and tied them to the trunk of a small plane tree on whose broad branches they perched themselves to watch the parade.

Eight abreast the soldiers marched, stepping in time to a four-square tune played by a small band of pipers. The rhythm of the song was punctuated by the jangling of breast plates and the slapping of leather soles on the hard-packed clay road. Some soldiers struck the ground with their lances for accent. They marched by, their helmets thrown back on their heads, their grinning faces blackened with a mixture of sweat and dust and blood. One young man, with only a bloody socket for his left eye, bawled out a bawdy victory lyric which his fellow soldiers took up lustily and tossed from rank to rank. The cartful of painted ladies that had passed them earlier rolled along in the middle of the group adding their high-pitched laughter as a countermelody. The urchins darted through the ranks trading sausages for souvenirs from dead Messenians.

Following the first contingent came the glorious Spartan dead. Row upon row of youths, or at least such pieces as had been salvaged, lay atop shields shouldered by helots. Behind these limped the wounded, men with stumps for arms, parts of their faces cut away, holes in their sides stuffed with bloody rags. And behind them, more helots carrying shields laden with more dead.

"The glories of war," commented the peddler. "How proud their mothers will be to have dead sons to add to the roster of heroes. Pity the poor mothers of sons who managed to come back alive. They will just have to wait until the next war."

Lykaina was staring at the soldiers of the next contingent, more whole men prancing to pipes. Under the sweat and dirt of one burly soldier, she recognized a face—Arete's husband. She shrank back into the leaves of the plane tree, but it was too late.

"Ho, comrades, look up there! A little helot lady in a plane tree. The very one, in fact, that lives in my wife's house. And where do you think you're going, little slave? Sparta's in the opposite direction."

He stepped out of his rank, swaggered to the side of the road and stood looking up into the plane tree. One of his comrades followed. They leaned on their lances, their upturned faces broken by smug grins of victory. The stench of their sweat swept over Lykaina. She tightened her grip on the branch and held her head high.

"May it please you, your grandmother-in-law has sent me to give greetings to Arion, your friend in Corinth. I am to invite him to come and help us celebrate your glorious victory."

"Has she now? And what fine wines have you got in your donkey's pack there? My friend and I have been marching all morning. We could use a bit of liquid refreshment."

He scrambled up the bank and jerked at the leather fastenings. The donkey started. Lykaina jumped down from the branch and quickly pulled an amphora of wine from the basket before the soldier could loosen the whole gear. The peddler and his boy were already moving up over the hill with their mules.

"Laconian wine, the best in the Peloponnese," said Lykaina, "to start the celebration early."

The soldier uncorked the jug and took a long swig.

"So," he said, passing the wine to his comrade, "the old woman sends you abroad as messenger. How am I to know you have not fled of your own will?"

"No more would I flee of my own will than you would leave a half-drowned poet on a sandy shore. Your courage in battle calls for a song. Who better to celebrate you than the man whose life you saved?"

The soldier took the amphora from his friend and drained the last drops.

"Well spoken, little helot. You are good with words, whether your pipes play or not. Pass me a few more of those amphorae, and I will let you pass freely on your way."

Lykaina unstrapped the remaining wine. The soldier and his friend tucked the jugs under their arms and, without a backward glance, jumped down the bank. Lykaina led the donkey up the ridge to where the peddler stood with his mules.

"So that was your soldier master," he said, when she reached him. "Muscle everywhere including between his ears. Let's wait here until they pass."

They sat on the hilltop and watched the parade until the last pair of tramping feet had carried its war-torn load into the distance. They took up their journey again, picking their way past discarded helmets and blood-soaked rags. A few minutes down the road, they found a disheveled figure slumped in the middle of the road. Barely more than a boy, his face was streaked with blood and dirt. One swollen leg lay twisted under him, and blood seeped from the rag he held to his side. His helot stood at a distance leaning on a lance, a sword and shield lying on the ground beside him.

"I am dying," the boy said simply as she approached.

"Let me look," said Lykaina and knelt beside him. Pulling the bloody rag away, she saw a gaping wound where a sword had been plunged in and twisted. She called to the helot.

"Bring me the waterskin from my donkey there."

The helot stared at her without moving, his face expressionless. She looked around and saw that the peddler and his boy had gone on down the road.

"Water!" She yelled it this time, using the voice she had heard Spartans use to bark orders to helots. "Now. Fetch it."

The helot slowly and deliberately laid down the lance and went to the donkey. He brought the waterskin and handed it to her without a word. Then he went back to stand beside the weapons. Lykaina took off her shoulder cape, wet it with water, and washed the wound which was nasty with infection. The leg was worse. The boy must have gotten both wounds early in the battle. The gash in the upper thigh was green and swollen and hard to the touch. The knee was badly twisted, and he had lost a lot of blood. Still, he needn't die. She could lance the leg wound, and with a good poultice of dragonwort on it and cold willow tea to drink, he would live, even though he would never walk straight again. She hunkered back on her heels.

"I can give you something that will cure both wounds. Tell your helot to make camp here. You will have to rest for a few weeks. You may always walk with a crutch, but you won't die."

"I will die!" The boy spoke vehemently. "I won't go home a cripple. But I pray that the gods let me die soon. If they arrive in the city without me, it will be too late. My family will think I have run away. They will be dishonored."

Lykaina stared at him.

"You would rather die?"

The boy grimaced with pain. His breaths were short, and his chest heaved with the effort of speaking.

"I will die. Our great poet Tyrtaios said, 'He who falls among the champions and loses his sweet life blesses with honor his city, his family, his people.' I would die like that. My helot will bear me home in honor."

Pain crossed his face again. He reached out and tugged at Lykaina's tunic.

"Do you have something," he whispered, "that will make it go quickly?"

Lykaina frowned and looked away. The boy's death wasn't inevitable. How could she assist in a killing? But she understood him. He would never fight again. When the next war came, he would stay at home with the old men and the other cripples. If he refused her healing and she did not help him die, his final end would be slow and agonizing.

She stood up and looked around her. She remembered a swampy place she had seen at the side of the road. Hemlock will do it, she thought.

"Build a fire," she called out to the helot, as she jogged back down the road.

She waded around the edges of the swamp until she found several small plants with finely cut leaflets and white flowers. She pulled them up and trotted back to where the helot was still leaning on his lance, fire unmade. She looked at him angrily.

"Wood," she commanded sharply. "Now!"

The helot again laid down the lance deliberately and moved off to gather wood. Lykaina cut up the hemlock and mixed it with water in a bowl. With the dry branches the helot brought, she built a small fire and set the bowl of hemlock on it. Unable to look at the boy, she sat back on her heels and watched the fire. When the brew had turned a deep brown, she took it off the coals.

"Sit up," she said softly, "and drink this. It will stop the pain and put you to sleep. You can go home in honor."

The boy sat up, fear and relief in his eyes. He took the bowl and drank the tea down.

"Thank you," he whispered. "My mother thanks you, my father thanks you." He lay back in the road. "One more favor," he said, his voice husky. "Will you wait until it is over and make sure my helot carries me away? I think once I am on his back, he will not put me down. But if no one's here, he may leave me in the road."

Lykaina nodded and sat back on her heels. The late afternoon sun had dipped low to the horizon, and the sky was turning purple over the hills to the west. Sounds of night insects were beginning to take over the evening air. A few moments later she looked at the boy and saw that he was still. She felt for his heartbeat; it was gone. She turned to the helot, still motionless by the sword and shield.

"Leave the weapons and put him on your back," she ordered.

His face expressionless, the helot walked over and pulled the lifeless boy up by one arm and flung him onto his back like a sack of barley.

"All the way to Sparta," she commanded. "Else Demeter will ride her night mare into your dreams. Persephone will reach out of the black earth and take you, too."

The helot grunted and moved off down the road. Lykaina watched him walking in the fading light. She picked up the waterskin and her bloody cape, kicked the ashes of the fire, and started off with her donkey in the opposite direction. A few miles down the road, she caught up with the peddler and his boy, encamped.

"You sent him off to his eternal reward, then? Glory to his family, glory to the state." He handed her a bowl of lentil stew.

"He knew no other way," said Lykaina, as she dropped to the ground and took the bowl gratefully. "He was happy that he lived up to his family's expectations. Who are we to think ill of him?"

They ate in silence and bedded themselves down for the night. Lykaina was bone tired, but she lay sleepless for hours, listening to the low hoot of an owl. The encounter with the army had brought home to her the truth of the words spoken first by the old woman and then by the peddler. Spartans—men and women—lived their lives in blind obedience to a war monster. The boy's choice was for his mother as much as his father. She would stand tall in other women's eyes. The wound in his side would become a badge of honor, a symbol of the courage with which he had faced the enemy.

Even the Spartans she loved—Arete who laughed at the women who lined up at the well in order of their husband's rank, the old woman whose favorite entertainment, aside from Lykaina's songs, was a lively discourse on the feeble-mindedness of Spartan society—were loyal to the state. Arete had refused to even think about coming away with Lykaina, and the old woman had agreed with her. They both accept the young matron's role as baby-maker. Arete nurtures her children, thought Lykaina, knowing that at the age of seven they will be torn from her side and she will rarely see them again. She is proud of their perfect little bodies. But what will she do if the next one is born less than perfect and is sentenced by the elders to be left out on the mountainside? Will she acquiesce to the state then? She sees herself as having no choice. The gods have willed it so. But the gods the Spartans worship are a mere reflection of Spartans themselves. The old woman had said that. Their blessed Apollo, a god of poetry and music to other peoples, was for them only a politician to be bribed to prophesy their victories.

Lykaina reminded herself that Arete had defied Spartan custom to love her. But her mind instantly flickered to Arete's unwavering insistence that nothing would change when the army returned. Her thinking that everything would be all right showed that she saw things only as she wanted them to be, not as they really were. If Lykaina had stayed, and Arete's husband had sent her back to the village, or worse, killed her, what would Arete have done? Would she have cast down her eyes and said simply that the gods had willed it?

The waxing moon broke through a cloud bank and sent its pale light earthward. The owl moved to a tree farther away. Lykaina snuggled deeper into her goatshair cloak. No more, she thought. It is time to put all that behind me. I am a poet, and I walk a lonely trail. Two days more and we'll be in Corinth and then away to Lesbos. She drifted to sleep.

"This is your shortcut to Corinth?"

Lykaina stood at the foot of the Arachnaion Mountains, looking up at the rough switchback trail that seemed almost vertical in places. Stunted bushes crowded the path, and scraggly trees stuck straight out from the rocky soil.

"A little steep in places," responded the peddler, "but no challenge to a Taygetan goatherd such as yourself. You and your donkey go first. I may have to use gentle persuasion on these mules." As soon as she had passed ahead, he landed a fierce blow on the lead mule's haunches. "*Hai*, you dundering son of a swayback mare and a braying jackass, get up there! Move!"

Lykaina and her donkey scrambled ahead while the peddler continued his invective and his boy jerked on the bridle. She climbed steadily, dislodging rocks as she went, stopping only when dense underbrush barred the way. She hacked at the shrubbery with her knife to clear the path. By the time she reached the top, her body was soaked with sweat. She threw herself on the rough ground and lay panting. I haven't climbed like that since I left Taygetus, she thought. My lungs are bursting. The blood pumping through her heart felt good though, and the breeze carried the sure scent of the sea.

The grunts and shouts of the peddler and his team came nearer and finally they, too, were on top. The peddler flung himself down beside her while the boy gave a ration of water to each animal. The two of them lay in silence listening to the snorting of the mules and the beating of their own hearts. Then the peddler sat up.

"There it is," he said, "golden Corinth, the end of my journey, the beginning of yours."

Lykaina sat up, too. Below them lay a lush plain with a ribbon of river winding through a sea of olive trees. She squinted through the midday sun and looked past the plain to the sea. Two seas! To the north, white-capped emerald water led to purple mountains topped with snow. To the east, a calm transparent blue stretched to the horizon. In between, low green mountains rose from a narrow neck of land.

"Allow me to acquaint you with the geography," the peddler said. "There, where you are looking now, is the Saronic Gulf. Beyond that is the great Aegean where you will soon be sailing. The other sea is the Gulf of Corinth. Raise your eyes and you will see double-headed Parnassos reigning on that farther shore. Now swing them back to the land between the two seas—Megara with its bulwark of mountains."

Lykaina swept her eyes back and forth over the landscape. The distant peaks to the north began to turn golden from the sun striking them.

"Lower your eyes a little now," the peddler continued, "and look there at god-built Corinth. Or rather, the great rock of Acrocorinth, the sacred citadel. When you climb its western face, you will pass a multitude of sanctuaries, should you feel the need of a blessing before you enter the graceful mistress of two seas. Demeter, Athena, Isis, take your pick. Or leave an offering at each to cover all potentialities."

As Lykaina stared, she felt her heart beat faster. The trip thus far had been familiar: a road like other roads she had traveled, a companion of her own kind. Now she would be entering a strange place with strange people. Corinth was not like Sparta, the old woman had said, where helot and ruler alike lived simply. Here there would be elegant houses, fine food, and people who dressed with style and spoke with eloquence.

The peddler broke into her thoughts.

"Do you know where you will be going in Corinth?"

"I will go to find Arion first. The old woman said he lives at Periander's court. I am hoping you can direct me."

"Direct you to the court of Periander?" The peddler laughed gently. "You will just go up and announce yourself? 'Greetings, Periander, I am Lykaina of Anabretae.' My dear, Periander is king. You cannot just walk into his court."

Lykaina frowned.

"But how will I find Arion then?" she asked.

The peddler scraped away a clearing on the ground in front of them.

"Here," he said, drawing in the dirt with a sharp stick, "is Acrocorinth. You can climb over it or go round it. On the other side is the agora. To the south of the agora you will see a paved road that runs to the sea. Take that road, and you'll soon come to the temple of Aphrodite. Next to the temple are a number of houses. The women who live in those houses know your Arion. One of them will give you a proper introduction."

Lykaina looked at the map, then at the peddler.

"You won't be coming with me into Corinth?" she asked.

"No, my good friend," he replied. "You and I shall come to a parting of the ways at Tenea, there below us." He pointed to a tiny village set at the foot of the mountain. "I have decided that I have no need of golden Corinth this trip. I'll steam these weary bones at the bath of Helen. See, you can just make it out over there on the coast. Then I will go straight to the sanctuary of Poseidon at Isthmia. The games will begin soon. There'll be throngs of visitors—from Athens, from Syracuse, even from far-off Lydia. I can charge twice for my drinking cups, and my fighting cocks will fetch a gold coin apiece if I'm clever."

Lykaina looked away. She had relied on the peddler to guide her. Now, when the way was the hardest, she would be on her own.

"This journeying with you has been good," she said finally.

"Ah, we're not done with each other yet. Going down these Spider Mountains will be even more difficult than coming up. It will take most of the afternoon. There's a stream where we can bed down just this side of Tenea. Then, in the morning, you'll go your way and I'll go mine."

He stood up and waved his stick at the boy. "There, boy," he shouted, "secure the cinches, make sure the packs are fast. Let's not lose our load so close to the finish."

Chapter 3.
Stopping at Corinth

Almost to the summit of Acrocorinth, Lykaina turned back to survey the sweep of the Nemean plain where she had parted company with the peddler. A hand touched her arm. A small girl held out a clay figurine, a basket filled with more figurines on her arm.

"Votives?" the child piped. "For the temples?"

Lykaina took the figurine and turned it over in her hand. "Which temple shall I go to, child?" she asked, as she gave her one of the peddler's trinkets. "Which one is best for a stranger to your city?"

"I like Isis best," the girl replied instantly. "I like her moonboat. We celebrate her holy day in the spring, and we all have our own little moonboats and sit her in them and take them down to the sea and let them sail away. My grandmother says she was the goddess who made everything, she gave birth to the sun itself. She says she sets the stars in the heavens, and she makes the winds blow gentle over the seas. When my grandmother was initiated into her mysteries, she says she saw a light coming from her. She says when she goes down to the underworld, Isis will be there. Her light will light up the gloom of Hades."

The girl shifted the basket to the other arm and slipped her free hand into Lykaina's.

"My mother's favorite temple is Demeter's. She says she honors mothers especially. She governs the fields and all the crops, but she doesn't have a moonboat. I never go to the temple of the Three Fates, they're too scary. They're fierce, and I don't want them to cut my life's thread. I like Persephone. I like to imagine that my mother is Demeter and that I'm her daughter, but I don't want any man to come and carry me away. I want to stay with her and my grandmother always. I don't mind the men when they visit our house, but I don't want to have to go to their houses."

Lykaina welcomed the girl's chatter. She had missed the peddler as soon as he and his train had disappeared from sight on the road toward Isthmia.

"Take me to your Isis temple then, and I will leave this offering for her. But first, tell me your name."

"Timia. My mother says I am both honorable and precious."

"Well, I am Lykaina from the mountains beyond Sparta."

Timia led her to a stone hall. Tall wooden columns fronted its porch, and bright paint covered its outer walls. Across the terra-cotta frieze over the lintel, a procession of women carried large vases. Directly over the doorway, Isis herself sat calmly holding an infant to her breast, her blank eyes staring ahead. In front of the temple, another Isis sat in a carved stone moonboat set on a pedestal. Lykaina placed her offering at the foot of the pedestal and raised her arms in silent prayer. When she had finished her supplication, she turned and found Timia still standing beside the donkey at the edge of the path.

"I've sold nearly all my votives. Shall I show you the agora?"

Lykaina smiled and took the outstretched hand. Timia led her down the slope toward the marketplace. They stopped at a large rock out of which clear water fell into a stone basin below.

"This is the Peirene Spring," said Timia. "It's the best-tasting water in the city. My mother sends me all the way up here whenever we have special guests. They say it comes out just where Pegasus struck the rock with his hoof. I don't like Pegasus, though. It would be fun to ride him through the heavens, but he helped Belerophon kill the Amazons, and I like the Amazons. When I grow up, I'm going to carry a bow and arrow and ride horseback from country to country, too."

Lykaina knelt and washed her face. She cupped her hands to catch the cold clear water and drank deeply. Her donkey nudged her, and she made room at the pool. When she had finished refreshing herself, she looked up. Timia was pointing to a small stone temple at the base of the rock.

"That's the old temple of Aphrodite," she said. "We have a new one now, close by where I live. You'll come with me to my house, won't you? And meet my mother and grandmother? And stay with us?"

Lykaina smiled and took the child's hand again.

Farther down the path, they came to a broad open area lined with long porticos and buildings—some open to the air, others with sloping red-tiled roofs and bright walls that reflected the morning sun. A half-built temple with double rows of marble columns dominated the square.

"That's Apollo's temple. They're still building it. They're going to put the roof on it this summer. I like Apollo when he plays his lyre. We have a lyre at my house. I want to learn how to play it. My mother used to play, but she doesn't anymore. She says that maybe Arion will teach me the next time he comes to visit."

Lykaina stopped and looked closely at Timia.

"Arion?" she echoed. "Do you mean the poet who lives at Periander's court?"

"That's the one," replied Timia. "He used to pass by the house to see my mother a lot, but he doesn't come so often anymore. My mother says it's because he's so busy making songs for the festivals, but I think he's got someone else he likes to see better. He stopped by once last month, but he didn't sing any poems and he didn't stay very long."

Lykaina smiled. The peddler's directions had seemed so vague, but she should have trusted his knowledge. The child lived near the temple of Aphrodite, and her mother knew Arion. It had been as simple as his words had implied.

"Come, let me show you the other Peirene Spring," Timia was saying.

She led Lykaina past the temple to a roofless enclosure where water flowed out of a pipe embedded in the rock and fell into a series of draw basins connected to each other by means of stone-carved troughs. The reflections from the water glanced off the stone walls and danced before her eyes. Seated beside the pools of water, men sat playing draughts.

"I like to come here in the summer when it's hot," said Timia. "It's always cool here, and the water tastes almost as good as the water at the upper spring. These men are supposed to be the most important men in the city, but I don't see why. They never do anything but sit around and talk."

Lykaina squeezed Timia's hand. The water had refreshed her, but her skin was still sweaty from the long climb up from the Nemean plain. She had seen enough of Corinth for now.

"Can we go to your house now?" she asked. "You can show me the rest of the city tomorrow."

They left the agora on a stone-paved road that looked toward the sea. Timia led her past the new temple of Aphrodite into a maze of houses behind the temple. The agora had been filled with men—men laying the stones to build the temple, men sitting at tables changing money, men standing in groups talking or sitting quietly playing board games. Here everywhere she looked, Lykaina saw women—old women, young women, small girls, infants. The children were dressed in tunics much like her own. The women wore long gowns that draped over one shoulder, leaving the other shoulder bare. Their faces were whitened with powder; round dots of red rouge highlighted their cheeks. Gold bracelets and rings graced their arms and fingers. Some of the women called out a greeting as they passed by, others merely glanced up from their work. Timia stopped in front of a small house where two women stood at a double loom in a tree-shaded courtyard.

"Mama, Babi, look here. This is Lykaina. She comes from Sparta, and she wants to meet Arion."

Both women turned from their shuttles and examined Lykaina. One was regal with white hair that flowed out from under a jeweled headband and down her back; the other, about her own age, had a softer face framed by light brown curls tied up with a purple ribbon. Lykaina gaped at their beauty, acutely aware of the childish tunic that didn't hide her grubby knees and brush-scratched shins.

The older woman spoke.

"Well you have come, stranger. Please enter our courtyard. Sit and tell us your story." She turned to the child. "Fetch a cup for our guest, Timia. Bring a basin and wash her feet. Then you can take care of the donkey." She turned back to Lykaina. "I am Erinna, and this is my daughter Telesilla. Clearly you have already met my granddaughter Timia."

Lykaina came into the courtyard and sat on a low seat carved out of sandalwood.

"Well I find you, my hosts. I am Lykaina of Anabretae in the Taygetus Mountains. As Timia has spoken, I have just come from Sparta, and I bear a message for Arion."

"And who told you that you might find friends of his here?" The woman was smiling, but her eyes were cool.

"On my journey here I traveled with Demostratos the peddler," responded Lykaina. "He advised me to seek out the women who lived near the temple of Aphrodite. He said someone here could make arrangements for me to meet Arion."

She stopped and took the double-handled clay cup Timia offered her and drank slowly. It was water from the upper Peirene Spring. She wiped her mouth and handed the cup back. The two women sat facing her, watching her carefully.

"His advice was good," said Erinna, her eyes softer than before. "I know Demostratos from many years ago. He was the most elegant peddler of all who came. He used to bring me the finest woolens from Milan and silks from Lakhori. Now he rarely visits. Tell me, how does he fare?"

Lykaina thought of the peddler's caged hens and fighting cocks, his tin keys and trinkets, his rough dogskin cap. Life had changed for him, then.

"He fares well enough," she replied. "He decided to bypass Corinth this trip to go to the Isthmian games. He said he would pass through when the games are over."

"Ah. He will have coins from all over the realm in his pocket then—if he doesn't exchange them for wine. But tell me about this message you bear for Arion."

Lykaina shifted her weight uneasily and leaned forward.

"In Sparta I lived in the house of Theadora, grandmother of Arete who is wife of Mabriotis the soldier. It is Theadora who has sent me on this journey. She tells me I must travel to Lesbos. She instructed me to seek out Arion whom she knows well. She said he would help arrange the rest of my journey."

The older woman waved her hand gently in the air.

"Mabriotis, isn't he the young man who rescued Arion when those pirates sent him overboard to what they thought was a watery grave?"

"He is the same," replied Lykaina. "Arion stayed at the house while he recovered. He continues to send messages from time to time."

Timia had brought a basin of water and set it on the terra-cotta tiles that covered the courtyard floor. She unstrapped Lykaina's sandals and began to wash the dust off her feet.

"You shall meet him then. I will arrange it."

It was the daughter Telesilla who spoke, her voice sounding like mountain water springing over rocks. She was looking at Lykaina out of eyes the color of the distant sea—light blue flecked with golden sunlight. Her full lips were painted a bright coral, and two matching coral spots dotted her cheeks. Lykaina had never seen beauty like this. Women from her village were dark, with black hair and black eyes set on olive skin. Spartan women were fairer, although in summer their skin, too, turned brown from the sun's rays. Telesilla's face was chalk white, and her painted mouth and cheeks made it seem even whiter. It was an artificial beauty, yet Lykaina felt herself wanting to reach out and stroke the painted cheeks, touch the coral lips. The older woman, Erinna, broke into her thoughts.

"We are about to take our midday fare. You will join us, of course, and then we will all sleep away the day's heat. This evening we will send a message to Arion and see when he will honor us with a visit."

After the soft white cheese and purple grapes had been washed down with sweet wine, Timia showed Lykaina to a small room off the courtyard. Lykaina sank down on the large mat spread on the floor, stretched herself out, and was asleep before Timia had gone out again.

She awoke to the sound of laughter in the courtyard. The music of Telesilla's and Erinna's voices was joined by deeper men's voices. Lykaina sat up and found a long gown made of the softest material she had ever touched. A comb and a gold pin lay on top of it, and next to them a water jar and basin.

She took off her travel-soiled tunic and washed herself carefully. She looked at the flowing material and tried to remember how the Corinthian women had arranged their dresses. She finally wrapped the material around both shoulders and fastened it with the pin over her breastbone. The skirt dragged the ground, so she hitched it up with a silk cord drawn around her waist. She looked in a small hand mirror that lay beside the pitcher and ran her fingers through her short black hair still dusty from the journey. She frowned at her image and then laughed. She was not a fine lady, she thought; she was herself. They could take her as she was. She threw back her shoulders and slipped into the courtyard.

She needn't have worried about her looks. The courtyard was dark, and no one took notice of her. She found a low bench on the fringe of the group and sat down. In addition to Telesilla and Erinna, there were two other women and seven or eight men. The women looked about the same age as Telesilla and wore their gowns draped low over their full breasts. The men were mostly older with gray in their beards and heavy worry lines creasing their foreheads. Across the low table laden with fruits and cakes, a younger man was sitting next to Telesilla, telling her a story. Telesilla's laughter rippled like water pouring into a bronze cup, and she rested her hand lightly on his arm. Lykaina looked away quickly and turned her attention to the group conversing closer at hand. They were talking about the new laws of the city.

"These sumptuary statutes," a man with a square face and neatly cropped beard was saying, "are all well and good for those who would spend their daily bread on wanton luxuries. But to extend their coverage to those of us who have the means to balance our outlay, to forbid the purchase in the marketplace of those goods which, if not of vital necessity, certainly make life more agreeable, this is absurd. You and I have no need of a tyrant's hand overseeing our accounts. We are not spendthrifts, and our purchasing should not be limited by law. We are responsible citizens and have the right to enjoy whatever mode of life we choose."

He raised a cup to his lips and drank deeply.

"Well spoken," responded a baggy-eyed man. "He oversteps his bounds. If I want to honor my friends with the extravagance of a banquet and have coins to do so, what right has Periander to send his chamberlains to close it down? He is unable to manage his own household. How dare he attempt to manage ours?"

He plucked a grape from a purple bunch lying close to him and tossed it into his mouth.

"Is it true," spoke a man whose belly pushed out his soft linen tunic, "that he took the clothes right off the backs of the women of the city? I have been lately abroad and heard this absurd story that surely is out of a taleteller's imagination."

"It was no exaggeration you heard," the baggy-eyed man said, "although you may not have heard the entire tale. He sent his trusted manservant to Thesprotia to consult the oracle of the dead. It seems that after murdering his wife last year in a fit of jealous rage, he was tortured by remorse and wanted to get in touch with her spirit. The three wood pigeons there gave interpretation to the whispering of the winds that his beloved Melissa was cold, that her extensive wardrobe had not been given entry into the world of the spirits with her, and that she walked naked in the dim world beyond."

"He believed them, of course," broke in squareface. "They quoted from her the very words that he threw in her face the night he slew her. 'The oven is cold when I bake my bread in it.' As well it might have been even if she had had no other lover—the man was even more a tyrant in his own house than he is in the city. Of course, those words were all over Corinth the day after he spoke them. His supposedly trusted manservant has a notorious bent for palace gossip."

"Well, cold as her oven may have been," continued baggyeyes, "our good Periander still burned hot for it. Nothing would do for his dear dead lady but to send her a wardrobe such as would bedazzle all those who walk in Hades. Of course, he determined that we should all contribute to it to show our respect for the dead."

He cut a sliver of cheese from the lump on a silver tray and washed it down with a long drink of wine.

"So a proclamation was sent out," he continued. "We were to attend a great fête in honor of Hera. Our wives were to dress in their finest to show their love and devotion to the great mother of the gods. His new laws, of course, applied only outside his own house, and the banquet was such as no one had seen in years. Forty-seven wines from Samos, from Lesbos, even from far-off Thracia. Golden bread baked from Thessalian wheat, honey and fruit from Hymettus, spitted lamb and broiled tripe and sweet blood pudding.

"We made our offerings to the gods. We toasted the good Periander. We feasted and enjoyed ourselves. Arion sang his finest poetry, and little dwarfs from Sybarus juggled golden balls for our entertainment. At the height of the festivities, Periander stood and announced that the ladies should retire to the great hall. They left to be entertained delicately, we imagined, while a young man from Syracuse entertained us men with the most delightful ribaldry we had ever heard. We were laughing so roundly we hardly heard the uproar from the great hall. But uproar there was, and at the end of the night our good ladies had nought but their underclothes to cover their modesty. Guards were suddenly everywhere, and we were all ushered into the courtyard where we watched in utter amazement the beautiful garments of our ladies being consumed in flames, dedicated by the priests to the shivering Melissa."

The group laughed heartily.

"You see how it pays to be an unmarried woman?" one of the younger women commented. "We may miss a lavish palace banquet with good wine and food, but we are not required to help dress a tyrant's murdered wife in Hades."

Lykaina laughed with the rest. She was enjoying herself listening to the talk. There had never been anything like this in Sparta where words were short and mostly about war. She looked across the table just in time to see Telesilla leave on the arm of the young man and disappear into one of the rooms adjoining the courtyard. She flushed in her sudden realization of how these women lived. Of course they would dress well and fix their hair with fancy ornaments. The loom Erinna and Telesilla had been standing at when she first arrived was not the means of their livelihood but only served to help them pass idle hours before business. And these men who came to spend the evening were not there to enjoy only good food and conversation. One by one they would all take their turns in bed and leave refreshed to return to their wives at home.

Her cheeks aflame, Lykaina got up abruptly and slipped across the courtyard and out into the street. She passed dozens of lighted courtyards out of which came laughter and the clinking of wine vessels. The entire district, apparently, was dedicated to Aphrodite whose temple it adjoined. She walked out to the main road and stood in front of the temple looking up at the lights of Acrocorinth which set a blazing crown on the city. Then she turned and faced the sea, letting the salt breeze fill her nostrils.

Was there nowhere on earth where women did not govern their lives by the movements of men? In her own village women were strong and

○

free, yet when they married it was the men who decided where to lead the flocks to graze and what produce to take to the marketplace. In Sparta women lived their own lives in their own houses, yet when the soldiers came home from war, the women adjusted their lives to suit the men's desires. Here, too, she had found women who seemed to be free, yet whose lives were organized to accommodate the pleasures of men. At least these men paid for the privilege—and paid well, it seemed, judging from the luxury of the houses.

Lykaina wandered a long time, letting the night air cool her anger and disappointment. At last she let her footsteps carry her back to the court-yard. The men had gone now, and the women were sitting around the table where the remnants of the evening's food and drink lay scattered.

"You have come back to us," said Erinna with a smile. "You left in anger. We thought you might have gone to find somewhere else to stay."

Lykaina frowned.

"You have no husbands," she said. "You seem to be free, yet you serve men."

"Ah. We hear of the moralizing stance of Athenians, but Spartans are reputed to be looser in their attitude toward the pleasures of the body. But perhaps they are no less rigid, only different." She poured some wine into a cup and handed it to Lykaina. "We are companions here, hetaerae that live together. We live without men during the day. Evenings we bestow the gifts of charm and grace upon those who honor us with their company. We are compassionate toward ourselves, and we are compassionate toward the men who come to us to mellow their behavior. We give them tender motherlove mixed with enlightenment. In our minds they find inspiration, in our delicate beds of love they pick the fruits of happiness necessary to gods and mortals. Can you be offended by that?"

Lykaina struggled for words. "I am not offended, only disappointed that women can never live free of men."

"Are you yourself entirely free of men?" It was one of the other women speaking, a short woman with golden ringlets framing her round face. "Would you pass a dying man in the road and not offer him comfort and healing, if possible?"

Lykaina remembered the young soldier.

"Of course I would not," she said, "but—"

"Well, we are healers, too. We attend to a man's spirit. Sometimes we provide a remedy for his physical ailments as well. Let a man dive into the healing waters of our vaginas, and he can be cured of any disease. Is such behavior to be frowned upon?"

Lykaina pondered her words. Was there a difference between her softening the final pain of the boy soldier, a stranger on the road, and the solace these women offered men who came to them?

"No woman is entirely free of men." Erinna was speaking now. "Even the Amazons take men to their breasts once a year in order to continue their race. We take no men for husbands, but we do invite them into our houses for brief periods. For companionship and love we turn to each other. But our Isis disapproves of the man and woman who remain coupled only to each other, so we invite men of the city to join our group marriage to appease her. Then we send them on their way."

"We are Corinthians, and we live in this city, not on some wild Amazonian plain." Telesilla's musical voice entered the conversation. "We own our own houses, and we pass them on to our daughters who follow in our footsteps. If we married, under Corinthian law our wealth would become our dowries and belong to our husbands to be passed on to our sons. Corinth is not like Sparta. Here women who are wives or daughters of men cannot go to school. They are locked away never to see anyone other than their husbands and children. When they appear at festivals or funerals, they look pale and unhealthy. Our daughters go to school. They learn about ideas, they study music. When they join us in our profession, they can converse with any man or woman."

"Our work is of the temple." Erinna was speaking again. "Like goddess Hestia, we are of the hearth, but our hearth is public. Just as every woman's hearthfire is her altar, so our hearthfire is the navel-stone of the temple. We are daughters of Aphrodite—she who rules birth and life and time and fate, she who reconciles man to all of them through love. We worship her in her temple and in our beds."

Telesilla's coral mouth formed a delicate yawn.

"I forgot to tell you. While you were gone, a messenger came from Arion. He will visit us tomorrow night. Now it has been a long evening, and I have need of sleep."

Her graceful body rose and floated away from the table. The two other women said good night and left the courtyard. Erinna took Lykaina's hand and looked into her eyes.

"You are welcome to stay as long as you like. Sleep well, my child."

And then she, too, was gone. In her own room, Lykaina slipped out of her new clothes and lay down. So much was different here. She had not meant to judge the women, and their words now made her judgment seem childish. It might be well to stay here for a few days before beginning the journey to Lesbos.

Lykaina woke the next morning to find a fresh water jar at her side and her own tunic laundered and neatly folded. She rinsed her face, dressed, and went into the courtyard. Timia sat on the freshly swept courtyard, a wet lump of clay taking on the shape of a small figurine in her hands. She looked up at Lykaina and pushed the hair out of her eyes, leaving a broad streak of clay across her cheek.

"The others are still asleep, but I've been up since dawn. I was hoping you'd rise early, too. I want to take you to my favorite place this morning. Do you like my Hecate?"

She held up a delicate figurine. It looked like the ones she had been selling yesterday. But the arms of this one were raised over her head, and they had finely shaped snakes wound around them.

"It's wonderful," said Lykaina. "Go on and finish it. I'll watch you work."

"No, no. I can finish it tomorrow. This is only the handle. She's going to hold a cup with her arms."

Timia wrapped the figure carefully in wet cloths and, as a final layer, stretched a goatskin loosely around it.

"We'll go visit your donkey first so that you'll be sure he's all right. Then we can go see where the real pots are made."

They left the courtyard and walked along a narrow path that led between the houses. A twisted fig tree by the side of a small hill sheltered Lykaina's donkey along with some nanny goats and a handful of chickens.

"I put your jugs over here where the animals won't knock them over. Your donkey gets along just fine with our goats. See, I tethered him so he won't wander away."

Leaving the stable, they retraced their steps until they came to the paved road. Just before the main square with its new temple of Apollo, Timia turned into a narrow passageway and led Lykaina past rows of stalls filled with pots and more pots. Amphorae, kraters, water jars, plates, beakers, and vases of all sizes and shapes stood on shelves and on the ground. Some of them were finished with bright black-and-red painted scenes; some of them were still being shaped by their makers. Timia and Lykaina stopped by a stall where a broad-shouldered woman sat in front of a small wheel, her large muscular hands embracing a shapeless lump of clay. She nodded at Timia and turned back immediately to her work.

"That's a potter's wheel," said Timia. "Did you ever see one before? It was invented right here in Corinth, no one anywhere else had ever thought of it. See how easy it is to shape the pot? You put one hand inside and one outside, like she's doing now, and the boy spins the wheel, and the clay goes round and round, and the pot gets its shape from how hard you press it."

The woman at the wheel spoke to the small boy at her side.

"Slower now, but keep it steady."

Lykaina watched the lump of clay become a broad-based vase with a narrow neck. The woman spoke again to the boy.

"That is enough now. Bring me the handles I made this morning."

The boy stopped the wheel. At the back of the stall, he carefully unwrapped two long rolls of clay. Lykaina watched the woman turn them into delicate handles that rose from the base of the vessel and returned to its narrow neck. When the handles were secure, the woman set it carefully on a shelf and turned to a group of pots that were no longer shiny and moist.

"Here," she said, "these are ready for firing."

The boy held out a wooden tray while the woman loaded the pots onto it. Lykaina and Timia followed him down the street to an open stall that sheltered a large, square clay chamber. A hairy-chested man wearing only a loincloth took the vases from the boy and set them one by one into the chamber. Then he opened a second chamber where wood was neatly stacked.

"You're just in time," the man told the boy. "We're ready to fire."

He placed a heavy stone across the opening of the first chamber. Then he took a flintstone and struck a spark into the tinder in the second chamber.

"Come back in three days," he said, tending the fire, "and it will be done."

The boy left at a trot. Timia pulled Lykaina farther along the street.

"Here," she said, as they arrived at a small stall where a group of women sat with paintbrushes and half-painted pots. "This is my favorite-favorite stall. Look at all the animals."

Lykaina looked closely at a water jar. A hare, a hound, and a goat, all with thin legs and gracefully arched backs, chased each other around the upper band. Next to the jar, on a fat wine jug, two red and black fighting cocks flanked a small black swan with folded wings. A siren whose dark head was twisted back over her outspread wings graced a small bowl, while next to that a solemn-eyed owl stared out from the middle of a scattering of dark lotus leaves at the base of a small amphora. They were wonderful figures. Lykaina picked up a shallow bowl etched with graceful curves and turned it over to find a dancing sphinx on its bottom.

"There you are. I thought I'd find you here."

Lykaina looked up, startled, and found Telesilla's pale blue eyes smiling at her.

"The child has no use for our loom. It's only potting she's interested in. I suppose I should send her here to apprentice, but it would mean her going outside our community."

Timia tugged at Telesilla's gown.

"Look, mama, see how the neck of the swan is curved like a snake?

I will make one like that, and you can give it to Arion."

Telesilla laughed. "If they taught potting in your school, I wouldn't have to come here to find you to tell you your teacher is waiting for you. Run now. I will entertain our guest."

Timia cast a longing glance back at the women painting and then ran down the street.

"My daughter is quite taken with you," said Telesilla, as she and Lykaina made their way past more stalls of pots.

"It was my luck to meet her yesterday," said Lykaina. "You must be proud of her skills with the clay. I thought the votives she was selling had been made by an adult."

Telesilla sighed. "Yes. She has a mind of her own. She talks of traveling. She says the best potters here are the Phoenicians, and she wants to go to their homeland. She is thrilled, I think, to meet a woman who is traveling to a foreign land."

They left the agora on a dirt road that led westward out of the city and climbed a hill that gave them an overlook toward the Saronic Gulf.

"Tell me about this journey you are taking," said Telesilla. "Where exactly are you going, and what do you expect to find? Since my daughter's intent is to travel, I should know something of the mind that drives a wanderer."

Lykaina frowned. It was hard to believe that she had not been journeying forever. Yet it was only days since she had left Arete and the old woman.

"I am a poet," she said as they sat down on a grassy slope close to a spreading plane tree. "I was born in the mountains. My grandfather taught me the poetry of my people. I was brought to Sparta to sing for the old woman Theadora who loves poetry."

"The woman whose message to Arion you bear," said Telesilla.

"Yes. She listened to my songs, and she told me about the poets she knew. But most Spartan poetry is praise songs for heroes or marching tunes to send the soldiers on their way. My poetry is not like that. It is about everyday things—how people feel when they leave their childhood home, how the mountains look in their springtime greenery, how a birdsong might be a message from a lover. That is the way my people sing."

Lykaina paused and looked out toward the blue water of the gulf. Soon she would be traveling there.

"The old woman told me about a poet," she continued, "a woman who lives on the island of Lesbos. She told me that I should go and meet her. When the soldiers returned from their victory last week, it seemed the right time to leave."

"Sappho, you mean," said Telesilla. "Arion has spoken of her. He even sang one of her poems once, I remember. It was a hymn to Aphrodite, a poem to inspire." She touched Lykaina lightly on the shoulder. "Sing me one of your poems. I love listening to poetry. I learned to play the lyre in school. I have sung the poetry of others, but I could never seem to make any of my own. Sing me one of yours."

"I always sing with my aulos," said Lykaina, hesitating. She looked into Telesilla's eyes. "Well...if you like, I will sing without it."

Telesilla's pale blue eyes regarded Lykaina's dark ones until she was forced to look away. She took a deep breath and sang.

> Early my beloved rises
> donning the sun for her face.
> The moon she puts on for her breast,
> for her eyebrows the wings of the raven.

"No wonder you want to meet Sappho," said Telesilla when the song was over. "You sing of the things she sings. Your poetry is different from the songs one hears here in Corinth. Your language is close to life, your images are strong and beautiful. I am moved by your song."

Telesilla reached out and touched Lykaina's cheek.

"Your rough country exterior belies a soft woman's heart. You are beautiful, Lykaina."

Lykaina's heart swelled into her throat. She let herself be pulled into Telesilla's arms, opening her lips to greet the coral ones. Her breasts felt the gentle brushing of Telesilla's fingers, and deep inside her warm pools seemed to spread outward in circles. Under the broad leaves of the plane tree the rough cotton tunic soon lay heaped with the soft saffron gown. They tasted each other's fruits; then, swollen and satisfied, they fell asleep in each other's arms.

The sun was beginning its journey into the western sea when they woke.

"We must hurry," said Telesilla. "Arion is coming tonight. We must not keep him waiting."

They dressed quickly and walked back toward the city. Lykaina's footsteps fell reluctantly on the stone path. From what she had learned last night, she knew that tonight she would lose Telesilla to the embraces of Arion. Flickers of anger licked her breast, and an image of Arete insisting that her husband didn't matter passed through her mind. As they passed the temple of Aphrodite, Telesilla spoke.

"You are angry. I can hear it in your walk."

"I am unhappy at the thought of you lying with Arion this evening."

"But that is my work, it is what I do. Are you jealous of a man who comes for a few hours? When he leaves I will come to you. We have much to learn of each other's bodies, but we have time."

"But your body will be filled with his body."

Lykaina's words slipped out through clenched teeth. She hated the thought of making love after a man had been with this woman. Telesilla stopped outside her courtyard and put her hand on Lykaina's shoulder. From inside they could hear talking and laughter.

"I am sorry you are hurt by what I do. But I can only love you; I cannot change my life for you. Soon you will be gone, and someone else will love me. I am who I am. You must accept that."

She kissed Lykaina's cheek and slid her arm around her.

"Come, we are late. We will talk of this later."

They entered the courtyard to find Erinna pouring wine into a cup held by a well-fed man with a meticulously trimmed beard. He stood up as soon as he saw them.

"To the most beautiful woman of Corinth. Greetings, my lovely Telesilla."

His eyes lingered hungrily on her body. Then he shifted them to Lykaina.

"And this is the young Spartan who seeks me out? Lykaina, I am told."

Lykaina blushed as everyone turned to her. She forced her eyes to meet his gaze.

"I am of Anabretae in the Taygetus Mountains. I have lived this past year in Sparta with Theadora, grandmother-in-law of Mabriotis who rescued you once from travail. I bring you greetings from her and request a favor for myself."

"My good friend Theadora! I spent many long evenings at her house. She was a devotee of my poetry. She kept me singing for hours. Tell me, is she well? Who sings poetry to her now?"

"She no longer walks, but her eyes and ears are still sharp. I was employed in her house to sing my mountain songs for her, and she liked them well. She told me to ask you for an introduction to your friend Sappho whom I am journeying to meet and from whom I hope to learn about the muse."

"She is an extraordinary poet already, good Arion," broke in Telesilla. "She will do well at Sappho's school. Her poems are like a fresh breeze blowing through sleep-stale rooms."

Arion cocked his head and looked first at Telesilla and then at Lykaina.

"So you will go to Sappho and her hetaerae. She has much to offer a young poetess. Her gift for words is as well known as her gift for love. Sing me one of your mountain lyrics, then, and let me see if your poetry is ready for Sappho's refinement."

Lykaina heard the gentle mockery in his voice and hesitated. What should she sing for Arion? What would the old woman say? Something short, perhaps, so that if he were only amused, it would be over quickly.

She brought out her aulos and played a long passage of twisting notes. The music placed a screen around her as she lifted her voice to sing.

Two suns, two moons came out today—
The one in your face, the other in the clouds.

When she finished, she dropped her eyes and waited. Finally Arion spoke.

"Your song has merit, yes." He paused, his eyes grazing Lykaina's body before turning to feast on Telesilla. "You may be right, my dear. Sappho may well like her poetry." He turned back to Lykaina. "Tell me, have you the poem in writing? I have a friend who would enjoy such a song."

Lykaina frowned and kept her eyes fastened on a single tile. The aulos almost slipped from her sweaty palms.

"You have no copy with you? Telesilla, fetch her papyrus and stylus. The poem is short. She can write it for me now."

A slow flush crawled up Lykaina's neck as she stared at the tile. Telesilla reached out and touched her hand.

"It is short indeed, dear Arion," she said. "You can surely remember it without a scroll. Come, she has sung for you. Give her some words for your countrywoman."

Arion stroked his beard. He pulled a gold ring from his little finger and handed it to Lykaina.

"Here, take this and give it to her. She will know you have come from me. As for passage there, a ship named *Skaftiri* is set to sail next week. The captain is a friend of mine. He is honorable. Tell him I sent you, and he will not overcharge you."

Lykaina placed the ring onto her middle finger and gingerly touched the signet—a dolphin leaping over the waves. Arion turned to Telesilla and took both of her hands into his.

"And you, my precious. How beautiful you look tonight. Shall I sing you some of my latest dithyramb? It will be presented at the Isthmian games tomorrow. A hundred virgins with voices sweet as their bodies will circle the altar and sing. But better than the virgins is my new chorus of wild satyrs. Oh, you must hear the verses they will sing to the virgins—even you will have to blush!" He reached out and stroked her cheek. "You will come as my guest. I will leave word for them to reserve a place for you and your mother—your friend here, too, if you think she would like that sort of thing."

He pressed Telesilla's hand to his lips. Timia appeared out of the shadows holding a small lyre. Arion sighed and took it to his breast. His fingers began to languidly pluck the strings. Lykaina moved into the shadows and sat down on the tiles next to Timia. His mocking words had engendered shame and anger. But the four strings of his lyre, she had to admit, seemed to be plucking notes out of heaven itself. The words of his song flowed from jubilance to wild sorrow, giving the poem a majesty unlike anything she had ever heard.

When Arion finished singing, he let the lyre fall from his lap as he raised Telesilla to her feet. They disappeared into a room, and Lykaina held her breath. She rubbed the dolphin signet and tried to blot out the scene with an image of herself listening to Sappho. Late in the night, as she lay on her mat, she heard the rustle of feet and felt Telesilla's soft skin touch her own.

"Don't worry," Telesilla whispered, "I went down to the sea and washed him out of me. I am a virgin again just for you."

The moon swelled to full while Lykaina waited for the *Skaftiri* to sail. She spent the days watching Timia shape her clay figurines, chatting with Erinna at her loom, or taking long walks with Telesilla. In the evenings, she joined the group in the courtyard, listening carefully whenever the talk turned to poetry. She learned to breathe deeply and still her heart each time Telesilla left in the company of a man. Late at night, when Telesilla joined her on her mat, she blocked out any thought of where this new and wondrous lover had just been.

Word finally came that the *Skaftiri* was loaded and ready to sail. Lykaina sold her donkey and the rest of her barter goods, added the proceeds to the first of the gold coins Theadora had given her, and bought passage from the captain.

The evening before the ship was set to sail, the full moon rose early into the spring sky. The hetaerae sent word that the district was closed. Lykaina let Erinna put a headdress of pure purple on her and walked with her to the temple of Aphrodite. Inside, she saw that the sanctuary was carpeted with shells strewn over the floor. Clay figures of sea anemones, cuttlefish, and sea urchins lay scattered around the base of the altar. On top, a large cone-shaped stone was surrounded by glowing candles. Each woman filed past and laid a coin next to the stone. Lykaina fumbled in her pouch and added the second of the gold coins. When they were all gathered, three women began to play a drum, a cymbal, and a lyre, while the rest of them formed a circle around the altar.

> *Goddess Aphrodite,*
> *who naked rode the scallop shell,*
> *your nymphs surround you.*

Hands upon each other's wrists, they danced a slow *syrtos*. They circled the altar, and the beat quickened. Erinna twisted her white scarf into a roll, extended one end of it to the woman next to her, and began to lead the women out of the temple and onto the moonlit road. They snaked their way to the seashore, the beat coming faster and faster until they were almost running. On the pebbled beach, Erinna coiled the

line inward until all bodies were touching, then turned and uncoiled
it until their arms were stretched wide. She led the women, twisting
her body and leaping high, never losing hold of the scarf for a moment.

The lyre stopped playing, while the drum and cymbal kept the quick
beat going. Erinna stood still, holding the scarf. Another white-haired
woman stepped forward and pulled a sickle from her belt. The rest of
the women dropped back and began to sing lustily.

> Cut off by a sickle
> those godded privates
> fell into the sea.
> You rose from the circle of foam.

The two women stamped their feet and circled each other, Erinna making the scarf billow while the other woman whipped the sickle blade
through the air. The rest of the women, arms upon each other's shoulders, swayed from side to side moaning a wordless tune. The drumbeat became frenzied, then stopped suddenly as the sickle dancer collapsed in a heap with Erinna on top of her. Moments of silence passed.
Then, barely seeming to move, Erinna rose and, holding the scarf over
her head, floated into the shallow water. The women all followed, stepping over the sicklewoman, who remained motionless on the shore.

When they were immersed up to their waists, the upturned drum,
now filled with honeycakes, was passed from hand to hand. The bell-
shaped cymbal, overflowing with wine, followed.

> Out of the drum I eat,
> out of the cymbal I drink.
> Now let me carry my sacred vessel
> into the chamber of love.

The chant was barely musical as the women milled in the water,
jostling each other and laughing. Lykaina stood still, uncertain of what
was happening. Everyone seemed to be splashing around her. She felt
a hand tugging her arm and let herself be pulled along out of the water
onto a stretch of beach where the pebbles were so fine they felt soft as
sand. Strange lips covered hers, new arms embraced her. All around
them sighs and moans of pleasure crescendoed, fell away, then rose
again. Lykaina lost herself in the love of this stranger—whoever she
was—and let herself float like Aphrodite over the foam-flecked sea.

Chapter 4.
A dolphin ride to Euboea

Lykaina followed Telesilla along the crowded quay. A small boy darted past them carrying a tray of food. A man clad in loincloth and sweat rolled a fat amphora up a narrow gangplank. Another pulled at the halter of a stubborn black bull. Somewhere in this disorder lay the *Skaftiri*, ready to take on a poet bound for Lesbos.

"Can it be my dear young friend of Anabretae?" A familiar body lurched out of a wine shop and accosted them. "And the lovely Telesilla, whose mother I have known in years of yore?" The peddler's slurred voice spoke through a wine-sodden beard. At his side, his loyal boy held his ragged purse. "By the looks of you, it would seem the young mountain poet is about to depart these shores. May I offer you my humble good wishes for the voyage?"

He bowed slightly.

"Have you sold all your goods at the games?" Lykaina asked.

"Every hen, every tin goblet." His eyes flashed. "You should have seen the price those two Argive cocks brought. And I was invited to attend the match between them." The peddler looked down at his bare feet. "Of course, I selected the wrong one on which to lay my wager." He looked up again brightly. "Ah, but the fight was well fought—my bird kicked even as his heart's blood ran."

Telesilla touched Lykaina's arm.

"We can't linger, Lykaina." She held out her hand to the peddler. "We must bid you good-bye. Her ship is scheduled to sail before the sun has passed its zenith."

The peddler clasped each woman's hand in turn.

"May Hecate guide you safely," he called after them, grasping his boy's shoulder for support.

The *Skaftiri*, a full-bellied boat almost half as wide as it was long, sported a single short mast from which furls of linen hung. Only a hand-span separated its gunwales from the waterline. On the afterdeck, a barrel-chested man with a red face bellowed orders to the seamen.

"That's not the captain who took my passage money," whispered Lykaina. "Arion's friend is older, not so—" She stopped mid-sentence as the new captain swung his fierce gaze over them.

"So! My female cargo has arrived!" The words exploded through a mat of greasy curls. The man folded his arms over his hairy chest. "Well, get yourself aboard. Or shall I have one of the men carry you up like a jug of wine?"

He threw back his head and guffawed. The four-man crew, who a moment ago had been scrambling to his orders, lined the rail and grinned at the women.

"Where is Testis, captain of the *Skaftiri*?" Telesilla's voice rang out clear.

"I am Skylandros, and I am captain of the *Skaftiri*! Your friend Testis has a pain in his belly, a broken leg, a whore he can't get up from. This is my ship now. A man shouldn't bet on a broken-chested boy. But if he does, so much the worse for him and so much the better for me. Come aboard now. I've got your passage money and I will oversee your journey to Lesbos."

He wiped the spittle from his beard with the back of his hand. Telesilla took Lykaina's arm.

"Don't go with him," she whispered. "He's not to be trusted."

Lykaina frowned. One of Arion's gold coins had gone for this passage, another for Aphrodite's honor. Even if she could find someone else who would take her for her last coin, she would be left with nothing for her arrival in Lesbos. She made her decision.

"It will be all right, Telesilla," she said firmly. "I am strong. He will not harm me. He is only showing off for his crew. Do not be concerned."

They embraced. Lykaina shouldered her pack and stepped up the gangplank. She found a spot at the rail on the forward deck and looked for the last time into Telesilla's beautiful face.

"Ready to cast off!"

Two sailors fore and aft held the heavy lines that kept the ship fast to the dock. The other two took their places at the oars.

"Cast off!"

The lines snaked onto the deck and coiled themselves into piles. Telesilla raised her arm, and Lykaina waved back. The boat moved slowly away from the harbor's enclosure until the quay disappeared behind a pile of rocks.

Once past the breakwater, the men shipped their oars and hauled on the halyards. A fresh breeze bellied out the linen, and ripples broke the surface of the water. The sail trim and the lines fast, the crew busied themselves splicing lines and mending sail linen. In the stern, the captain steadied the long, curved tiller and gazed ahead. Lykaina rested on her pack and watched the Megaran plain slip by.

Suddenly a gray head with a broad nose rose up from a wave. A sleek body dove over the foam of the bow's wake and disappeared under the ship. Dolphin! Lykaina caught her breath. Another one slipped out of the water and followed the first one under the bow, its shiny body reflecting the sun's rays in its momentary flight through the air. Lykaina counted seven of them, sliding in and out of the water, diving over the foam and under the bow. They played until the sun had traveled westward behind the boat. Then they vanished as suddenly as they had come.

The sun sank behind a growing bank of gray clouds, and the night air sent a chill breeze over the water. Eventually the waning moon found a hole in the clouds to shine through. Lykaina pulled her aulos from her pack and blew several long low notes out over the water. One by one the dolphins returned. Now, instead of diving under the ship's bow, they leapt high to catch the moonlight on their bodies. It was as if they were dancing to her music.

Watching the dolphins, she thought about her grandfather. The old man had taught her how to make her first sounds under a cloud-filled sky such as this one. He'd sharpened two reeds and made her blow them until she could produce a clear, brilliant sound that echoed across the hills. When he'd been satisfied that her lips could control the vibrations, he'd hollowed out an alder shoot, whittled it into a chanter, and placed the two reeds in one end. Then he'd taught her to play melodies that bent one note into the next.

Once she'd learned the tunes, they'd spent their days following the herd from one sparse pasture to another, blowing notes at each other across the backs of the animals and listening to the echoes bounce off the rocks. Nights, after a supper of bread and fresh cheese, they would sit under the stars and play the flocks to sleep.

"So you play a little shepherd's pipe, do you?"

The rough voice startled her. Lykaina turned to face a tall, lean sailor whose cheek was cleft by a scar running from ear to nose. She edged away from him.

"If you like to listen, stand back," she said sharply, one hand on the knife in her belt.

A second man, shorter and broader than the first, appeared out of the shadows.

"Play us a dance tune." His hoarse voice rasped. "Play us something we can move our feet to."

His muscles reflected the moonlight as he put his arm around the first man's shoulder. Lykaina stepped backward and stared at them.

"A little dance tune while the moon is still bright," he hissed again.

Lykaina put her aulos to her lips, her eyes fastened on the two men. She played a slow *syrtos*. The men lifted their feet high and brought them down softly onto the deck. The third sailor joined them and then the fourth. Hands on each other's shoulders, the men danced around the forward deck. Lykaina changed the rhythm and played faster. The man with the scarred face executed a series of leaps as he led the line from foredeck to midships and back again. The moon scuttled behind the bank of clouds that by now covered most of the sky, and the twisting line disappeared into the shadows. Lykaina listened to their bare feet patting a graceful rhythm on the wooden deck. She brought the dance to a close and paused for breath. The moon found another hole in the clouds, and the men were revealed once again on the foredeck.

"You play a pretty tune," rasped the broad sailor. "We thank you for your kind entertainment. We bid you good night, and sleep well under Orion."

They all bowed low and slipped off into the shadows. Lykaina sank down on the deck. They had seemed so menacing at first, yet all they had wanted was a dance. She lay back and watched the dark clouds cover the moon again. The wind had picked up during the dance, and now the boat was moving swiftly through the black water. Lykaina fell asleep listening to the snapping of the lines against the mast.

"Heave! Bring it down!"

Lykaina awoke to shouting voices and cold rain striking her face. The men who had danced only a few hours earlier were hauling on the lines that held aloft the sail, now torn and flapping in the singing wind. Ahead of the ship, a red horizon was squeezed between an angry sea and black clouds. The shoreline had disappeared. Lykaina could barely see to the stern where the captain strained to hold the tiller steady.

She scrambled to her feet and found that the deck tilted under her. Her pack slid away from her and lodged at the rail where water engulfed it. The ship pitched, and she fell to her knees. Water rushed past her. She slid back toward the edge and held on to one of the railposts while a wave smashed over the bow and streamed water over the deck. A portion of the rail gave way, taking with it her pack. The ship righted itself. Lykaina crawled to where the men were still trying to bring the flapping sail down. She locked her arms around the base of the mast and closed her eyes.

"Hecate, protect us," she whispered.

The ship rolled sideways. A loud crack over her head accompanied the wave that swept past her trying to wrench her arms from their sockets. She felt a sharp pain in her leg. Then nothing.

When she opened her eyes, she saw that she was covered with a tangle of torn sail and lines. Her leg was pinned to the deck by the broken boom. Blood oozed from a gash above her knee. She tried to move, but the tangled lines held her fast. She looked around. The boat was steadier now. The sea was still angry, but no rain fell from the black clouds. Except for the debris around her, the deck was clear. Looking forward and aft, she could see no sign of the crew. Only the captain, now lashing the tiller to the stern rail, remained. Lykaina freed her knife from her belt and began to hack at the lines.

"Evil spirit, begone!" Lykaina looked up into the captain's face even angrier than the sea. "Destroyer bitch, you plot to drown us all? You would take my newly won ship into the briny depths? I will kill you!"

The captain's fist glanced off the side of Lykaina's face. The boat swung with a gust of wind, and he fell to his knees. Lykaina slashed with her knife to free herself.

"You have cost me my sail and my crew," the captain roared, as he struggled to regain his footing. "You will pay me with your life."

Hacking desperately at the heavy lines, Lykaina felt the blade of her knife snap. Out of the corner of her eye, she saw the captain's arm drawn back with a marlinspike ready to hurl. One last pass with the broken blade and she was free. The boat pitched, and she slid across the deck and into the water. Even without its sail, the ship moved swiftly away from her.

"Deathmonger, let Poseidon take you! Let the fishes suck your bones! Let the...."

The final curse was lost in the wind, and the *Skaftiri* disappeared into the mist. Lykaina, alone in the water, looked around. Her whole body was numb. Tears of rage and terror spilled from her eyes. She had no idea in which direction a shore might lie. The journey, hardly begun, seemed over. Hecate, guide me, she prayed. Don't let these black waters swallow me. She struggled to keep above the waves. Each time she felt her body sink, she willed it to rise, to let her mouth gasp in the early morning air. I will not die, I will not die—the chant resounded again and again inside her skull.

Something nudged her shoulder. A sleek gray head rose out of the water next to her and small round eyes looked into hers. The head disappeared, and she felt one dolphin's body slide under her left arm, another slide under her right. So the story about Arion's rescue by dolphins may have been true! Exhausted, she hung between them and let them carry her.

The ride took her out of the storm. From time to time Lykaina glimpsed other dolphins swimming on either side of the two that bore her, their shiny backs breaking the dark surface of the water. They formed a broad phalanx riding through the gray waters. As the clouds lifted, they moved faster, swept along by some ingoing tide. Black shapes appeared out of the mist on either side of them, and Lykaina saw that they were moving through a wide channel. Trees and hills emerged from the gloom. A rocky shoreline came closer. Lykaina felt the dolphins slip away from her. She put her feet down and touched bottom. Both dolphins rose out of the water and executed simultaneous flips in the air as if to salute her. Then they were gone.

Lykaina stood on one leg in the shallow water. She touched her face with her hand and found it swollen and painful. The salt water had cleaned the gash on her leg, but she had lost a lot of blood. She hobbled out of the water. Exhausted from the ride, she lay down on the shore and slept.

She woke to the sound of voices. Opening her eyes, she saw that the sun was high in the sky. Four young girls spoke to each other with words that seemed familiar, yet she could not make sense of them. When she sat up, the girls stopped talking and backed off. She struggled to stand, but her leg, now stiff and swollen, would not support her.

One of the girls—a gangly child with red curls around her face—rushed forward and helped her to a rock. The girl knelt beside her and touched the skin next to the gash. She spoke, but her words fell too strangely on Lykaina's ears to be understood. Lykaina put out her hand.

"Speak slowly," she said, "I don't understand you."

The girl raised her brows astonished. She turned to her friends and then returned her blue-eyed gaze to Lykaina.

"You are hurt," she said, pronouncing each word carefully. "You must not try to walk." She smiled suddenly. "We will help you to our village. Wait here." She spoke rapidly to her companions, and they scattered into the piney woods that came almost to the shore.

Left alone, Lykaina touched her wound gingerly. Her whole body ached. She looked around her. Next to her rock, a scraggly stand of hyssop pushed through the pebbled soil. She stripped some leaves from the bushy plant, chewed them, and applied the pulpy mass to the cut.

Presently, the girls returned, each carrying sturdy short sticks which they proceeded to tie together with the cords from their tunics. The redhead beckoned to Lykaina.

"Come. Sit here. We will carry you to our village."

The morning sun filtering through the tall pines made soft patterns on the carpet of needles they walked over. The girls were strong. They stopped to rest only once before reaching the village of square mud-coated houses with flat mud roofs that climbed up the slopes of a hill. As they passed through the village lanes, wide-eyed children stopped their play to silently follow them.

In front of a large house on the third level of the hill, the red-haired girl called out. A woman appeared in the doorway. Stout and muscular, her face had the same look as the girl's, her hair the same copper color. Rapid speech passed between them. The woman turned to Lykaina and spoke slowly and clearly.

"My daughter says that you have come out of the sea and that you are injured. You are welcome to rest at my house."

"I had a misfortune at sea," explained Lykaina. "I hurt my leg, and I had to swim ashore. I am grateful for your kindness."

The woman waved the girls away. Lykaina hobbled to a low stool by the circle of stones near the doorway that held the remains of a fire. The woman disappeared into the house and returned a moment later with a clay bowl filled with clear liquid. She threw some twigs onto the not-yet-dead coals and blew until a flame burned steadily. The bowl, set at the edge of the fire, gradually turned a steamy brown.

"Willowbark tea," the woman said, as she handed the brew to Lykaina. "It will ease the pain."

Lykaina had not drunk willowbark tea since she left her village. Spartans, of course, were expected simply to endure their pain.

"What did you put on the wound?"

"Hyssop," replied Lykaina. "I saw it growing near the shore."

"You are knowledgeable in the ways of healing. Where is your home?"

"Far from here. I am Lykaina of Anabretae. I was born in the Taygetan Mountains near Sparta. I am journeying to the island of Lesbos. My ship met a storm, and I was washed overboard. I hope to find passage on another boat—"

Lykaina stopped, realizing that the woman was frowning at her.

"Sparta! This is Euboea. It will not be safe for you here when the men return. Sparta is our enemy." Lykaina stared at her. The woman broke off a heel from a loaf of bread that had been cooling on top of a round clay oven. "Here. You must be hungry. Eat this. Then you can rest inside."

Lykaina sunk her teeth into the dark barley bread. Her host moved across the dirt yard to a nanny goat tethered to an olive tree.

"There's no need to worry yet," she called to Lykaina. "The men are away on the Eretrian Plain fighting the Chalkidians. That is, we call it the Eretrian Plain. The Chalkidians call it the Chalkidian Plain. They fight over it every year. They go out just after seeding and battle until harvest time." She pulled the nanny's teats and squirted milk into a jug. "It should be a few more days before they return. If they win the war and the barley crop is good, it will be a happy year for all of us." She got up and brought the jug back to the hearth. "But not for you. You must be away by then. You should practice walking, even if there's pain." The woman reached up over the doorway and pulled down a long crooked stick. "Tomorrow you can walk with this crutch. My husband used it last year after a spear left his leg useless. Now you are tired, you need to sleep."

The woman helped Lykaina into the house and left her on a pile of fresh straw next to the chicken roost. Lykaina thought about her host's warm hospitality and the warning that she must leave soon. Sparta seemed so far away. How could these islanders consider her an enemy? She fell asleep wondering if the danger were as great as the woman had said.

The next morning, after her host and her host's daughter left for a day in the barley fields, Lykaina took the crutch and set out to explore. She hobbled into a square where a plane tree sheltered a row of old men sitting on a stone bench. Although the day was hot, they all wore heavy woolen leggings under their coarse tunics. One of them, whose white hair hung halfway to his shoulders, called to her.

"Ah, the young stranger is walking. Come closer so we may see you. Talk so we may hear your strange speech." He turned to the other men. "She appeared out of the sea. My nephew's wife is keeping her." He turned back to Lykaina. "Talk to us, woman. We are old men who have need of a new voice."

Lykaina stepped closer and stood on her good leg.

"I am grateful to your kinswoman for her hearth," she said.

"Ah, listen to the sounds of her words. Speak more. How did the sea spit you up? How is it that a woman can be so far from her home?"

Lykaina shifted her weight on her crutch.

"I was traveling by ship," she said. "A storm arose, and I fell overboard. I was carried to your shores by two dolphins."

Murmurs ran along the stone wall.

"Dolphins, you say," said the old man. "Poseidon watched over you, then. Now tell us your homeland and why you have left it."

"My home is in the mountains beyond Sparta and . . . ."

Too late Lykaina remembered her host's words of warning. The old men exchanged looks. The murmurs turned to rumbles.

"Poseidon has saved you for what?" muttered the old man with narrowed eyes. "You are of the enemy. Your Spartan kin are joined in alliance with the Chalkidians." He shrugged. "What matter, though? We on this bench are all too old for war. Enjoy your days with us. But you should know that when our sons come home, it will be another story."

A youngster ran by followed by a pack of boys waving sticks.

"Kill the Spartan dog! Kill the Chalkidians!"

The old man waved his hand after them.

"You see? That is how it will be for you when the soldiers return. Well, until then, enjoy the sunshine of our streets. We are good people, you know. We plant seeds in the brown earth and nurture their growth. It's only a little war each year that stirs our blood."

Lykaina, shaken, left the square. Back at her host's house, she fell onto her bed of straw. Her leg throbbed from too much walking, her head from the danger ahead of her. Will it heal in time? she thought. It was hard to believe that the friendliness she had encountered so far would change. Yet she knew from her days in Sparta how differently people behaved when soldiers returned from the battlefield.

That evening, the kinswomen of her host brought their distaffs to the outdoor hearth for a night of storytelling. Children at the feet of their mothers and grandmothers listened wide-eyed to tales of magic and mystery until sleep curled them into little balls. Lykaina struggled with her broken knife to transform an alder shoot she had taken from the tree behind the house into a new aulos. Between stories, the night air blended the sounds of spinning whorls with the drone of insects and the occasional soft hoot of an owl.

Away from the others, at the far edge of the fireglow, a lean-faced woman held a small box loom on her lap and passed a wooden shuttle back and forth. Her eyes were deepset over high cheekbones. Wild black curls streaked with gray were held in check by a blood-red kerchief. Her tunic, long and flowing, was a red so dark it was almost black. In a quiet moment during one long tale, the woman suddenly called out words that skipped unconnected around the edges of the story.

"The three-cornered cave spills blood into the blackness of night, but the silver moon rises."

For a moment there was silence broken only by the whirring spindles. Then the taleteller picked up the broken skein of her story and continued. When the circle had dispersed into the night, Lykaina asked who the woman was.

"She is Maia. She works spells. She is related to my sister-in-law." Her host turned abruptly and went into the house.

At the next evening's hearthfire, Lykaina found herself sitting next to the strange Maia. She watched the nimble hands pass the shuttles back and forth. The half-finished cloth was the same deep red as Maia's tunic, with warp threads all black and the weft the color of a late-summer berry. From time to time Maia slid a white shuttle in and out until gradually a row of moons—waxing, full, waning—emerged from the cloth.

"Your weaving is beautiful," remarked Lykaina, in a lull between stories. "What are you making?"

Maia looked up from her lap. Her eyes burned into Lykaina's.

"The shuttle pulls the threads of life forward and back. The weaving is of the hearthfire, its place is the edge of the circle. It does not frighten the children. Are you a child?"

Lykaina, taken aback, did not answer. She concentrated on her whittling. A wolf's head was beginning to emerge at the top of the alder shoot. She turned her attention back to a new taleteller who had begun to talk about a warrior woman of an earlier time. Later, in another silence between stories, Lykaina heard Maia's hoarse whisper again.

"A tree grows, and the wind blows life through its leaves. When the goddess danced upon the waves, the North Wind breathed life into her womb. When the poet breathes life into an alder shoot, all the children of Eurynome dance. Come to my house tomorrow, and I will show you divine things."

Lykaina stopped whittling and looked into two black eyes that burned like glowing coals from the fire. A shiver ran through her body, but she was not afraid. They locked eyes for a long moment. Then Maia suddenly wrapped her shuttles around her loom and vanished into the night.

The next day, Lykaina hobbled to the square. The old men waved to her to join them. Lykaina shook her head.

"I am looking for the weaver, Maia. Can you direct me?"

The old men looked at each other. The one with long white hair finally spoke.

"You would visit the Maia woman? What business have you there?" His eyes seemed less friendly than before.

"I would see her weavings," answered Lykaina. "She has invited me."

The men exchanged glances again. Finally whitehair pointed along the street.

"Take this past the well. Where it forks, take the downhill path. Follow that until you come to the woods. Look carefully in the trees. Her abode is there." He turned away from her as if to dismiss her, barely hearing her thank you.

Lykaina followed his directions. The path petered out at the edge of the woods. She peered through the leaves and saw a hut made of mud bricks and shaped like a beehive. A low wooden doorway decorated with double spirals marked the entrance. Lykaina ducked under the lintel and stepped down to a sunken floor of hard clay. Ochre-stained walls ended in a domed ceiling. A small hole at the top let out the smoke that rose from red coals on a three-legged brazier. Along the walls hung tapestries—black and red with white spirals or crescent moons or stars.

"You have come to the womb of my cosmos." Maia sat next to the brazier, a small reed snake cage on her lap. "Like every womb, it bleeds without being wounded, like a snake it sheds its skin and lives. Please be welcome."

Lykaina sat down on a low stool and laid her crutch beside her. She looked at Maia. Again she felt drawn by the dark eyes.

"You have made these all on your loom?" she asked, nodding toward the weavings. "They are wondrous. They seem as if they come from another world."

Maia opened the cage door and began to stroke the coiled python. Her voice was low and chantlike.

"It was in *this* world that black-winged night surrounded the Great Mother. She laid the silvery egg in the womb of darkness. It was *this* world that she shaped into heaven and earth. She breathes in, she creates; she breathes out, she dissolves. Everything flows from her—the wind and the mountains, the waters and the tides. She guides the shuttle to record her being."

A peacefulness embraced Lykaina. Her thoughts roved to her mountain grandmother, a small wiry woman whose leathery hand had held her own on their long walks in the mountain meadows. She closed her eyes and saw the special places where they had picked bunches of black hellebore and blue hyssop. She smelled the bundles they had brought home to hang from the ceiling. Maia's voice brought the old woman back so forcefully, it was as if she were present in the room with them instead of sleeping under the black earth. Maia brought her back to the smoky interior.

"The Great Mother walks the serpent path through the terrestrial earthflow. She climbs the winding spray of stars of the galaxy. You are traveling and still nameless to me. What is your origin? Where is your journey's end?"

For a moment Lykaina didn't realize that Maia's words held a question. The dronelike voice seemed only to spill mysterious words into the air with no mind to their destination. Then she felt a thread from

Maia's eyes pulling words from her mouth.

"I am Lykaina of Anabretae in the Taygetan Mountains. I am a singer of words. I have set my mind to meet Sappho, the poet of Lesbos. My journey was broken by misfortune, but as soon as I am healed I will find my way again."

Maia set the snake cage aside and touched the wound on Lykaina's leg.

"The demon is still inside you."

She took the kerchief from her head and stood up. Taking three cloves from a head of garlic hanging on the wall, she folded them into the kerchief and tied it into a knot. She passed the knotted kerchief over Lykaina's leg three times and chanted, "Great Gaia who creates and destroys, loose the demon from this woman's leg." Maia threw a lump of salt over her shoulder and spat. "The demon has returned to its owner. The pain will ebb."

Lykaina felt her leg. The swelling seemed to have diminished. Again she felt the tie to her grandmother. She remembered her crooked foot and the fenugreek her grandmother had rubbed on it. And salt. Whenever her grandmother finished a cure, she threw salt to the ground, saying it was the true blood of the earth.

Maia stood up.

"The sun chariot travels the paths of destruction. The sun hero slashes the timeless web of life, but the threads of fate reweave themselves. The life force ebbs and flows again. Where is the voice that sings under your words?"

Again Lykaina did not recognize the question for a moment, and again she felt her mouth open of its own will.

"I lost my aulos in the dark sea. The shoot I was whittling at the fireside will be a new one."

Maia rummaged in the dark of the hut. She returned to the fire and held out her hand.

"A broken blade cuts no wood. This will carve a voice worthy of your words."

Lykaina took the knife, her eyes wide with wonder. She had never seen such a tool. Around its haft wound a carved ivory snake with an egg in its mouth. She touched the black obsidian blade and drew blood. She looked up to speak her gratitude, but Maia had turned her back and was standing at the tall loom that stretched from floor to ceiling. Lykaina stood up. Her leg was strong again, and she could put weight on it without pain.

"I am indebted to you for many gifts," she said. Maia did not seem to hear her. Lykaina looked around the hut once more, taking in the signs on the woven icons. Then she picked up her crutch and left.

Outside, she found she did not need the crutch. She could walk on her leg, even run on it with no pain, no weakness. As she jogged through the narrow village lanes, she noticed that women and children alike drew away from her. Whispers followed her. They must be surprised to see me healed so quickly, she thought, as she joined her host and daughter at the hearth. Her host frowned at her as she passed a bowl of broad beans, but she said nothing. Lykaina herself remained silent throughout the meal. After the daughter had disappeared into the sleeping loft, the admonishment began.

"The whole village speaks of your visit to the Maia woman. You are a stranger, and your ignorance must be forborne. But from this day on you must be careful where you walk. The woman holds evil in her heart. She is not of this place, she is a stranger. Her family came from across the water. It is whispered that as a child she made the seas rise angry until they swallowed her brothers and father. Her husband, the uncle of my sister-in-law, had his lifeblood sucked from him. He was in the prime of his life and healthy, yet less than a season's turning after they were married, he withered and died like barley in a summer drought. His family knew she had worked the spell. They made her leave the village. They say she went to the mountaintop and there practiced forbidden rites. I was a small child when all this happened. Her evil ways were common knowledge. Even we children knew to stay away from her."

A lump of dough took shape under the host's hands. The woman threw it onto a flat rock and began to knead it.

"I was just betrothed when she dared return to the village," she continued. "It was the aunt of my husband-to-be who brought her back. She was our village weaver. She said she needed help with her loom. We did not want the woman, but we allowed her to stay to please our aunt. After our aunt died, we let her stay on. But we made her build her house outside the village so that any spells she might cast would have no power over us. We tolerate her at our hearth only because she is kin."

The rounded dough was set aside, and another lump was thrown onto the rock.

"Her talk is crazy and perhaps seems harmless. But she is not to be trusted by anyone. You must stay away from her. If she healed your leg, it was only to draw you into her web of evil. Do not go again."

Lykaina did not answer her host. She watched her shape and knead two more loaves in silence. Something deep inside her told her that Maia was not evil. She held power, that was clear, but not evil power.

Lykaina had learned to trust her own senses when she was very small. She thought about the time during her first year away from the wolf's den when she had gone with her mother and grandmother to the spring for water. She had lagged behind, and her mother had called to her impatiently. Without knowing why, she had stood frozen in her tracks. Her mother had shouted angrily, her grandmother had called quietly, but still she had refused to move. And then a tall pine, heavy with the weight of late winter snow, had fallen on the path in front of her.

If Maia were a danger to her, she would know it.

That evening Maia did not appear at the hearthfire. Lykaina missed her, although each slice of the obsidian blade brought up her presence. She lost herself in a long tale about the demands of a river god for a human sacrifice so that a bridge might be built across the water. Eventually the fire burned itself into a heap of red coals as the final sliver of the waning moon scuttled from cloud to cloud. Now that her leg was healed, Lykaina thought, she could travel. Tomorrow she would ask her host to direct her to a fishing village where she might purchase passage to Lesbos. The last of the three Corinthian coins the old woman had given her was still safely sewn into the pouch on her belt. Surely it was more than enough to continue the journey.

A chill breeze brought her out of her thoughts. She saw that the bobbins were hanging motionless, and that the women's faces were turned toward the trail that led to the barley fields. Lykaina listened, too, and soon made out a distant whooping voice echoed by another whoop.

"They're coming," said a woman, getting up from the fire. "They're in time for the harvest."

Spindles and bobbins were quickly gathered in, and each woman vanished into the night to her own home. The children ran off in the direction of the shouting.

"Build up the fire," her host called to Lykaina, as she went into the house. She returned with a chicken, its neck freshly wrung, and held it over the fire to singe its feathers. Lykaina helped her pluck it, clean it, and spit it over the flames. Then her host turned to her.

"You must hide now. Once he learns that you are from Sparta, he will declare you his slave. Go quickly and cover yourself with straw. When he is asleep, my daughter will show you the path to the mountain."

Lykaina hurried into the hut and burrowed down in the straw. The whoops, accompanied by tramping feet, were close at hand now. A chorus of barking, braying, and cackling resounded through the village. Lykaina watched the space next to the fire fill with a squat man in a pigskin tunic. His legs bulged with muscles. His sweaty arms hung loose from his shoulders. Above his short, ragged beard, a pair of eyes set deep under a wide brow reflected the blaze of the fire.

"Barley wine, woman!" The coarse voice cut through the late night air. "Bread and onions. Move quickly, your husband is hungry from his victories."

He took the jug held out to him and sat down heavily on the low bench by the fire. Lykaina watched his larynx bob as the wine ran down his throat. The jug empty, he turned to the bread and cheese on the bench beside him. The jug was refilled while he tore off hunks of bread and pushed them into his mouth. When he had washed down three small loaves of bread with as many jugs of wine, he pulled the half-cooked chicken from the spit and tore it apart with his hands. Sucking on the bones, his appetite at last sated, he belched and looked around.

"Where is the Spartan whore?" He belched again. "The children said my house had been defiled by the enemy."

Lykaina's host narrowed her eyes.

"She is waiting inside to please you." She handed him another jug of wine. "Here, you have hardly begun to celebrate."

His black brows met in the middle of his forehead as he stood up and drank the wine in one long swig. He wiped his mouth with the back of his hand.

"So she is here. Good. She will be my slave. We have just defeated the dog Chalkidians, so we have just defeated Sparta. I will beget little slave children on her."

Unsteady on his feet, he sat down suddenly and belched again. Lykaina touched the ivory snake in her belt and held her breath. The jug fell to the ground, and the soldier slumped forward, his head on his knees. The host hurried inside to Lykaina's hiding place.

"He will not wake up until the sun is high tomorrow," she whispered. She turned to her daughter who stood beside her with frightened eyes. "Bring her to the trail that leads past the great forked willow by the river." She turned back to Lykaina. "It will take you over Mount Dirfis. On the other side is a fishing village where you will find a boat to continue your journey." She gathered up the remains of the soldier's bread and cheese and put them into a goatskin bag along with a water jug. "It is a two-day journey, perhaps three if the pain returns to your leg. There are willows along the way. You can make tea if your leg swells again."

She went to a large black box that stood next to the entrance of the house and pulled out a tiny pigskin bag tied with a leather thong. Out of the fading fire, she picked three burnt-out coals and placed them carefully into the bag. Then she took a bright blue bead from the box, threaded it onto the thong, and sewed up the bag.

"Wear this," she whispered, tying the amulet around Lykaina's neck. "There is danger in the night. You will need protection from the evil eye."

She put her hands on Lykaina's shoulders and kissed her on the forehead.

"Go now to the good."

Lykaina picked up the goatskin bag and her almost-finished chanter and followed the daughter out of the firelight. They hurried along the path by the river until they came to the forked willow. Standing there, a dark night cloak about her shoulders and a large woven bundle in her hand, was Maia.

"I will guide you over the mountain. I will protect you. We will sail the dark sea together. We will meet your destiny."

The force was there, vibrating between them. Lykaina turned to the daughter.

"Go back to your family. Thank your mother and tell her that I have found my way. I will be all right."

Chapter 5.
The Great Mother's temple

A stone pillar marked the branching of the path. Maia paused and touched the rounded top lightly with both hands. Without a word, she turned onto an uphill trail barely visible under the thick pines that shut out the stars. She slowed her pace slightly as they climbed the trail that switched back and forth up the mountainside. Abruptly she stopped, unwrapped her cloak from her shoulders, and spread it on the ground.

"Black night, black forest," she whispered. "Black is the beginning of all things. We will sleep."

Lykaina shivered. The sweat that had earlier flowed from her body now took on the chill of the night air. She dropped gratefully onto the cloak, wrapped herself in a corner of it, and fell asleep. Only two or three dreams later, she felt a nudge at her shoulder and opened her eyes. Sun rays slanted through the cypress trees that encircled the cloak. She took the bowl of steaming nettle tea offered her. Maia seemed less mysterious in the early morning light. Lykaina drank the tea and watched her methodically roll the cloak into a pack and scatter the ashes of the fire.

Back on the trail, they climbed steadily, surrounded by birdsong and dappled sunlight. When they emerged from the forest, a rockier path led them between low shrubs and past the occasional twisted tree. The sun warmed them. When it stood directly overhead, Maia dropped her pack and pointed to a flat rock.

"The sun at its midpoint and we at ours, it is time to refresh ourselves. Sit."

Lykaina searched in her pack for the bread and cheese her host had given her. They ate slowly, looking back down over the pine forest to the narrow strip of water that separated Euboea from the mainland. To the north, in the distance, they could see the famous plain over which the Eretrians and Chalkidians annually fought.

"I am grateful to you," said Lykaina, "for leaving your home to guide me."

Maia turned to her.

"I am not leaving my home," she said. "I am going to my home. All of my homes. This night we will sleep in the place where I was a young woman. Tomorrow we will find our boat in the village where I spent my maidenhood. After that we will sail to the shores of my birth."

"You were born in Lesbos?" asked Lykaina in surprise.

"I was born in Lesbos."

Like her daylight appearance, Maia's speech was no longer mysterious. She spoke quietly, reminding Lykaina of women she had listened to all her life.

"My people were fishers," Maia said. "We lived at the edge of a small sea inside the island. I will take you. It is called Hieras. When you are there, you think there is no way out into the big sea. But if you sail with the rising sun over your left shoulder, you find a passage between two great rocks that opens into the Aegean. When the Aegean is angry and its dark waves are capped with white flying foam, Hieras is still blue, calm as the water in a bowl."

Maia tossed a piece of bread into a bush in front of them. A bluejay dropped from a branch and carried the prize away.

"Every night of my childhood," she continued, "my father and my brothers would go out, each in his own little boat, each boat with a lantern hanging out behind. The fish would see the lantern and come to the surface. They did not see the tridents poised, ready to drive home. The boats all returned with the sunrise. I waited every morning at the shore with my mother and sisters. The men threw the fishes into our baskets. We tied the baskets to the donkeys so that my mother and sisters could take them to the agora in Mytilene."

"Mytilene," echoed Lykaina. "Where is that?"

"Mytilene is the first city of Lesbos. Mytilene is where you will find your Sappho. You can walk the distance between the Gulf of Hieras and Mytilene in the time it takes the sun to rise halfway to its zenith. I will show you."

Maia turned and looked fully at Lykaina.

"I see they gave you protection against the evil eye," she remarked, fingering Lykaina's pigskin amulet. "They would do better to give you protection from their own warring gods."

She turned away and threw another piece of bread to the waiting jay. She talked softly, almost as if to herself.

"They think the evil eye is something that lurks in the night air waiting to harm them. But it is the eye of the Great Mother who watches them. They have forgotten that they, too, once worshipped her. They, too, walked in the path of her spirit. They have forgotten how they took her many faces and cut them away from her. Who is Artemis, Huntress of the Moon? Who is Hera, Queen of the Heavens? Who is Hecate, dark Goddess of the Night Sky? They are all our Great Mother—she who creates all things mortal and immortal. But *they* have forgotten."

Maia pulled a waterskin from her pack and drank. She handed the flask to Lykaina.

"My grandfather," said Lykaina, wiping her mouth with the back of her hand, "said that the gods and all living creatures came out of Oceanos, the stream that girdles the world."

Maia looked at her carefully, measuring the statement.

"And who created Oceanus?" she said. "Out of Chaos," she spoke slowly, letting each word take its space, "our Great Mother emerged and gave birth to sea and mountain and sky. To amuse herself, she mated with Ouranos, the sky god. From that union she brought forth titans and cyclops and hundred-handed creatures. She loved them all. Ouranos, like fathers everywhere, was jealous of his offspring. He hid them in her depths. But they would not stay. The sons rose up and killed the father. In time, they tried to kill their own sons to prevent the turning cycle. It distressed the Great Mother to see these male creatures killing themselves. It was she, in her ever-giving nature, who saved the infant Zeus from being a morsel in his father's greedy mouth. She took him to a mountaintop and nurtured him with her breasts."

As she talked, Maia's hands described in the air the words she was speaking. She went on.

"She continued to turn the seasons, to pull the tides in and out, to draw out of black earth the fruits of abundance and return them to earth in their time. Sometimes she left the lesser gods to their bloody quarrels, sometimes she intervened. But those who tilled the earth and fished the dark seas forgot who turned the seasons and who governed the tides. They became taken with this Zeus creature. They made him a god above her. They set his sons up with him. They took their fragments of the Great Mother and set them under him—his wife, his daughter, his consort. They began to call him the supreme father of us all."

Maia stood and brushed the crumbs from her lap.

"Remember this, Lykaina. It is all in their minds. His palace on Mount Olympos, the underwater one where Poseidon stables his white horses—they do not exist. The Great Mother exists. *She* is the earth and the sea, the moon and the stars. She is the mountains and the rivers. She is this very stone we sit on and the wiry grass that grows around it. She is our birth and our death, our time and our fate. Who can deny her? Let them tell stories of their Zeus and how he did this or that. They are only stories. It is Earth that is real, and the Earth is our mother."

Maia got up and went to lie down in the shade of a nearby elm. Her gentle snore reached the rock almost before Lykaina realized the space beside her was empty. Lykaina continued to sit and stare at the wisps of clouds that changed and rearranged themselves as they floated. The heat of midday passed slowly as she mused on Maia's words. Her thoughts were interrupted by Maia's hand on her shoulder.

"Let us put our feet onto the pathway of Earth's spirit again. We will reach the summit by nightfall."

It was black night when they mounted the final crest. No moon lit the way, and the stars hid behind banks of clouds. Lykaina followed Maia by sensing her on the path ahead. Thorns tore at her arms and legs as she pushed through thick underbrush. Maia disappeared between two large stones that held a third slab across the top. Lykaina followed and found a great rock blocking her path. She felt its face and discovered a cleft near the ground. On her hands and knees, she crawled in the direction of Maia's shuffle. When the sounds ahead stopped, Lykaina found herself in a space with enough headroom to stand. A triangular break in the cave roof opened to a slice of the sky. In the time she had been crawling through the passageway, the clouds had parted to reveal the faint halo of the new moon. Maia stood with her arms upraised, the pale starlight reflected on her dark face, her lips moving in silent prayer. She dropped her arms, rummaged in her bag, and pulled out the water flask, a bowl, and a small cloth packet. The liquid she handed Lykaina was milk-white with yellowish flakes floating in it.

"Drink this fruit of the moon. Like the new moon, you will swell and increase, you will nourish yourself."

Lykaina, thirsty from the long climb, drank deeply. She sank onto Maia's cape spread out on the cave floor. She felt safe in this dark, warm space, its black velvet silence enfolding her. Maia's drone lapped around her ears as she drifted into unconsciousness.

Lykaina felt herself swelling, slowly at first, then faster until the silence around her burst into a thousand singing stars. She raced through the night, circling each star, coming close to its pulsations, then shooting off to the next one. The black expanse seemed endless, the stars infinite. She sailed through the Pleiades and dipped into the Great Milky Way, moving so quickly that the song of one star melted into the music of the next. The stars took on colors—reds and yellows and deep purples—and their songs faded into silence. They grew wings and moved about her motionless self. The air became bright gold with sunshine. She was standing on soft earth watching butterflies flitting near and dancing away. All was silent.

Lykaina felt herself growing smaller and smaller until the wings of the butterflies became like willows waving above her. The eye of a single butterfly became a deep pool that drew her in. She swam down, down into its depths. Everywhere she looked, small creatures peeked out of spiraled shells. Surrounded by sounds tinkling like goatbells on a country path, she swam in and out of the shells. The dark sea washed her.

Now her feet touched down onto a solid floor, and she was motionless again. Brown earth caressed her. The shells became tiny rhizomes sending their silent shoots upward. Thousands of seeds everywhere sprouted and pushed their way through the soil. A gnarled tree root took hold of her and carried her down, down to the lower world where she heard the whispering souls of the dead. "Gaia, Gaia," they murmured, "Gaia, Gaia." The tree root let go of her. A tendril just breaking out of its seed caught her hand and pulled her up and up until she burst out of the ground and into the bright air.

She opened her eyes. A small fire burned in front of her. The opening at the top of the temple framed the Great Bear of Artemis. Maia looked at her with eyes that seemed to stare into her soul.

"The Great Mother has shown you her realm."

"What happened?" asked Lykaina, blinking her eyes in the firelight.

"The Great Mother has taken you on a journey. She offers the journey to all, but only a few have the courage to go. You are blessed."

Lykaina shivered. She put her hands out to the fire and again felt the surge of life go through her body. No wonder the villagers were afraid of Maia, she thought. She holds great power. Or rather, the power is the Great Mother's and Maia the channel through which it flows.

"You are blessed," repeated Maia.

A wedge of sunlight opened Lykaina's eyes. The cave room was empty, the fire a pile of gray ashes. By daylight, she could see that the walls were covered with black-and-ochre paintings. The high-domed ceiling peaked in a blue triangle of morning sky. She crawled out of the tunneled entrance and found Maia pushing sticks into a fire.

"The one who is newly blessed greets the morning."

Lykaina took the steaming bowl offered her. She sipped the nettle tea, feeling her body strong and her heart clean. She rewound the visions of the night through her mind's eye.

Maia walked to her bundle and pulled out an armful of sticks and yarn. She drove one stake into the ground and quickly transformed the others into a bow loom, passing a woven girdle around her hips to pull the warp threads tight. Her low voice accompanied the shuttle movement.

"When I was younger than you, I lived in this temple. There were many priestesses then. I helped them in the ceremonies and brought them the things they needed—oil for the lamps, laurel leaves for the fire. We needed to be secret even then. But worshippers came. Women told their families they were gathering herbs or visiting a sick cousin. We ate whatever they brought us. If it was too dangerous for them to leave their villages carrying food, we gathered wild berries, nuts, and honey. After seven years I became a priestess, too, and stayed another seven years."

Lykaina looked at the overgrown entrance to the temple, the thorn bushes and the wild brush that choked the path leading to the clearing. Once this place had been a busy community of priestesses. She went to her own pack and pulled out the alder tube. If Maia were going to tell a story, she would finish the aulos.

"Then came the years of the barren fields," Maia continued. "The first year, the rains were few and the crops poor. We ate more roots and berries that year, but no one worried. The next year even fewer raindrops fell. What grain they brought us was stunted, the fruits pale and small. More people began to come to the temple, but the gifts they brought were fewer. The third year there was no rain at all. The temple was filled with people from all the villages—men as well as women, people who had almost forgotten the Great Mother, but who turned to her in their time of need. We prayed to her to release the rains. We came out of the temple and prayed to her in the open air."

Maia's fingers deftly reknotted a thread that had broken. She picked up a bare shuttle and wound white thread onto it. Lykaina knew a figure would soon emerge from the black and red.

"She heard us. There was a promise of rain—you could smell it in the air. Dark clouds began to gather. The first drops were gentle, almost like dew falling. A rainbow touched earth. Then the clouds rolled in, and the fields drank their fill. The barley lifted its withered heads and rose upright to greet the cool moisture. Everyone saw that it was she who gave us our lives back."

Maia's voice stopped, and only the sound of the shuttles and the obsidian blade disturbed the mountain air. The story of the temple touched a memory inside Lykaina's head. She stopped her carving to pull up the dim image. A temple on the mountaintop. . .having to go secretly. . . fear of being discovered. Her hands took up their task again as she saw herself a child climbing the mountain with her grandmother. They were supposed to have been gathering oregano, yet the path they had taken led away from the meadows. Steep and rocky, in places it had been no more than a ledge between a wall of rock rising above and a deep gorge falling away below. At the top, exhausted, she had curled up under a cypress tree to sleep.

When she had wakened, she had been frightened, she remembered, because she had not been able to see her grandmother anywhere. Then she had heard voices, several voices in a drone. The long-buried image came back to her vividly. A domed hut—now she recognized it—a beehive made of stones. She remembered how she had crawled through the long low entrance just as she had last night. Her grandmother had been standing with four other women, all chanting and swaying. Human language had been still new to her, and she had not understood the words. But one word had come again and again, engraving itself on her memory. *Gaia*, the name had resounded each time it was chanted. *Gaia*, the name Maia chanted when she sang to the Great Mother.

Her grandmother had gathered her up after the ceremony and hurried her down the mountain path. She had not spoken to her until they were far below, back in a field of oregano.

"You will not speak of this to anyone," her grandmother had whispered, as if the rocks around them had had ears. "We have been gathering herbs all day. If they know about us, they will destroy us."

So. Gaia was not just divine earth, a lesser goddess. She was the Great Mother. Perhaps on every mountain there was a temple for those who knew where to find it, in every village those who secretly crept out to worship. Lykaina looked over at Maia, now cutting an altar cloth off the loom. Back in the village she had been called evil and crazy. Yet the things she said were neither crazy nor evil. How better to discover others who followed the ancient path than to utter disconnected threads of an overall weft. If they were recognized, the hearer would be part of the secret. If they were not, the hearer would only think the speaker crazy.

"This Great Mother," said Lykaina, "she had a temple in my Taygetus Mountains. My grandmother took me. I had forgotten until now."

Maia grunted.

"I know. I saw her in you at the hearthfire. You had forgotten her, but she had not forgotten you."

Maia looked into her eyes, and Lykaina felt the pull again. A white bird with an egg inside it flew across the altar cloth. Lykaina looked down in her lap and found her own work was finished, too. Six holes marched up the aulos, each carefully spaced as her grandfather had shown her. Hollow wolf's eyes stared out from under the carved mouthpiece. She carefully unwrapped the two reeds she had taken from the shore, tested them to see if they were still wet and fitted them into the mouthpiece. She blew tentatively. Maia nodded to her. Reflections of the late morning sun danced over their faces. Lykaina began a simple shepherd's dance from her childhood, but the sacredness of the place around her changed the melody's shape. Lykaina's heart filled as she sent the notes circling around the clearing. She sang.

> Look at the amaranth, where does it bloom?
> At the fork of the road, on the stones, on the rocks.
> Whoever cuts it, cuts herself,
> but she who eats it never dies.

They spent the rest of the morning clearing the brush away from the front of the temple and scrubbing the entrance stones. Sweeping the cave floor inside, they found shards of clay vessels amid the animal debris. Lykaina picked up two unbroken votives and handed them to Maia, who placed them reverently near the libation stone. They were silent as they worked, each task seeming to be understood without words. From time to time, the song of a blackbird fell through the dome's triangle.

The peace was broken by shouts and the sound of feet trampling the brush. Maia and Lykaina both froze.

"Here! Look at this! Didn't I tell you this old path would take us to it?"

The voice outside the cave had the uncertain pitch of an adolescent male.

"What? Where? I don't see anything," a second squeaky voice responded.

"There. See those two stones standing upright? And the third one laid across the top? That marks the entrance. Here, let me have a drink of that."

Lykaina looked at Maia and saw her eyes wide open, an ancient terror reflected in them.

"How'd they get that stone up there?"

"It looks heavier than an iron ox cart. Here, let me step on your back, I'm going to hoist myself onto it."

Grunts and scuffling sounds were followed by a whoop.

"Look at me! I'm the king of the mountain!"

"Here, give me a hand, I'm coming up, too."

The women heard the scraping sound of rock on rock.

"Watch out, it moved! Hey, maybe we can rock it off and jump free."

Maia gripped Lykaina's upper arm, her fingers digging deep into the flesh.

"Fools," she whispered. "They play with sacred things. Let them be struck down for their blasphemy."

They listened to the sounds of leather soles striking the rock again and again. Eventually the scuffles were replaced by panting.

"I could have sworn it moved before. It doesn't look so secure."

Feet thudded to the ground.

"Forget the old stone. Let's see what's inside the cave."

Maia pulled at Lykaina's arm and disappeared behind a rock jutting out next to the libation stone. Lykaina followed her into a passageway barely wide enough to slip through. At its end she had to crouch and squeeze herself through an even smaller hole. She could feel that she was in another large chamber, although she could see nothing in the pitch black air. She put out her hand and touched Maia's arm. Maia pulled her close to her.

"We are safe here," she whispered. "No man can pass into this chamber. They will amuse themselves, and then they will leave."

Lykaina took the reassurance into her quaking belly although she could still feel her heart—and Maia's—beating wildly.

"See?" The voice was close at hand now. "I told you it was a house of evil. Great Mother, they called her. Great smelly hag, I say. Let's smash her to bits!"

The breaking of clay against stone reached their ears.

"Tssst! Careful!" the second voice whispered. "It's dangerous to offend even the old goddesses. They may try to avenge themselves. Let's go back to the deer tracks."

"Afraid, are you? What can she do to us? We are almighty. We are under the protection of Zeus. Here, take a swig of this and then let's see how this altar cloth tears."

Maia and Lykaina stood holding each other, listening to the desecration of the temple—the smashing of the clay votives, the scratching of the wall paintings—all accompanied by high-pitched shouts.

"Here is a roaring bull's dung to suck into your slimy maw, you death-dealing bitch. Choke on it, haw!"

"And here is winepiss to wash it down. Let's see your power now, old sow of the universe!"

Maia buried her head in Lykaina's shoulder. Lykaina's own ears pounded along with her heart.

"She smells just like any old woman now, doesn't she?"

The voice was panting.

"Phew, yes. Did I ever tell you the story my great-grandfather used to tell? About how he came here once with his regiment when there were still priestesses doing their evil things?"

"Tell me now while I catch my breath."

"They'd been enticing the villagers up to ensnare them in their deathtraps. The old hags had gotten bold. So my great-grandfather's regiment stole up the mountainside one fine morning and took them by surprise. There were lots of them, he said, young ones, all luscious and ripe for plucking and old ones all withered and dried up. What a time they had of it. They surrounded them and herded them all together like a pen full of sows. Then they went at them. Stuck their boar's rods into every hole they had, including the ones their swords made. They strung them all up. You should have heard his description of the hag-fruited trees. You would have roared with laughter."

"We missed all the good times, didn't we? Born too late."

"Maybe not. Didn't you notice the ashes out there in the clearing? And that altar rag looked just woven. Maybe there's a priestess or two here yet. Their slime always seems to be oozing back. We'll give them the same as my great-grandfather did."

"You're right. There is the smell of female crotch in here. Let's go stick them."

Lykaina held on to Maia, their two hearts pounding so hard she was sure they would be heard. The footsteps crashed around the outer chamber for an eternity.

"Nobody here. Maybe they're outside."

"Let's go hunt them down."

Her ears followed the sounds through the tunnel of the entrance and out into the brush beyond the clearing. Finally there was silence. The two women stepped back from each other. Maia's voice was low and hard.

"May the Great Mother shrivel their seed and the rod that plants it. May their blaspheming tongues swell and blacken until their mouths rot. May a thousand moon-mad furies pursue them into eternity."

The curses cut through the fear-drenched air. Lykaina felt Maia brush past her. She followed her into the outer chamber where, without speaking, they worked to cleanse the room of the boys' filth.

Later, out in the clearing, they ate their noonday meal of bread and cheese. Maia's face held no expression. She chewed slowly and stared into the ashes of the dead fire.

"Is it true what the boys said?"

Lykaina was afraid to ask, but she needed to know the answer. Maia continued to stare at the ashes. Finally, she spoke.

"It was just after the rains. We had been so eager, we had forgotten to be careful. Some of the new people did not understand how the temple must be kept a secret place."

Maia picked up a burnt stick and drew it aimlessly through the ashes.

"The soldiers waited until the rains had started to fall. Even they, in their blasphemy, knew that only the Great Mother could bring the rain. Their Zeus, their Poseidon—what did they care about the farmers? Their women called on Demeter, but their prayers were all wrong."

The bird and the egg from the weaving took shape in the ashes.

"After the rains had fallen, after the crops were renewed, they came. On horseback with swords, with torches, they climbed the mountain. They set fire to the altar. They destroyed everything."

Maia's hand stopped moving. She stared straight ahead.

"I had been out in the woods picking mushrooms. I heard the terrible cries, I saw the flames from afar. But I was a valley away. By the time I could run back, the men were gone. The temple stones were scattered. My sisters were hanging from the trees."

Maia stared sightlessly. Her eyes were wet, but no tears fell to her cheeks. Her voice dropped to a whisper. She broke the stick across her knee.

"I cut them down one by one. And one by one performed the burial rites. I cleared away the ashes of the altar and carved a new one out of oak. I set the temple stones upright again. The Great Mother gave me the strength. I worked for forty days, and for forty days I did not eat. The Great Mother kept me strong. If the soldiers came again, I thought, they would see how the Great Mother still lives. But the soldiers did not come again. No one came."

Lykaina felt a volcano rumble in her stomach.

"Why do they hate us so?" she whispered.

She almost choked on the words. Maia looked at her.

"Hate us? Before hate there is fear. We carry within us mysteries they cannot understand. They want to be masters of all, but they cannot be masters of what they cannot understand. So they deny our knowledge even as they cut us down."

Maia stood up.

"Women understand the cycles of life. We are of the moon. We know that the slender sickle of light grows nightly until it waxes full, then diminishes to darkness again until the new moon rekindles the sky. Men are of the sun. Every day it is the same, every day they are the same. They are afraid of the changing faces of the moon."

Lykaina got up and stood next to Maia. They watched a squirrel climb up a tree, its cheek bulging with a nut.

"The movement of the moon governs our lives," continued Maia. "We carry within us its cycles. At the dark of the moon we bleed without being wounded, in its fullness we pass the seed that promises life. Our wombs carry the power to bear moonfruit. When man enters us in search of the life-giving seed, he feels himself diminished while we swell. When he sees life growing within us, he fears his own death. We know that within every life is the seed of death, that our immortality is in the never-ending cycle of our children and our children's children. But man is greedy, he longs for immortality for himself. He envies our wombs—the source of life—because he sees in them the source of his own death."

Maia took Lykaina's hand and held it tightly.

"They call our sacred openings devouring gullets. They think we use them to suck out their precious life spirit. They will destroy the earth trying to destroy us. But in the end we will survive them. Come, we will gather the honey and almonds. Tonight you will enter the Great Mother's circle."

The headband Maia wove for Lykaina echoed the silver moonboat of the night sky. She led her deep into the brush to a place where spring water emerged from an outcropping of rock and fell into a crystal pool below. The night air was cold. Lykaina shed her tunic and stepped into the water. She shivered as she immersed herself. She stepped out and let Maia dry her with rough material and rub a musk-scented oil over her chill-roughened skin. Maia tied a withered mandrake root around her waist. Shaped like two lovers embracing, the rough tuber scraped Lykaina's bare skin. Something deep inside her navel quivered. Lykaina closed her eyes and let the wordless rhythm of Maia's chant connect with the rhythm flowing through her body. Sensations that began in the outer skin moved inward until her whole body glowed.

Inside the temple, a small votive lamp sent shadows dancing over the cave walls. Lykaina's oiled body gleamed in the soft glow. Maia raised her arms and chanted in a low voice.

> Virgin Gaia who rides the clouds,
> many-breasted mother of the earth,
> dark crone of the underworld,
> accept what is already yours.

Still chanting, Maia took Lykaina's hand and led her in a dance. They circled around the libation stone and past the jutting rock that had hidden the secret tunnel from the boys. Maia's voice rose and fell wordlessly. The rhythm of her chant quickened at each turn around the cave. Sweat ran freely from Lykaina's body, down her rib cage, down her inner thighs. The quiver inside her navel spread throughout her lower body, reaching places that usually only a woman's touch could rouse. The rhythms pushed faster and faster as Maia now stood her in the center of the cave and whirled her around. Sweet juices flowed inside and out, and her body shook uncontrollably. Maia raised her arms until Lykaina was standing on her toes, her feet still, her body jerking in wild gyrations. Her breath came in short gasps. Something seemed to push out from deep inside her. Her motionless outer body made a shell around the inside pulses. A white heat exploded in her core and spread out to her toes, her fingertips, the ends of her hair. Now Maia was rubbing her again, mixing her sweat with fresh oil. So alive was her body with sensation that she could not tell if Maia's hands were under her skin or outside it.

Maia stopped rubbing her. She opened her eyes. Maia was holding out the newly finished aulos.

"The Great Mother is inside you. Praise her."

The hand that took the aulos seemed detached from the glowing body. The fresh reed in her mouth tasted of brine. She began to play, feeling each note resonate deep in her belly before it passed from her lips out through the alder tube. She heard the music as if it were being played by someone a mountain away. Yet every note slid over her body, circled around the cave and rose like a night swallow through the triangular opening up to the waiting crescent moon. The words that flowed through her mouth seemed to come from somewhere outside of her, yet they resounded in her core. She sang.

> *Virgin Gaia who rides the clouds,*
> *many-breasted mother of the earth,*
> *dark crone of the underworld,*
> *I emerge from your delta of life.*

Chapter 6.
Arrival at Lesbos

A steep downhill path led the two women to a fishing village stretched along the side of the mountain above a rocky shoreline—a balcony over the blue sea. Under the noontime sun, shadowless streets zigzagged between rough-cut stone houses. Below, under the shade trees along the shore, half a dozen fishermen sat cross-legged mending their nets. One man, knee-deep in water, scraped barnacles from the waterline of his boat.

"Wait here," hissed Maia, and disappeared into one of the stone houses. Lykaina stood and watched a dark shadow on the eastern horizon emerge from the morning mist to become a large island.

"That is Skyros." Maia's voice was at her side again. "Beyond that— six days, perhaps seven—is Lesbos. We have a boat."

"Someone will take us?" asked Lykaina.

"We have a boat," repeated Maia. "We will take ourselves." She smiled at Lykaina's puzzled face. "The boat is my cousin's. I grew up sailing, you know. I will teach you. Come."

They took a rocky footpath down to the harbor. The men lifted their heads from their work as the two women passed by.

"Good day to you," one of them called. He turned to a small boy who was lining up dried sea urchin shells on a stone. "Go and assist the women in whatever they need. Quickly, now."

The boy left his shells and trotted after them. They followed the shoreline until they came to a cove where a small coracle lay overturned. Several of the skins that stretched over its round bottom were torn. The keel was cracked. A pile of torn linen, poles, and ropes lay tangled beside the boat. Maia eyed the scene. She pulled a long bone needle from her bundle and knelt next to the upturned hull.

"Take the boy and find some pine tar," she said. "You will need to mend the keel. If we work quickly, we will set sail by sundown."

What had seemed a hopeless task began to take shape as the sun crossed from the sea in front of them to the mountain behind. The hullskins patched and the crack of the keel filled with pitch, the lightweight boat slid easily into the water. Maia showed Lykaina and the boy how to fit two poles together with a third one crosswise over the top. They stepped this bipod mast into the wooden frame and fastened it securely with lines. The sun had dropped behind the mountain when they hoisted the newly patched linen onto the mast. A gentle breeze ruffled the sail.

"Our time is right." As the sea took on the shadows of dusk, Maia's voice became low and mysterious again. "It is fifty days from the waning of the Pleiades. The Etesian will blow us straight to Lesbos. Get in."

Lykaina climbed into the boat and crawled forward. Maia followed her and crouched in the stern. The silent boy pushed them away from the shore and waved. Maia paddled with a short, flat oar until the boat was beyond the harbor mouth. Then, as the stars began to emerge from the darkening sky, she placed the oar firmly under her arm. The sail bellied out, and Maia steered the wind-pushed boat over the dark waters. When the lights of the village above the harbor had disappeared into the night mist, she called Lykaina to the stern and pointed to the stars overhead.

"You will learn to sail now. It is the Seven Sisters that must be watched. Keep them over your right shoulder. They come from our Great Mother. She birthed them to bring good weather to sailors. When they begin to wane, the seas rise and the storms blow. When they reach their zenith at the end of the new year, the Mother's consort must die and let another take his place. You will watch them carefully."

Maia placed the oar under Lykaina's arm and the line into her hand. She sat close to her, watching her every move. Each time the coracle veered off course, she reached out her hand to correct the oar. When wind spilled from the linen, she took the hand that held the line and helped Lykaina adjust the sail. By the time the sky ahead of them had reddened into dawn, Lykaina was feeling the joy of the wind in the sail and the boat gliding over the water.

They sailed for seven days, taking turns at the steering oar. When Maia helmed, Lykaina slept in the shade of the sail. When Lykaina took the oar under her arm, Maia stayed close by, showing her how to keep a steady course even when the wind blew gusts and the waves danced.

"How do you know the ways of sailors?" Lykaina asked her the first day out.

"I learned to sail as a baby," replied Maia. "Every day, after my father and brothers came back with their catch, my mother and sisters took the fish to the market. While they were away and my father and brothers were sleeping, I crept down to the shore and raised the sail. From out on the water, I could see a piece of the footpath my mother and sisters took. When they appeared on their return from the market, I sailed back to shore."

Maia reached out to adjust the oar under Lykaina's arm.

"When I was only twelve suns' turnings, it was decided in our sorrows that my mother and sisters and I should come to the house of my mother's brother. He had married a woman from the village where we took this boat. That land seemed barren after the green of Lesbos. My mother's brother took us in reluctantly—we were four females, and in that village they did not value women."

Maia looked back over the stern, and Lykaina followed her eyes. Skyros, which had been a pale blue shadow on the horizon all morning, had disappeared. They were alone on the water. Maia continued.

"They did not value women, and they did not pay attention to the goddesses. In Lesbos we worshipped the Anatolian Artemis from whose many breasts flow the bounties of life. But no one there gave great reverence to Artemis or even to Demeter. Poseidon gave them the fruits of the sea, they said, and Zeus held reign in the sky. Even the dark underworld they had given over to Hades. To them Athena was only Zeus' daughter, Persephone the wife of Hades, Artemis Apollo's sister. Everywhere the ceremonies were different from those I had known. Their gods were always in the center. Sometimes I would hear a small piece of a familiar prayer in the middle of their strange incantations.

"My mother and my sisters went to the temples with my cousins. 'What can we do?' they said. 'It is not the same here as at home. We are foreigners, we must learn to belong.' But I found some old women who took me to the temple on the mountain. And there I found the one who creates and destroys, the one who makes peaceful harmony out of opposing forces. We had to go secretly at night. They said it was dangerous to be seen worshipping the Great Mother. And her high holy days—we celebrated them in secret. My mother and my sisters warned me. They told me not to follow the old women."

The sun passed momentarily behind a bank of clouds. Lykaina shivered.

"It was when my uncle found out about my night visits," Maia went on, "that he arranged for my marriage. I had just had my first blood, and I did not want to marry. In Lesbos it is our custom to know ourselves well before we join with another. But my uncle said marriage would cure me of my stubbornness. The man was a widower. His first wife had died in childbirth. It was whispered that the infant, a girl, had been born living and that he had snuffed out its life when he learned his wife was dead. He told my uncle that I looked strong enough to bear sons and work his fields. He said he would take me without a dowry. So I went from one barren land of exile to another."

"Was the village where we met the village of your husband?" asked Lykaina.

"It was," answered Maia.

"It seems strange for a woman to go to her husband's village," remarked Lykaina. "Even in Sparta it is the woman's home that the man comes to."

"Just so it was in Lesbos," Maia replied. "But these Euboeans—they not only make the male gods the center of worship, they make the man the center of the family. I went to my husband's house. I was a foreigner twice over. They treated me like a pack donkey. I worked from dawn until long after dark. And then . . .," a frown creased Maia's brow, "and then when I went to his bed, he could not raise his rod to plant his seed. He said I was bewitching him. I who had not seen fifteen winters, I knew nothing of how a man plants his seed. His family screamed at me, they called me dry wood. They brought an old woman to do her magic with the mandrake root. They brought me into the village square where little boys beat me about the belly with willow switches. But it was not I who was the dry wood. The black earth does not send forth its shoots unless the seed has been planted."

The sail hung limp for a moment. Then a fresh breeze caught it and sent the boat surging ahead.

"Finally, he could no longer raise his hand to beat me," she continued. "His face took on the color of dead ashes. He complained of a pain in his belly. They brought an old woman with herbs, but he continued to wither. One morning he did not waken. His family said that I had poisoned his soul. They stoned me and drove me away from the village.

I remembered the Great Mother's temple on the mountain. The priestesses took me in. They said I could be of the Mother, that she would look after me."

Lykaina remembered the story her host had told her. Here was the truth.

"But you came back to the village that turned you out. Why?"

"It was years later. A woman lived there who wanted me." Maia sighed. "After the massacre, I observed all the rituals for my dead sisters. One day, this woman came to the temple. She told me that it was too dangerous for people to come there again. She said that I should come to the valley and live like a villager. She was a weaver. She said I could earn my bread making cloth.

"I did not go at first. I needed to stay with my dead sisters. And there I lived for seven more years. Every year this woman came, at first alone, then with two or three others. In the end she persuaded me to come with her. We went up to the mountaintop every full moon. From time to time others came, too. But one by one they died, and the young people would have nothing to do with the Great Mother. It is true, they called on Demeter to help them. But they knew her only as Demeter, guardian of the crops, not as the Great Mother of all. And they never came to the temple on the mountain. When my weaver friend died, I was left with her loom. For these last twenty years I have gone alone to the temple. Until you found me."

"And you never returned to the land of your birth?" asked Lykaina.

"I have been waiting for the sign. If we read carefully what the Great Mother sends us, we do not step falsely."

"It is so many years since you came, how can you still know the way?"

"When I sailed that first journey, I looked carefully at the night sky. I memorized every star and how it fit with the other stars. I knew that one day I would find my way back. When I learned that your destination was Lesbos, I knew the Great Mother had sent you as a sign. I knew that the time had come to return to my homeland."

Lykaina looked closely at Maia's face. She could not guess her age. Her dark curls were streaked with gray, her brown face was deeply lined, yet her body did not have the movement of agedness.

"And you?" asked Maia. "You, too, left the village of your childhood to go to a strange place. Tell me how that came about."

Lykaina closed her eyes for a moment, remembering her mountain village. She has told me her story, she thought. Now I will tell her mine. She took a deep breath.

"My brother tricked me into leaving my mountain home," she began. "He and my cousin always went to Sparta to sell our goat cheeses. My cousin pretended he had hurt his ankle, and my father told me to go in his place. It was a difficult journey. We not only carried cheeses, we drove a dozen kids with their nannies. Dawn had not broken when we left, but the sun had almost completed her journey westward before we arrived. We slept outside the city. The next dawn we went into the marketplace."

Maia reached out and took Lykaina's hand to pull the sail tighter. Lykaina felt the boat surge forward on a fresh breeze. In her mind, a memory of the Spartan market engulfed her.

"I was terrified," she continued. "I had never seen so many people nor heard so much noise. There were animals everywhere—sheep and goats bleating, chickens cackling, donkeys braying. The men shouted and pushed each other for space to set their goods. My brother shouted along with the rest of them. I stayed close to the nannies. They didn't seem to mind the noise, although the kids were as frightened as I was, I think. I took out my aulos and played, to soothe myself and to quiet the kids."

Lykaina saw herself in the midst of the hubbub, blowing her aulos to bring order to the chaos in her head. The nannies and kids, she remembered, had huddled around her—the nannies, it seemed, to comfort her and the kids to be comforted. Her brother had called out to every passing stranger to come and taste the fresh mountain cheese.

"While I was playing," she went on, "a shadow suddenly fell over me. I looked up. A soldier stood there. He frightened me even more than the peasants and their animals. He seemed tall as a mountain, and his legs looked like small tree trunks. He told me to sing."

A strong gust made the boat surge forward on the crest of a large wave. A glance from Maia told Lykaina that she must hold the steering oar firmly. The wave passed, and the boat steadied itself.

"I had been longing for my home, so I sang a song about the mountains that wait in the springtime for the nannies and kids to climb their paths. I was afraid of him, but I did not let my voice tremble. When I finished, he turned to my brother, and they whispered together. My brother told me to go with the soldier. I stood in terror, but the soldier took my arm. The nannies bleated after me. I thought my heart would crack. He led me into the courtyard of a large house where an old woman was asleep on a litter. 'Sing!' he commanded again. So I sang. When the old woman opened her eyes, she seemed as fierce as the soldier. But then her face softened when I sang about a young girl washing her clothes with musk tears and hanging them on the bitter almond tree."

"So your brother sold you."

"My brother sold me. But the old woman did not treat me like a slave. I sang for her, and she told me stories of her childhood. If Sparta was strange to me, it was strange to her also. So much was different from her childhood. The gods had changed, she said. And the ways of men. The poetry she loved went unsung. That was why she listened to me."

Lykaina had never spoken so much before. In the mountains she had talked only to the goats; in Sparta she had usually been the listener. But Maia's eyes seemed to pull words out of her. She seemed hungry for knowledge of Lykaina's life. She seemed to understand the thoughts that lay unspoken behind the words.

Maia slept in the late afternoon, leaving Lykaina to steer the boat alone. She was coming to love the feel of the water surging under the skin hull, the wind ruffling her hair as it bellied out the sail. She watched the surface of the water, looking for the dark areas that told her a gust would soon tip the boat sideways unless she adjusted the oar. She looked back over the stern. Behind the little boat, the sun hung suspended for a moment above the horizon and then slowly inched its way into the sea.

Dusk spread over the water. Maia, now awake, stood up abruptly and took the oar from Lykaina. The boat swung gently into the wind, its patched sail flapping. Maia touched the oar to her brow three times, then laid it in the bottom of the boat. She stepped out in front of the mast and faced the low-hanging crescent moon.

"Gaia, Gaia."

The chant melted into the darkening sea. The night air chilly, Lykaina pulled her cloak around her and waited. Maia let the chant die away. Then she stepped back into the center of the boat and picked up the oar.

"You will sleep now. I will sail."

They changed places, and Lykaina gratefully curled up in her cloak. Lying in the bottom of the boat, she watched the stars become bold and bright as the dark sky chased the fading light. She woke up several times during the night and listened to the hull slapping the waves. A thousand stars filled the black sky, their pattern revolving slowly around the double mast. Each time she woke, Maia was motionless, her eyes peering into the darkness. Once when Lykaina opened her eyes, she saw for an instant a glow surrounding Maia's head, but when she blinked, it disappeared.

The next morning Lykaina's sailing lessons resumed. Maia showed her how to keep the boat on an even keel even when the wind whipped up the waves until they crashed over the stern and into the boat. As the sun climbed the morning sky, they shared the last of their provisions.

"This evening we will pull fish up from below," Maia promised. "The Great Mother will direct them to our boat. Tell me how you came to be called woman of the wolves."

Lykaina smelled the fresh breeze and the salt air as she plunged back into her memories.

"For my first years, I was raised by a wolf," she began, remembering the dark, damp cave filled with animal hair. "I don't remember how I got there or how long I stayed. I remember the den and my mama's warm belly. We huddled against her—my littermates and I—while the wind blew snow to cover the cave's mouth. When the sun drew buds from the waiting trees, she pushed my littermates out of the cave. Her belly swelled, and then there were new littermates, tiny and almost hairless. She must have pushed me out, too, because I remember running with the others through the forest, picking berries and catching moles. One day I fell into a trap. My brothers and sisters tried to help me, but the ropes held me fast. They ran away when the humans came. Two hunters took me to a village and gave me to a family. They told me to call the daughter of the house Mother. Her mother and father became my grandparents."

The sail fluttered. By now Lykaina knew to tighten the line in her hand. The sail filled as she continued.

"I had a crooked foot. When I ran on all fours with the wolves it didn't matter. But my new mother made me walk upright, and my foot dragged behind me. My grandmother wrapped it in a fenugreek poultice every night and pulled at it. Little by little she straightened it, and I learned to walk on two legs. And to wear a tunic."

Lykaina closed her eyes, remembering the first time her new mother had pinned the coarse goathair material around her. She had struggled and screamed. As soon as her mother had set her free, she had torn at the cloth until it fell from her. Her mother had picked up the tunic and roughly pinned it on again. It had taken many pinnings and more tears before she had allowed the material to remain on her body.

Gradually she had learned the ways of people. She had learned how to take food with her hands and place it in her mouth to chew. She learned to follow her mother carrying water jugs up the mountainside to a place where the stream fell from rocks into a deep pool. She had learned to walk carefully with her grandmother over the mountain meadows repeating names after her—thyme, hyssop, goat's rue.

"I had only been with my new family a season's turning," she continued, "when they brought my mother her groom from the next village. Everyone danced for three days and three nights. Then my mother's new husband went up the mountain with my grandfather and the goats. Soon after he left, her belly began to swell just like my wolf mother's. Only it wasn't easy for her like the wolf. She screamed in pain. She threw herself from side to side. My grandmother gave her wormwood tea and hung a sprig of thyme over her head. She called on Hecate for assistance. But Hecate decided to take my mother to the underworld and leave us my brother in her place. Two winters after that my grandmother began to cough and to spit blood. By then I knew how to make the wormwood tea. I had learned the chants for Hecate. But before the trees had opened their buds, she had gone to join her daughter. When my grandfather and my father took the flocks up the mountain again, they left my baby brother with a cousin and took me with them."

Lykaina stopped talking. She had not even told the old woman in Sparta this much of her life. Deep inside her, the memories had created a whirlpool. She turned her attention to Maia's hands, which were knotting the threads of the torn net that had been lying in the bow. They sailed in silence, letting the sun make its journey westward behind the boat. She thought about Maia's tale of exile, how they had both come to leave the lands they loved.

"You said you came to Euboea with your mother and sisters. Why did you leave Lesbos?" she asked. "And where were your brothers and father?"

Maia kept her eye on the net in her hands. Her brown face showed no expression as she spoke.

"It was late summer. The skies were already beginning to foretell the coming winter storms. One night the smelts began to run, great schools of them. For these you don't use tridents, of course. They are too small to catch that way. Instead you have nets like this one—all strung from one boat to another. Smelt fishing is best done when the sea is calm so there is no danger of the nets becoming tangled. This day the sea was not calm. My mother argued with my father while he readied the boat. 'Wait,' she said, 'wait until the winds rest.' My father scoffed at her. He said it was for women to fear and for men to conquer fear. She said that Thetis sent them the fresh wind as warning. He said that no woman held realm over the sea, that the sea belonged to Poseidon. In the end, he and the others went out. My mother and I took votives to the temple and prayed for the sea to become calm."

Maia stopped talking and let her head sink to her breast. She seemed to sleep. Lykaina held the oar steady and kept her eye on the belliedout sail. A silver fish jumped out of the blue water, caught the sun for an instant, and disappeared again. A few moments later, Maia opened her eyes and continued the story.

"Not a single boat returned," she said flatly. "In one night, there were no more men in the village. I was the oldest of my sisters. I was almost as tall as my mother. I was strong for a child of twelve suns' turnings. I knew how to sail. I begged my mother. 'Let us stay here,' I said. 'I will catch the fish. I will teach my sisters.' But all the other families were scattering to relatives. So we left, too."

Maia stood up and dropped the mended net over the side of the boat. For a long time there was no sound except for the waves on the boat's hull. Then a slap of water. Maia quickly drew the net up. A large white fish flopped into the bottom of the boat.

"Whiting," Maia said. "Give thanks to the Great Mother. We will eat well tonight."

Lykaina handed Maia her knife and watched her scale the fish, slice it lengthwise, and throw the guts to the sea.

At dawn on their seventh day out, gulls began to circle the boat. Ahead, a dark cloud on the horizon grew. Shapes separated themselves into mountains and hills. They slid along the side of the island until the solid shoreline opened a crack. Maia maneuvered the boat between two great rocks and into a small sea surrounded by forests and low hills on one side, mountains on the other. A sandy beach presented itself for landing, and the hull touched bottom. Lykaina was in Lesbos.

Maia dropped the sail and hopped lightly overboard. She and Lykaina dragged the boat onto the beach and left it slightly atilt on its keel. They scrambled up the bank to a meadow of tall grasses and bramble bushes. Maia picked up a stick and poked in the weeds. Back and forth she criss-crossed the meadow. Lykaina, puzzled, followed her. Finally Maia stopped and grunted.

"There," she said, "that's all that's left of the home of my childhood."

A few large stones marked out a foundation; smaller ones lay in a pile. A mole scurried from its disturbed nest. Lykaina looked back toward the gulf where the water lay blue, the sun's reflections dancing on its patterned surface. Across the gulf a range of mountains rose from the narrow plain that bordered the shore. One tall peak towered over the rest.

"Olympos," said Maia, following Lykaina's gaze. "But not the one where their posturing Zeus lives. This one is our own Olympos. When I was a child, they said that once a year Artemis would come from her mountain in Anatolia, bringing with her her lions and her snakes and her dancing maidens, and take up residence on Olympos. We all went, the whole village, every midsummer. We climbed the mountain on stone steps that went first one way and then the other up the mountainside. Halfway up there was a plateau where we gathered. We danced. By day, our rhythms joined the rhythms of the bees dancing, by night we danced with the stars. And Artemis led the dance. She danced us close to death and drew us back to life. We leapt on her path of joy, and we stepped carefully on her path of fear. Midsummer next year I will take you there to dance with her."

The trees at their back rustled as a light breeze blew up from the water. Maia turned abruptly.

"Now we must build our camp."

As they worked, Maia spoke little. Single words and abrupt gestures showed Lykaina what she should be doing. They built. A stand of aspen saplings became a lean-to hut. The double poles of the mast, separated by the boom and with a warp beam set near the top, became a standing loom. Maia folded the sail into a small bundle and tucked it between two rocks near the lean-to.

"We have no need of a sail," she said. "The steering oar will move the boat as much as we need it. Now. Food. We have nothing to eat. Berries. Rabbits. Tomorrow you will go out."

Climbing the mountainside the next morning, Lykaina was in her own element. She had loved being in the boat with Maia and learning the ways of the wind and the water. But now she reveled in the freedom of being on her own—running, setting traps, and searching out berry bushes. With Maia, she was always off balance. The strange rituals made Lykaina feel as if she were in another world. Maia's way of working without talking made Lykaina feel like a child. She was glad to be on the mountain foraging. She picked mulberries, gathered mushrooms, and set a line of traps. If Artemis were willing, their meals would soon be like home.

She returned to the camp in the late afternoon. The loom was strung with saffron-colored yarn. Maia's fingers sent a shuttle through the warp threads. She pulled the heddle rod forward, battened the weft upward, and sent the shuttle through again. Lykaina went down to the shore and watched the sun dip behind the dark mountains across the water.

"*Hai!*"

Maia's call startled her. She loped across the meadow to the campsite. The loom was empty. Maia stood next to it dressed in a long saffron gown like the ones the women of Corinth wore. More saffron material hung over her arm.

"Stand still," Maia commanded. She draped the material around Lykaina and pinned the folds over her shoulders. Long folds fell to the ground. Maia adjusted the pins and stepped back.

"Walk," she commanded.

Lykaina took one stride. The material caught on her foot. She stumbled and stopped, frowning.

"Pick it up," said Maia. "With one hand, like this."

Maia grasped the edge of her skirt and walked gracefully to the hut and back. Mouth open, Lykaina watched. Maia's movements were usually quick and abrupt, but she now moved like the coracle over the water. Lykaina picked up a fold of her skirt and tried to imitate the walk. She stumbled again.

"The material is beautiful, Maia," she said, "but it is too long for me. I wear my tunics short so that I can move freely."

"No," said Maia severely. "You are in Lesbos now. You are going to

93

the home of its most famous citizen. You must dress like someone who belongs."

"I am going to learn poetry from Sappho," said Lykaina sharply, "not to stand in Hera's beauty contest. Poetry has nothing to do with how long or how short my tunic is."

"She will not hear your poetry if you dress in mountain rags. Her slavegirl will not permit you to enter her house. You will be treated like a slave yourself. Do you think Lesbians listen to the poetry of slaves like your old woman of Sparta? Gather up your skirt and walk."

Lykaina obeyed. She managed to reach the hut and return without falling, although every step made her feel like a fish thrown onto a sandy shore.

"Better," said Maia, after several trips. "Tomorrow we go to Mytilene. You can watch the Lesbian women walk and learn more before you go to Sappho's house."

Lykaina's heart jumped. The journey had taken so long that the goal had become almost unreal, a dream receding like an island into the mist. But tomorrow she would see the city where Sappho lived. And soon she would see Sappho herself. Her journey would be over.

Before the peak of Mount Olympos had caught the morning sun's rays, Lykaina and Maia were struggling up a path long overgrown with wild brush. In the dense forest, the air was damp and cool. They stopped for a moment in a clearing where they could see the gulf water that had turned from dawn gray to early morning blue.

"This is the spot I watched to see my mother and sisters pass," commented Maia. "By the time they had descended below, my boat was pulled up on the shore, and I was busy at my chores again."

They plunged back into the forest and continued to climb. Eventually the trees thinned, and the path joined another, this one worn from travel. A small village clung to the side of the hill, its square sun-baked houses lining the single street that traversed it. Here the way was open to the sea. Although the village still lay in shadow, the gulf sparkled with sunlight. Other people joined them on the trail, some leading donkeys loaded with produce. The path broadened into a road and led them past terraced gardens, groves of olive trees, and carefully pruned vineyards. They passed through another forest, less dense than the one below.

The road crested the hill and began a steady descent. Through the trees, they could now see water kissed by both sun and wind. The trees thinned, and a city appeared before them. The white-capped sea rolled up to a long breakwater. Inside, a fleet of merchant ships lay in neat rows. The sun-bleached temples of an acropolis looked down on the city from their perch atop a tiny island just beyond the harbor. Below the acropolis, red-tiled roofs peeked out from under giant trees that turned green and silver in the breeze. Lykaina saw that a narrow bridge connected the island to the rest of the city, which spread around the harbor and up the low hills behind.

Mytilene, thought Lykaina. I am looking at Mytilene. I am close to the home of Sappho.

Maia pulled the new gown from her bundle. She drew Lykaina behind a bush and unfastened her rough tunic. The new fabric felt soft on Lykaina's skin, and she touched the draping folds gingerly as if they might disintegrate if she grasped too hard. Maia pinned her shoulders and stepped back.

"We will purchase the proper shoes for you in the market," she said, eyeing Lykaina's rough sandals with their broad straps. She ran her fingers through Lykaina's short hair. "You will let this grow. For now, it will have to do. You can practice walking before we reach the city."

Descending into Mytilene, Lykaina practiced the birdlike steps that kept her from stumbling. By the time they had crossed the bridge and climbed the stone steps to the agora, she could walk without tripping, although her thigh muscles ached from the strain.

The marketplace, like the one in Corinth, mingled smells of perfumes and sizzling sausages. Shops under the high-arched porticoes offered piles of richly colored carpets, while tables in the open air overflowed with bright hyacinths and oleander. A barber was trimming a young man's blond beard; a manicurist groomed his long, slender hands. Men and women alike moved so gracefully that it seemed as if their feet did not touch the ground. Lykaina strained to hear their Aeolian speech, muted like bells ringing from another valley. The vendors' voices, as they sang out their wares, blended into a rich chorus. The children playing in and around the stalls seemed to be dancing. Even the animals— baby lambs, chickens, loaded donkeys—were subdued, as if the music around them had made them content with their fates. Above the market, Lykaina could see several temples, the morning sun glancing off their painted marble columns.

Maia found a small, empty space next to a carpet stall and opened her bundle. Lykaina helped her spread out her wares.

"Go," said Maia. "Your task is not to sell but to observe."

Lykaina looked around the agora. She tried to imitate the way the Lesbian women moved their bodies. The tiny steps she had almost mastered; the easy sway of the hips was more difficult. She noticed that while the men strolled up and down, or sat talking with their friends in the porticoes, the women usually entered the market in twos or threes, visited different stalls, picked out the items they desired, and then left, followed by a small child carrying their purchases.

At midmorning, when Lykaina passed Maia's pile of woven goods, Maia held out a pair of sandals with thin soles and tiny straps. The leather was stiff, and the narrow strap cut into Lykaina's flesh. After three turns around the agora, her feet ached, and she had a cramp in one toe.

As the sun neared its zenith, the crowds thinned. Merchants closed the shutters of their stalls, and goods that had been laid out on the smooth stones of the square were loaded back onto waiting donkeys. Her weavings all sold, Maia's bundle now held cheese, grains, and olive oil. Lykaina and Maia carried it between them on a stick. Across the bridge in the main part of the city, Lykaina took in the soft blues, greens, and ochres of the buildings that lined the waterfront. She admired the finely carved wooden balconies. As they left the city, her blistered feet and stiff back made her no less eager to return and to immerse herself in this life.

They walked home in silence. Lykaina's head was full of the images of grace and elegance, her body alive in anticipation of her coming meeting with Sappho. Back at the campsite, she sat at the hearth, carefully rubbing olive oil into her new sandals to make them soft. Maia stood at her loom.

"It is the most beautiful city I have ever seen," began Lykaina, the thoughts inside her head demanding voice. "It is more beautiful than Corinth. Did you listen to the voices of the people? Their speech is so soft, it sounds like music. And their hands wave so gracefully you'd think they were dancing. Did you see the gowns with fine embroidery at the hems? The men were gentle, too, don't you think? Did you notice their hands? As soft as the women's, and they gestured just as gracefully. Even the boys playing blindman's buff moved as if they were dancing. The girls looked just like little ladies, their gowns flowing, their little feet stepping like birds. Oh, Maia, I am so grateful to you for making this gown and showing me how to walk. Tomorrow when I go to meet Sappho—"

She broke off, aware that Maia's hand was holding the shuttle motionless.

"I am ready to meet Sappho, don't you think? My walk is not so graceful as the Lesbian ladies, but I will remember to walk slowly."

Maia lifted the heddle rod and slid the shuttle home.

"You must be careful." Her voice was a drone. "This meeting with Sappho is not the end of your journey, it is the midpoint. You will not find the Great Mother in Mytilene, although they have used her bones to build temples to her offspring. You must carry her within you. The center is a deep and chaotic place. You can spiral in by yourself, but you will need her help to spiral out."

The rhythm of the loom filled the silence that followed Maia's speech. Lykaina puzzled over the words—riddles like those of their first meeting in Euboea. What was the center she was talking about? Of course she would not forget the Great Mother, but she was going to Mytilene to learn poetry, not to worship. She waited for Maia to continue, but only the loom spoke. After the sun had dropped its flames behind Mount Olympos, Maia held out her hand to Lykaina.

"Come," she said. "We will ask the Great Mother to give you a mantle of protection."

Lykaina looked up and met Maia's eyes. Her images of Mytilene scattered under the intense gaze. She followed Maia silently into the forest. They climbed a rocky trail until they came to a large upright stone slab. Maia stopped and touched it reverently and sent a muffled wordless chant to hover in the air around them. Lykaina reached out to touch the stone also, but, without breaking the chant, Maia deflected her hand. As Lykaina stood waiting for a sign from Maia, her thoughts began to return to Mytilene. She wondered if perhaps Sappho had been one of the women she had seen today. What did she look like? Would she have been walking with other poets, would she have been out with her hetaerae? Suddenly she remembered that her aulos was still new and that one of the notes was not quite true, one of the holes needed adjusting. And she must cut new reeds to fit in the mouthpiece and soak them so that they would be soft and pliable.

"She is ready to receive you. Come. We will go to her altar."

Maia's voice pulled her, but now Lykaina's thoughts of tomorrow were also compelling. She knew Maia's ceremony could last all night. When would she prepare for her meeting with Sappho?

"Maia," she said hesitantly, her eyes fixed on a tree just to the right of Maia's head. "Maia, I must prepare for tomorrow. I must make sure my aulos is properly tuned. I want to search out the right poem to sing to her. Do not worry about me. I will keep the Great Mother within me. But the purpose of my journey is to meet Sappho, and I must prepare myself."

Maia's eyes burned into Lykaina's. Lykaina dug her toe into the moist leaves underfoot, resisting the thread pulling her. A moment of silence passed. Then Maia turned and walked away. Lykaina felt her feet pulling to follow, but she stiffened her legs until her knees locked. When Maia had disappeared, she stumbled down the path, her palms wet with moisture and a deep quivering inside her belly.

She stood at the water's edge for a long time, her mind wiped clean of any thought of either Mytilene or Maia. She slowly walked along the shore until she found a stand of reeds. She cut several, chewed them lightly, and held two together with her lips. A high piercing sound echoed from the mountains across the gulf.

Back at the campsite, she spent a few minutes enlarging the third hole of the aulos. She fitted the two reeds into the mouthpiece and went back down to the shore. The waxing moon had risen over the gulf. The long notes that rang out over the water melted the hard knot in her belly. All the greens and blues and ochres of Mytilene fused in her mind to color the music. She sang.

> *Tomorrow white sky, tomorrow white day,*
> *tomorrow the wild swallow flies to the dove.*

Chapter 7.
Sappho's courtyard

Hidden behind a pillar, Lykaina stared at Sappho. Like a goddess she seemed, her head crowned with black curls regally bound with a purple ribbon. The snow-white folds of her gown draped over an inlaid chair. Embroidery stitches added the colors of early dawn to her shoulders and late sunset to the hem of her skirt. Around her sat seven younger women, their sleeveless gowns gathered around them in folds.

Sappho's head was inclined toward a plump young woman who was singing and playing a lyre that looked like Arion's except that it seemed to be made out of a tortoise shell. A wrong note fell from the strings. The woman faltered and blushed. Sappho put her hand on the woman's arm, sang a few words herself, then motioned the young poet to continue. The girl smiled gratefully and went on with her song.

Lykaina kept herself hidden behind the pillar. Despite her day of practice in the marketplace, she felt awkward with the long folds of material around her legs. The thongs of her sandals cut into her legs, and she had a blister on one heel. She had walked too quickly up the street to Sappho's house, and her breath was short.

"Who is that hiding behind my pillar? Is it you, Atthis, come back for a visit?" The voice that called to her was soft and low. "Come out and show yourself—if you are Atthis or another."

Flustered, Lykaina forgot to pick up her skirt. She emerged into the sunlight of the open courtyard, snagged her foot on a fold and stumbled. As she caught herself from taking a full-length sprawl, she heard giggles and whispers.

"It is certainly not Atthis."

Lykaina blushed, furious at herself for not remembering. She stood and stared at the ground.

"Hush, my sisters. You have forgotten your manners." The giggles stopped. "You are not my beloved Atthis. You are a stranger. Come closer so that we may see you. Do not mind my companions, they mean no harm."

Lykaina clutched her gown and stepped carefully, her heart now beating as if she had just run after a kid frolicking too close to a cliff.

"I am Lykaina of Anabretae," she said slowly, and heard her own words fall like rough stones beside the silverwork of Sappho's voice. Sappho waved her hand to silence the suppressed giggles of the others. Lykaina held out Arion's gold ring. "I have come from Sparta and from Corinth. Your friend Arion sends you his greetings and begs that you listen to my song."

She directed her rehearsed speech at Sappho's feet. When she finished, she raised her eyes tentatively. A faint smile graced the perfect face. A thrush in a mulberry bush sang. Sappho took the ring from the outstretched palm.

"Arion is my friend and colleague. What he asks, I do with pleasure. Sing for me then. But first, you must have refreshment." She clapped her hands softly. "Gongyla, pour our guest some wine. Praxinoa, run and fetch a stool for her to sit on."

A tall, freckled girl leapt up and ran inside the house. The plump girl who had been singing when Lykaina came in took a silver goblet from a small three-legged table and poured first water and then dark red wine into it. Lykaina, still staring at Sappho, took the goblet and tasted sweet grapes with a hint of musk. The tall girl returned with a delicately carved stool and set it beside Sappho who motioned Lykaina to sit.

"We are ready to listen."

Lykaina set the goblet back on the table. She started to wipe her mouth with the back of her hand, then stopped and blushed. She pulled her aulos from under the folds of her gown and began to play. A series of quick notes circled out of the courtyard and back again. She sang.

O

Let her become a flowering quince by a stream
and I snow on the mountaintop.
Melted, I rush over rocks to water her roots.

Whispers and a brief giggle followed the poem. Sappho herself was
silent, the half-smile still on her lips. The thrush continued its song.
Finally, Sappho spoke.

"Arion was right to send you. You sing well; your poem is good." She
turned to the girls around her. "Gongyla, pour wine all around. We will
drink a toast to our new companion."

Gongyla poured the sweet red wine for everyone, and they raised their
goblets to Lykaina. Lykaina looked closely at each of the seven young
women. Some had long hair that fell over the front of one shoulder in
braids or ringlets; others wore curls bound up with brightly colored rib-
bons. All of them wore garlands of flowers around their heads, gold
necklaces, bracelets, and rings. The pale skin of their faces was highlighted with dots of red on their cheeks and black lines around their
eyes. Scents of rose and jasmine mingled in the air around them.

"We have work to do," Sappho was saying. "The wedding falls on the
full moon of this month. We have been commissioned to write songs
for dressing the bride, songs for the groom's arrival, and of course," she
lowered her voice with amusement, "songs for the bridal chamber." The
girls giggled. "Tomorrow we will start. Each of us will write one poem
for each event. We will choose the best ones to sing at the wedding."

Two of the women whispered to each other. One of them spoke hesitantly, her eyes on the ground.

"Are we to attend the wedding even if our songs are not chosen?"

"Of course, we need everyone's voice. We will go as companions. Our
new companion, too." She smiled at Lykaina and reached out to touch
her arm.

A silver bell sounded from within the house.

"Luncheon, friends. Let's see what fine foods they have prepared for
us today."

Sappho rose, and Lykaina saw that she was tiny. Barely reaching the
shoulder of any of the others, Sappho led the way into a large white
room beyond the sunny portico. Tall candleholders set on tripods held
dozens of white candles, and flowers were scattered over the floor. Sappho took Lykaina's arm and guided her to a long wood-and-ivory couch.
Several young slavegirls dressed in short white tunics entered swiftly.
The first stopped in front of Sappho and set down a small table that
held a silver tray. Sappho lifted the cover and cried, "Quail, companions! Mushrooms and truffles! We dine well today." With a delicate twist
of her hand, she broke off a leg and offered it to Lykaina. "Here, you
must have the first taste and tell us if it is well done."

Lykaina took the leg and bit into the tender flesh. Aware of the eyes on her, she managed to nod pleasure in Sappho's direction, although she had no sense of the taste at all. She was grateful when Sappho turned her attention to her own food. Lykaina ate slowly, her eyes moving from woman to woman. She tried to memorize the crook of the finger as one tossed a truffle into her mouth, the toss of the head as another sipped her wine. Feeling Sappho's presence beside her, she found it hard to concentrate on eating properly and listening to the flowing conversation, too.

"You know who the groom is," Sappho was saying. "He is nephew to our venerable Pittakos." She turned to Lykaina. "Pittakos governs all of Lesbos. He was born a peasant but became ruler of us all."

"Still a peasant, too, from the looks of him," remarked one of the hetaerae.

"Shuffle-foot," said another. "He drags his cracked toes through the marketplace like a crippled duck."

"A crippled duck with a sausage belly," giggled a third. "They say he eats without candles, just gobbles his food like a wolf in a cave, and grease runs down his chin with his wine."

"He thought he could buy his way into a good family, but his wife is so old she needs a donkey cartful of powder to hide her wrinkles."

Lykaina wondered what the young women would say if they knew of her peasant background. She had managed to walk from courtyard to dining room without stumbling; she had sipped her wine as daintily, she hoped, as anyone else. A thought came into her mind—*What difference does it make if he rules well?*—but her voice remained mute. She made sure her disfigured toe was well hidden beneath the folds of her gown.

The silver bell sounded again, and everyone stood up to leave. Sappho took her arm.

"Will you take your afternoon sleep here? Then we can walk and talk in the evening air. I want to learn more of your journey."

Lykaina let herself be led up a stairway to a small white chamber with latticed windows. Sappho kissed her lightly on the cheek and vanished. Lykaina unwrapped her gown and lay down in the undergarment Maia had woven. Sure that she would lie awake with all the new thoughts in her head, she was asleep almost instantly.

She dreamed her gown was a billowing sail caught up on a breeze, skimming her over the treetops. All around her other women glided, singing to each other. She opened her eyes to find a young slavegirl fanning her gently, the late afternoon rays of the sun casting a latticed shadow on the tile floor. The child had hair the color of wheat and eyes a pale blue. She smiled and beckoned to Lykaina. Lykaina followed her into another room where she watched the child pour water into a large marble basin in the center of a mosaic floor. Lykaina splashed her face and arms and dried herself with the soft towels offered her. Back in the sleeping room, she let the small hands deftly adjust the folds of the gown and pin the material at the shoulders.

"Thank you," said Lykaina. "What is your name?"

The young girl shook her head and put a finger to her lips. Then she slipped out of the room, motioning Lykaina to follow.

In the courtyard, Sappho was waiting for her.

"Are you refreshed now? Come and join me for an evening stroll. I will show you our Mytilene."

Walking beside Sappho, Lykaina felt tall and ungainly. Sappho's tiny feet seemed to glide over the stone cobbles.

"See how the houses on this side are all covered in the shadow of the mountain?" Sappho pointed to the view in front of her. "Only the acropolis on the hill over there is still touched by the sun. Look how it makes a golden crown upon our blue-veiled city."

Along the wide steps of the street ran a dry streambed filled with white boulders, red, flowering oleander, and wild pomegranates. They passed scattered houses, most of them like Sappho's—a blank wall facing the street with a large wooden door and knocker. From behind one walled garden, a tall cypress rose; from another, the top of a myrtle tree. When they reached the waterfront, Sappho led Lykaina across the stone bridge that connected the acropolis to the city. At its midpoint, she guided Lykaina to the rail.

"This northern harbor keeps the fishing boats," she said, "and the boats that take us to the mainland. See, there in the distance is Mount Ida and the Troad, still bathed in sun."

They crossed to the other side of the bridge and looked out at the other harbor.

"Here are anchored our ships of war. This was a busy harbor before the Peace. Now, thankfully, the ships rest."

They passed over the bridge and began to climb the hill to the acropolis.

"Your music reminded me of my childhood," Sappho said as they climbed. "I was born not here but in a smaller city on the other side of the island. Eresos. Perhaps you saw it as you sailed toward Lesbos. It is built on a rocky headland, and its beacon is well known to sailors."

Lykaina remembered the light that had appeared ahead of them the night before they had landed.

"Two rivers run down from the mountains," Sappho's soft voice continued, "and in the spring the fields are covered with violets and hyacinths and anemones. Where the rivers run into the sea, the naiades call out to the nereids. The shepherds that tend the goats on the hill-sides play pipes like yours. Your music reminded me."

Listening to Sappho, Lykaina forgot her ungainliness and began to walk freely, not worrying whether her hand was holding the extra folds properly.

"Tell me, how did you come to poetry?" Sappho asked her. "Who has taught you? What schools have you attended?"

Lykaina looked toward the dark sea and remembered her grandfather, his crook across his shoulders, calling out a song to the valley below. She thought about the old woman in Sparta, listening to her intently, telling her if a song was too short or a melody unclear. Well, I am who I am, she thought. She took a deep breath and spoke.

"I grew up a goatherd in the mountains of Taygetus. My grandfather taught me how to play. My poems—they come to me. They are the songs of my people, and yet they are also my own. Words seem to come out of some place inside me to join with the words my grandfather taught me. I lived with an old woman in Sparta who knew your poetry. She sang me your poem about the moon once. She knew Arion, too. It was she who told me to come to you."

Lykaina stopped talking. Sappho smiled.

"And how many poems have you written? Have you brought them all with you?"

Written. Lykaina remembered the scratchings on the horn-colored scroll the old woman had shown her. She still could not bring that image into any relationship with the words that came out of her mouth. And how many poems? Poems were not things to be counted like goats. You sang a song one way for one event and another for another, and it was the same and yet it was different. She took another deep breath.

"The old woman showed me your moon poem on a scroll. But I...I don't understand how those marks can mean what your mouth sings."

"You must learn to write, then," said Sappho. "When you write your words, they belong to you, no one can take them from you. When you only sing your poems, you touch those who sit with you and listen and no one else. Someone may take your words, change them, and call them their own. Then they are no longer yours. But if you write them down and sign your name to them, they can travel the world over and still belong to you."

"But my poems are not all mine," protested Lykaina. "Some of the words are words my grandfather sang. He learned them from others before him. How can I own words that belong to other people?"

"It's the way you sing those words that makes them yours," replied Sappho. "It's the way you put them together that belongs to you."

"And when you change the poem, does the writing change, too?"

Sappho raised a black eyebrow.

"Once a song is written well, there is no need to change it, is there? If you have different thoughts on the subject, you write a new poem."

"No," said Lykaina, "I mean the same poem. When I sing a song, I watch my listeners, and the poem often changes."

Sappho smiled at two men who passed them speaking a low "Good evening." She turned back to Lykaina.

"If a poem is truly yours, it shouldn't matter how the audience listens. The poem comes from you, not from the audience. You can't let others control what you sing."

Lykaina was silent. What did it mean to own a poem? How could a poem be always the same, no matter where it was sung? It all had to do with this magic called writing. Her mind could not stretch to see how it all fit together.

"Writing is not difficult," Sappho said. "I will teach you. You will learn first to write your own name. Then I will show you how to put your poems onto a scroll. We'll start with the poem you sang today. It is a perfect gem." She took Lykaina's arm. "Come, the night shadows will soon be upon us. Let us return to the house. The room you slept in is yours."

Lykaina let the puzzle of writing subside under the thought of living at Sappho's house. Then she remembered Maia and frowned.

"I am staying with a friend on the Gulf of Hieras. But I would like to return tomorrow, if I may."

"Of course. You must come. And every day. You are our companion now. You are one of us."

They returned to the stone bridge. By now, the sun's last rays had been cut off by the mountain. An old man was lighting, one by one, the lights along the quay. Sappho turned to Lykaina and embraced her lightly.

"Until tomorrow, then."

Lykaina's cheek glowed from Sappho's kiss. She watched the diminutive figure float into the darkness. Then she picked up the folds of her skirt and ran past startled faces. When the last house had been left behind, she stopped long enough to take off her sandals and her gown. Then she began running freely, her arms outstretched, the gown flowing like a streamer behind her.

At the campsite, she found the lean-to dark, the hearthfire in front of it a bed of glowing coals. In the shadows she could barely make out the design on the half-finished weaving that hung from the loom—a single red egg in a sea of black, a white snake wound round the egg. Down at the shore, Maia swayed in a trance. Breathless, Lykaina went into the lean-to and lay down on her mat, tired from the mountain run. She closed her eyes and listened to the soft drone of Maia's chanting.

It seemed only a few moments later that Maia was standing over her, waving a small milk snake over her head.

"Be wary." Maia's voice was a whisper. "The moon force is double-edged; it spins in two directions. The center is dangerous. Only the serpent has the power to move the universe. Remember."

Lykaina slept again.

In the morning, she emerged from the hut to find Maia squatting over the fire, pouring hot nettle tea into a bowl. Lykaina sat down on a log and held the bowl in both hands, the steam rising to her nostrils.

"She liked my song." The words fell quickly from her mouth. "We ate quail, and she let me sleep in one of her upstairs rooms. There was a special room just for washing with a marble basin in the center of the floor. There were slavegirls for everything—one was the doorkeeper, six served the food, one helped me wash and dress. Sappho took me for a walk through the city. She is tiny, she barely comes to my shoulder, her hands are like a child's. Her voice is pure music, she speaks so softly you have to be very still to hear her. She—"

"You are smitten." Maia's sharp words cut her off. "You have come to learn poetry, not to walk a lovesick lane. Remember who you are."

Lykaina's brow furrowed, and anger pushed into her throat. It was Maia who had insisted she dress like a lady, learn to walk like a lady. Now she didn't want to hear about her success.

"She is a rare and precious bird. She is the one you dressed me for. Why are you angry that she likes me?"

Maia poured the remaining water over the coals and stood up. She cast a long look at Lykaina.

"There is danger in the center," she said finally. "If you forget who you are and whose spiral it is, you will never pass to the other side."

She turned abruptly and went to the loom. Lykaina stared at her back. If Maia was going to be difficult, she thought, then she would go and stay with Sappho as she had been invited. She went into the hut and carefully draped the gown around her, sure this time of how the folds were supposed to fall. She came out again and stood at the edge of the hearth.

"You are not pleased with me," she said carefully, her anger still flickering. "I am not a child. I know how to take care of myself. If you don't want to see how I have gained my goal, then Sappho has invited me to stay in her house."

Lykaina waited for a response, but all she heard was the sound of the shuttle. She turned and walked quickly up the mountain trail, trying to cool the hot flush of her cheeks with an image of Sappho's courtyard. At the clearing in the woods, she stopped. Never leave a friend's hearth without good parting words, her grandfather had counseled. She turned and called clearly down the mountain.

"You have been a gift to me, Maia. I will not forget you."

At Sappho's house, Lykaina felt she had begun a new life. Every day a new discovery gave her a different way of seeing things. In the wash-room, she could make water flow out of three bronze lionheads to splash over her body and into a marble trough. In her bedroom, next to the embroidery-covered mattress, a carved chest held dozens of pots and bottles arranged neatly on ceramic trays. The blonde slavechild fixed a chignon of someone else's tresses over her too-short hair, combing it first with a piece of carved ivory with long slender teeth. Long bone pins attached ornaments and flowers as a crown, and a round piece of polished metal with a long handle gave her a reflection of herself.

The slavegirl showed her how to take white powder from one of the little pots and spread it carefully over her face. Another pot provided a red-ochre grease which she learned to daub with her finger onto her lips and cheeks. Black kohl from still another pot made a shadow on her eyelids. Her lashes she stiffened with a paste the slavegirl mixed from eggwhites and mastic.

When her face and hair were finished, she learned to take a drop or two of a scented liquid from one of the tiny bottles and place it care-fully on the back of her neck. One day she smelled like fresh roses after a rain, another day like spring violets. One bottle held a mixture of spices—musk and myrrh, ginger and cardamom, cinnamon and saffron.

Mornings Lykaina woke as soon as the first bird song began to spill through the windows. While everyone else slept, she put on a short tunic she had found in a chest and slipped out through the garden at the back of the house to the hills behind. Here she ran to feel the earth under her bare feet, the early morning breeze in her face. From time to time she might flush a quail or startle a deer in a thicket; once she came upon a wild peacock preening itself on a rock. She would stay out until the red sun had lifted itself above the mountain range across the water. Then she would descend the hill again. In the moment be-tween leaving the footpath and entering Sappho's garden, a voice from the mountains seemed to call. But thoughts of the coming day would crowd her mind, and she would run eagerly up the stairs to her room where the slavegirl waited to help her dress.

In addition to Sappho and the slaves, two other young women lived in the house. After a breakfast of nuts and fresh fruit, the women whose homes were nearby would arrive, and they would all gather in the in-ner courtyard at Sappho's feet to begin their day of poetry and song.

They sat in a circle, Sappho on a chair with inlaid ivory on its back, the others on low stools. Each woman had her own lyre—a tortoise shell strung with four strings—on which she took her turn plucking out a melody and singing. Sappho would listen carefully, suggest a new word, ask the woman why she had chosen one image or another. Then she would listen again.

The aulos didn't seem to fit here. Its double-reeded mouthpiece made notes piercing so they could carry across the valley to other mountains. Here the sound rocked the small courtyard. Sometimes she heard a snicker when she put it to her lips. She tried to dampen the sound, but even the softest notes seemed too loud. Eventually she took to playing only a few notes before beginning to sing.

When all the companions had sung their poems, Sappho would set them to carving their words onto the soft, wet rolls of papyrus that had been soaking at the edge of the courtyard all morning. While the others wrote, Sappho would sit with Lykaina next to a shallow box of sand and show her how to trace letters with her fingers.

"Just the way each line of poetry is made of many separate words, so each word is made of many separate letters. Each letter stands for a sound. Look." Sappho drew an elegant lambda in the sand. "This letter stands for the first sound of your name. Say it—*luh*—just the beginning."

Lykaina echoed the sound and stared at the letter in the sand. She placed her finger in the sand and tried to make the same graceful curving line. Her lambda was crude, crude as her country accent now seemed. She drew again, and this time her finger curved just right. Pride surged through her chest. This was her letter, it belonged to her name. The third try was lopsided again. Lykaina sighed her disappointment, and Sappho touched her cheek.

"It takes practice. But you must never be discouraged. I will always be right here. You have lovely hands, you know, you are going to make lovely letters with them."

Sappho's light touch guided Lykaina's hand. When Lykaina drew a letter alone, Sappho's murmurs of encouragement made Lykaina's hand move along the perfect curve. With Sappho's breath on her shoulder, Lykaina felt like she was immersed in a deep pool of spring-fed water.

Then suddenly, with no warning, Sappho would stand up and call out, "Time for our dance!" and lead them out into the garden. Lykaina found herself stumbling in the circle around the old stone well, stumbling as much from the sudden change as from trying to learn how to hold the hand of the woman next to her without dropping the fold of her gown. The young women sometimes laughed at her clumsy steps, but a glance from Sappho turned the laughter into smiles of encouragement.

Dancing finished, they would return to the courtyard for the part of the morning Lykaina found the most exciting. With the sun now high in the sky, the women would gather a little closer to Sappho's feet. Sappho, her tiny hands gesturing intensely, would sing her own poems to the accompaniment of the lyre. Many of the poems were about Atthis, a woman Sappho seemed to have loved deeply and then lost. One day Sappho was persuaded to tell the whole story.

"She came to me," Sappho began, "when she was no more than an awkward child. I was still in the bloom of my own girlhood, and I loved her little monkeyface from the moment I set eyes on her. My own little Kleis was still a baby, and we used to go, the three of us, to the mountains to spend the summer. The air was fresh up there, and the breezes cool. We picked sweet irises and wove them into garlands for our hair. We crushed their rose petals to perfume our bodies. We wandered through nightingale-filled woods. We lay together in sacred groves and bathed ourselves in still waters of deep pools. Ah, listen to the first song I made for her."

Sappho nodded to Gongyla who scrambled to pick up the lyre at her feet. Sappho's clear voice sent its silver notes into the air.

Love—bittersweet, irrepressible—
loosens my limbs and I tremble.

No one spoke, letting Sappho, her eyes glistening, remember her love. She took up the story again.

"Once she was annoyed with me because I stayed too long in the country. She wanted to return to the excitement of city life, and I wanted to linger in our pools of love. One morning she left a letter at our bedside. She threatened not to love me anymore if I did not bestir myself. Well, we left. And at a dinner party the very next week, I found myself watching her send her silver laughter to charm a boy—a god he seemed to me, so perfect he was in body. Flames seared my skin, a roaring entered my ears, I could not speak. I had showered her with gifts, I had given her all that a young woman could desire."

Sappho paused, her hand half-raised, her eyes fixed on the mulberry bush in the corner of the courtyard. She went on.

"Yet finally, she left me. She forgot everything. My love and the beautiful life we led together meant nothing to her anymore. She went to Andromeda, that wrung-out old dishrag who dares call herself a poet and teacher of song." She shrugged. "Oh, she cried when she left; she said she was going against her own wishes. I told her to go and be happy but to remember our love and how precious it was. So she went. For months I heard no word from her. Then she came back to visit. But there was no glow in her eyes to see me. It was clear to me then, she hated even the thought of me."

Again Sappho nodded to Gongyla, and again she sang.

The honey nor
the honey bee is
to be mine again.
The tear that had been hovering on her lower eyelid made a path down her cheek. Several of the other girls were crying, too; their sighs joined the song of the thrush.

The morning before the big wedding, the women sat in the courtyard finishing the embroidery on their new gowns, chattering about who had been invited to the ceremony. Lykaina had never embroidered before. While the other girls of her village had sat at their grandmothers' feet, she had been out on the mountains herding goats. She struggled to make the stitches even.

Praxinoa paused her needle.

"Will Andromeda and her companions be at the wedding, do you think?"

"The peasant woman with her peasant clothes?" Sappho laughed softly. "No. Our Pittakos may be low-born himself, but at least he has learned enough from our society not to invite a swineherd's daughter to snort her poetry."

"Imagine if she came," said Praxinoa, "how her gown might look with great clumsy stitches making a silly peasant pattern."

"Oh," Gongyla added, "I wish she *had* been invited. We could have amused ourselves watching her clutch at her skirt as she stumbled along."

Lykaina, blood creeping up her neck, looked at her clumsy embroidery stitches and then at the small neat ones the others were making. It felt as if they were talking about her, not about this poor Andromeda woman. Suddenly she heard her own voice ringing out angrily.

"Why do you make fun of her? It doesn't matter where she was born, only what her poetry sounds like."

Her gown with its half-finished embroidery fell to her feet as she stood, now embarrassed, not knowing what to say next. Sappho looked at her.

"When anger fills the breast, restrain the idly yapping tongue," she murmured, and the other women, averting their eyes from Lykaina, laughed softly. Lykaina grabbed her skirt roughly and strode out of the courtyard. She ran through the garden and threw off her gown as soon as she was beyond the last house on the hill. Her legs ached from having been still for so long, and her lungs, choked with humiliation, could not seem to fill themselves with air.

She was descending the other side of the mountain before she realized where she was running. The blue Gulf of Hieras lay before her, a breeze rippling its surface. She slowed to a trot, her heart beating both from the exercise and from the thought of seeing Maia again. But when she came to the spot where she and Maia had encamped, there was no sign of either the lean-to or the loom. Maia was gone, leaving no trace except for some ashes in the firepit. Lykaina slumped onto a log and stared out into the gulf. Shame from the scene in Sappho's court-yard mingled with shame for the way she had left Maia. She sat very still for a long time, listening to the gulls call out to each other as they swooped over the water.

Presently she sensed that she was not alone. She looked around and saw that the slavegirl—the one who helped her dress each morning and slept outside her door each night—was standing a few feet behind her carrying her cast-off gown over her arm. Lykaina looked into the clear blue eyes, glad for the presence of another human being. The child took a few steps toward Lykaina, cocked her head, and held out the gown.

"Come and sit down with me and tell me your name," said Lykaina, patting the log next to her. The child shook her head and, just as she had that first day when Lykaina had asked her her name, she put her finger to her lips.

"It's all right," said Lykaina. "I'm not one of them. I'm a slave, too. They knew it all along. They've been having their fun with me." She waved her hand toward the place where the lean-to hut had been. "Now I've lost my friend, too."

The girl shook her head vigorously. She made some circular motions with her hands and then pointed out toward the opening to the sea. Realizing that she had never heard the girl speak, Lykaina decided that the child must be mute. What was it she was trying to tell her? That Maia had remade the coracle's mast and sailed away? How could she know that? Lykaina watched the girl's gesturing hands closely but could not guess their meaning. The girl stopped, shrugged, and then held out the gown again. Lykaina shook her head.

"No. They're laughing at me. They think I'm another Andromeda. I can't go back."

The girl shook her head again. She mimed playing an aulos, then stepped to the side and clapped her hands softly. She pointed to Lykaina, clasped her hands to her breast, and pointed toward the hills that lay between them and Mytilene. Then she held out the gown again.

Lykaina frowned. Was the child saying that she should go back? That Sappho liked her music? She traced her finger in the cold ashes and watched a perfect lambda take shape. She frowned at the letter. Per-haps she had jumped to the wrong conclusion. Perhaps they had not been laughing at her after all. Sappho's words, *Restrain the idly yapping tongue*, danced through her head. She took a deep breath and stood up. There was so much to learn. She would apologize for her outburst.

If Sappho liked her poetry, she would be forgiven.

Lykaina let the child drape the gown around her and followed her up the path. At the top of the mountain pass, the slavegirl bent suddenly, picked up something from the path and whirled around, a long iridescent feather in her hands. She stepped back and ran slowly in a circle, her arms flapping, raspy croaking noises coming from her throat. She stopped, pointed to herself and to the feather. She circled again, holding the feather out behind her. Lykaina stared uncomprehendingly. The child's body was so light, it seemed as if she were flying. When she stopped again, it was as if she had landed on the bough of a tree. She folded her wings and looked intently into Lykaina's eyes.

Finally Lykaina understood. It was a magpie's tailfeather.

"Magpie?" she asked, pointing to the feather. "Your name is Kissa?" She flapped her own arms and pointed to the girl.

The slavegirl's eyes lit up, and she flew again. She seemed to rise above the path and glide past Lykaina. She circled back and ceremoniously handed the feather to Lykaina. Then she ran ahead, flapping her wings and croaking happily. Lykaina smiled as she watched her fly down the mountainside. Whatever happened with Sappho, she had a friend in Kissa.

When Lykaina arrived back at the house, Sappho was seated alone in the courtyard, her hands resting lightly on the carved arms of her chair. She looked up as Lykaina entered and smiled at her.

"I thought we might have lost you. I was hoping you would forgive our thoughtless chatter."

Lykaina blushed and sat down on a stool.

"It is I who must apologize for my behavior. You were right to chide me."

Sappho laughed.

"Well now, we have both said our *I'm sorry*'s. Let's put it behind us and concentrate on our festive day tomorrow. It is your poetry, for the most part, that we will be singing."

Lykaina blushed again, this time from pleasure. Sappho was not displeased with her, she had forgiven her her country behavior. How lucky that Kissa had brought her back! After all, she had come to Lesbos for poetry, and poetry was all that mattered.

The slant of the sun told Lykaina that she had slept late. She sprang out of bed, her stomach fluttering at the thought of the events to come. Today is the day, she told herself, as she applied the kohl to her eyelids. Today my poetry reaches beyond Sappho's courtyard. Other poets—and statesmen and all the important people of this island—will hear my words. She hummed her newest melody while Kissa draped the gown over her shoulders. The blessed child had embroidered fine stitches in and around her own clumsy ones so that it all looked part of the pattern. Lykaina squeezed her hand and then ran down the steps to join the others.

"Aphrodite has lighted your face with her own beauty!" Sappho kissed Lykaina's cheek. "Come, we are on our way to her sacred spring. Take this ewer to carry her water."

The other companions, too, greeted Lykaina warmly. She sighed relief that her outburst of the day before was apparently forgotten. She took the hand offered her by Praxinoa and joined the snakelike dance that led over the hill behind the house. At the sacred spring, she gathered jonquils and anemones with the others and wove a garland for her head. She smiled at her reflection in the water. I look as fine as any of the others, she thought, as she tucked a stray strand into place. I am one of them. And my poetry—I'm sure that Sappho likes it best; we are singing all of my songs.

"Come, fill your jug. We are ready to go and bathe the bride."

Sappho's touch on her arm startled her out of her reverie. She blushed and quickly filled the silver ewer from the bubbling spring.

Water held high, the companions danced back into the city, to the old section near the acropolis. They found the bride's house decked out with branches of evergreen and bay. The bride, shy and ungainly in her underchemise, was waiting for them in a marble-tiled bathroom.

As Aphrodite's water sparkles and shines
so shines our bride all ready for love.

The bride's ungainliness disappeared as the women wrapped a soft rose-colored gown around her and crowned her head with a long veil of transparent cambric. Rowdy shouts from below interrupted their finishing touches and signaled the arrival of the groom and his friends. The companions led the bride into the inner courtyard where a canopy of bright green foliage hung over the gathered guests. The bridegroom strutted to the center; the hetaerae led the bride to him and danced in a circle around the pair of them.

This courtyard is a harbor
and the groom a golden ship,
the bride and all her bridesmaids crystal water.

Laughing and shouting, the company crowded around the bride and bridegroom to wish them well. A bell rang, and the odors of roast kid wafted into the courtyard. Sappho drew Lykaina aside and let the guests sweep by them.

"Come and meet my oldest and dearest friend," she said, putting her arm around Lykaina's waist. "He's just back from a sojourn in Carthage." A tall, handsome man stood before them, his shoulders slightly drooping, his trim beard a distinguished gray.

"So this is your newest protégée." He smiled warmly at Lykaina. "I am Alkaios. She tells me that you are a special poet. If that bridegroom song was yours, I agree with her. Come, shall we dine?"

He offered one arm to Lykaina, the other to Sappho, and led them into the dining room.

"Now you two ladies shall sit together, and I shall admire the view," he said, as he escorted them to a low couch. He turned and clapped his hands. "Here, boy, bring us some of that roasted pheasant. You, with the anchovies and sardines, put a tray down here. Ah, and if that is Samian wine, let it flow."

A half-dozen naked slaveboys hovered. Small inlaid tables heaped with delicacies appeared before them. Wine fell into their silver goblets. Lykaina looked around in amazement at the other guests eating. In Sappho's dining room, the companions and their guests ate slowly, each bite separated with conversation. A plateful of roast lamb begun at sundown might only finally disappear when the stars came out. Here the guests gobbled their food and hurriedly washed it down with wine. Mouths full, they competed with each other to embarrass the bride with details of the night to come. Sappho and Alkaios seemed an island in the midst of a tempest.

"So, my dear," Alkaios was saying to Sappho, "your face is more radiant than ever, your eyes dance. Such a joy is it to you to have a new companion?"

"Ah, friend Alkaios," replied Sappho laughing, "look at her—a face fresh as the mountain air. Wait until you hear the poems she has made for the marriage chamber."

Lykaina quickly put her goblet to her lips to hide the crimson spreading over her cheeks.

"Ah, sweet shame." Alkaios leaned forward and touched Lykaina's wrist. "When I was a mere boy, I blushed like that every time I saw this delightful piece of innocence sitting next to you. I tried to woo her, but, alas, she wouldn't have me. Remember, Sappho, the letter I wrote you? *Innocent Sappho, violet-haired, how shame prevents me from speaking. . . .*"

"And what you had in mind to tell me, as everyone knew, was not for young innocent ears to hear," replied Sappho. "Besides, your drinking parties were already notorious. I never understood how you could write such exquisite love poems while swilling wine and carousing with your young boys."

Alkaios waved the pheasant wing he was holding and smiled at Lykaina.

"Has she told you about my early dishonor? No? Well, I will then. It was during that dreadful war with the Athenians. It went on and on, year after year, drinking the blood of my dearest friends. And I, I loved the fight but not the dying. It seemed so squalid to embrace black earth when all of life and liberty lay before us." He held out his goblet to a passing slave. "Wine from where? Rhodes? Let it flow." He turned back to Lykaina. "Now, let's see. Oh, yes, my love of life and liberty. It was so great that under the walls of Sigeum I gave up my shield and arms to the Athenians and took to my heels. It seemed the better side of valor." He turned to Sappho. "Do you remember the letter I wrote you?"

Sappho smiled. Lykaina could see how much she was enjoying the memories of their youth.

"You said, if I remember, *Your Alkaios is safe, but not his arms*, and then something about how the Athenians had hung your shield before the altar of Aphrodite. Oh, how pleased they were with themselves!" She took a pomegranate from a passing tray and broke it into three pieces. "One for each of us, may we live a thousand years and love in all of them. You know," she said to Lykaina, "he was not at all a coward. After the war, he provided the fire for our rebellion against the tyrant. His poetry was a call to arms: it roused us all and made us know the true value of liberty." She turned to Alkaios. "My favorite poem of yours, dearest, will always be that one that likened our beloved Lesbos to a ship on a storm-tossed sea. *Our black ship laboring under the giant storm*, you sang, and we were all ready to rise up and lay the tyrant low! Ah, Alkaios, do you ever think what might have been had our little plot been successful? If we'd toppled the tyrant and made our dreams of a fair and reasoned government come true?"

Alkaios tossed an almond into his mouth.

"Why, you'd have never gone to Italy nor I to Egypt. You have to admit, exile wasn't all that bad. Look what you brought back from yours— the ever-graceful Kleis. Which reminds me, where is she? I haven't seen her tonight." He turned to Lykaina. "Have you met your mentor's beautiful daughter yet?"

Sappho reached over and placed a grape between Lykaina's lips.

"She hasn't had the opportunity. My dearest Kleis is confined. By next full moon, you will know me as a grandmother."

"Never!" Alkaios leaned over the table and kissed Sappho's hand. "I will always know you only as daughter of Aphrodite, lovelier than the sea out of which she rose."

"Flatterer! If I am daughter of Aphrodite, then you are son of golden Apollo."

"If I am son of golden Apollo. . . ." Alkaios turned to Lykaina. "When we were younger, Lykaina, this violet-wearing goddess and I used to duel at poetry. Do you remember, Sappho, how we used to trade lines? Until one of us found a line so perfect the other could not match it."

He cast his eyes around the room. A tall bowlegged man with a protruding forehead was noisily toasting the bride. "Aha. Tonight a man and a woman begin their life's journey together. Come, Sappho, I challenge you on love. Love is. . . ." He furrowed his brow for a moment and then brightened. "Love is bittersweet."

Sappho laughed. "All right," she said. "Sweet-bitter love, fiction-weaver love."

"Weaver of fictions, love," Alkaios quickly responded, "and bearer of pain."

"Pain-bearer, yes, but sweeter than the lyre's song."

"Sweeter than the song of the lyre and whiter than the egg of a swan."

"A swan's egg. . ." Sappho paused. "Concealed in a hyacinth, a swan's egg showed itself to Leda."

Alkaios set down his wine goblet. "Changing meters? Well, then, Leda found an egg and a swan found Leda."

Sappho placed her goblet next to Alkaios' and carved her words carefully. "Ah, Zeus, a down-flying swan. . . ." She pushed her goblet until its rim touched the other, sending a silver tone to ring under her words. "And love, a down-rushing wind that shakes even the mountain oak."

Alkaios clapped his hand to his brow. "Beautiful Sappho, I give you the final word. As usual. Your gift is unsurpassed." He stood up. "Listen! The bell's ringing. It's time to lead the bride to her new home. Come, my silent Lykaina, take this arm, and you, my dearest and best, this other one, and let us follow the chariot of love to the marriage bed."

They flowed with the crowd out into the street where the bride and groom were being installed in a brightly painted chariot drawn by two sleek brown horses. Slaves held flaming torches high to give light to the procession as it wound its way through the narrow streets. Outside another house bedecked with evergreens and bay branches, the groom's mother waited. She kissed the bride. The crowd cheered as the groom took the bride's hand and led her across the threshold.

Lykaina lost Alkaios and Sappho as the crowd squeezed into a tiny room where hundreds of candles lit a small altar. The offering to the household gods was brief, the bride's tremulous prayer barely finished, before she and the groom were pushed and pulled up a staircase strewn with flowers. At the top they were hurried into the marriage chamber, and the door was pulled shut behind them. The guests all stamped their feet and called out advice for the joining. Lykaina heard Sappho's voice above the crowd.

"The moment has come! Sweet bride, rosy with love, get thee to the marriage bed. Let the towering groom pour sweet nectar into your golden cup."

At length the bridegroom emerged, naked and holding high the bed-

116

○

sheet with its telltale spot of pale blood. The company cheered and pushed him back into the room. Most of the guests left to continue their merrymaking elsewhere. Sappho touched Lykaina's arm and led her to where the other companions were standing.

"Now," she whispered, "it is time for your best bridal song. We will sing to their loving." She turned to Alkaios, who was standing back against the wall, a smile on his lips. "Listen! You are going to hear something special."

The young women's voices were pure and strong.

Lady bride, your trembling doves—
tonight the eagle flies into the nest.
Lady bride, your golden courtyard—
tonight the dewdrop opens the rose.
Lady bride, your sacred cave—
tonight you unlock the mystery of life.

Alkaios embraced Lykaina warmly. "You are a true poet. I wish you well." He kissed Sappho quickly on the lips and then turned to follow a young man down the stairs. "Until we meet again," he called back.

The hetaerae sat on the floor of the hallway and sang song after song. As the night wore on, their giggles turned to whispers, their songs to lullabies. Lykaina felt Sappho's head fall against her arm. The wine from the banquet had left a warm glow in her body. She put her arm around Sappho's tiny shoulders and pulled her close. When their eyes met, Lykaina felt as if she were singing to Sappho instead of to the bride and groom.

Finally they left. Walking through the predawn streets of Mytilene, the tired companions linked arms and let their voices join the birdsong that was just beginning to break the fading night. Sappho, her head on Lykaina's arm, smiled up at her.

"You have sung well at your first wedding. Did you hear what Alkaios said about your poems? He never issues empty praise. Everyone is asking who you are and where you have come from. You are going to be famous on our island and beyond."

Lykaina, glowing from wine and song, felt her heart beating at her rib cage. How silly she had been to have run away, to think that the women had been making fun of her. They accepted her, they admired her poetry. They didn't care about her country origins. She squeezed Sappho's arm back.

"It has been a day of wonder for me. I will not soon forget it."

One by one the companions left the group to go into their own houses. At Sappho's door, the two who lived there slipped inside, but Sappho held Lykaina back.

"Wait a bit," she said. "The sun is almost ready to break the horizon.

There's a place nearby that looks straight to Mount Ida. Let's go there and watch the morning splendor."

She took Lykaina's hand, and together they followed a footpath that crossed the dry streambed and led to a small pine grove. They sat down just as the golden rim of the sun began to push back the red dawn over Mount Ida. Sappho stroked Lykaina's arm.

"You are not so lithe or graceful as my Atthis, but no one can match your poetry. It touches me deeply and makes me long to touch you deeply. Come with me, my Lykaina. Let us make the journey together into love's sweet valley, let us taste the honey of the sacred bee, let us lay the poetry of our bodies before Aphrodite's temple of love."

Lykaina, her heart now pounding in her ears, let Sappho draw her down onto the soft bed of pine needles. They kissed. The flowers fell from their garlands, making a bright halo around their two heads. Gowns cast off, the two smooth brown bodies moved into one another. Like the predawn glow of the eastern sky, a fire spread slowly over Lykaina's body until the flames were licking her everywhere. The fire grew hotter and hotter. Finally the soft center exploded, sending scorching spirals rolling outward to burn the very tips of her toes. The red fireball in the sky climbed from Mount Ida to a position high over the city as Lykaina, consumed, lay looking into Sappho's eyes. She let the fire burn slowly into glowing embers.

Sappho whispered to her, "Sing to me," and Lykaina, her eyes never leaving Sappho's face, sang.

> Day begins.
> Now the dawn breaks,
> now the birds,
> now the swallows,
> now the partridges,
> now the baby partridges,
> now they're all singing.

Chapter 8.
The magic forest at Eresos

"Listen, my dear young poets!"

Sappho clapped her hands as she entered the courtyard. Lykaina and the other hetaerae looked up from their writing, their styluses poised over their papyrus scrolls. Everyone recognized the tone of voice that meant a pleasant surprise.

"We are going on a holiday excursion. All of us. We leave next week."

Sappho bestowed her smile on everyone in turn. Styluses clattered to the courtyard floor.

"Oh, we're going to the country!"

"I love being out where it's all green and quiet."

"Is it to be the mountains or the sea?"

Lykaina remembered Sappho's tales of the summers she spent with her companions away from the heat of the city—sometimes in a village in the mountains, sometimes at a resort on the seacoast.

"No, no, my friends." Sappho lowered herself gracefully into her chair.

"Not the country this time. A city. A city on the farthest side of the island. Eresos, the most beautiful city on Lesbos. Eresos, the city where I was born."

The women crowded around her.

"Tell us, Sappho, what is it like there?"

"Where will we stay?"

"Is it hot?"

"Is it near the sea?"

"How will we get there?"

Sappho raised her hand.

"Sit. Sit down, all of you, and I will tell you."

They sat and folded their hands in their laps, their faces eager and expectant.

"The city is in a wonderful valley that lies between wild, wild mountains. The rivers that run down from the mountains bring fresh water to all the gardens. And the gardens, such gardens you have never seen. Oh, the gardens here are nice, the flowers are bright, the melons are round. But in Eresos, in every courtyard, there are lush greens and bright reds and oh, so many wonderful colors. The city's main square faces the sea. It is shaded by a magnificent plane tree—it would take all of us touching hands to encircle its great trunk. And then you step forward to the sea, and the sand stretches until it reaches a high headland with a stone lighthouse that sends its beacon all the way to western Greece. The breezes from the sea are cool and fresh always, and the water is emerald green. Oh, my friends, you will love it."

Sappho's face was full of color as she talked, her hands described circles in the air. Lykaina loved to see her animated like this. It was as if all the life inside her could not be contained in one small body.

"But it is so far away," said Praxinoa, "how will we get there?"

"Oh, yes," said Sappho, "it is far away from here. I have hired a boat for us. No road can cross the mountains between here and there. And the mountains, they are like no mountains you have ever seen. Their shapes are strange—it is as if some god had taken rocks and molded them like clay into fantastic forms. In fact," she lowered her voice to a hush, "they say Hephaistos has a fire under the mountain, a fire so hot that it melts the rocks underneath the earth until they flow like boiling water. Whenever he is angry, he opens up one of the mountains and lets the boiling rock flow out. Everyone must flee until his anger subsides. Then the mountain closes up once more, and the molten rock hardens into wonderful and fantastic shapes."

Shudders rippled around the circle.

"Oh, it's nothing to be afraid of now. Hephaistos has not been angry since he caught Aphrodite and Ares in his bronze hunting net and exacted tribute for their deception. But the strange shapes remain to remind us of the anger of the gods and how their whims can change our lives. But come," she stood up, "let's go into the garden, and I will tell you how my beloved city of Eresos came to be named."

The women gathered their skirts in their hands and went out into the garden. When they were all seated at the well, Sappho tilted her head to one side and began to speak.

"You may remember how Poseidon, ruler of all the seas, once fell in love with the nymph Halia of Rhodes and fathered on her a daughter and six sons. The sons, unfortunately, inherited their father's surly and quarrelsome nature. Once, to amuse themselves, they sat on the shores of Rhodes and hurled insults at Aphrodite who was passing on her way to Cyprus. She struck them mad on the spot. In revenge, they turned on their own mother and ravished her."

Gasps of horror interrupted the story. Sappho waved her hand.

"Those things happened in those days," she said with a shrug. "Anyway, Poseidon punished them by sinking them deep underground, and Zeus sent a great flood from which all the people of the island fled in terror. Halia, in her shame, flung herself into the sea. Which left only the daughter, the nymph Rhode, who floated on the waves until the island reemerged.

The shudders subsided, and Sappho continued.

"Now Helios, he who drives the chariots of the sun, had at that time been left out of Zeus' grand allotment of cities and islands to all the gods. So he, as he drove his chariot across the sky, saw Rhodes rising from the sea and claimed it and the nymph, too. On her he begot seven sons, all of whom became learned astronomers."

She looked from face to eager face.

"Unfortunately, several of these sons, too, were less than nice. Four of them conspired to kill their eldest brother, the most handsome and wisest of them all, after which they fled—one to Egypt, one to Kos, another to Ikaria. The fourth one, Makaras by name, came to Lesbos. Fratricide had apparently subdued his nature somewhat, and he became a wise and just lawgiver. His four sons and five daughters gave their names to the cities of Lesbos. It was Eresos, youngest and most handsome of all, for whom my beloved birthplace is named. Mytilene, of course, is named after one of his daughters."

"I thought Mytilene was named by the Amazon Myrine for her sister," broke in Gongyla.

Sappho gave her a long gaze.

"Oh, some say that, too. Come, it's time to go back to your writing."

As they started back to the courtyard, Lykaina pulled Sappho aside.

"I want Kissa to come with us."

"Kissa?" Sappho raised her dark eyebrows. "We are staying at the house of a cousin. His servants will provide all we need."

"No," said Lykaina, "I don't mean as a servant. I mean she should come with us so that she can swim and play in the sand. She's only a child, she should have time to play."

"But she does play," said Sappho. "All the slave children play. They have their own games. They play Figs-and-Raisins and Hide-and-Go-Seek and lots of other games. Haven't you ever seen them out there in the field behind the garden?"

Lykaina dug her sandal into the soft earth.

"She has never swum in the sea. It is so close, yet she has never gone. I want her to come with us."

Sappho plucked a flower that was drooping its bloom over the path. She reached up and set it into Lykaina's hair.

"Have I ever told you how I came to have her?"

"No. I wondered," said Lykaina. "I know that she cannot speak or hear, but she seems to understand my every thought even as I think it. And she expresses herself wonderfully with her movements. She told me her name by doing the most exquisite dance—I could almost see a magpie swooping low and chattering."

"Kissa, yes. The other servants called her that because a magpie sat on the garden wall while her mother was giving birth. But come, let's go back into the garden, and I will tell you the whole story."

They turned back along the path and sat on the old stone bench across from the well. Sappho began to weave the flowers she had gathered into a garland.

"Her mother gave birth to her right here. She was a strange one, that one. A giant of a woman, from Thrace, which many of our slaves call home. They long for it as anyone longs for their homeland, even though it is often their own fathers who sell them into slavery."

Sappho stooped to pluck a violet at her feet and place it into the wreath.

"Anyway, when they brought Kissa's mother to the slave market, she was wild. They had her in shackles because she had fought the slave sellers all the way to Mytilene. She was heavy with this child already, but that did not prevent her from dealing out blows to all who came within her reach. I had gone to the market with my brother because I needed someone to help with the laundry. The woman was filthy, her clothes were torn. Her face was covered with cuts and bruises from where they had beaten her, and her screams were like some wild animal in pain. It took three men to hold her. I could not bear to see it. I laid the money down and told them to unshackle her. My brother tried to dissuade me. He said she would never work as a slave. And the trader said, 'Oh, madame, we cannot unshackle her, she is wild.' 'Take off her chains,' I said, 'she is no longer yours to command.' They scowled at me, but they had pocketed my coins, so they had to set her free. As soon as the shackles dropped, they ran from her. My brother was more dignified, but he, too, stepped back. I walked straight up to her. I did not know if she understood Greek, but I said simply, 'Come with me,' and turned and walked away. The men were amazed. She might have run, but when I walked up to her our eyes met, and something passed between us, I don't know what. She stopped screaming and followed me without a word. We came into the garden, and there she stopped. She refused to come into the courtyard. I said, 'Fine.' If she wanted to wash herself at the well instead of in the shower room, she could. When she was clean, I tended her cuts and bruises and gave her fresh clothes. She fell asleep leaning against the well."

As Sappho talked, Lykaina watched her face soften with caring.

"She never did come into the house," Sappho continued. "Each morning, after I finished with my companions, I sat with her and stroked oil into her bruised skin. In bits and pieces, she told me her story. It was her own father, apparently, who was father to the child inside her. He sold her as soon as she began to swell. The man who bought her took his pleasure, too, but he paid for it. She covered herself with filth so that wherever he tried to sell her, no one wanted her. It was only a few weeks after she came to me that the child began to push its way out. It was well before her time, but the injuries forced the birth. She screamed in pain. I sent for the doctor, but we lost her anyway. The injuries were too deep—the blood would not stop flowing."

Sappho paused, her eyes filled with tears. Then she went on.

"The infant lived. She was tiny, but she lived. I think her ears were damaged from the injuries of her mother. I had a wet nurse come. We gave her all we could. But she will always be small, I think. Her disposition is so sweet, the other slaves were delighted to raise her. I thought she would suit you well—that's why I gave her to you."

Lykaina, engrossed in the tale, started. Of course, she thought, the child was a slave to be given away or sold at the whim of its mistress. But now she who had known the other side of slave barter held a human life in her hands. If she was no longer a slave herself but equal to Sappho and her friends, was the only choice then to hold others in slavery? Sappho stood up and placed the wreath on Lykaina's head. Then she stooped and kissed her.

"If you like, we will take her with us. It will be fun to see her on the sand."

The day of the excursion arrived with sunshine and fair winds. Lykaina and the others stood waiting on the quay surrounded by baskets and trunks and earthen vessels. A blue caïque bobbed at the pier, its captain engaged in a heated conversation with Sappho. Sappho finally threw up her hands and returned to the group.

"The thief wants more. He says the weather may change before we arrive at Eresos. Look at the sky, there's not even a hint of a cloud. He thinks we are at his mercy." She shrugged her shoulders. "Well, we are. No one wants to carry all this back, and no one wants to spend precious hours looking for another boat. Look, here's Alkaios!"

Lykaina felt a strong arm grip her waist.

"So, you are off to a better clime," said Alkaios, his eyes smiling. "Are you taking the muses with you and leaving us bereft of our inspiration? How are we to compose our own poems without the presence of your graces?"

"Come with us, then, dear Alkaios," said Sappho, as she raised her lips to be kissed. "You have never seen my birthplace. There is room for you at my cousin's house. Come and join us."

Alkaios laughed and shook his head. "Much as I enjoy the pleasure of your company and that of this poet-wonder of yours, I have other plans. Carthage calls me once again. You should travel there with me sometime. It, too, is a magnificent city. People from all of civilization pass through. Everywhere you go you see faces of many colors and robes of unknown materials. Where I stay they love your poetry, my dearest. And once I have arrived this time, they will come to love the songs of our Lykaina. I will make sure of that."

He opened his satchel to reveal several scrolls tucked along one side. Lykaina looked from Alkaios to Sappho.

"I gave them to him, my precious," said Sappho. "Remember when I told you that your poems could travel the world over when you learned to write? Alkaios here is your carrier pigeon. Your fame will soon reach to the other side of the Mediterranean."

Lykaina, color rising to her face, looked toward the caïque.

"I see she has not lost her crimson glow," laughed Alkaios. "That is good. So long as you blush from praise, my dear, you will not be spoiled. But look now, your boat is loaded. It's time for good-byes." He took Sappho in his arms. "I do not like this pain of separation," he said as he held her close. "We do it so often, yet it never gets easier." He released her and turned to Lykaina. "Take good care of her. She is a fragile petal. You are the one who must shelter her in a storm."

He kissed her on both cheeks and stood back. The other companions were waiting for them at the boat's rail. Kissa appeared at Lykaina's side and took her hand.

"Yes, little one, we are coming," said Lykaina.

The three of them scrambled up the gangplank.

"Ready to cast off!" roared the captain. Two men on the pier untied the heavy lines and threw them to the crew. The little boat moved away from the quay under the power of two sets of oars. Outside the harbor, the captain gave orders to raise the sails. There was a moment of stillness when the oars stopped, and then the wind caught the sails and bellied them out. The boat began to move swiftly along the coast.

Lykaina was happy to be on the water again. The gentle motion of the waves made her feel as if she were part of the sea. When they passed the narrow opening that led into the Gulf of Hieras, the image of Maia's dark face burned before her. Where was she now? she wondered. Why had she left the shores of her birthplace? Lykaina felt her loss. Yet it had been Maia who had forced her to choose. She had almost pushed her away, it seemed. It was as if the things that Sappho had to teach her could not be part of Maia's world. *Remember who you are,* Maia had said. But who I am is a poet, she thought. And it is in Sappho's world that I can best be that. Here my poems are heard by the ears of other poets. And now—a surge of pride entered her breast—they will be heard beyond the great Mediterranean. An arm encircling her waist interrupted her thoughts.

"The wind and the salt air become you," Sappho whispered. "Are you happy with me?"

Lykaina looked down at the radiant face.

"I am happier than I have ever been."

In Eresos they took up residence in a large house on a hill overlooking the sea. The city was as Sappho had described it—a small but perfect jewel set between two ranges of wild mountains. Trellised grapevines drooped clusters of dark purple fruit over courtyards full of flowers; the shiny leaves of the creeper clung to the courtyard walls. Every night the sun sent out a blaze of golds and fiery reds. Long after the fire had disappeared into the western sea, the clouds remained tinted with its colors.

Mornings they swam in the calm blue water or played on the sandy beach. Noontimes they dined in a public house by the water's edge— every day a different kind of fish grilled over an open fire and garnished with lemon and herbs. Evenings they sat in one of the seaside taverns outside the city with other musicians and poets, singing and watching the moon rise over the mountains. At each evening's end, Lykaina, saturated with sun and sea, good food and company, found herself invited into Sappho's bed for long moments of ecstasy and love. It was a summer that seemed to stretch forever.

Eventually the days began to shorten, and the late evening breezes carried a faint hint of cold air. The other women became restless, ready to return home. Sappho lay beside Lykaina one morning and sighed.

"It seems to be time, my love, to leave this idyll."

Lykaina reached over and stroked her cheek.

"The others don't want to linger as I do," complained Sappho. "It is always this way. I want to take as many magic moments as I can and let them pile up on top of each other. But the others grow bored with perfection, they always want change. When we are in Mytilene, they want to go to the mountains. When we are in the mountains, they want to go to the seashore. When they are at the seashore, they want to go to the city. They are never where they want to be."

Sappho rolled over and kissed Lykaina's lips.

"Never mind. We will go back and make ourselves another perfection there. Come, let's find our captain and see how much the thief will make us pay."

They dressed slowly, each drinking in the other's body, reaching out to touch a hand, a shoulder, a cheek. As they descended the gray marble steps to the harbor, Lykaina said, "Let me do the haggling. Let me see if I can secure a fair price."

Sappho smiled, and Lykaina passed ahead of her to the boat tied up at the quay. The surly captain was swearing at a small boy who had brought him a bottle of wine.

"Mule's piss," he yelled, spitting the contents of his mouth onto the side of the boat. "Take this back and bring me something made from grapes." He turned to Lykaina. "And what are you bringing me, air to fill my sails with? There's plenty of wind out there already, I don't need any more."

Lykaina squared her shoulders and jutted out her chin.

"We want passage to Mytilene—nine women, our baggage, and a child. You are right about the wind. It is strong, and it blows toward Mytilene. You can take us there in half the time you brought us and at half the price."

"Aha. You want to strike a bargain. The wind is not that strong, and it may change at any moment. I'll give you a fair deal, though, at three-quarters the fare you paid to come."

"It is the time of the Etesian," said Lykaina firmly. "The wind is steady from now until the setting of the Pleiades. Half the price, and we'll load our own baggage."

The captain narrowed his eyes.

"The lady knows the sea. Anyone who calls the winds correctly sails for the fare they ask. The deal is struck."

He held out his grimy hand, and Lykaina shook it with a strong grasp.

"Under those soft robes lie the bones of a sailor," he muttered, as he turned away.

Sappho was delighted with Lykaina's bargain.

"You have shown him that women can deal in a man's world. Come, I have a treat for you. Since this is our last day, I am going to show you a magic place." Sappho took Lykaina's arm and steered her toward the city square. She called to a young boy playing with a dog under the plane tree. "You there. Go to the stables and bring us two good horses. Make sure they are steady ones, we are going into the mountains." Sappho turned back to Lykaina, her eyes sparkling. "I have only been there once, when I was small. The shepherd who grazed his flocks on the slopes behind my father's house took me. I remember how tall I felt seated in front of him on his horse. It was long ago, but I know I remember the way—I can see it right now before my eyes."

The boy returned leading two smartly stepping mares. Lykaina looked down at her flowing gown and frowned. How could she ride horseback? She watched Sappho step up onto a small wall and slide gracefully sideways onto her horse's back, one leg raised forward, the other hanging down. Lykaina followed suit. She did not have the control that came with straddling the horse, but she found that she could balance herself well enough.

Praxinoa broke away from her companions playing ball and ran to Sappho's side.

"Where are you going?" she asked. "When will you be back? Are we going home soon? Everyone is asking."

Sappho leaned over and ruffled her hair.

"We are going for a ride. We'll be back by suppertime. And yes, tell the others to pack, we sail tomorrow morning."

Praxinoa waved them off.

"Actually we are going to see a forest," said Sappho, as they passed between the two rows of gently swaying poplars lining the long straight road that led directly away from the sea. "But this is not just any forest. It is magic. It is a forest made of stone!"

Lykaina looked at her.

"Do you mean there are stones that look like trees?"

"No," replied Sappho, "they are real trees. You can see the grain of the wood, you can see every knot. But some god has turned them into stone. Some of them stand upright, and some are fallen down. Where they have fallen over, you can see the rings of the inner tree. I remember the old man showing me a broken piece that had the imprint of a leaf inside it. Every vein was clearly marked. And the colors, oh, Lykaina, the colors will amaze you. Reds and yellows of all different shades, so bright and shiny that you'd think some jeweler had just polished them."

They had been traveling up the road for nearly an hour when they came to a small village with crude stone huts that reminded Lykaina of her own mountain village.

"Here is where we find the path," said Sappho excitedly. "I remember it was between two old fig trees, and there was a stone wall just beyond."

Lykaina pointed up the road.

"There are two fig trees just ahead."

"That's it—there's the wall. Now you will see something."

Sappho kicked her horse into a trot. They headed toward a range of the grotesquely shaped mountains. Lykaina looked up and saw swiftly moving clouds rolling along the tops.

"Those clouds, Sappho," she called out, "they might mean rain."

"It's just a little way," Sappho called back over her shoulder. "It will only take a few minutes."

Lykaina urged her mare on. They rode at a steady pace through a landscape that was barren and wild. No brightly colored gardens grew here, no lush green fields, no fruit trees. Only rocks and small round thorn bushes clung to the sides of the hills. In the distance Lykaina could hear echoes of sheep bells. Otherwise they were entirely alone. The trail climbed steadily uphill.

"We're almost there," called Sappho over her shoulder. "It's just beyond this bend."

But they rounded the bend only to find another bend and then another. The horses were soaked with sweat now, and Lykaina could see that Sappho was tired. Her usually graceful body drooped forward, and she clung with both hands to the wooden saddle. The roiling clouds had by now turned from ash gray to angry black. Lykaina could hear a low rumble of thunder roll across the mountains. She knew that they must turn back, but the path was too narrow to come abreast of Sappho, and Sappho was deaf to all her entreaties.

Suddenly a bolt of lightning glanced off a rock just ahead of them. Both horses reared in fright. Sappho slid from her saddle and began to tumble down the rocky slope below the path. Lykaina steadied her mare and jumped down. She scrambled down the bank after Sappho who was caught in a scrubby fig tree growing out of a rock. Sappho clutched the branches and wept.

"Oh, I wanted to show them to you, I wanted to make a perfect end to our perfect holiday."

Lykaina held her tightly and stroked her neck.

"It's all right, my love. We'll have plenty of holidays together. We'll see the stone trees another time. Look below you, you are lucky to be alive."

The fig tree was at the edge of a sharp drop-off. Below them rocks and thorn bushes jutted out from the bank. Another bolt of lightning flashed. The horses reared, turned on their two hind legs, and plunged down the mountain path. Thunder now rolled on every side, and sharp drops of rain fell out of the sky like stones.

"Hold on to me," said Lykaina. "We'll get back to the path and find somewhere to shelter ourselves. We'll have to stay here until the storm passes."

Sappho let Lykaina half carry, half drag her up the slope.

"Are you able to walk?" asked Lykaina.

"Yes, except that I've lost a sandal."

Lykaina retrieved the sandal lodged in a bush and strapped it onto Sappho's foot. Sappho sat still, her arms clutched across her breasts, her lips murmuring.

"I wanted to show you the pretty colors, I wanted you to see the stone trees."

By now the rain was pelting them, each drop hard and icy. Lykaina looked ahead to where the trail turned and passed along a ridge. The black clouds that covered the sky made it difficult to see, but a flash of lighting showed her a dark round hole in the rocks just below the path ahead.

"We'll probably have to share it with animals," she said, as she helped Sappho along the path, "but it will shelter us from the worst of the storm."

The cave was low and dark and smelly, but it was dry. Lykaina left Sappho at the entrance and crawled on all fours to explore. Her hand came across first some dry twigs and then some dry branches. She picked up a rough stone. Struck against the side of the cave, it sparked. Flint, she thought. Some shepherd has used this cave for shelter before us.

Later, as they huddled naked around the fire, their clothes spread out to dry, Sappho leaned her head onto Lykaina's shoulder.

"You told me you were of the mountains," she said, running her finger lightly along Lykaina's arm. "But I never understood what you meant. Your poetry is so fine, you always seemed to be one of us. Oh, of course, you are not so graceful as the others when you walk, and you used to play that funereal aulos. But somehow I never really believed your stories about your mountains and your herds of goats. How could anyone learn to sing like you do with only a cave like this for shelter?"

By now Lykaina had recognized the odor of the cave. It was a wolf's den. If she explored farther back, she would probably find tufts of baby fur and little piles of cub dung. She breathed deeply, letting the rank odor fill her nostrils. An image formed of a mother wolf and four cubs.

A she-wolf with silver-and-black markings was calling to her. Memory fragments chased each other: a basket on a ledge...a warm den like this one...a warm sleek body...a teat filled with warm milk....

But Sappho was still talking.

"You know about these things. Clearly this is as familiar to you as my courtyard. But tell me, how could a song come out of a dark, smelly place like this?"

Dark and smelly, thought Lykaina, a spark of anger rising in her breast. It shelters you from a storm we should never have gone into. But when she glanced down at Sappho who was looking at her now with loving eyes, the spark of anger extinguished itself. How could Sappho understand?

"We did not live in caves," she said evenly. "We lived in houses. Not so fine as yours, but they had walls and roofs. I learned to sing out in the open, on the mountain. The old man, my grandfather, taught me how to bounce a note off the opposite rock. It was all light and open air up there."

"Still, you were singing only to mountains and sheep."

"Goats," corrected Lykaina, her voice stiff. "What I sang came out of the songs my people have sung for thousands of seasons' turnings. I sing what is in my heart, but its shape comes from many people."

Lykaina hunched forward and pushed a piece of wood into the fire. Sappho reached to touch Lykaina's cheek.

"Ah, my strange mountain-woman. You are so proud. Do not be angry with me. I have been stupid today, not once, but twice. First I led us into a storm from which you, with your knowledge of the mountains, have saved us. Now I have been ignorant about your mountain poetry. Forgive me and love me again."

Lykaina looked at Sappho's small, dark body glowing in the firelight. The woman had a daughter now grown to womanhood, and yet her breasts might be two ripe pears, her nipples plump raisins. Thunder still rolled outside, and lightning lit up the wild mountains from time to time. But the cave was warm from the fire, and the anger that had risen in Lykaina's breast melted as their two bodies reached into each other and loved.

Lykaina shivered. Sometime during the night the fire had gone out. She rearranged the gowns to cover the sleeping Sappho and crawled to the cave entrance. The rain had stopped, but clouds still covered the sky. Directly across the valley from the cave, striations of clouds—bright pink, ash gray, and charcoal—moved swiftly toward a mountain peak whose grotesque shape was wrapped in black shrouds. As each pink layer reached the mountain, it was swallowed by the gray and the black.

Lykaina looked in the direction she thought the sea might lie. The clouds there, a yellowish hue, were not so thick, and occasionally she could see behind them a hint of blue. A wind with a cold bite blew through the valley, but no rain was falling.

Her belly growled. They had last eaten some apples as they left the city. She longed for the obsidian knife, now hidden with her aulos in a corner of her room in Mytilene. No way to make a bow without a knife. Nor fashion a trap. What animals—besides the absent wolves—lived here anyway? She hadn't seen a rabbit or any small ground animal. Then she heard the morning cry of a wild partridge. Her eyes scanned the nearby shrubs and rocks looking for the nest. She slipped out of the cave, picked up a rock, and climbed down in the direction of the cry. After several false turns, she located the nest on a ledge. She could see from the distance a mother feeding four fledglings. She poised herself for the throw and breathed a soft prayer.

"The Great Mother blesses you for your gift of life. May she show your babies how to live without you."

The Great Mother, she thought as she carried the warm feathered body back up to the cave. I have not said a prayer to the Great Mother since I left Maia.

Back at the cave, Sappho was up, clutching the gowns around her.

"I'm cold and I'm hungry," she complained, her face drawn. "How will we ever get home? Oh, why did I ever care about those stupid trees!"

"Hush," said Lykaina, as she blew sparks into flames. "We will eat first and then we will find our way home. I'm afraid that we cannot re-trace our steps—the storm has washed away part of the path we came on. We will continue forward. The path must eventually lead some-where. And we will find someone who will help us to Eresos."

She spitted the plucked bird and set it over the fire. By the time they had eaten, the gray clouds were white, the mountaintop had un-shrouded itself, and patches of blue sky could be seen in several direc-tions. They left the cave and began to walk.

The footpath neither climbed the mountains above nor descended into the valley. It simply wound around, following the curves of the hills. From time to time the sun, as it climbed its morning uphill path, pushed a fistful of rays through a break in the clouds. Lykaina could see that they were moving not toward Eresos but at least not directly away from it. She walked ahead, stepping carefully on the path still slick from yesterday's rain. She thought how hard this must be for Sappho who had never walked on any road not paved with marble or clean hewn stone. Lykaina was proud that she did not complain even when she stumbled.

Suddenly the sun broke through and covered the whole slope before them with light. Relieved, Lykaina breathed deeply. She surveyed the now-golden valley, her eyes slowly moving over every scrubby tree, every stone, looking for a sign. Her eyes passed over, then came back to rest on something below in the middle of the barrenness. Several lumpish shapes—were they tree or stone? The sun striking them reflected many colors—reds and yellows, blacks and browns. Lykaina reached back for Sappho's hand and pointed. But Sappho had already seen them.

"That's it!" she cried. "Those are the stone trees! Look at the colors! Look how they shine!"

Lykaina held her breath, the sight was so dazzling. As she watched, she saw that something was moving amongst the trunks. Black figures, three of them, moved in and out.

"Look, there are people there," she exclaimed. "We have found our help!"

They set off again, and soon Lykaina's sharp eyes picked out an almost invisible trail that left the path and descended in the direction of the stone trees.

"These are not the ones the old man took me to see," said Sappho, as they drew closer. "There were only a few of them and most were fallen over. Look how many there are here!"

"Perhaps there are several stone forests scattered over these mountains," responded Lykaina, still dazzled by the colors.

They drew close to the trees, and Lykaina saw that the three figures—all women—were moving around the largest of the trunks in a solemn fashion. She began to hear a familiar drone.

"Stop," she whispered to Sappho. "This is a sacred place. The women are praying."

"Nonsense," said Sappho. "It's not a temple. You can see that no one built it. It's beautiful, but it's only a group of stone tree trunks."

She started to push ahead.

"No," said Lykaina, holding her back firmly. "It is a temple. The Great Mother built it. These women are praying to her."

"The great mother?" echoed Sappho. "Who is the great mother? There is no *great mother*—only Zeus is the great father."

Lykaina looked at her. All the time she had been with her, the Great Mother had seemed like something from another time, another place. In Sappho's courtyard, at the temples in Mytilene, only the Olympian gods seemed present. She had never spoken of the Great Mother to Sappho, she hardly ever thought of her. But now, in this place, she felt her presence; she felt pulled to the stone trees not for their great beauty but for their sacredness, their belonging to the spiritual realm.

"Wait here," she said to Sappho. "I will speak to the women, they will understand me."

Sappho looked at her curiously but remained where she was. Lykaina walked slowly ahead. As she reached the first tree, she saw that the women had stopped the ceremonial dance and were leaning against the great trunk, their hands pressed hard onto the smooth colored surface. Lykaina slipped into place and laid her hands on the stone trunk also. She felt a surge of life enter her hands and spread through her whole body. She took up the familiar chant with the women.

> *Virgin Gaia who rides the clouds,*
> *Many-breasted mother of the earth,*
> *Dark crone of the underworld,*
> *We worship you.*

The chant died away. Lykaina stepped back from the tree and looked at the women on either side of her. The third woman came from around the other side of the trunk. All three seemed ageless. Ragged black clothes draped their bent bodies. Their faces held masses of wrinkles, and their dark eyes were sunk into their skeletal heads. They stared at Lykaina, but Lykaina could not tell from their faces whether or not they were angry at her intrusion. Finally one of them spoke in a voice low and rumbling like the thunder of the night before.

"Then you are one of us. But what about her?"

She jerked her head in the direction of Sappho.

"She is my friend," said Lykaina. "She is not of the Mother, but she will not endanger you. We need safe passage to Eresos. We were lost in the storm last night."

The three women looked at her for a long time. Then the speaker raised her hand in a sharp gesture and let it fall.

"The Great Mother sends thunder to clear our ears and lightning to open our eyes."

Lykaina blushed and lowered her eyes. The only sound in the whole valley was the low call of a far-off ground dove. She looked up and saw that the three women's eyes were no longer fierce.

"Go back to the footpath on the hill and continue in the direction you were going. Before the great light has moved halfway to her resting place, you will be at the seashore. There is a village there. Ask for Onasilos. He will take you to Eresos in his boat."

Lykaina touched her hand to her forehead and turned away. When she reached Sappho, she did not speak but took her hand and led her back to the trail. They walked in silence until the blue sea filled their eyes. The village the women had spoken of sat nestled against a large black rock. A breakwater harbored a handful of fishing boats.

"They told you about this village?" Sappho's voice broke the silence.

"Yes," said Lykaina. "A man named Onasilos will take us to Eresos."

"Something happened back there," said Sappho. "I saw you touch the tree, and I felt something. Who is this great mother you worship? I do not know her. Who is she, and why does she have no temples?"

Lykaina looked at Sappho. She loved and trusted her. But she remembered her grandmother's words, *Tell no one.* And Maia's warning, *They will destroy us if they know.* She reached out and held Sappho's shoulders with both hands.

"If you love me, you will not ask. And you will not tell anyone what you have seen."

Her voice, both fierce and gentle, hung in the air. Sappho looked at her for a long time. Then she pulled their bodies together. Lykaina could feel their two hearts beating, but each to its own tempo.

"I have now seen two Lykainas," whispered Sappho. "In my courtyard, there is a Lykaina who speaks softly and sings rare songs. She follows me wherever I go and delights my friends with her perfect words."

Sappho pulled her body away and put her two hands on Lykaina's cheeks.

"Now I have seen another Lykaina, a Lykaina who knows wild places and secret things. A Lykaina who walks in front and tells me where to step. This Lykaina is also beautiful, but I don't know her and I am afraid of her. I am afraid that she will draw back into her wild and secret places and leave me alone in my courtyard." Sappho dropped her hands and looked toward the sea. "I will do as you wish, my beloved Lykaina. I will speak no word of what I saw."

Together they turned and began to move toward the village.

Chapter 9.
Journey to the center

"Please, where is the mistress Sappho?"

Lykaina looked up from the lyre she was plucking. A small boy in a slave's tunic hesitated at the edge of the courtyard.

"She is in her room. You may give me the message."

The slaveboy bowed his head and came a few steps closer.

"My master Alkaios says—"

"Your master Alkaios? Is he home again? Tell me your news!"

Lykaina motioned for the boy to sit on the stool next to her, but he remained standing, his eyes on the floor in front of him. Words fell out of his mouth in a rapid monotone.

"My master says he is once again home and requests the pleasure of his most precious friend and her friend, too." He stopped for breath and raised his eyes just enough to meet Lykaina's. "Tonight after sunset. He says you will find at his house a wondrous surprise."

Lykaina held out her hand, but the boy kept his fists clenched at his sides.

"Tell him we accept his invitation with pleasure. I will deliver the message to Sappho myself."

She grasped one of the clenched fists and forced a coin into it. The boy turned and fled. Lykaina smiled after him. He reminded her of her first day in Sappho's courtyard—how she had stood embarrassed, afraid to speak the lines she had memorized to introduce herself. That was long ago. Now she was first among the hetaerae. Messengers arrived regularly to ask her to compose a hymn to Apollo or a song to inaugurate an official. Scrolls of her poems filled a wall of pigeonholes in Sappho's library. Slaves need not always be slaves, she thought. It is simply a matter of determination.

She began plucking the lyre again, letting the notes fall aimlessly onto the courtyard tiles. How noble an instrument, she thought, how well it suits the poetry of the courtyard. Her aulos now languished in a corner of her room, touched only by Kissa who polished it every morning.

She looked toward the staircase. It was not like Sappho to stay in bed so late—especially on a day she had set aside for the two of them to be alone. A commotion upstairs made her stop playing.

"Leave me alone! Let my hair be like Medusa's! I am as wretched as she!"

Something clattered to the floor, and footsteps scurried down the hall. A moment later, a disheveled Sappho stormed down the stairs. She waved a torn scroll at Lykaina.

"She's nothing but a common slavewhore!" Sappho stamped her foot on the tile. "They call her beautiful. Fa! She uses her beauty, public property that it is, to extract gold coins from innocent men. She smells out fortune like a hound smells out a rabbit."

Lykaina laid aside her lyre and went to Sappho. Sappho paced in front of her, her voice sharp and acrid.

"And now she has smelled out my beloved Charexos, my baby brother, and sucks his fortune from him. She spent all last summer inveigling him to buy her lavish gifts. Now he has bought her her freedom and intends to marry the bitch."

Sappho collapsed on a chair. Small furrows cut through the powder on her cheeks. Lykaina knelt beside her and touched her arm.

"Calm yourself, my love. Who is this you are talking about? What has she done?"

Sappho turned dull eyes to her and sighed.

"Doricha. The vixen's name is Doricha. Rhodopis, they call her—like a rose. A rose in a briar bush. I met her years ago on Samos. We were being entertained by the tales of Aesop. She was his fellow slave, still just a pretty young face used to adorn the dinner parties. She danced a little and played the flute sweetly while we ate. Then she was sent away since it was Aesop we had come to hear. No one paid any attention to this Doricha."

She tossed her head angrily.

"A man called Xanthes bought her," she continued, "fitted her out in finery, and took her to Naukratis to service the military—a career well suited to her charms. But she was not content with being the pride of the navy. No, she had to lay her snares for my brother. She sees in him her great opportunity for wealth and respectability. And marriage now, that she-lynx has set her ill-smelling snout to the ground and connives at becoming my sister-in-law. My brother behaves as if besotted by wine. He fawns on her, he jumps to satisfy her every whim. It was one thing to pleasure himself with her body on his trips away from home. But now he intends to bring her back to Lesbos as his wife. I am shamed and dishonored by him—bringing a slave into the family!"

Lykaina stroked Sappho's arm. Slave, she thought. I was once a slave, does she not remember? And I am accepted into her family. She pushed a flicker of unease aside to tend to Sappho's anguish.

"Listen!" Sappho unrolled the letter. "'Dear sister,' he writes. 'You must congratulate me. I am to be married next full moon. Then we set sail immediately, and soon I will be bringing my beloved Doricha for your marriage blessing.' Does he really think I will bless a union begun in the cesspool of harlotry? Oh, I am shamed by him."

She crumpled the papyrus and threw it aside.

Lykaina, still stroking her arm, murmured, "It will not affect your place in society, what your brother does. You must find a way to forgive him and accept her. After all, she plays the flute, you say. Perhaps she is a poet, also."

Sappho stood up abruptly, shaking off Lykaina's hand.

"You! What do you understand of family? You who have none except for some goatherds in the hills! You speak of acceptance as if I were a peasant welcoming a stray dog into my hut. I am Sappho, descendant of Penthilos, son of Orestes, son of Agamemnon. I do not accept slaves into my family!"

Sappho turned on her heel and left the courtyard. Lykaina felt as if she had been slapped. She stood up shaking. This woman I love, she thought, what does she really think of me? How can she accept me if she feels that way about slaves? An urge to run overwhelmed her, a need to feel the earth beneath her feet again. But Sappho's face twisted in pain remained in front of her. She does not know what she is saying, she thought. I must find a way to comfort her.

Lykaina fetched a jug of Samian wine from the storeroom and set it on a silver tray. On her way through the courtyard, she picked up the lyre. She found Sappho in the garden, sitting at the stone well. She set the tray down beside her and, without a word, began to play and sing.

> As the plains thirst for water,
> as the mountains thirst for snow,
> so I thirst for your laughter again
> and the light in your eyes.

Sappho lifted her head and sighed.

"Only a country woman could sing that. Oh, my sweet Lykaina, you bring joy to a heart that is heavy. All right, for you I will smile again. We will forget this letter for now and walk together. But I tell you, no matter what song you woo me with, I will not permit that obscene and evil bitch in my house!"

They spent the morning walking the hills behind Mytilene. Clusters of wild marigolds, all reds and yellows, called out to be plucked. Sappho began to talk about her childhood.

"My father's bones were watered with tears when I was only six. We lived then in Eresos. Remember that lovely jewel of a city? I was so happy there. I helped my mother tend my baby brothers, I played with my little friend whose father herded sheep on the hills behind our house."

Sappho took the garland she had been weaving and placed it on Lykaina's head.

"Then the war came. Those greedy Athenians, always wanting what belongs to others. They laid claim to our way into the Hellespont. We Lesbians were just a group of cities then, each living as peacefully as we could. You know Pittakos, our governor, the man whose nephew was being married at your first wedding here. Well, he was rough and woolly. But he was an exceptional soldier, so he was asked to lead an army to protect our rights. All the men took up arms and boarded warships and sailed out to engage the Athenians. My poor father was killed in the very first battle.

"My mother bundled us up, myself and my three brothers. Charaxos you know about, he is two years younger than I. Then Eurygos and Larichos. We came here to Mytilene to stay with an uncle. It seemed safer. Eresos sits so unprotected on the open sea." She sighed. "The war lasted ten years. My uncle's house had full view of the harbor and the sea, so daily we watched our ships of war move back and forth, lying in wait for the Athenian pirates."

They came to a cypress grove with trees so thick that the sun did not penetrate. Sappho took Lykaina's hand and kissed it.

"So it was here in Mytilene that I passed my girlhood," she continued. "Poetry came early to me. My mother chose for me a group of companions, and there I found my strength in words. When I was fifteen I was wooed by our friend Alkaios." She laughed. "I was afraid of him then, but I never showed my fear. I simply looked the other way whenever he tried to talk to me. He would come to my house drunk to serenade me, and he sang my praises at every dinner party on the island. I resisted his advances. He was so uncouth in his drunkenness. But his poetry was good even then, and I learned from it."

They stopped as a doe, followed by a spotted fawn, jumped from behind a tree.

"I almost forgot," said Lykaina. "Alkaios is back from his travels. He sent a message this morning. We are to join him for dinner tonight."

Sappho clapped her hands.

"Oh, praise be," she cried. "I am longing to see him. Perhaps he can tell me how to dissuade my brother from this folly!"

Her fist clenched. Lykaina took it between both her hands and uncurled the fingers one by one.

"Tell me about your early days with Alkaios," she said. "Tell me how you tried to make a revolution."

"Do not think that I am ignorant of your devices," pouted Sappho. "But all right. I said I would put it out of my mind and I will."

They walked in silence for several minutes, emerging at last into the sunlight. They were at the edge of a cliff overlooking the emerald sea. A salt breeze ruffled the flowers on their heads.

"After the Peace was made," said Sappho, "we thought all our troubles were over. I was sixteen then, and people were just beginning to ask for my poetry, thanks to Alkaios. Our cities had been joined together only for the sake of the war, but there were those who had come to love to rule. The rest of us were longing to go back to our free and easy ways, and now we were appalled to find ourselves restricted by new laws made by a tyrant. Alkaios and I and others joined together in a political group. Oh, we were so idealistic. We thought our angry poems alone could overthrow our oppressors. For our troubles we were sent to live in exile—Alkaios to Egypt, I to Sicily. It is beautiful there, the water is warmer than here, and the winds don't blow so cold in the winter months. But, oh, how I missed my Lesbos. It was as if a piece of my heart had been cut out of me and cast into the sea. I bled daily."

The footpath followed the edge of the marble cliff. Below them, a pine-shadowed cove harbored children swimming.

"It was not all bad," Sappho went on. "I met my husband there and bore my beautiful Kleis. We were not unhappy. I made poetry. And became the talk of the Adriatic. Perhaps that was why Pittakos called for my return—to bring my growing reputation back to its native soil for his own glory. But I forgave him, I was so happy to feel the cobbles of Mytilene under my feet. My husband had been lost at sea some months before. He was a merchant, and a storm took his ship to the bottom. So I returned alone with my beloved Kleis. She is a grown woman now, as you know, married and with her own family. But I have my companions."

Sappho turned to Lykaina and reached up to touch her face.

"See how life flows like a river? The riverbed is the same for everyone, but the water is always changing. When I lost my Atthis, I thought I might as well be dead. My other sweet friends were kind and loving, but they only reminded me of her beauty and my loss. But now, like a fresh mountain stream, you have entered the course, and again my life is changed. Stay with me, Lykaina, stay with me always. We will make an eternity of poetry and love, not knowing where one ends and the other begins. Forever I will put you to rest with me on soft cushions, and forever we will rise together with the queenly dawn. Every day of one thousand years I will touch your breasts that are softer than fine raiment and drink the sweet nectar of your body."

The path sloped down to a cove protected from the inquiring sea by large gray rocks. A scrubby bush served as rack for their abandoned clothes. They floated in the clear blue water and let the sun wash their faces. Later, resting against Sappho's breast and listening to the waves lapping just beyond her feet, Lykaina felt like a queen. This is a palace of love, she thought. This is a land of poetry. Here I belong.

Alkaios' white house, on one of the hills to the south of Mytilene, stood alone in the middle of a luxurious garden, its arches curving up to a red-tiled roof. The crescent moon hung over the hill behind. Sappho and Lykaina entered the house through a great double door carved with a frieze of goddesses. A slave woman rushed to bathe their feet and annoint their heads with perfumes. They wandered from room to room, pausing and chatting with other guests. Finally they came to the dining room. Lykaina heard Sappho gasp beside her.

"There he is," she whispered, "but who is that with him?"

Lykaina looked in the direction of Sappho's gaze. Alkaios stood talking to a large majestic woman whose skin was the color of the obsidian knife blade. Lykaina had seen black-skinned men before—sailors at Corinth, merchants in Samos. But this woman looked like none of them. Her head was crowned in hundreds of tiny braids, tightly interwoven with strands of gold. A high forehead sloped down to black arches over a pair of eyes that sent out blazing fire. Her long straight nose broadened into a pair of flaring nostrils. Thick sensuous lips parted slightly to reveal a set of ivory teeth. The woman's immense body was covered with folds of the brightest material Lykaina had ever seen.

Alkaios saw them and beckoned.

"Come and meet the treasure I have brought back with me."

He steered the woman toward them. Lykaina felt the black eyes take her in and hold her. The woman pressed her two hands together and slightly inclined her head.

"May I present Soudiata, princess of Ghana. Her country is many days journey from Carthage. She came by camel across the desert."

The royal woman opened her mouth, and bubbles of speech fell from it. The sounds were like music, her broad face like an instrument playing it. A young attendant translated.

"She is honored to meet the great Sappho and the other Sappho, too. She has listened to the poems of both and admires them well."

Sappho's face radiated.

"Tell her that I am well pleased to know a princess from this faraway place. I hope she is finding what she seeks in my homeland."

The broad black face beamed back pleasure. More bubbles fell from the lips.

"She says," said the attendant, "that she, too, is a singer of poems and that she would be honored to exchange songs with the greatest poet of the Mediterranean."

A bell rang. Alkaios gave his arm to the princess.

"There is much for all of us to talk about, but food must be eaten when it is presented. Come, Sappho and Lykaina, seat yourselves on this couch while the royal Soudiata and I sit close by on this one."

As she sat down, the princess spread her flowing gown with such grace that Lykaina suddenly felt as awkward and tongue-tied as she had in her first days at Sappho's. She concentrated on the breast of roast duck a slave had set before her.

"You must hear the music of these Ghanaians." Alkaios picked up a sardine wrapped in a fig leaf. "They have an instrument that they make out of a calabash. Some are large and some small, but all of them make sounds like a crystal fountain. It is a royal instrument—only the reigning queen and her daughters are allowed to play it. Soudiata will bring hers to you tomorrow, you will see and hear."

He offered an anchovy to the princess.

"Why is she traveling so far from home?" Lykaina surprised herself with her words. "What is a camel, and what is a desert?"

The attendant, standing behind the princess, whispered into her ear. Soudiata's face broke into a broad smile.

"The desert is a sea where there is no water, only sand," the attendant said. "The camel is the ship of the desert. He is big, and he has a great hump on his back. Hundreds of them make a long trail across the sand. The princess' land is beyond the desert. Her city sits at the bend of a great river that flows both north and south. It is the tradition of her people that the queen's daughter journey before she takes up her reign. She carries with her the royal calabash so that she never loses touch with the foremother who guides her journey. When she has seen the Great Mother's world, she can return to the bend in the mighty river. When the time comes to mourn the passing of the old queen, the people will accept the young one knowing she has seen all the places the Great Mother created."

The Great Mother, thought Lykaina. She knows of the Great Mother and speaks her name aloud. She looked around to see if anyone had noticed, but Alkaios and Sappho were feeding each other roasted oysters. She looked back at the princess and locked eyes with her. A current passed between them. Lykaina tried to imagine a sea of sand, a river that flowed in two directions. She wanted to ask more questions, but could not find words. Instead she watched the princess watch a troupe of dancing acrobats display their skills.

The next morning the princess arrived at Sappho's house attended by her translator. As she entered the courtyard, the strands of gold woven around her neck caught the morning sunlight and reflected a glow onto her face. Sappho stood up to greet her. Lykaina and the other companions scrambled to their feet. Palms together, the princess inclined her head for the royal greeting. Her wide full mouth let flow bubbles of sound.

"She says it gives her much pleasure to come into the presence of the great Sappho," the attendant translated. "In her travels she has heard Sappho's poems often quoted. She has been eager to meet the composer of those fine words."

Sappho smiled.

"Tell her I am deeply honored by her visit. May my hospitality please her." Sappho turned to the companions. "This is Soudiata, princess of a country beyond the great desert that rims the other side of the Mediterranean. She is friend of my friend Alkaios and a poet herself. She has come to share her song with us."

Lykaina's eyes followed the princess as she glided across the courtyard to the carved highback chair Sappho had prepared for her. The attendant stood behind her. Sappho poured wine and water into a silver goblet and handed it to Soudiata who took two delicate sips before setting it down on the little table beside her.

"She will be pleased to hear the great Sappho's song, if Sappho will so honor her," said the attendant.

Lykaina plucked the lyre while Sappho's clear voice filled the courtyard with golden song.

When sun dazzles the earth

with straight-falling flames,
a cricket rubs its wings
scraping up a shrill song.

Sappho finished, and everyone turned to Soudiata whose eyes were closed. Her hands were folded in her lap; a single crease of concentration lay across her broad black forehead. She opened her eyes and spoke.

"The song is even greater from your lips," the attendant translated.

Sappho smiled. "Now," she said, leaning toward Soudiata, "it is our turn to be pleased by your song."

The attendant knelt before Soudiata and held out the calabash. Lykaina saw that it was covered with black and white moon designs. Stitched to the rim were bands of bright beads and smooth shells. Soudiata held the calabash on her knees so that the hollowed-out portion was hidden from view. She tilted her regal head to one side, closed her eyes, and reached into the calabash. The sounds that poured out were amazing, sounds that Lykaina felt as much as she heard. Penetrating and warm, the notes flowed through her body and out and around her. Over the cascading melodies, Soudiata's deep rich voice melted into the air.

Lykaina closed her eyes. There were so many sounds with one tone overlapping another, she thought other instruments must have appeared out of the air to join her. But when she opened her eyes, there was only the single calabash on Soudiata's lap. Gradually, note by note, all the sounds fell away.

"The song is about the rainbow spirit who divides the dark sky like a knife that cuts a too-ripe fruit," said the attendant quietly.

"Tell her," said Sappho, "that her song has a beauty that we have not heard before."

"Ask her," said Lykaina, driven by curiosity, "if we might see how her sounds are made. What magic lies inside the calabash?"

Soudiata laughed when Lykaina's words were translated. She beckoned to her to sit beside her. Inside the calabash, Lykaina saw a small box from which a set of narrow iron prongs curved gracefully upward. The prongs were different lengths, with the longest ones in the center and shorter ones on either side. The square box on which the prongs were fixed was delicately carved with more crescent moons. A white opaque membrane covered a hole in its center. Soudiata reached her thumb inside, pressed one of the prongs and released it. The membrane over the hole quivered and buzzed as the note resonated.

"We call it a kalimba," said the attendant. "The quiver of the prong makes the sound in the calabash, just as the quiver of your lyre string makes the sound in the tortoise shell."

Soudiata guided Lykaina's hand into the calabash. Lykaina pressed a prong and felt the sound travel up her arm and through her body.

Soudiata began to play with both hands, her thumbs striking different prongs to send different tones tumbling out of the calabash. She stopped, placed the calabash into Lykaina's lap and gestured to her to play. Lykaina reached inside and struck the prongs with first one thumb and then the other. The sounds resonated through her whole body, making the tips of her toes tingle. She felt as if she were in a trance. She kept striking the prongs and feeling the sounds until she suddenly heard Sappho's voice, cool and distant.

"Our Lykaina looks as if she will disappear into the magic calabash."

The companions laughed. Lykaina felt the blood rush to her cheeks. Soudiata spoke.

"I would be pleased to hear this Lykaina sing her own song," translated the attendant.

Lykaina blushed even deeper. She started to pick up the lyre, but Sappho held up her hand to stop her.

"Not that," she said, the coolness still in her voice. "Play for her with your own instrument, let her hear a mountain song. Quick, Praxinoa, run fetch her aulos from her room."

Lykaina heard the sharpness in Sappho's voice. Why the aulos? she thought. It had been Sappho who had encouraged her to take up the lyre, who had said that the aulos was inappropriate to the poetry of the courtyard. When Praxinoa handed her the instrument, she felt a rush of delight at its smooth grain. She chewed the double reed, dried out from disuse, until it was soft again. An old joy seeped up from deep within as she started to play. She closed her eyes, imagining the long penetrating notes flowing north and south with the princess' river. When she stopped finally to sing, the words that came out were words her grandfather had long ago sung.

> Tall like a willow,
> your hair braided with gold,
> your hands are like reeds in the water,
> your body is straight like a cypress,
> even your footprint has charm.

She opened her eyes and found Soudiata's dark ones looking into her own. Soudiata reached out her hand and took the aulos. She put her lips over the mouthpiece and blew, but no sound came out. She tried again, puffing out her cheeks, but still no sound. She laughed and handed the aulos back to Lykaina.

"She says your instrument has a sound that could carry magic to the mountaintop and speak to the Great Mother. She thanks you for your song. She would like to meet you again and trade secrets."

"Ah." Sappho's voice broke in coldly. "Our Lykaina will not only fall into the magic of the calabash, she will fall under the spell of the magic-maker." She stood up. "Your visit has been an honor to us. We hope you will come again."

Soudiata also stood up, one eyebrow a quizzical arch in her mobile face. She placed her palms together and inclined her head. Then she glided across the courtyard, her attendant following with the calabash. Lykaina stood up in confusion. There was so much to ask the princess, but only the princess' musk scent remained in the air.

During the rest of the morning, Sappho seemed distant, giving her attention only to the other companions. After lunch, she disappeared and did not return until late evening. That night, she did not invite Lykaina into her bed. Lykaina hardly noticed, though, her thoughts were so much on the magic calabash and its rich sounds. What, she thought, would it sound like to have both calabash and aulos playing together?

In the days that followed Soudiata's visit, no one spoke of her. Each time Lykaina made a reference to the rainbow song or to the magic calabash, Sappho cut her off by changing the subject or by turning to another companion as if Lykaina had not spoken. The princess' poem had been, Lykaina thought, exquisite; the sound of the calabash instrument extraordinary. She wanted to talk about them and about the wonderful black-skinned woman from the faraway land. She swallowed her disappointment and concentrated on composing a poem for the installation of a new governor.

Softly the rain drizzles
and softly the clouds part.
Softly a rainbow cuts the sky. . .

she began one morning, carefully plucking the strings of the lyre to accent each *softly.*

"A rainbow," broke in Sappho with a tight smile. "Perhaps you will need one of those barbarian gourds to accompany this song. You should be more careful of your influences."

Lykaina blushed and stopped playing. She hadn't been thinking about Soudiata, but even if the rainbow image had come from her, why was it wrong to use it? She felt Sappho's touch on the back of her neck.

"There, my love, you can sing about a rainbow if you like. Just don't have it cut the sky like a knife cuts a too-ripe jungle fruit."

Sappho continued to stroke Lykaina's neck. The image of the mountain rainbow was replaced by one over Mytilene's acropolis. Lykaina finished the poem.

Softly a rainbow places a halo
over the still white marble.

"Well composed, my dearest," declared Sappho, and the other companions murmured their approval. "That will be a fine song for the governor."

In her room later that afternoon, Lykaina picked up her aulos and rubbed her finger over its burnished surface. An image of her grandfather crept into her head, his cheeks sucked in, the mountains behind him dotted with scampering goats. She listened to the sound in her head that she could imagine echoing off distant rocks. The old man's image receded as she thought of her life here, her love for Sappho. Her poetry was finer now and, Sappho was right, it demanded the finesse of the lyre. But surely, she thought, there were times when the dark piercing tones were appropriate.

At the governor's reception, held in the open-air market below the acropolis, all the officials of the city stood in a row, their purple and gold robes flowing in the breeze. Lykaina stood in front of them, her lyre in hand, looking out over the hushed crowd. She sang her rainbow song, received polite applause, and stepped back to let the ceremony continue. She looked over the crowd and admired the mixture of soft colors of the elegant gowns. Suddenly her eyes stopped at a robe of bright oranges and reds, blues and greens. Standing between two marble columns, Soudiata caught the late afternoon sun in the gold in her tiny braids. Over the crowd, their eyes met in recognition. Even at that distance, a current passed. The speeches finally ended, and the crowd began to move in a procession to the temple of Apollo. Lykaina lost sight of Soudiata, and then suddenly the majestic figure was beside her, touching her arm.

"She asks, where is your aulos?" the attendant whispered. "It suits you better than this tortoise shell with strings."

"Tell her. . .," Lykaina began. But tell her what? That the aulos is not appropriate for ceremonies such as this? Lykaina smiled at Soudiata and shrugged. Soudiata spoke rapidly again.

"She says to tell you she is leaving this island soon. She wishes to see you. She wishes to trade secrets with you. She wishes to hear your aulos again. Will you come to the house tomorrow when the sun is high overhead?"

Sappho would disapprove, thought Lykaina. She called the sounds of the calabash barbarian. But Lykaina would not pass by this opportunity to speak with the princess and to hear the magic sounds once more.

"Yes," said Lykaina quickly, holding out her hand. "I will come."

The next morning Lykaina woke early, even before the song of the thrush began to fill the courtyard below. She picked up her aulos and slipped out through the garden. She climbed the hills behind the city, thinking how she had not come out into gray dawn for such a long time. So many dinner parties and ceremonies, so many nights of love with

Sappho had left her rising long after the sun had started its journey across the sky. Now she stepped lightly, enjoying again the feel of the earth under her.

She found a big rock and climbed onto it, letting her feet dangle as she watched the long red fingers streak the clouds above Mount Ida. She raised the aulos to her lips and played songs from her childhood— mountain songs, cheese-making songs, goat-herding songs. She closed her eyes and let the sound ring through her body and out over the city below. Gradually she realized that she was not alone. Opening her eyes, she saw the slavegirl Kissa hunkered down a stone's throw from her, watching her. Lykaina smiled and beckoned to the child.

"Come and sit with me, even if you can't hear my music."

Kissa came and stood in front of the rock. She placed her hand over the end of the aulos and nodded at her. Lykaina blew a note. Kissa's face broke into a smile. Lykaina played a quick shepherd's tune, and Kissa laughed with joy. She hears my music with her hands, thought Lykaina, just as I felt the sounds of the calabash in my body. Lykaina stopped playing and shook her head in wonder. Kissa reached up, took Lykaina's hand from the aulos, and placed it over her heart. Lykaina felt the small steady ka-thump under her fingertips.

"Of course you have rhythm inside you," she said. "It is the heart-beat that sets life's tempo."

Her fingers back on the aulos, Lykaina played a slow *syrtos*. Kissa touched the end of the aulos with both hands. After a few moments of hand-listening, she stepped back and began to dance, slowly and gracefully, in perfect time to the music. Lykaina brought the dance to a close and began another, livelier tune. Kissa stood still for a moment, perplexed. She touched the aulos briefly, then started to dance in time to the new beat.

They played and danced until the sun had cleared Mount Ida and was sending sparkles to the foam-flecked waters below. Lykaina's cheeks were exhausted. She had not played so many dance tunes since the last wedding in her village. Her face streaked with sweat, Kissa ran to Lykaina, embraced her, then whirled around and danced away down the hillside. Lykaina followed, filled with a deep sense of peace she had not felt for some time.

The companions were all seated when she entered the courtyard, quietly copying their poems onto their scrolls. Sappho glanced at her, then continued to speak in low tones to Praxinoa, pointing to the words she had written. Lykaina hurried to put away her aulos and returned to the courtyard with her own scroll and stylus.

"We all heard your country music," remarked Sappho with a wry smile. "Do you plan to abandon the songs you have composed here and go back to your peasantries?"

Lykaina's face clouded. She could still feel the joy of her playing. Why was there no room for her aulos on this island? Why could there not be different kinds of music for different times? This was Sappho's house and Sappho's courtyard, but the hills belonged to no one but the gods. Did the gods approve only of the lyre?

"Sometimes it is good for me to remember my past," she said evenly, her voice firm and steady. "There is room for the aulos in the hills. I will play it there when I feel the need."

Sappho raised her dark eyebrows, opened her mouth to speak, and closed it again. She came to Lykaina and laid her head against her shoulder.

"I meant no harm. Forgive me if my voice is sharp. My brother will soon be here with his wretched bride, and I have no patience for those sounds. They remind me of the flute of the vixen that bewitched my brother. I cannot bear to hear it. Be patient with me, my love."

A single tear fell from Sappho's eye. Lykaina brushed it away with her hand and kissed Sappho lightly on the lips.

"It's all right, Sappho. Everything will be all right. Here, let me pluck a melody for you to cheer you up."

Lykaina picked up the lyre and let her fingers pull the strings lightly. It was a beautiful instrument with a beautiful sound. Sappho was right, it suited her poetry, it suited their love. Before that, everything paled.

Sappho dismissed the companions early and retired to her room, complaining of a headache. Lykaina took her some willowbark tea and kissed her on the forehead.

"Sleep the rest of the day. It will be good for you."

She closed the door gently and motioned to Kissa. They walked quickly through the city and found Soudiata in Alkaios' garden, seated on a low stool next to a stone well topped with a large wooden cogwheel. While oxen plodded an endless circle turning the creaking wheel, Soudiata drew on a piece of smooth bark with a half-burned stick of wood. She set the drawing carefully aside before standing up to embrace Lykaina.

"She says they live at the bend of a wide and deep river," said the attendant. "The water is plentiful there. But there are places in her land that are far from the river and have only a water hole that dries up in the summer. A machine such as this would be useful for the farmers there."

Lykaina marveled at the detail of the drawing with its precise rendering of every stone on the well and every cog in the wheel. On another piece of bark, Soudiata had drawn the network of irrigation ditches that carried the well water out to the rows and rows of terraced grapevines.

"She says she has drawn enough. She invites you to come with her to the sacred grove where the spirit of her foremother has taken up residence."

Soudiata took Lykaina by the hand and led her beyond the house and vineyard to a promontory that overlooked the sea. The small procession—Soudiata and Lykaina in front, Kissa and the royal attendant behind—followed the path along the cliff's edge until it turned inward. After a short climb, they came to a small grove of chestnuts that surrounded a bubbling spring. They sat in the cool, damp air listening to the sound of the water on the rocks.

"She comes here every day," said the attendant, "to speak with the spirit of the ancestor who accompanies her on her journey. She has no choice, she says. Even if she is tired, the calabash leads her, it has a will of its own."

The attendant placed the calabash on Soudiata's lap and stood back. Soudiata closed her eyes and began to play. Lykaina took Kissa's hand and placed it on the outside of the calabash and watched the look of bewilderment on Kissa's face turn to delight as the sounds of the instrument entered her hands. Lykaina found herself in almost a trance as the music of the calabash mixed with the sounds of the bubbling water. Soudiata began to sing, her low voice weaving in and around the notes of the calabash. The attendant whispered into Lykaina's ear.

"She sings about the wandering spirit of her foremother who leads her in her travels. This woman was a queen who took off her royal robes and dressed like a common woman in order to travel to every corner of the land, to walk and talk among her people. The queen's house sits at the bend of the wide river that flows both north and south. The foremother walked all the way to the source of this mighty river, and then she turned around and walked to its mouth. Everywhere she went she carried with her the royal calabash so that she could speak with the Great Mother whom she found in the trees and in the grass, in the river and in the rocks.

"When this foremother came to the mouth of the mighty river, she found that it poured its waters into the great sea where the sun goes to rest every night. The people along the shore told her that one could sail toward the setting sun for days and still not see the other side. She asked them to take her, but they were afraid. They took her along the shore instead, as far as the Pillars of Hercules. The foremother returned home, but she was not satisfied with her travels. She had her shipbuilders build a mighty ship, one that required one hundred oars and a great sail to send it over the water. She was determined to sail into the setting sun until she could see the land of the other side.

"When the great ship was ready, she sent word through all the land, calling the bravest and the strongest to the shore. Thousands of women and men came. For days they held contests of strength and endurance and courage. When the final one hundred women and men were chosen, they filled the ship with food and water and took their places at the oars. The ones who remained sent them off with prayers to the Great Mother and then waited for their return. But the great ocean swallowed them. The ship and its brave crew never returned."

Soudiata stopped singing and let the calabash alone tell about the empty waves washing the waiting shore. Kissa held her hands on the calabash until the last echo had died away. Finally Soudiata laughed and broke the spell. She pulled Kissa by the hand and showed her how to pluck the tongs with her thumbs. Tentative at first, the child's fingers soon found a rhythm and a music—different from Soudiata's, but strong and beautiful. Lykaina was amazed at Kissa's skill. Then she remembered Kissa's heartbeat and her dancing feet. She is dancing with her fingertips now, she thought.

They spent the rest of the afternoon in song and dance. Lykaina played her aulos while the other three danced. Soudiata returned to the calabash and began to play notes that moved in and out of the dark wails of the aulos. The sun's last rays had long disappeared from the grove before the dancers collapsed in front of them. Lykaina and Soudiata laid aside their instruments and joined hands with the other two. A force entered Lykaina's fingers and flowed through her body. It was almost as if the four of them were one, as if they were all part of the earth they sat on. They held on to each other without speaking until darkness had closed over the sacred grove. The spring bubbled, night insects sang their song.

Soudiata broke the circle finally and led them away from the spring. Under the full moon, the procession made its way along the promontory and back to the well in the garden. Soudiata whispered to her attendant who ran into the house and returned a few moments later with a small calabash with the magic tongs inside it. Soudiata handed this to Kissa and stroked her blond head.

"She says it is a royal instrument," said the attendant, "but who is to know when a slave is the daughter of someone else's queen?"

Soudiata removed one of the gold strands of her necklace and placed it around Lykaina's neck. She embraced her, speaking low into her ear.

"She says her foremother is pleased with your song," whispered the attendant. "But she reminds you not to forget your own foremothers who also speak with the voice of the wind and the water."

They embraced, and Lykaina felt the charge of energy flow through her body again. She stood back, smiled farewell, and took Kissa's hand. Together they made their way back through the streets of Mytilene to

Sappho's house.

The rooms were all dark when they entered. Kissa scurried off to the slave quarters behind the storeroom, and Lykaina felt her way along the wall of the passageway to the stairs. As she placed her foot on the first step, a cold and imperious voice rang out from the courtyard.

"Where have you been that you need to enter my house like a thief in the night?"

Startled, Lykaina turned toward Sappho whose face, lit by the pale moon, was frozen in anger.

"I spent the afternoon with Soudiata." Lykaina spoke hesitantly, knowing that her words would grieve Sappho. "She sails next week to her homeland. She wanted to exchange songs before she left."

"I see. You took your peasant pipe to play with the barbarian gourd. And left me to suffer alone the impending destruction of my family honor."

"Sappho! The kalimba is no barbarian instrument. It makes beautiful sounds. They may seem strange to our ears, but they have their place in the world. She speaks to her foremother with her calabash. It is a bridge between the real world and the world of the spirits. She has respect for your poetry, you must have respect for hers."

Lykaina stopped and held her breath. She had not meant to say so many words, but something compelled her.

"Ah," responded Sappho with a bitter smile. "The little goatherd has become the teacher, and Sappho is to be her pupil. Next you will be instructing me to play your crude peasant pipe. You will have me singing your peasant songs. You will dress me in country rags and make me like Andromeda, the laughing stock of the Aegean."

Sappho drew herself up and folded her hands in front of her.

"I am Sappho whose fame has spread through all the civilized world. Even that black barbarian has heard of me. I took you in when you didn't know how to pick up your skirts. Your poetry showed promise, and I devoted myself to you. I gave you every luxury—soft beds and fine clothes, food fit for gods, and cultured company. But you, you spurn my gifts of love and turn to your own kind—slaves and barbarians!"

Sappho's voice, at first cold and distant, was now filled with passion and anger. Her words hit Lykaina like lashes of winter rain. Lykaina felt herself splitting into two pieces. One part of her wanted to run to Sappho and kneel before her, to bury her head on her breast and beg forgiveness for her transgression. Some of what Sappho said was true. She had helped her fulfill her every dream. The poetry she was creating now was better than any she had composed before. Sappho's love filled her with an ecstasy she had never known. If she went to her now, if she kissed her on the lips, Sappho would forgive her, Sappho would take her in her arms. Everything would be all right again.

But the other half of Lykaina was listening to the parting words of Soudiata: *Do not forget your foremothers.* If she felt ecstasy with Sappho, she experienced a more peaceful joy this morning on the hill with the slavechild Kissa. If her poetry with Sappho had become refined and well crafted, her music this afternoon added a spirit that she never felt in Sappho's courtyard. And the oneness she had been part of in the sacred grove, the energy that flowed from fingertip to fingertip and into the earth, made her feel connected to all women and nature. Here she was connected only to Sappho. The other hetaerae remained always aloof from her. They all danced in a circle, but no current ran from hand to hand. Lykaina stood rooted to the courtyard floor, unable to speak over the warring voices within her.

"Who knows," Sappho continued, "if your precious princess is really the daughter of a queen. Perhaps she, too, is a slave, run away from a civilized master. When my brother's wretched wife arrives, the three of you could form a slave troupe. You could tour the islands selling your slave songs and your filthy slave bodies. Everyone would marvel the way they do at a dog who walks on two legs."

Sappho took a step toward Lykaina, her black eyes darting flames of anger. Her voice was again cold and controlled.

"But in my house," she said, pacing each word carefully, "I will have no slaves pretending they are otherwise. Go! Leave me in my misery. Let me weep once more the giving of my heart to an ingrate!"

Sappho brushed past Lykaina and swept up the stairs. Lykaina stared after her. A small voice inside said, *She does not mean what she says, she is in pain. Go to her, it is not too late.* But the other sounds in her head drowned it out. The strong rhythm of the calabash pummeled the soft pluckings of the lyre strings. Over it all the aulos wailed, groaning like an ancient oak bending to a gale.

She turned and ran. Out of the courtyard, through the garden, onto the hill. She ran up the stony path, tearing the clothes from her body. She threw the gown into the wind. She pulled the band of embroidery from her head and tossed it into a bush. Her instinct for sure-footedness was dull now, and the sharp stones cut her feet. Low branches tore at her face and arms. Around the mountain and down to the Gulf of Hieras she ran, the mixture of sounds inside her head becoming a greater and greater roar. At the water's edge she stopped, panting, blood oozing from her scratched face. She looked down and saw that she was still clutching the aulos in her hand.

The full moon scuttled behind a bank of clouds and emerged again. A sharp wind blew white caps over the surface of the dark water. A force took hold of Lykaina, a force too strong to resist. She let it draw

○

her arm back. In the woods behind her, a tree cracked and a large branch fell to the ground. In front of her, the carved wolf's head of the aulos caught the light of the moon as it sailed out over the water and disappeared.

Chapter 10.
Spiraling out

Howl. Rimmed by black mountains and dark forests, the Gulf of Hieras waited for the dawn. An owl hooted. Lykaina crouched in the reeds by the shore, gray mud streaking her face, her limbs, her bare brown body. The single gold strand that encircled her neck caught a ray of the waning moon and sent it back heavenward. She howled, and echoes returned from the mountains.

Inside her head, a curled memory drew her inward. Fetal limbs suspended in dark silence waited for her. She held her breath and waited, too, waited for the memory to uncurl itself and take her on its terrifying journey. . . .

The narrow passage is dark, the force relentless. No light at the end, only the too-swift propulsion from behind, pushing, pushing. Something holds her back, she cannot let go. A tiny twisted foot, everything is wrong. The force pushes, the silence roars. Spasm after spasm threatens to tear the limb from the body. Like a broken branch caught in a fast-moving mountain stream, she cannot move.

The turning. A strong grip twists the body right. The foot lets go, the memory emerges. Howl.

Where there was darkness, bright light. Where there was silence, harsh roaring. Hard slaps buffet the tiny limbs.

"Too small."

"Look at the foot."

"Maybe they won't notice."

"Maybe."

Now the memory huddles in a tightly woven reed basket. Five giant shadows with rough hands lift her up, turn her around. A poke in the rib, a swat on the rump, a pull on the arm. And the foot, the twisted foot.

"Too small."

"Look at the foot."

Howl.

Passed to a fleet-moving shape, the woven reed basket is carried out of the circle of light. The memory shivers in darkness. Tall shadows blend into taller shadows, broken only by a distant sliver of curved light. A low and mournful wail cuts through the chill.

Leaves rustle, and a warm rough tongue licks the eyes, the nose, the now-silent mouth. The basket overturned, gentle teeth grasp the nape. A journey through underbrush, a warm dark cave. Enclosed in fur, the memory is warm again. A full nipple fills the mouth. Lifeblood.

Four other mouths pull with her at the swollen teats. Furry bodies push her this way and that. The mother is firm but gentle.

Outside the cave, cold and dark turn to warmth and light. Brown and gray become green. The mother nudges the cubs into the new spring air. The furless memory sits at the edge of the dark cave and watches and listens. Small bodies grow big, baby fur becomes black and silver. Yips are answered by howls. Then she is alone with the mother.

The moon scuttled behind the dark clouds. A cold night wind ruffled the gulf waters. Lykaina, alone in the reeds, raised her voice to the moonless sky. Howl.

Lykaina gave one final howl and crawled on all fours to the empty site where the lean-to and the loom had once stood. She nestled herself against a log. The mountains on the far shore were beginning to take on the color of dawn. Except for the howls echoing in her head and the tight knot in her belly, nothing was left inside her. She lay watching the water reflect the reddening sky. Then she slept.

A cascade of sounds startled her out of her sleep. A small figure stood upright at the edge of the circle, its forepaws hidden behind a large round gourd that hung from its neck. A familiar body, a cub she knew, but why was she standing so awkwardly? What were the strange sounds that seemed to be coming out of her round belly? Too much to ask a howling head. Lykaina lowered her chin onto her paws and closed her eyes again.

In her dream, she was climbing a mountain, moving from rock to rock. One rock began to slide, then another, then the whole mountain shook. Stones from above pelted her body as she slid with the rocks, turning over and over.

The crash, when it came, was soft. A rough tongue licked her brow. She opened her eyes. It was not another cub, this creature. It was Kissa stroking her forehead with her hand. Lykaina sat up and shook herself. Kissa brushed pine needles from her shoulders and back. Lykaina shuddered at her touch and hugged her knees to her chest.

"Too soon." The words clawed their way out of her throat. "Too soon. She pushed me away." Kissa snuggled against her arm. "I wasn't like the others, but she took me in. She cared for me. Then she pushed me out. I tried to drink one day, and she snarled. I tried to burrow deeper, and she nipped. She pushed me out, she wouldn't let me stay, she—"

Lykaina stopped. Kissa's blue eyes, round and unblinking, stared at her. The strange sounds hung in the air. Lykaina let her head fall onto her knees and closed her eyes. A jay called, a nuthatch twittered. She felt Kissa leave. She was alone again, deep in her cave that smelled of milk and must and damp fur. She watched again as the light at the front of the cave turned from gray to golden, the bushes from black to green. She watched her cub brothers and sisters ramble away. She watched herself lick berry juice from their lips on their return. She watched their mother chew the burs from their coats. She let the warmth, the safety surround her.

And then, sure as green leaves turn to reds and yellows, and chill mists replace early morning dews, she watched her mother push them all out. Not herself at first. She was allowed to stay. She was allowed to take her place at a teat when the new ones arrived. Not at the first turning of the seasons nor the second nor even the third. But at the fourth turning. . .at the fourth turning, snarls and cruel nips drove her out. The cave was no longer hers. She had to look for her own place to sleep. She had to provide her own warmth.

A strand of smoke curled under her nose. Lykaina opened her eyes. Kissa hunched naked in front of a small fire. Two fresh mullets were turning mottled red over the flames. The sun had passed behind Olympos leaving the gulf waters dark again. A lone gull cried. Kissa pulled one of the fish from its roasting stick, wrapped it in a plane leaf, and handed it to Lykaina. Lykaina saw that Kissa, too, was caked with gray mud, that gray streaked her face and arms.

"Look at us," she called to the long shadows, "are we human or animal? If my first mama threw me to the wolves, my second one threw me back. The third one taught me to walk on two legs, but when her belly swelled, I lost her, too. And the old woman and Maia and Sappho. . . ."

Lykaina hunched forward and stared into the fire. Kissa licked the juice from her fingers and picked up her calabash. She closed her eyes, tilted her head like Soudiata, and began to play. Her sounds were small, her patterns uneven. As she plucked, her body swayed back and forth. Lykaina leaned against the log and let the sounds resonate through her bones. Each note seemed to strike a different spot on her body, as if she herself were an instrument being played. Tears pushed their way through her half-closed eyes. Wolves howl, she thought, humans cry. And let the tears flow.

Lykaina slept for days, waking long enough only to smile at Kissa and eat the berries or nuts or roasted fish offered. Once she dreamed she was a prancing black mare, lifting each hoof to step daintily on round stones that became upturned calabashes leading to a bridge made of alder saplings. In and out of her dreams, the sound of Kissa's music floated, sometimes gentle and soothing, other times quick and darting. Once the wail of an aulos joined the kalimba, but when she opened her eyes, she found it was only a strong wind whistling through the trees.

One morning, it seemed that her body had slept enough. She opened her eyes and, instead of shadowy shapes and muffled sounds, she saw bright sunlight touching each leaf of each tree. She walked to the water's edge. A gannet sat on a rock, its piebald body reflected clearly in the water. Out from the shore, she caught sight of a single large fin moving slowly toward her. She thought of the dolphin that had saved her life. Was this a sister, a cousin? The dolphin broke surface and leapt high, its sleek gray back reflecting the morning sun, its broad mouth curled in a silent laugh. Underwater again, the silent fin moved away from her and out toward the narrow neck of the gulf. It is my own time to turn, thought Lykaina, as she moved into the water. She dove deep and rose again, feeling the water drops fly from her body. She turned and waved to Kissa standing on the shore.

"Come into the water, little one," she called. "We'll wash the mud from our bodies. We'll become human again."

Skin scrubbed shiny clean, snarls unraveled from their hair, they emerged from the water. Kissa caught Lykaina's hand and pulled her up one of the paths leading away from the clearing. They came to a waterfall, and Kissa squatted in front of a pile of stones. She lifted the flat one that lay on top and stood back. Lykaina caught her breath. Inside the cache, the black obsidian blade of her knife rested against the last of the gold coins the old woman had given her. Her old belt was there, too, and the amulet she had been given in Euboea.

Kissa tugged at her arm again and pointed. Three straight alder shoots leaned against a tree trunk. Kissa picked up one of them and put it to her mouth, pressing her fingers over imaginary holes and making gutteral noises in her throat. She picked up the other two and held out all three. Lykaina laughed.

"You are always two jumps ahead of me, aren't you, little one?"

She hefted the three alder shoots and picked out the middle-sized one. "This looks like the best one." She ran her finger over the smooth bark. "So. We were born into a world where we do not belong, you and I. We will make our own hearth, then. We will sing our own songs."

Kissa picked up her calabash and hung it around her neck again. She poised herself like a great bird and began to run down the mountainside. Lykaina dropped the knife and the gold coin into the pouch on the belt and tied the amulet around her neck. She ran to catch up, feeling the strength return to her legs. The howls in her head had already begun to turn into songs. Whoever she had been, she still was. Whatever she needed in order to go forward, she could make with her own two hands.

Days began to fall into a rhythm. Each morning Lykaina and Kissa ranged through the forest, setting traps and gathering chanterelles and wild blackberries. Late afternoons, Kissa showed her how to take a spear and stand motionless on a ledge over the water until a golden bass slid out of its resting place to catch the spear in its side. Evenings they sat at the fire, Lykaina carving her new aulos, Kissa plucking notes from her calabash. Each chore took Lykaina's full attention. Yet always hovering at the edge of her focus was an image of Sappho. A fish leaping out of water would turn into Sappho dancing at the well. The juice of a berry tossed casually into the mouth would suddenly explode into a kiss. The must of a broken chanterelle would draw her into Sappho's secret place. It was always when Lykaina felt strongest, her feet most solid on the ground, that the wave of lost passion would engulf her. At those times, one poem of Sappho's would ring in her ears.

Pain penetrates

me drop
by drop.

She learned to become very still in these moments, to wait, like the hunted hare, until the moment of danger had passed. As the summer days grew shorter, the moments came farther apart, and when they came, the pain throbbed more gently.

One evening, when the wolf's head that decorated the aulos mouth-piece was taking its final shape, Lykaina's thoughts turned to Maia.

"She carried with her another world," she began, speaking to Kissa as if she could hear. "It was a world where everything was connected through the Great Mother. When I was with her, it made sense. I felt the Great Mother in the earth between my toes, she touched me with the salt breeze. When I was with Maia, the pulse of the earth seemed to flow through me. The force in her eyes made me feel connected to the very center of the earth."

While Lykaina talked, Kissa played softly, letting the notes fall between them.

"Yet when I went to Mytilene, the Great Mother seemed to fade. I did not feel her presence. And Maia. . . ." She paused, remembering her last morning with Maia. "It seemed as if Maia were pushing me out, Kissa, as if she were driving me away. She called me to the Great Mother, but she nipped my heels just like my wolf mama. If she knew what was going to happen, why did she turn me out? Why did she abandon me?"

She heard the calabash drop to the ground and looked up to see Kissa standing up, her child's body striking an angular pose that made her look for all the world like Maia at the loom. Her small hands darted back and forth, and Lykaina could almost see the heddle rod lifting, the shuttle sliding home. Kissa's feet began to move, and Lykaina watched her dismantle the loom and rebuild the coracle. Kissa danced the boat away from the shore and out into blue water, her body bending to the wind, the steering oar under one arm, the other steadying a wind-filled sail. She danced the boat moving swiftly under the wind, tacking first one way, then turning to catch the wind from another direction. As she sailed, her child's face, now stern and ageless, scanned the sky for weather signs.

Lykaina held her breath as she watched the dance unfold the story. Maia arrived at a distant shore and joined others like her in a procession that wound up a rocky mountain path. Again and again Kissa multiplied her Maia image until Lykaina seemed to be seeing hundreds of Maias moving up the trail. At the top, Kissa made the multitude dance, whipping priestly bodies around a great rock that stood tall under the moon-filled sky. Lykaina could almost hear the frenzied drumbeat urging the dancers to move faster and faster.

Now Kissa drew her Maia figure away from the dancing circle, straining her ears to hear a different sound. She danced her away from the mountaintop and back down to the sea where a strong on-shore wind blew. Kissa's body became the wind pushing the coracle back to shore again and again. Finally she let the boat sail but sent it far off the straight path to Lesbos, bobbing tiny in the vast sea.

Then Kissa became Kissa again. She sat down beside Lykaina and leaned her small body against Lykaina's shoulder. They rested together, listening to the drone of the night insects.

"So, little one," said Lykaina finally, "you are telling me that she is coming back. I don't know how you know what you know or how you can tell the story with one small body, but I will believe you. I will believe you because I want to believe you, because I want her to come. I want to feel her presence again, I want to reach through her to the Great Mother."

Following the trapline one early morning, they came across a tall pine tree with broken bark.

"Deer," Lykaina told Kissa. "This is where they rub the fuzz off their antlers. Come, let's follow their tracks."

The detour led them away from the trapline. It doubled back and descended the mountain until they came to an open place edged by a marble cliff hanging over the water. Almost directly below they could see the clearing where the ashes of their morning fire were scattered. Far out on the blue gulf waters, a small boat caught the wind in its sails.

Kissa touched Lykaina's arm and pointed to a column of steam rising from a pile of slate gray rocks at one side of the clearing. They climbed up onto the first rock, and Lykaina felt a wave of warm moist air wash over her body.

"A hot springs!" she exclaimed, as the rocks opened to reveal the pool of clear water from which the vapors were rising.

Kissa crouched and reached over the water to feel the steam. Lykaina let her big toe ease slowly into the wet warmth.

"Come on, little one, it's not so hot."

Splashing with their hands, they let their feet explore rocks where bubbles tickled their toes. The nearly round pool was surrounded on three sides with great slabs angling upward. The rocks on the fourth side were low, letting them look right from the pool out to the sea.

When their bodies became too hot, they climbed out and let their feet dangle in the water while they watched the sailboat they'd spotted earlier move closer and closer to shore. Kissa gripped Lykaina's arm as the boat beached itself just below their camp. Two figures climbed out and pulled the boat up onto the shore. Lykaina had seen many boats on the gulf before. A village at the far end sent its lanterned shells out to fish every night and return in the gray dawn. The village she had passed on her way to Mytilene had a small harbor below it into which larger boats occasionally sailed. But no boat had ever come close to their shore. They watched the figures move past their ashes and disappear into the forest.

"Come, let's finish the trapline," said Lykaina standing up. "They're probably just exploring to amuse themselves. By the time we get back, they'll be gone."

But the boat wasn't gone when they arrived back at the campsite. Kissa looked at Lykaina.

"I don't know, little one," said Lykaina. "But I do know that we can't be here when they come back. Let's go up to the waterfall and wait."

They hadn't taken three steps before Lykaina heard voices. They scrambled into a dense thicket and hid behind a large bush. Two men emerged into the clearing, both of them wearing the long flowing robes Lykaina remembered from her days in Mytilene. One of them was tall and spindly with light curls around his boyish face and a neatly trimmed beard. The other was shorter and round and nearly bald. It was the bald one speaking.

"It's a natural place, don't you agree? It's like an amphitheater with the whole sea for a stage. Can't you see those rocks with people perched on them, steaming their bodies in midwinter? We can make our fortunes."

"It is a spectacular view," the tall one agreed. "It's not very big, though. No more than a dozen could bathe at a time. The hot springs at Loutra can hold a hundred."

"We can make it bigger. I'm thinking of pulling out all the lower rocks and sinking tile for a real floor. We'll get an artist to do a dolphin mosaic. Listen, it won't be for a hundred bathers. We don't want a hundred bathers. This is going to be for the elite. We'll pull out all the rocks, replace them with marble. We'll carve marble steps into the side of the mountain. Down here we'll have the bungalows. This clearing is perfect—the boat landing is just below, and there's room for a dozen or so bungalows, each with its own privacy. We'll build a public house over there, serve only the finest fresh fish. We'll bring in chefs from the mainland. We'll be the talk of Mytilene. Everyone will want to come, but we'll take only those with connections. I've got Alkeios' cousin interested. If he comes, we can get the whole Sappho crowd."

"Whose land is this, anyway?" The tall one stooped to trace a finger through the ashes.

"Who knows who built that fire," baldpate responded. "Probably some wandering vagrant. Nobody's lived on this land for years. There used to be a village around here, but some disaster overcame them, and they all left. When I was a boy, it was said that the place was home to evil spirits, but now even that tale is forgotten. Come on, what do you say? With my connections and vision and your money, we'll be famous."

Tallman stood staring at the ashes.

"I'll have to talk to my uncle. It's his money, you know."

"Well, come on then, let's go talk to him. You shouldn't delay, though. There are others who might be interested."

The two men walked down to the shore.

"We'll bring him out to look it over, then," was the last phrase that drifted up before the boat got under way.

Lykaina and Kissa crawled out of the thicket and watched the boat move toward the opening into the Aegean. Lykaina rubbed a long scratch on her arm that a briar in the thicket had made. Listening to the men's voices, she had felt as if a huge net had dropped over them, a net like the one that had ensnared her four-year-old cub self and brought her into the world of humans.

"No, no, no!" she shouted. "They won't do it again! No!" She picked up a rock and hurled it after the departing boat.

Kissa pulled her to the firepit and sat her down on a log. Lykaina's head dropped into her hands. Numbly she listened to Kissa build the fire and skin the rabbit they had trapped. Without relish, she ate the leg offered her and stared into the fire until the stars came out. Then she slept.

By the time Lykaina opened her eyes, the sun was already painting Olympos golden. She started up, wondering why she had slept so late. Then the events of yesterday flooded over her, and she lay back again, barely breathing. This would be her last trap run—make sure they're all sprung so that no wild thing is caught without purpose, she thought. And then where would they go? She sat up and realized that Kissa was not sleeping beside her. She looked around, but Kissa was nowhere in sight. She fought the panic pushing into her throat—nothing happened, she just got tired waiting for you to wake up, she told herself.

Then she heard the calabash—wild sounds, not at all like Kissa's songs. Following in their wake, an apparition—hareskins stitched together with vines hung from Kissa's small body, charcoal and ashes covered her face and arms, twigs and leaves crowned her head. She was dancing grotesquely, leaps that jerked her body through the air, steps that brought her close to collision with the trees. Lykaina laughed out loud.

"An evil spirit, are you then?" she called out.

Kissa held out another cloak of rabbit skins, and Lykaina threw herself into the costuming. She rolled in the remaining ashes and rubbed the ends of half-burnt wood over her face and arms. She put on the hareskin cloak and let Kissa heap her head with dried leaves and twigs. She pulled her aulos from its hiding place, and when she put her lips to the mouthpiece, she found notes she'd never made before—wild screeches that seemed to belong to neither the human nor the animal kingdom. Kissa threw her body this way and that until she fell down in a heap. Lykaina stopped playing.

"All right, little one. Let them come with their plans. We'll drive them away. This land is ours. It is not fit for the elite. They'll have to find themselves another hot springs."

It was several days before the men came back. Every day Lykaina and Kissa scanned the gulf looking for the sail. The day it came was cloudless, the sky a perfect blue. Lykaina's skin prickled in anticipation as she smeared the ashes over her body and put on the rabbitskin cloak. They looked each other over, grinning broadly. Then each took up her instrument and a handful of stones.

Three men stepped out of the boat this time. The third one was tall like the younger one but with gray curls and just a fringe of gray beard. Lykaina and Kissa kept far enough ahead of them on the trail, each tossing a pebble now and then into the bush behind them. Kissa sent a few quick notes plummeting through the forest air. The men stopped, not sure of what they had heard.

"You didn't tell me it was so eerie," a deep older voice said. "Seems almost as if spirits inhabit these woods."

"Must be some kind of birds." It was baldpate's voice, nervous but reassuring. "I can't quite recognize it. It didn't sing long enough."

"You know the story of the villagers who left here," continued the older voice. "It used to be said that by accident a child was left behind, and that it ranges the mountains crying for its mother."

"Just a story, surely, uncle. Besides, that child would have long ago died or grown to adulthood."

Kissa dropped a few more notes while Lykaina tossed the rest of her pebbles.

"Well, I don't like the feel of the place. You can't expect people to pay good money to hear strange sounds."

"Whatever the creature is, it will be gone by the time the people arrive. Wild things don't stay around when there's building going on. Look, here's the hot springs."

The men had arrived at the clearing. Lykaina and Kissa, ahead of them, were hidden among the rocks over the springs. They let the men admire the view, test the water, and talk about the money to be made. Then Kissa began to pluck the kalimba wildly, letting the sounds jerk from rock to rock. Lykaina blew a single long wail on her aulos. They both stopped and scurried silently to another rock. The men strained to see where the sounds had come from. Lykaina and Kissa separated. Soon strange sounds were bouncing off all of the rocks. The men backed away toward the edge of the cliff.

Kissa showed herself first, darting out from behind a rock, an unearthly shriek rising out of her throat. She ducked out of sight, and Lykaina stood up and let her aulos answer with a shrill cry. Kissa bobbed out from another rock and disappeared, leaving a trail of kalimba notes behind. Lykaina leapt from one rock to another sending a lone wolf howl to ring off the trees. The men stood frozen, their ash-white faces moving one way and another. Without speaking, they turned and ran into the woods. Moments later, Lykaina and Kissa watched the boat push out from the beach and catch the offshore wind. They threw off their rabbitskins and jumped into the warm water.

"This land is indeed inhabited by spirits," Lykaina called out to the speck-sized sailboat. "We are the spirits, and the spirits are us. We belong to this land."

One morning, when the late-summer air had covered their sleeping bodies with dew, Lykaina woke to Kissa shaking her shoulder. She had barely opened her eyes when Kissa grabbed her hands and pulled her to her feet. Sensing urgency, Lykaina got up and followed Kissa down to the shore. She saw white caps on the water and patches of dark blue where gusts were touching down onto the rippled surface. Kissa was standing absolutely still, looking toward the mouth of the gulf. Lykaina followed her gaze, squinting her eyes, and finally made out a small dark shape bobbing in the distance. She followed it as it moved across the mouth, then turned to sail in a new direction. Before she could see it clearly, her heart was pounding. Eventually the double-poled mast became visible, the patched sail, the round black hull. Maia, seated aft with the oar under her arm, tacked the boat back and forth skillfully, catching the wind to keep the sail full. Her dark face was expressionless as she steered the little coracle up to the shore. Lykaina waded out to her and helped her drop the sail.

"I heard you calling from the center." Maia spoke matter-of-factly. "The wind did not cooperate to speed the boat, but the Great Mother kept you whole on your journey, I see."

They unstepped the mast and hauled the coracle up to the campsite. With six hands, the work of making camp went quickly. Before the sun stood straight overhead, the lean-to was built again and the loom set up. Kissa took her spear and brought back three red mullets for their meal. Maia had not spoken since she first landed on the shore. In her usual way, she had directed the building with abrupt gestures and occasional grunts. Now with the campsite built and the fish in their bellies, Lykaina felt the need to talk.

"I did not know when I left you what lay ahead for me. Sappho was all that I had imagined and more. She made me part of her world. She drew a voice out of me that I did not know I had."

Maia poked the coals under the clay pot of nettle tea.

"I did not know," Lykaina continued, "that I was leaving part of me

outside her courtyard. I did not know that. . . ." Lykaina faltered. Maia
handed her a steaming cup. She blew on the tea and pushed on. "When
I left her, I thought I was split in two. I felt that I had plunged into a
place so deep that no light would ever come again."

Silence fell between them. When Maia spoke, her voice resonated.

"It was well you went in so deep. The Goddess leads you into the
center so that you can see how both creation and destruction come from
the same source. You are ready now for purification. Last night was the
new moon; tonight she begins her journey to full. We will proceed."

Maia eyed Lykaina's nakedness.

"You will need something to put on afterwards. The loom is ready.
But you yourself must choose what to hang on it."

Maia opened a large bundle of yarns and spilled out a multitude of
colors—soft pinks, dark reds, bright yellows. One skein was undyed
goatshair that ran from black and brown to gray and pale yellow. An
image flashed into Lykaina's mind of her grandmother carding and spinning goats' hair the winter before she died. She picked up the wool and
handed it to Maia, who grunted and began to string it onto the loom.
Lykaina pulled out a saffron skein and held its softness to her cheek,
thinking of Sappho.

"Can you put in some moon designs with this?" she asked.

Maia looked her in the eye.

"Is there anything else that needs to go in it?"

Lykaina shook her head no.

"Then take Kissa and prepare the other things. Bring a wild sea onion, fill this jug with pure spring water and this basket with barley
groats."

Lykaina took the clay jug and the basket and set off with Kissa. The
sea onion was easy. Kissa ran right to a large bed of them. Lykaina
remembered that there was a barley field just before the village on the
road to Mytilene, and the waterfall next to Kissa's stone cache would
provide the clear spring water. They returned with their harvest just
as the sun was falling behind the mountains. The new material hung
on Maia's loom. The grays and blacks and yellows and browns of the
goat's hair were broken by a narrow strip of saffron that ran diagonally
from bottom to top. Across the hem, waxing and waning crescents
flanked a single full moon in the center. Maia looked over the sacred
items and nodded.

"The first step to the Goddess is through the sea water. Everything
must be clean."

She took the material down from the loom and handed it to Lykaina.
Kissa lifted her small tunic from the bush where she had hung it the
morning she had found Lykaina. They all walked silently to a rocky place

at the shore. Maia took off her own gown, and the three of them stood naked, scrubbing the garments. They wrung them out and laid them on the rocks to dry. When the slender silver crescent lifted itself over the low hills that separated them from Mytilene, they raised their arms in greeting as Maia chanted.

> *Gaia riding the sickle moon,*
> *let the one who dove into the center*
> *spiral out into fullness.*

They left their garments on the rocks and walked naked to the campsite. Maia handed the basket with the barley groats and sea onion to Kissa, took the water jug for herself, and led the procession up the mountainside. At the waterfall, she veered onto a narrow path Lykaina had not noticed before. She led them deeper and deeper into a thick woods that blotted out the starlight. The path was rough, but Lykaina's feet seemed to know where every root jutted out, and she did not stumble. The path turned sharply, descended over some rocks, and spilled into a clearing. An ancient plane tree stood in the middle, its majestic limbs spreading out until they touched the forest around. Pale discs hung from its branches and moved silently in the night breeze. Behind the plane tree, a bank of rocks rose straight up. From a cleft in the largest rock, a trickle of water ran down and disappeared into a hole in the ground. In front of the tree, a flat stone lay across two stumps.

Maia brought the procession to a halt in front of the altar and set down the jug.

"The fire must be fed by alder."

She waved Lykaina away to look. When Lykaina returned, a small fire was blazing. Taking the alder branch from Lykaina, Maia placed it in the fire. Then she stepped back and raised her arms.

"Great Goddess, we begin."

She picked up the jug and poured water over first her own hands, then the hands of Lykaina and Kissa. She motioned for each of them to take a handful of barley groats and throw them into the fire. Then she picked up the blazing alder branch, poured water over it, and waved it sputtering back and forth over Lykaina's head. When she had finished, she gave her the sea onion.

"Peel each layer," she commanded, "until nothing remains."

Lykaina peeled the onion. Tears spilled out of her eyes and flowed down her cheeks. When the last layer had been pulled back, Maia turned away from the fire and raised her arms. Lykaina and Kissa turned also. The pale sickle moon had just come into sight through an opening in the branches. Below it stared the unblinking star of Aphrodite. Maia began a wordless chant in her low voice. The tears continued to flow down Lykaina's cheeks. She was drawn into the chant as if she herself were one of the sounds floating off into the night.

"Let her pour the libation. Let her cleanse herself. Let her put it all behind her."

Lykaina, still half in a trance, felt Kissa touch her arm and hand her the water jug. A memory of her grandmother purifying the house after her mother's death told her to tip the jug backwards and pour the water out behind her. As the last drop trickled onto the ground, she felt a prayer surge up from within her.

The water flows from the center.
What is spilled cannot be brought back.

The three of them stood in silence until the silver moonboat had traversed the opening in the forest and had lost itself once more in dark branches. Maia turned and led the procession back down the mountainside, past the campsite and down to the rocky shore. They each put on their freshly dried tunics. Lykaina felt the rough goatshair and remembered her childhood home. The soft saffron strip circling round her belly and breasts reminded her of Sappho's gentle lovemaking.

Suddenly shrill rhythmic sounds broke the still night air. Maia was whirling and singing a frenzied chant. She grabbed Lykaina with one hand and Kissa with the other and drew them into her wild dance. Up and down the shore they moved, circling and spinning. The knot that had formed in the pit of Lykaina's stomach when she left Sappho, that had been slowly unraveling since Kissa had found her, now loosed itself entirely and became an undulating ribbon leading her around and around. They danced until the sliver of moon had faded into the morning sky. Then Maia pulled both Lykaina and Kissa close to her and held them in a strong embrace.

"You are of the Goddess," she whispered into Lykaina's ear, "but you are also of yourself."

Chapter 11.
Climbing the mountain

Late summer stretched toward early winter. Reds and yellows streaked the sides of Olympos. A sharp wind from the gulf promised cold, and mackerel skies heralded rain. The loom reflected the changing season as rugs and blankets took shape under Maia's hands. Once each moon Maia left the clearing loaded with her loom's harvest to return in the evening with barter. The hearth expanded to include a small donkey, two nannies, and a billy goat.

Evenings, around the hearthfire, Lykaina blew the melancholy of her new aulos into the surrounding forest. What is spilled cannot be brought back, she thought, but it is not forgotten.

One evening Maia remarked, "Music fills the open spaces, but poems need human ears."

Lykaina looked at her. It was true. She did not sing these days. Neither the mountain songs of her childhood nor the poems she had composed with Sappho came out of her mouth. The few songs she began fell empty into the hearth. In her childhood, when she had first learned to sing, she had sung to her grandfather's ear. Then the old woman in Sparta had been her listener. In Sappho's courtyard, she had become used to singing to someone who listened carefully, someone who made her search for the most perfect expression. When she had learned to inscribe her words onto the soft papyrus so that the song was "finished," she found that the song could change no more. Those finished songs— songs that she had sung many times and for which she had received lavish praise—now seemed frozen into a time she could no longer enter.

Maia was right, new songs needed new ears for creation. Kissa heard Lykaina's dance tunes with her body. She seemed to understand Lykaina's thoughts almost before she spoke them. But she did not hear words. Maia heard words, but she did not care how they were put together or how they fitted themselves to music.

"You are ready to sing new songs," Maia continued, "but you need ears to hear them. Tomorrow a fair begins on Olympos. I am taking my weavings. You take your songs. You will find ears there."

A fair, thought Lykaina. A village fair, perhaps like the ones I went to as a child in Taygetus, where farmers brought their harvest produce and hunters their prey. There had been musicians and jugglers, she remembered, and storytellers and people with masks. She raised her aulos to her lips and blew a dance tune into the fire.

Early the next morning, Lykaina and Kissa helped Maia load her weavings onto the donkey. In addition to the blankets and rugs, Maia had bundled up several moon tapestries. Lykaina stuck her aulos in her belt, and Kissa slung her kalimba over her shoulder. The three of them set off, the donkey trailing behind.

They followed a dirt path along the shoreline until they reached the reedy end of the gulf. A deeply rutted road led them around toward the base of Mount Olympos. At the foot of the mountain, the road turned northward; in front of them, a narrow stone switchback staircase worked its way back and forth up the mountainside. By now others were with them, some with loaded donkeys, some carrying bundles on their backs. Children skipped up and down the steps, running from group to group, laughing and calling out to each other.

They climbed for several hours. The stairs ended at a narrow plateau lined with cypress trees. Above and below it, small stone houses with red tile roofs poked through the greenery. All along the plateau, vendors had set up stalls filled with farm produce—vegetables, fruits, chickens, sheep, and goats. Several stalls displayed freshly killed rabbits, quail, deer. Half a dozen booths held pottery, weavings, and tinware.

Lykaina, admiring a collection of hunting knives, felt Kissa tug her arm. She turned and looked in the direction of Kissa's pointed finger.

The narrow plateau opened into a square where a plane tree spread its branches in all directions. Kissa pulled her by the hand until they were in front of a wide stone wall upon which two men shouted at each other. Both men wore masks with tusklike fangs, round goggling eyes, and jutting ears. The smaller of the two—a hunchback—waved his arms and danced with mock fright.

"Quick, hide me," he cried, as they came up to the edge of the crowd surrounding the wall. "They're going to beat me!"

"Why?" said the taller man, "what are they going to beat you for?"

"Because they don't want me to die."

"They don't want you to die?"

"Yes. I was trying to die a nice quiet death, and they wouldn't let me."

"But why were you trying to die?"

"Because I'm hungry! I'm always hungry. My master makes me work all day and gives me only scraps for food. So I thought, instead of waiting to starve to death, why not die right now?"

"And how did you decide you were going to die?"

"Well, I thought I might go and drown myself. But I got to the well, and I looked down, and there was water in it. So I thought if I jumped in, I might die of a chill, and I didn't want to die of a chill, I wanted to drown."

"So what did you do then?"

"Well, then I decided that if I was going to die, I might as well enjoy myself. So I decided to die a sausage death."

"A sausage death? What's a sausage death?"

"Well, my master was having a dinner party. And the cooks had been making sausages all morning. So I thought that if I ate one or two hundred of them, my stomach would have such a shock that I would die immediately. But I'd eaten only thirty, or maybe forty, when they started beating me. They didn't want me to die!"

The hunchback did two backward somersaults and hid behind the plane tree just as two burly men jumped onto the stone wall, each of them waving a long wooden club. Kissa clapped her hands in delight.

"There," remarked Maia as she joined them, "is where you will sing. You will wait until evening—it is all buffoonery during the day. When the sun sets, there will be ears."

They left Kissa at the plane tree watching a trio of jugglers who had replaced the mummers. Lykaina helped Maia unload the donkey and set out her wares between two other weavers. She left when Maia began to haggle with a young woman who was fingering one of the blankets. Back at the plane tree, the jugglers had given way to a large hairy man in skins who was beating a hand drum while a small black bear with a bronze collar and chain stood on its hind legs and shuffled.

Kissa slipped her hand into Lykaina's and leaned against her arm. Eventually the two of them grew tired of the noise and the crowd and climbed the slope above the plateau.

The entire island lay stretched out before them. Below them, the Gulf of Hieras sparkled blue whenever afternoon sun broke through a bank of high-sailing clouds. Beyond the low still-green hills that hid the city of Mytilene, Mount Ida was shrouded in a gray mist that hung low over the white-capped waters of the Aegean. Staring at the water that lapped the shoreline where she and Sappho had walked, Lykaina began to feel a place deep inside her where emptiness still reigned. It was as if a part of her had died, a piece of Lykaina that existed only with Sappho—the Lykaina-with-Sappho part of her self. Other parts of her were alive and whole, but that part was gone.

She felt Kissa's small head fall against her shoulder and looked down at her. Mouth slightly open, the child was sleeping. Small quiet breaths rose and fell on her chest. Lykaina laid Kissa's head in her lap and stroked the soft blonde curls. She had lost Sappho, yes, but she had gained Kissa. And Maia, too. When her connection to Sappho snapped, she had felt bereft. But Kissa and Maia made her feel connected to the world again.

Was this what love was about? she wondered. Something deep inside stretched out its tendrils to intertwine with someone else's tendrils. The connection was as fragile as new climbing buds and as easily broken in a storm. But often when one intertwining was severed, another tendril seemed to reach out and find a new connection.

The shadows of the cypress trees below them had stretched far beyond the edge of the plateau. The shouting and noise of the fair seemed quieter as vendors began to pack up their booths in the early evening air. Lykaina shook Kissa awake.

"It is time for our music now."

They climbed down the slope and made their way to the large plane tree. An old man, white bristles on his chin, his head tilted back, his eyes half-closed, was singing a song about heroes of a long-gone war, a war on the mainland that had lasted for ten years and been lost only when a great wooden horse was pulled inside the city walls. Lykaina had heard parts of the tale in her childhood and smiled to hear the same words in this faraway place. The audience standing around the plane tree was hushed, hanging on every word the old man sang. A girlchild with large brown eyes squatted at his feet, silently mouthing words she remembered from past singings. The old man stopped and coughed. Someone handed him a bowl of clear liquid which he drank clumsily, trickles running out of the corners of his mouth.

"And then?" a voice called out.

The old man raised his gnarled hand.

"No," he said, "no more tonight. My throat needs more than one bowl-ful to wet it. Tomorrow." His eyes fell on Kissa's calabash. "And what manner of instrument does the child have?" he asked, motioning her forward.

Lykaina pushed Kissa gently and followed her to the old man's side. He took the calabash in his hands and peered inside it.

"What sort of sound does it make? What god invented it? Play, child, let us hear this thing."

Kissa ducked her head at the attention. Lykaina helped her onto the wall where she sat with her feet straight out, the calabash on her lap. Lykaina pulled the aulos from her belt and stood beside her. Kissa tilted her head and began to play. There were murmurs from the crowd, then hushes to silence them. Kissa's rhythms were strong and even, her tones rich and resonant. Lykaina let her play for a while, then raised the aulos to her lips and let its notes weave around the rhythms. Gradually she felt a song begin to take shape inside her.

> Whoever loves the rose must have patience
> and not cry out when the thorns draw blood.

The words came out freely and, like the aulos music, danced in and out of the plucked sounds. The crowd nodded in recognition of a truth they all knew. A deep voice called out, "Her voice is strong. Her words have truth. Let her sing some more."

Lykaina stretched the love song into a story, letting it unfold like the rose, each petal in its own time. The small brown-eyed child who had listened to the old man's song sat at her feet, her open mouth trying to follow Lykaina's words. Lykaina's heart pulsed each time a well-turned phrase rose out of her throat to meet the waiting ears.

At length they gave the plane tree over to a young man with a harp. Someone handed them both bowls of the clear liquid which they drank, relishing the sweet licorice taste and the burning sensation as it trav-eled down their throats. Maia was at the edge of the crowd, waiting for them. She put her arms around Lykaina and kissed her on both cheeks.

"Your voice has found ears. You are the strongest poet you have ever been. The Goddess is with you."

Lykaina hugged both Maia and Kissa. Maia was right. The song she had found tonight was like the ones she had sung with Sappho and yet it was more. She ate the stew Maia had prepared and savored the memory of the audience. She looked around at her new family. Life changes, she thought, and we change with it. It is not for us to decide when, it is only for us to recognize the moment when it comes.

The fair lasted three days. With the hushed audience, Lykaina found her songs growing in length. She began to tell stories—tales her grand-father had sung to her, stories of her own adventures on her journey to Lesbos. She found words and phrases from other songs to fill out the new lines of poetry so that each song wove together the old and the new. The audience hung on every word and called out for more each time she finished.

After their last performance, a stout woman with a walking stick came up to her.

"The fifth full moon after the Anestheria marks the moon mysteries of Sigri. Come and offer your gifts to Selene. She seeks poets such as you. You will reap the reward of the goddess if you come."

She looked around furtively and hurried away. Lykaina watched her slip through the crowd, wondering at her words.

The fair broke up the next morning. Lykaina and Kissa loaded the food and supplies they had bought onto the donkey. They all began the descent down the stone staircase. Lykaina led the donkey, feeling a new sense of peace and well-being. With a place for her poetry in the world, there was purpose to her life. With Kissa and Maia, there were the con-nections that made day-to-day life meaningful. Both were necessary for life, she thought, yet they needn't reside in the same person, as they had with Sappho. Perhaps, in fact, it was better they be separate.

She picked her way down the narrow stone staircase, steadying the donkey's pack. She thought about the coming festivals and fairs she had promised to attend and then about the woman who had spoken to her the night before. She caught up with Maia.

"What are the moon mysteries at Sigri?" she asked.

Maia did not seem to hear her. Lykaina shrugged and put her atten-tion to helping the donkey navigate through the crowd of other animals and people. Dusk had fallen by the time their feet felt the familiar dirt of their own footpath leading along the gulf. Maia came alongside her.

"The moon is subject to the Great Mother's law of becoming. As it waxes and wanes, it gives women our inner cycle of ebbing and flow-ing. You yourself have felt the double-edged moon force spinning in two directions. You have known the power of creation and destruction that flows out of the center." The night wind from the gulf made Lykaina pull her shawl closer around her. "The fifth full moon after the spring sowing," Maia continued, "was always the celebration of the moon. Once the mysteries were everywhere, on every island, in every village. When those with the chariots brought their new gods of destruction, they ruth-lessly sought us out, trying to erase the Great Mother from her own earth. But they cannot destroy her, for it is the moon in her perpetual state of becoming that gives fruit to the earth. And they cannot destroy those who remain faithful to her. Every year there is a gathering in

Samothrace, an island one day's sail north of here. Men and women go there. Those with authority permit the rituals. But in Sigri, it is only women that go. I was in Samothrace when you went into the center of darkness. Next midsummer, we will go together to Sigri."

Maia stopped abruptly and looked Lykaina in the eye.

"You who have seen the center will celebrate her power with others who have made the same journey."

A nighthawk called softly from the forest. Clouds covered the night sky. Lykaina listened to the water lapping the shore and pondered Maia's words.

When they arrived at the campsite, a young woman in the short tunic of a slave was seated in front of the firepit. As they approached, she stood up and held out a papyrus scroll.

"My mistress bids you read this and give me your reply." The woman's voice trembled as she spoke.

Frowning, Lykaina dropped the donkey's lead and took the scroll. The scent of lavender rose to her nostrils. Tears hovered at the back of her eyes, blurring the carefully inscribed words. She looked over at Maia, but Maia had turned her back to unload the donkey. She felt a hand on her arm. Kissa pointed up the mountainside toward their waterfall. Lykaina squeezed Kissa's hand and set off up the trail at a trot.

When she came to the waterfall, she sat for a long time listening to the splashing of the water over the rocks. The nighthawk had followed her, or sent its cousin. She let a tear make its way down her cheek. She had thought herself whole again and in harmony with her surroundings. But the mere sight of the papyrus had thrown her off balance. She wiped her eye, unrolled the scroll, and began to read.

"The moon has set," the papyrus began, "and the Pleiades are gone. It is midnight. Time passes, and yet I lie alone, longing for the sound of your voice. Come down from the mountains, my dearest, and let my two arms embrace you once more."

Lykaina sat very still for a long time. Inside her a battle raged. The Lykaina-with-Sappho, still very much alive, struggled with the Lykaina who felt her center with Maia and Kissa. She felt as if she were perched with the unseen nighthawk watching pieces of her self wrestling below. One cried for her right to love, to feel the touch of her lover, to abandon herself to those moments of ecstasy when her whole body became a spinning wheel of fire; the other turned over each moment of ecstasy to show her the pain lying in wait on the other side. Maia's voice echoed in her ears: *Remember who you are, remember who you can be!*

At last the voices faded, and the rumblings in the pit of her stomach subsided. She hid the papyrus in Kissa's stone cache and walked slowly down the mountainside.

"Tell her," she said to the waiting slave, "tell her that I still love her, but that I cannot come. I have other work to do."

Maia, squatting at the hearthfire, grunted. Kissa reached up and traced the tear dried on Lykaina's cheek. The slave bowed and set off up the trail.

Protected from the worst of winter's winds, the Gulf of Hieras was never so cold as the sea around Mytilene. But when she had lived with Sappho, Lykaina had rarely ventured out of the fire-warmed house to feel the winter air. Now when the winds turned the water gray and capped it with angry foam, she knew them from the chill in her bones. She felt the leaves as they fell from the trees around her to lay a wet carpet over the ground. She watched Olympos hide itself in dark clouds for a week and then emerge covered with snow. She and Kissa propped up logs to make walls for the lean-to and then hung rabbitskins inside to keep out the wind. Maia wove them all long goatshair cloaks. Evenings, when they huddled together around the fire, Lykaina thought of the long winter nights of her Taygetan childhood. This winter, like those, seemed to last forever. And then one day, warm winds from the south arrived to force buds from the trees and pull violets and hyacinths from the wet ground.

Lykaina's herd multiplied with the spring, each nanny producing twins that scrambled and jumped almost as soon as they burst out into the spring sunshine. Market days now saw the donkey loaded with cheeses as well as woven goods, and Kissa began to accompany Maia to Mytilene. Each time Lykaina watched them start up the trail, she felt a longing to go with them just to see the city again. But she did not move to follow, nor did Maia invite her.

Lush spring gave way in its time to brown summer as the rhythm of their lives continued. Lykaina was measuring out the clabbered milk one evening when Maia put a hand on her shoulder.

"Tomorrow is the new moon. We must be in Sigri for the mysteries. We will leave tomorrow evening."

The moon mysteries. Lykaina had not forgotten. At each fair she had attended this summer, someone had touched her and whispered, "We will see you at the moon mysteries."

"The flock is too big by now to leave on its own," she said. "Who will tend them while we're gone?"

"Kissa," said Maia shortly.

"Kissa? But surely she is coming with us."

Maia stepped in front of her and hung a small triangular rose-colored stone around her neck.

"Only those whose bodies hold moonblood can draw down the moon.

Kissa is not yet moon-touched. She will go another year."

Lykaina looked at Kissa who was cleaning a large bass. With her as a constant companion, Lykaina often forgot she was still a child. She knew that there were some things a child could not do.

They set sail at sunset the next day. Lykaina kissed Kissa on both cheeks. Kissa's face clouded, and she jutted out her lower lip. Lykaina tried to think of some way to tell her that the year of her firstblood they would go together, but she was not nearly so adept as Kissa at talking with gestures. Instead she hugged her.

"Milk the nannies before the kids have a chance to nurse. They have to learn to find their own food."

Kissa pulled away from her sharply and ran off toward the goat pen. Lykaina started after her, but Maia pulled on her arm.

"No. It is time to leave now. She will understand when she is ready."

Maia climbed into the coracle. Lykaina pushed off and hopped into the stern. She looked back toward the goat pen, but Kissa was nowhere in sight. A fresh breeze caught the sail, and she turned her attention to steering the coracle through the dark water. She had not sailed since the journey to Lesbos, but she found she had not forgotten how to keep the sail full and the steering oar steady.

The back of the moon lifted itself above the treetops. Lykaina felt a warm flow between her thighs. Her own moonblood was beginning, just as it began every month, with the rise of the new moon.

"We celebrate the moon," Maia's low voice came to her, "because the Great Mother created us all out of her own ocean of blood. She is like the moon. She governs the tides of life and death. She pulls the child from its mother's womb on the incoming tide. She pulls the soul from the dying person on the ebb. Each month she sends us blood to remind us that out of our blood new life is formed. When no moonblood flows, we know that life is growing within us. Or else the blood has become wise blood to create a pool of wisdom inside us."

They followed the shore along the lee of the island. When dawn began to lighten the sea in front of them, they rounded a headland. Lykaina saw the lighthouse that had been both her first sight of Lesbos and a daily part of her long summer with Sappho in Eresos. She pushed the memories aside and kept her eyes on the water ahead. Finally they left behind the long sand beach of Eresos and rounded the cape of Sigri. Maia took the steering oar and maneuvered the boat between a small pine-covered island and the mainland. They rounded the tip of the island and swung into a cove filled with other small boats. On the beach, hundreds of women were embracing and laughing. Others were climbing a high promontory that jutted out into the sea.

Afterward, Lykaina thought that it was not the mysteries themselves that were remarkable. In pieces she had experienced it all before—the drinking of the milky soma followed by visions of the Great Mother's universe; the dancing of naked limbs that made her quiver deep in her core; the familiar chants sung with arms upraised to the silver moon that nightly grew rounder. Even the beautiful stone tree trunk around which they danced was like the ones she had seen with Sappho. What *was* remarkable was the community of women, women whose moon-blood, like hers, was flowing. Except for those like Maia whose blood remained inside, a pool of wisdom.

Joined together, the women's life rhythms seemed almost visible, pulled by the goddess moon. The bodies all different, the rhythms the same, Lykaina lost herself in the joining. She let the point between her own self and others blur and fade. Her songs seemed to come both from within her and from the bodies around her. In her visions, she saw herself red like the heart of a flame glowing in a red hollow cavern. She felt her flame spread and join with other flames until she became part of a mighty roaring fire pouring out of the cavern and rising into the night sky. She felt the vast tide of nature whose ebb and flow is governed by the moon. A thread seemed to come out of her navel to join a matrix encompassing all heaven and earth. As much as she felt the pull of the moon, she also felt herself, with the others, pulling the moon, drawing it down into her own belly.

The night the moon rose full and round out of the sea, she felt she no longer belonged to her body. Instead she and it were all part of one great whirling dance that flowed like the sea around the great stone trunk. When the moon reached its zenith that night, the dance stopped, and the whole universe seemed to stand still with them. The perfect matrix unraveled itself, and each thread wound itself back to the navel where it belonged. Lykaina looked at her sisters and saw them one by one again.

Silently they embraced each other and descended to the beach. Lykaina fingered the moonstone amulet as she followed Maia to the waiting cora-cle. She was herself again, yet she would always be a part of this whole.

It was a late afternoon several months later, when chilly winds had already begun to blow the leaves from the trees, that Lykaina returned from her trapline to hear Maia speak brusquely from the loom.

"You have a visitor down by the shore."

Lykaina stopped short.

"Who is it?" she asked.

"Go and see for yourself."

Lykaina looked down at the shoreline. A short dark figure in a flow-ing gown was silhouetted against the reflection of the water. Beyond her, a small ferryboat waited in the water, a young man at the oars. Lykaina stood frozen staring at the woman.

"She is a guest. Go and welcome her," said Maia, throwing the shuttle through the threads again.

Lykaina walked slowly toward the shore. What would she say? What would Sappho say to her? She stopped a short distance from the boat.

"See how the water grows lighter as the sky grows darker." Sappho waved her arm toward the gulf. "It is peaceful here. Only the sound of the water lapping the shore." She turned to face Lykaina. "You are looking well."

"I...yes, I am well. And you...you are...?"

"I am well also, thank you." Sappho smiled and gestured to Lykaina to come closer. "Come. I won't bite. I won't even carry you away to ravish you."

Lykaina stepped closer.

"It is said amongst my kitchen slaves that a new voice is in the mountains. Someone who sings at country fairs, someone whose poetry is peerless. They say she sings poems of love and tales of adventure, that when she opens her mouth, the gods take time from their idle pursuits to listen."

Lykaina looked down at her feet.

"I found a voice that blended what I learned from you with what is deep inside me." She paused and then added, "Kissa plays, too."

"So I have heard. Who would have thought that a deaf child could make music?"

"She hears it with her fingers, with her whole body. She is happy."

"I am glad I gave her to you. She would have been a serving girl all her life."

"She is free now." Lykaina's voice took on an edge. "She stays because we are friends."

Sappho looked away.

"Yes," she said quietly, "so I would think of you."

They stood together watching a group of small lanterned fishing boats move silently out toward the mouth of the gulf.

"I came to ask you...," Sappho began and then stopped. "No," she said, "the hard words must be said first. I came to say that I am sorry for the things I said. You were right to leave me."

Lykaina looked at her.

"I left because what you said hurt me. But I have stayed away because I cannot live in your world."

"My world...," Sappho's voice held a touch of anguish, "...my world is barren without you. I came to ask you to come back, if only for a visit. For one night. My friends ask for you. 'Where is your poet friend?' they say. They miss your songs. And I miss you."

Lykaina was afraid to speak. She had kept her thoughts of Sappho in a far corner of her mind, allowing herself only a glimpse now and then. Standing beside her, she felt overwhelmed by love for her. It seemed as strong as when they had been together every day.

"I cannot come," she whispered. "I have my life here. I—"

"Just for one evening. A few friends whose conversation you would enjoy. Your old companions will be there. I beg of you."

Lykaina thought about those evenings in that other world. She missed the long conversations about poetry, about music, about travel in the world beyond. She missed Sappho, too. One evening....

"All right. I will come."

"Wonderful!" exclaimed Sappho. "Tomorrow evening. I will invite Alkaios. He may have news of your friend Soudiata."

Lykaina looked down at her tunic.

"But I will wear this," she said firmly. "I will not dress your way."

"Come in a bearskin, if you like. Your tunic is wonderful, it suits you. You are as beautiful as ever."

Sappho took her hand and kissed it. They walked to the boat together, and Lykaina helped Sappho step in.

"Until tomorrow, then," whispered Sappho, leaning over to kiss her cheek.

"Until tomorrow."

Freshly bathed and with a garland of rosebuds in her hair, Lykaina stood nervously in front of Sappho's red door. She remembered her first days in Mytilene with the billowing gown catching her legs and the stiff sandals biting into her feet. How long ago that was. She raised her hand and knocked. The doorslave greeted her and anointed her with rosewater. Inside the house, everything seemed familiar and yet so strange. It was as if she were seeing things reflected in a smoky mirror. She paused at the entrance to the dining hall. Her old companions stood in groups talking with other guests. Sappho was talking with Alkaios. One or two faces were unfamiliar. A beautiful young woman standing off to one side was certainly a new hetaera.

Sappho floated up to Lykaina and took her by the arm.

"I was afraid you wouldn't come after all. Come and sit beside me." She rang a silver bell. Instantly the room was filled with slavegirls bearing steaming trays and kraters of wine. Throughout the meal, Sappho plied Lykaina with a taste of this dish and that, calling out to her slaves to bring just one more delicacy. Lykaina laughed at her.

"You must think I am starving in the woods. We eat there, too, you know."

Sappho laughed, too. "Of course you do, but I don't get to watch you."

At length the dishes were cleared away, and Sappho stood up.

"It is my great pleasure," she announced, "to bring back a beloved friend to sing for us."

The guests looked at Lykaina as if they were seeing her for the first time.

"Lykaina, our former companion from the mountains of Sparta," Sappho continued, "and more lately from the mountains of our own Lesbos, has agreed to sing for us a new song."

Amid the scattered applause, a thin voice whispered, "Do bare knees and hairy legs fend off wolves in the mountains?"

Lykaina, feeling mellow from the wine and conversation with Sappho, looked over at a group where several of the hetaerae were sitting, their faces frozen in perfection, their red lips pursed. Sappho frowned in their direction and then turned back and nodded at Lykaina. Lykaina pulled her aulos from her belt and began to play. Watching Sappho, she let the notes surge out of her into the still air. The music rang too loudly in the small hall, but the warmth of Sappho's eyes led her on. She began to sing one of the tales she had been creating at the fairs, a song that wove the story of her own rescue by dolphins with a tale about a young girl from Troy setting out to find the Amazons to help the Trojan army against the Greeks.

Low murmurs came from the hetaerae again. A tossed grape missed an open mouth and rolled across the mosaic floor. A wine goblet clinked against a bowl. Lykaina's eye caught one of the painted mouths in a yawn behind a ring-decked hand. She faltered, her words momentarily lost. Sappho's eyes drew her on again, and she finished the line with a phrase she hadn't sung since childhood. She played some notes on the aulos while she recovered the song. Her eyes roved the room, and she caught other polite yawns, other low whispers. Sappho's eyes darted from group to group, trying in vain to pull them into the song.

The aulos stopped mid-note. Lykaina began the lines that told about the Trojan girlchild struggling to climb the mountain. Then she stopped. Her audience lost, she could not go on. She felt the blood rush to her cheeks. She dropped her eyes to the floor. The room grew silent. Alkaios began to applaud enthusiastically; others politely joined him.

"A bold and interesting tale, my dear," he said, ignoring the frozen faces around him, "and quite an unusual meter. You must tell me how you came to it."

Lykaina looked over and saw Sappho slumped in her chair, her hand to her forehead. The companions and other guests were standing now, talking again in groups as if she had never sung.

"It is a meter common in the mountains," she said shortly, as she wiped the reed of the aulos. "Mountain ears hear its beauty even if city ears cannot."

"Please," protested Alkaios, "do not think we do not appreciate its beauty. It is extraordinary. We are always eager to hear new poetic styles. I am grateful to you for bringing your rare gift to us once again." He waved his hand toward the chattering hetaerae. "You must forgive your old companions. Your voice is strange to them. They do not understand that beauty has many shapes."

Lykaina looked around. The women she had spent so many seasons with were behaving as if they did not know her. And they didn't. Without a flowing gown and a painted face, she had the voice of a stranger. It was as if she had never been a hetaera. She felt Sappho's touch on her arm.

"My dearest...," Sappho began. Her words hung in the air. Lykaina tucked the aulos in her belt. "You are going?" said Sappho, her brows knit, her eyes dull and lifeless. "Will you come again? I want to hear the rest of your song."

"I have ears that can hear in the mountains," Lykaina answered. "Come there if you want to hear me."

She strode to the door. At the threshold she turned back. Sappho was leaning on Alkaios' arm, her perfect face pale and weary.

"I love you, Sappho," Lykaina whispered, tears ready to fall, "but I don't want your world. It is yours. I have my own."

She left the house quickly. Once again she was running with tears spilling from her eyes. But this time the tears were not for herself. They were for Sappho—a woman full of grace and love and the finest poetry ever sung trapped in a world that could see beauty only if it were properly attired. Lykaina would love her, perhaps forever. But never again in that world.

Chapter 12.
Return to Sparta

"The old woman is dying."

Lykaina struggled out of a dream. She had been rowing the coracle through dense reeds to open water, but the oars had become entangled. The reeds had turned into skeins of gray wool that she was combing with a sheep's curry. The voice came again, low and clear.

"Go to her, she is dying."

Lykaina, now fully awake, shook her head. She looked out of the lean-to. Stars still dotted the sky, and the waning moon hung low over the gulf. Kissa slept on her mat, her thumb resting lightly against her lips. Maia's corner was empty.

Lykaina got up and wrapped a skin around her shoulders. She stepped out into the clearing and looked down to the shore. Maia stood motionless in the pale moonlight, twin milk snakes curled around her upraised arms. Lykaina walked down and stood a little way from her, letting the cool night breeze clear her head of the remaining strands of her dream. She watched a group of lanterned fishing boats returning from their night's work.

The moon had completed its cycle several times since the ill-fated dinner at Sappho's. For a while, the memory had stuck at the edge of her mind bringing sharp pain into focus at unexpected times. Finally it had receded, taking its place with other more pleasant visions of Sappho, all of them resting in a not-often-visited part of her memory. Her days now were filled with tending her small herd of goats; special days she performed with Kissa at fairs, weddings, and other country celebrations.

"The sleeping ground of the dead reaches out for its bloodseed." Maia stood beside her, her hoarse voice piercing Lykaina's thoughts. "Only in death can there be rebirth. The dark of the moon must be fed for the new seeds to grow. Your old woman has offered herself. She calls to you for one last song."

Lykaina started. The words of her waking dream came back to her: *The old woman is dying.* Who had spoken them? She furrowed her brow. Maia gripped her by her shoulders.

"There is no time for delay. You must go to her now. She is dying. The Goddess is waiting for her."

A sharp vision came into Lykaina's mind. The old woman lay on her litter, her long gray hair tangled like the wool skeins of her dream. A force surged in the pit of her stomach. Wherever the words had come from, Lykaina knew they were true. She nodded numbly at Maia, then turned and ran back to the campsite. She ducked into the lean-to and dressed quickly. Her aulos in her belt, her goatshair cloak, bread and cheese in her pack, waterskin, knife—everything was ready. She turned to Kissa whose wide-open eyes stared at her.

"I am going home to Sparta," she said. She motioned in the direction of the setting sun. Her mind scrambled for a way to say *home* with her hands. Kissa frowned. Lykaina knelt and hugged her. There was no time to explain, even if she could find the gestures. She stood up and handed Kissa the shepherd's staff.

"Take care of the nannies," she said, shouldering her pack and stepping over the threshold. "They are yours now."

Maia held out a bundle of weavings.

"These will gain your passage. Find a merchant ship bound directly for Corinth. Talk to no one but the captain. Go quickly now."

Lykaina embraced her and turned to go. A bevy of hoarse croaks stopped her in her tracks. Kissa stood in front of the lean-to, her face dark red, her mouth twisted around the sounds that emerged from it.

"Uh-uh-uh-uh!"

Kissa broke the shepherd's crook over her knee. Lykaina turned to Maia.

"Go," said Maia. "I will explain to her. If you delay, it may be too late."

Lykaina set down her pack and held out her arms to Kissa.

"One more hug, little one. You are precious to me. I grieve the parting, too."

Kissa hurled herself at Lykaina and began to beat her with her fists. "Uh-uh-uh!"

Maia shook her head, but Lykaina pulled Kissa close to her, letting the blows fall on her shoulders. The memory of Theadora sitting with the children, showing them how to thread broad beans floated into her mind.

"Hush, hush now, Kissa," she murmured. "You're going to be all right. I have no choice. I am honor-bound to help the old woman prepare for death's journey. She is my family."

Kissa's croaks eventually dwindled into exhausted sobs accompanied by the rhythmic heaving of her small frame against Lykaina's body.

"One day I will return," whispered Lykaina into her hair. "I promise you."

Maia took Kissa firmly by the arm and led her away. Lykaina turned reluctantly to the trail. At the first bend, she looked back. Maia sat on a log at the hearth holding Kissa's head in her lap and stroking her hair. A bolt of pain twisted through Lykaina's heart. She had found peace here, and her heart had healed. Yet the old woman was calling her. She had learned what she needed to know in Lesbos. Now it was time to go home.

The sun was halfway to its zenith when she arrived at the Mytilene harbor. Large boats and small ones rocked at their moorings while men in loincloths carried cargo up and down the gangplanks. The air was filled with the cries of traders, eager to cut a good deal. Most of the boats, she learned, were on their way to Rhodes or Crete and from thence to Egypt. One or two small boats were bound for Corinth but planned to stop at all the islands in between.

Finally she located a Phoenician gaulos set to sail at midday. It was scheduled to be in Corinth in seven days. One of the sailors directed her to the captain, a tall bent man with gray hair crowning his weathered face.

"I want fast passage to Corinth."

Lykaina spoke quickly, as if the speed of her words would make the journey go faster. The captain turned from his business with a merchant and scrutinized her.

"And I have a fast ship bound for Corinth," he finally said. "What have you got that will make room for you on it?"

Lykaina opened the bundle of Maia's weavings and spread them out on the quay. Several merchants turned from their haggling to stare at the fine materials. Some pushed their way into the circle that now surrounded her and began to finger the fabrics. The moon symbols Lykaina had become so familiar with were subtler on these weavings, almost fading into the surrounding patterns. One portly merchant began to drape several pieces over his arm. The captain narrowed his eyes.

"Half this bundle will take you to Corinth. Here, Mikilis," he called to a young sailor. "Pick out the best half of these, and let the woman sell the rest as she pleases."

He left the circle. Lykaina let the sailor select what he wanted and then rolled the remaining pieces back into the bundle.

"There are more where these came from," she said to the portly merchant. "Ask for the weaver Maia at the agora. Someone will direct you to her."

The gaulos was fast. Almost as wide as it was long, it nonetheless cut the waves cleanly. The island stops were brief and the winds steady. Lykaina spent her days on deck keeping a vision of the old woman before her eyes. Each time the stern wrinkled face threatened to slide into the foam, Lykaina pulled it back, sometimes by singing to it, sometimes by sheer will. She will not die without me, she thought. She will hear my song once more before she journeys to the underworld.

After what seemed an eternity, the gaulos arrived in Corinth's port. Lykaina followed her bundle over the rails and onto the dock. She elbowed her way through throngs of merchants eager for fresh goods from the east and ducked into one of the shops along the quay.

"A horse," she said shortly to a young man who was carving thick slices from a spitted lamb. "I want to hire a horse."

The young man continued slicing.

"What have you got to hire one with?" he said, barely looking at her.

Lykaina opened her bundle enough to show corners of Maia's weaving. The young man glanced at them. He laid down his knife and wiped his hands on his tunic. From the doorway of his shop, he let out an ear-splitting whistle. A young boy detached himself from a group of knucklebone players and trotted over.

"Go to Petriklis the peddler. Tell him to bring his nag."

It was only a matter of minutes before Lykaina found herself astride a small black mare heading out onto the road that led to Sparta. It had taken four days to travel from Sparta to Corinth by foot; on horseback she could make it in less than two. The old woman's face frowned at her from between the mare's ears.

"Hang on, granny," Lykaina muttered between clenched teeth. "I'm almost there."

The old woman lay on her litter. Black eyes stared fiercely up into the gnarled fig tree that shaded the courtyard, long gray hair lay tangled and unbraided around her shoulders. Lykaina stood in the arched doorway for a few moments as daylight faded into evening. Arete sat next to the litter and wiped the old woman's forehead with a damp cloth. The baby, now a husky four-year-old, crouched at the side of the courtyard building a tower out of stones and sticks. Niki was nowhere in sight. A wail from inside the house broke the silence. Arete got up hurriedly and disappeared. Lykaina slipped into her place and began to stroke the old woman's arms.

"I'm here," she whispered. "I heard you calling."

The fierce black eyes turned to rest for a moment on Lykaina's face, then they closed and a sigh escaped from the old woman's breast.

"Fix my hair." The voice was almost a growl. "I let no one else touch it, and now my hands won't work like they used to."

Lykaina took up the long bone comb and began to gently work the tangles.

"I'm dying." It was a whisper.

"I know. I came to sing you onto your journey into the underworld."

"I'm afraid. No one's ever come back to tell about it, you know."

"Hecate will guide you."

"So they say. Sing for me."

Lykaina put down the comb and pulled her aulos from her belt. She began with a long low note that quivered and rumbled. She let it spiral upward toward a sky just beginning to show the first evening stars.

The world is a tree and we are its fruit.

Hecate, the vintager, gathers us all in time.

Lykaina sang until the old woman fell asleep. She watched the beloved face in repose as darkness fell around them. The boy came and stood beside her, leaning against her arm.

"She's getting ready for a long journey," he said. "She says I can't go with her."

"She's right, you can't. It's a journey everybody gets to take, but each of us has to go on it by ourselves. Hecate looks after us, though."

Lykaina felt a hand on her shoulder and looked up. Arete, beautiful as ever, stood holding an infant on her hip.

"You have come home."

"Yes. I came to help her prepare."

Arete smiled down at her.

"She's sleeping now. You must be tired from your journey. I'll watch her while you rest."

"I'm not tired. I'll lie down here beside her. I see you have a new one to take care of."

Arete looked down at the child on her hip.

"She's seen two full moons already. She fills some of the space for me since they took Niki away."

"She is in the gymnasium now?"

"Yes. I rarely see her. When I do, it's hard because she's so different. She's tough—I like that—but she doesn't want me to touch her. She'll get along better than I did. I cried for my mama, and everyone laughed at me for it. She'll be a better Spartan."

Lykaina thought about the affectionate Niki becoming one of the pack-children racing through the streets, knocking over anyone in their way. Better Spartans, yes, but not better children. The new baby began fretting, and Arete pulled aside her tunic to nurse. Lykaina looked at the child-attached-to-breast scene that used to take her breath away. Arete as nursing mother was as beautiful as ever. Lykaina lay back and watched the stars now poking their way into the darkening sky. This had been her first real home. Had it not been for the soldier, she never would have left.

The old woman stirred. Lykaina sat up and took her hand.

"I'm here, granny."

"I was afraid you were just a dream. You're not, I see, you're real flesh and blood. Tell me about Sappho. Did you find her?"

"Yes. She took me in as one of her hetaerae. I learned to play the lyre and to sing a new kind of song with her. I learned to write my poems on papyrus—just like you showed me. They went to other islands that way. They even traveled to Egypt."

The old woman squeezed her hand.

"And do they live a life of luxury there? Do they eat fine foods and dress in soft materials and sleep on soft beds?"

Lykaina remembered her first days at Sappho's. How to tell the old woman all of what had happened?

"It is a fine life," she began slowly. "We wore long gowns made of soft Persian linens. Every morning we sat in Sappho's courtyard and sang our songs. When we finished, she sang for us. We took our mid-day meal together; in the evenings we ate with other poets and musicians—and those who govern Lesbos, too. It was just as you said. Everyone talks about poetry there, everyone is eager to hear a new song."

Lykaina paused, remembering her last evening at Sappho's house. She made her thoughts change direction.

"I felt my poetry coming from a different place in me. When I sang with the lyre instead of the aulos, the songs came out softer, more . . . ." She paused again.

"More like Sappho's?"

"Yes."

"You loved her?"

"Yes, I loved her."

"And?"

"Her world," Lykaina hesitated and then rushed on, ". . .the people in her world are all alike. You have to become one of them to belong. I wore a soft gown, and I learned to walk and talk like them, but there were times I felt the need to be out on the mountain blowing my aulos. She didn't really like that part of me. She even called the aulos barbaric. And I. . .I couldn't erase who I had been."

"Who you still are."

"Who I still am. In the end I had to leave."

"So. Was it worth it?"

Was it worth it, Lykaina thought. Lykaina-with-Sappho is still part of me. Who I am now grew out of who I was with her.

"It was worth it."

"Sing me one of her songs."

Lykaina remembered an old lyre that had hung in a corner of the house. She took it down, dusted it off, and tuned the strings. She began to play softly and sing.

> Come, holy tortoise shell,
> my lyre, and become a poem.

Singing those words now, she felt Sappho inside her. The woman was not a simple person. She had been cruel sometimes, yes, but she had more often been generous and loving. She had given herself to Lykaina, and she had not held anything back. And truly, this poetry was the greatest anyone had ever made.

The old woman sighed and closed her eyes.

"Now sing me one of yours."

Lykaina started to trade the lyre for her aulos. Then she thought of the song she had tried to sing that last night at Sappho's. It was a long tale, it told of wild adventures. Better to contrast those adventures with the quiet of the lyre.

She began to sing, plucking a soft ostinato under her words. She let her young Trojan heroine, daughter of Cassandra's nurse, begin her journey by foot, climbing the mountains behind Troy to escape notice of the encamped Greeks. She sang about the dark way along the Hellespont to the Black Sea where the girl set off in a small coracle with a double-poled mast. A Poseidon-sent storm smashed her boat, but dolphins carried her to the Amazon city of Sacastene. She was awed by the strong women astride horses whose upraised moonsickles caught the glint of the midday sun. Their queen, Penthesilea, gave her a winged black mare with a gray mane and gray tail, and she flew over the mountains with the Amazon army—down to the plains of Troy to engage the

Greeks in battle.

By the time the song ended, the night was black and the last sliver of the waning moon reigned high in the sky.

"It was worth your going if only to bring me that. I am ready for Persephone's dark underworld now."

Lykaina laid her head on the old woman's breast.

"Stay a bit longer, granny, just until I've drunk my fill of you."

She spent the night holding the old woman in her arms and singing softly into her ear. Arete sat next to her. Other kinswomen arrived and stood on either side of the litter. Around midnight, the soldier and other male relatives came and stood talking in the outer courtyard. Theadora's breaths became raspy, as if her lungs could no longer take in the night air. Lykaina continued to sing—songs she had learned from her grandfather, songs she had composed with Sappho, songs she had sung with Kissa. Just as dawn's glow was beginning to push back the black night, the old woman's eyes flashed open. She sat straight up and opened her mouth. Lykaina supported her, holding her tightly. The relatives moved closer.

"Speak, granny," whispered Lykaina.

A hoarse croak came out of the old woman's throat, and she fell back. Lykaina laid her cheek against the withered breast.

"Go to the good, granny. Safe passage to you."

She closed the old woman's eyes and mouth. Shrill keening sounds broke from the kinswomen's mouths as they moved in to wash and anoint the still body. Arete brought out a long white robe and wrapped the old woman in it. They lifted her onto the bier, placing her with her head toward the house, her feet toward the street outside. One of the women brought out a bundle of wild marjoram and sprinkled the fragrant leaves over the body. Another wove a garland of laurel and celery to place on her head. The soldier tacked a cypress branch over the door of the outer courtyard.

Lykaina stood motionless at the old woman's head, still holding her hand, a low cry shaking her throat. One of the kinswomen started to pull Arete into the position of chief mourner, but Arete shook her head.

"No, she is in her rightful place. My grandmother loved her best."

By now the women were all swaying around the bier, shrill wordless wails falling out of their mouths. From time to time one would reach out and touch the body, then pull back to beat her breasts. Some of the women drew blood as they scratched at their cheeks. Others tore their clothes and smeared their faces with ashes. Lykaina listened to the rising lamentations. She felt the grief swelling in her heart, and she opened her mouth to sing.

Here in this courtyard,

beside a shady tree a fountain flowed.
Sisters and cousins sat in the shade,
her granddaughter sat with her children.
Today the fountain dried up,
today the tree is uprooted.

The sun climbed into the eastern sky, crossed westward, and descended behind the Taygetus Mountains. The lamentations rose and fell around the lifeless body. From time to time Lykaina picked up the aulos and let it fill the air with a shrill ululation that seemed to reach to the underworld itself.

When the sun rose again the next morning, the soldier and Arete's brothers and cousins entered the inner courtyard for the first time and lifted the bier to their shoulders. A tall, thin man with sallow cheeks held up his hand just before the procession began.

"Remember the law," he said solemnly. "No one is to lament or tear her clothes as we go. No cries, no blood. Women are to walk in silence behind the men. Any woman who breaks the law will be punished severely."

Lykaina remembered the funeral of Theadora's sister who had died soon after she had come to Sparta. After the funeral banquet, Lykaina had asked the old woman who had made the law and why.

"Who made all our laws?" the old woman had responded, her lips curled in disgust. "Old Lykourgos. He knew what he wanted. The ending of a life is an important time. The inheritance is divided, the family takes on a new shape. This all happens during the ritual for the dead. Those who lead the lamentations are the reshapers. Before Lykourgos, women took charge of the final journey to the underworld. After giving back to the earth what sprang from the earth, they turned to the living. Too much power, says our Lykourgos. So he made a law that said women should continue to do the work of preparing the dead for their journey to the underworld, but that they must not be prominent in the reshaping of the family. A simple law with a heavy penalty, that's all it took. When the time comes for my own funeral, you will see how my soldier grandson-in-law takes charge after the preparations are all done."

The soldier did indeed take charge. At the gravesite, he slaughtered a lamb and let its blood flow into the pit. He and Arete's brother poured the libations and placed the old woman on the pyre. After the burning, he stepped forward to extract the bones from the ashes and place them in the tomb. When the time came for the offering of gifts, the women all waited for his nod before bringing forward their honey and flowers. Once or twice one or another of the older women stepped out to assert her rightful place, but each time Arete waved her back. They glared at her but bent to her wishes.

Back at the house, Arete supervised the women as they prepared the funeral feast. The older women grumbled at her docility, but they served the food to the men seated at a long table, and they hovered in the background ready to refill wine carafes and meat platters. Lykaina watched as the men drank toasts to the old woman. One by one they stood up to sing praise songs. They didn't know her at all, she thought, yet they control what she owned. And Arete, model of the new Spartan woman, accepts it.

In the days following the funeral, Lykaina stayed with Arete. She helped her purify the house and took barley broth, milk, and honey to the gravesite to pour down the libation tubes. Lykaina did not talk much during these days. She wanted to relive each day of her life here, to remember each word the old woman had said, each look she had given her.

On the morning of the eleventh day, the soldier entered the house for the first time since the funeral banquet. A young girl in a white tunic trailed behind him. He set a black kidgoat down on the courtyard floor and stared blankly at a spot between Lykaina and Arete.

"Since my grandmother-in-law purchased your freedom," he announced, "you are free to leave. By law, mourning is officially over. There is no further need for you. This kidgoat will pay for the laments you sang for my wife's grandmother. Take it and return to your village." He turned to Arete. "This is the daughter of one of my comrades-in-arms. She will assist you in your wifely duties." He turned on his heel and left.

The two women listened to the slap of his leather soles as he strode off down the street. Lykaina looked at Arete, but Arete had already turned away to pick up the baby. The young girl stood where he left her, her eyes fastened on the ground.

"You accept what he says without challenge." Lykaina's voice barely controlled her anger. "This is your house now. He has no rights here. You could tell *him* to leave. You could divorce him, if you wanted."

"Please, Lykaina, I don't want to argue. It doesn't matter. He's hardly ever here. He won't even come back to see if you've gone. Ignore him."

Lykaina shook her head. What was the point in talking? If Arete was happy with the way things were, what right did she have to question her? What did it matter if he pretended that he was in charge of her life, if in fact Arete listened to him quietly and then did as she pleased? Except that, to Lykaina, it did matter. Symbols were important. If he thought he controlled things and didn't, it was only because he chose not to. If the time ever came when he wanted to, it would be easy to enforce the rules he had laid out.

She touched Arete's arm.

"I have made the journey back this far. I will take this kid to my village. I have not seen my family now for many seasons' turnings. It's time I went home." She kissed Arete on the cheek. Tears filled Arete's eyes. "It's all right. You have to live your life the way you think best. I will go to my village. You will take care of the mare for me while I am gone, yes? When I have visited with my family, I will come to you again."

She lifted the kid, placed it around her shoulders, and left the house. Heading out of Sparta, she passed through the now-bare fields where helot men, women, and children were bent over sowing wheat. Life for them was an endless cycle of plowing, planting, and harvesting, she thought. Their backs were always bent to one task or another. In the end, all they produced went to their Spartan masters.

She thought how in every city where she had traveled, there had been humans whose lives were dedicated to the service of others more powerful than themselves. Everywhere there were hierarchies where this person commanded deference while that person deferred. You could only live in such a society if you understood the order. In the village of her childhood there was order, too, but it was different. The people there who commanded deference were older people—a healer like her grandmother, a seer who interpreted the signs of the heavens. Their lifework was to give. It was a life self-chosen. No one was born to it. The deference they gained was from their gifts to others.

By now she was climbing a rocky trail between two mountains whose jagged peaks towered above her. A few light snowflakes had begun to fall, and she was grateful for the warmth of her cloak and the kid around her shoulders. She began to recognize familiar rocks and trees. She knew she was not far from the first of the seven villages that marked the ridge on which Anabretae was set. Up here it was still winter, with only a few anemones poking through the hard ground to tell of the spring soon to come.

She entered the village as dusk was falling. The snow had stopped, but the air was still cold and damp. The small huts were dark and shuttered, the village square empty. At the far end of the pathway, a light in a half-open door drew her to a wineshop where several old men were huddled around an open hearth listening to a gray-bearded man who wore the cloak of a peddler.

"But these are no ordinary beads," he was saying. "They come from the bottom of the sea. They were strung together by the hands of the nereids. I have them because once I was married to a nereid."

The man paused, looking around to see the effect of his words.

"When I was a young man," he went on, "I was handsome and carefree and spent my days wandering the seashore playing my pipe. There was a group of nereids who used to dance on the sand, and they persuaded me to play for them. I would go every night after the sun had gone down, and they would dance until the first light of dawn broke at the edge of the sea."

He dropped his voice and smiled, as if remembering days long past.

"I fell in love with one of them. She had a beauty unsurpassed—and I believed she had a fancy for me, too. But she disappeared with her sisters into the sea every morning. There was no way to keep her there."

The peddler paused and rubbed the bright blue beads with his fingers.

"So I asked a wisewoman from the village," he continued, "how I could make her my wife. And she told me that if I could catch hold of her kerchief and not be afraid of whatever happened, but to hold fast to it, the nereid would be mine."

The peddler looked around, making sure he had his audience's attention.

"That night, just before dawn, I threw down my pipe and took hold of her kerchief. Her sisters all fled, but I held fast. It was as the wisewoman had said: without the kerchief, she could not leave. She turned herself into a lion first, and then a snake, but I remembered the old woman's words and I held on. She turned herself into a fire, shooting out flames in every direction, but still I held fast. At last she returned to her own form, and I took her home with me as my wife."

Sighs escaped from the lips of the men around the hearth. The peddler went on.

"I wore her kerchief around my belt and never let her have it. The next year we had a baby, and everything seemed fine. I thought she was mine forever. But one night," the peddler paused dramatically, "it was the festival of the blossoming of spring, and my wife was leading the dance. Everyone praised her beauty and grace. She told them the dance would be even finer if she had her very own kerchief to dance with."

The peddler shrugged his shoulders and rolled his eyes upward.

"What could I do? They all told me to give it to her. She danced one long dance for us, the most graceful anyone had ever seen and then, poof, she disappeared in a cloud. I never saw her again."

The peddler bowed his head, as if remembering a great sorrow.

"But she loves me still," he continued, a faint smile teasing the corners of his mouth. "She leaves me these, once a year, on our baby's birthday. And although they are precious to me as she is, I can be generous, too. I can share my wealth with others for a very small price."

By the end of the story, Lykaina's face had broken into a wide grin. Who else should she meet but her old traveling comrade, the peddler.

As the blue beads were passed from hand to hand, she approached the hearth and laid her hand on his shoulder.

"You still tell a fine story, friend. And no need to worry about blue beads flying out of their cages, eh?"

The peddler clasped her hand.

"If my eyes are not too faded and dim, then I am perceiving the wolf-woman singer of tales. Have you been to Sappho then and returned to tell the tale? Or did your ship's captain fail to answer the riddle of the gorgon of the sea and lose his boat in a storm? Come, shopkeeper," he turned to a man who was tending a large pot set on the edge of the hearth. "I have thirst from my story and hunger from the trail. My friend and I desire some victuals. And a bowl of milk for the goatling."

He led Lykaina over to a corner where two round stools were set on either side of a low wooden table. Lykaina lifted the kid off her shoulders and set it onto the dirt floor. It shook itself and wandered away to sniff at the men at the hearth.

"Tell me of your journey. Did you find her? Was she all you had hoped for and more? Have you returned to your homeland to bring us her songs? In my travels I heard of a new voice in Sappho's court, a voice almost as great as hers. Another Sappo, some said. I wondered if it were you. Ah, before we talk, we'll eat."

The shopkeeper set two steaming bowls in front of them along with a jug of wine and a half loaf of black bread. Lykaina pulled out her knife and carved off two hunks. She was as hungry as the kid who was back at her side, lapping greedily at a bowl of milk. She dipped her bread into the thick broth and ate. When she had wiped the bowl clean, she looked up at the peddler. He had planted his elbows on the table and was resting his chin on his hands, waiting.

"Yes," she said, "I found Sappho. And she was all I had hoped for and more. She is truly the tenth muse. Her voice, I could not have imagined such a voice."

"And did you learn from her? Is it really you they have been telling tales about? If so, why have you left her?"

"I do not know what tales you have heard, but yes, I did sing with her. I learned a new kind of song and. . . ." Lykaina stopped. No point in trying to fool the peddler. "I was like your nereid out of water. I could sing, but it wasn't my home. Those of Lesbos have their way of living, and I have mine."

"Then you have come home?"

"I have come home. The old woman I first sang for in Sparta was dying and needed me to help her on her way." Lykaina leaned back against the bare wall. "Now let me ask you a question. Have you been traveling these parts long?"

The peddler leaned back and half-closed his eyes.

"Long enough. I took sick at the Dionysian festival. I thought it was too much wine, but it didn't go away. I finally had to go to my brother's house. I was dizzy, I had no appetite, the pains turned me like a whirlwind. My brother brought a healer who said I was suffering from a wandering navel. She brought it back by tying a thread around my waist and twisting her spindle. It was gone in an instant."

The peddler drank from the wine jug.

"You asked not after my health, though, but if I had been here long."

"I am sorry for your ill health, but yes, I thought if you had been in these parts, you might have news of my brother, my father, my old grandfather. I am on my way to Anabretae to see them."

The peddler sat straight and looked at her, sadness in his eyes.

"You are traveling in the wrong direction, then. It has been two seasons' turnings since the old man, your grandfather, made his journey to the underworld. Your father took himself a new bride from one of the villages deep in the Mani. He divided the flock and took his share to her family. Your brother," he paused and scratched his beard, "I heard he joined flocks with his cousin. But then there was talk of bad blood between them. He left Anabretae, they say, and no one seems to know where he has gone. Your cousin took his family and left, perhaps into the deeper Mani, too. I don't know."

Lykaina's shoulders drooped.

"I am sorry for you," said the peddler. "You were looking for your family, and they are scattered to the winds."

Lykaina clenched her teeth. She looked down at the sleeping kid and thought of the child she had been. Born out of time and orphaned early. And orphaned, it seemed, again and again.

The hearthfire had burned low, and most of the men had left the wineshop. The proprietor came over to the table and laid the blue beads in front of the peddler.

"We liked your story, old man, but who would wear beads in this village? If you have tin pots, I could look at them."

"If you have a stable for us to bed down in tonight, tomorrow I will show you tin pots that will light up your eyes," said the peddler. "I've got every size and shape of a pot you could think of, made of the finest tin ever mined."

"Tomorrow, then. The stable's behind the store. Make yourselves comfortable."

Lykaina picked up the kid, and they made their way to the stable where the peddler's donkey was already chewing barley groats. Lykaina spread her cloak, curled up next to the kid, and slept.

At dawn the next morning, she left the old peddler asleep on his pile of straw. The cool air made frost of her breath as she stepped outside the stable. She drew her cloak around her tightly. The kid rested safely on her shoulders. She took the trail out of the village and forked to the left onto a smaller footpath that led up the mountain instead of to the next village on the ridge. No point in going to Anabretae, she thought. No home there now, no family. Some might remember me, but to what purpose? If they avoided me as a child because I was not of their blood, why would they open their arms now? Better to go and blow some notes to my childhood rocks and then return to Sparta.

She climbed steadily through the morning. A low cloud shrouded the mountain, spitting flakes of wet snow and blotting out the sun. When the trail gave out, she climbed from rock to rock, following the curve of the mountain. No trees up here to break the cold wind, not even a scraggly bush. Only the wet cloud pressed against her face, hiding even her feet from her.

At the top, there was no sound at all—no cry of a bird, no breath of wind. She set the kid down and watched it scramble over a rock. This is my homeland, she thought, yet I have no family here. And if there is no family, how can it be a homeland? She sat down on a frozen rock and tried to peer through the mist.

Why do I call this my homeland? she thought. An accident of birth placed me here. Or rather, the deliberation of a council of old men who put me on a mountain ledge. Still, it was here that I first learned to run, it was here that I found my first voice. I owe my life to a she-wolf of this lonely place.

She looked closely at the bare earth where a tiny white flower was trying to poke through the stones. Home is where the family is, she continued her thoughts, and I·have no family now. The she-wolf, the young mother of my brother, the old woman of Sparta—all gone, all taken into the black earth. All journeyed to the inner chambers of Hades while I still breathe the air above.

The cloud, holding tight around her, washed her face in cold rain. She drew her aulos from her belt and began to pierce the cloud with wails. With the mournful dirge still ringing from the other mountains, she sang.

> Oh, pitiless Persephone,
> you came to the wrong house,
> you came at the wrong time.
> You should have laid your hands on my Spartan mother
> before she gave birth to me,
> I who sit on this desolate mountain weeping tears,
> without family, without homeland.

The cloud lifted slightly. The kid, who had been nibbling at the bare ground around her feet, raised its head, sniffed the air, and scampered off. On a slope partway down the mountain, Lykaina saw two wild mountain goats pulling at the branches of a dried bush, an old scarred nanny with great ringed horns and a younger one with smaller nubs. The kid ran to the old nanny and put its nose up for a nuzzle. The nanny butted it away. The kid came back, now looking for an udder on the younger goat. The nanny moved sideways, and the kid was butted again, this time a little harder. The kid stood back for a moment, then approached once more, slowly this time, and stood a few feet away. The younger nanny shook her head and pawed the ground. The kid pranced in place. The old nanny lowered her head as if to charge, then lifted it and stood still. The kid approached gingerly and took a nibble from the branch hanging from the old nanny's mouth. All three goats remained motionless. They eyed one another, chewing. Then the nannies turned and trotted off, the kid following.

Born out of time, thought Lykaina, but you find your feet, little goat, you find a new nanny, you find a new home. She watched the three goats move off down the mountain slope. Suddenly she saw an image of Kissa, curled up in sleep, and Maia, arms raised to the moon in prayer. They are my family now, she thought. My home is where they are. We were not born to each other, but our lives are hewn out of the same hard rock. We are kin because our minds are kindred. We are family.

She stood up and stretched out her arms. The cloud around her separated and let a single ray of the pale winter sun fall onto her face. The wetness of the drizzle mingled with the tears on her cheeks, but in her heart she felt a strong root growing. She turned in the direction where the goats had disappeared and called out.

"Wear your new home well, little goat, and I will mine."

As the cloud lifted and floated away, she began to leap from rock to sunlit rock down the mountainside.

Back at Sparta late that afternoon, Lykaina found the city buzzing. Soldiers in full battle dress moved importantly around the agora. Helots followed in their footsteps carrying supplies. Mules stood patiently, their backs half-loaded, sheep and cattle lowed in their pens. Women and old men talked excitedly in groups. Children everywhere staged mock battles, shouting war cries and thwacking wooden sword against wooden sword. Passing through the agora, Lykaina suddenly found herself surrounded by a band of small children with shields larger than themselves and long bamboo spears.

"Stay, stranger," one of them cried. "Explain yourself. Are you Spartan or Messenian?" The boy edged toward her and poked her tentatively with his spear. The others, excited by his boldness, pressed closer.

"She can't be a Spartan, look at her funny tunic," said a little girl whose face was exaggerated into a frowning grimace.

None of the children was more than ten, most of them younger. Lykaina felt a sinking sensation in the pit of her stomach.

"And she's certainly not a helot, look how she looks us straight in the eye. So she must be a Messenian. Prepare to die, dog!"

The first boy pushed his bamboo spear a little harder into her side.

"Hold your spears, Spartan soldiers," Lykaina called out over the hubbub. "You are brave and fierce warriors, I can see. But I am not Messenian, I am from your own Taygetus Mountains, I—"

One of the smaller children at the outer edge of the group caught her eye.

"Niki!" she cried.

The girl narrowed her eyes and pushed her chin out. The other children turned their eyes onto her.

"Niki," Lykaina repeated. "Don't you remember me?"

"Who are you calling Niki?" jeered one of the boys. "There's no Niki in this army. Niki's a baby name. That girl's name is Eunika."

Niki's face darkened into a fierce frown, while her lower lip, still thrust out, trembled.

"Eunika, then," said Lykaina. "I knew her before she became a soldier, and we called her Niki. Come, Eunika, tell your brave fellows that I am friend not foe."

Lykaina tried to catch her eye, but Niki averted her face and looked instead across the square.

"There!" she suddenly cried. "There's a Messenian dog! After him!"

She sprinted after a small yellow hound. The others turned and took up the chase. The dog laid back its ears and ran. Lykaina stood for a moment, shaken. She had forgotten how rough the children's games were, how seriously they took themselves. And the sight of the new Niki as one of the pack made her tremble with anger. The child has seen no more than seven winters, she thought, yet she must deny those who nurtured her and gave her love. A good Spartan, she had developed a taste for blood.

Lykaina walked on, unable to erase Niki's twisted face from her mind. She slipped through the streets and up the steps to Arete's house. Arete was in the inner courtyard showing the young woman the soldier had brought how to knead bread. Her face broke into a smile when she saw Lykaina.

"Back so soon? I thought you would stay longer with your family."

"I have no family in Anabretae, they tell me. My grandfather has died, my father remarried into the deeper Mani. My brother, it seems, has fought with his cousin and both have disappeared."

She related the news in a monotone, her thoughts still on Niki. Best not to tell Arete of what had happened.

"Oh, Lykaina, I am sorry for you."

Arete put her arms around her and pulled her close. Lykaina leaned her head onto Arete's breast and felt an old sensation begin to push upward. Then she pulled back.

"It's all right," she said. "I miss the old man. I wish I had seen him before he died. My father and brother? I think I have not yet forgiven them, even though leaving their hearth was right for me."

"You know, Lykaina, this is your home now. The old woman even left you a parcel of land. The soldier was furious, but there was nothing he could do about it. She had it witnessed by three members of the council. It's that olive grove you always liked on the other side of the river."

Lykaina didn't answer. Coming down the mountain, her desire to take up her life with Maia and Kissa had grown with each footstep. Her encounter with Niki made her want to put the city of Sparta behind her for good. Yet she cared for Arete, and she knew Arete wanted her to stay.

"Come," said Arete, "the girl can finish the bread. Let's take a walk and look at your land. We'll avoid the agora. You must have seen all the war preparations. The planting's almost done, so they'll soon be off."

She picked up the baby, and they left the courtyard. Arete stepped in front as she always had, but now Lykaina felt resignation instead of anger. She followed her in silence down the wide steps toward the center of town. Before reaching the agora, Arete turned off onto the narrow street that led to the path to the river. The infant fell asleep on Arete's shoulder. At the riverbank, they watched the crescent moon rise over the river. Arete finally broke the silence.

"Do you remember standing here that other time, just before the soldiers came home? It was the crescent moon then, too. I remember thinking how complete my life felt with you and the old woman and the children. Then you left and then Niki and now the old woman. There seems to be nothing I can hold on to."

"Yes," said Lykaina. "Sappho told me once how life is like a flowing river. The riverbed is the same for everyone, she said, but the water is always changing. We never know when a new stream will enter the course and change our lives."

"Are you home for good then?" Arete's voice was hopeful. "I have missed you. I kept hoping you would come back. The soldier only stayed long enough to give me this one." She patted the infant's soft head. "Now he sleeps every night in the barracks. As soon as spring comes, the war will start. He'll be gone from the city entirely. I want so much for us to be together again like we were. You have no family now. Let me be your family."

Lykaina looked up at the slender moon.

"Who *was* my family anyway?" she asked, half to herself. "The woman who birthed me and let the council of old men abandon me to the mountains? The she-wolf who suckled me and pushed me out of the den when it was time for me to become one of the pack? The woman who took me in and then died birthing my brother? The old woman who taught me the secrets of herbs? The old man who taught me to open my mouth and sing to the farthest mountain? My father who sent me to Sparta, my brother who traded me to your soldier husband? Your grandmother who heard my song and sent me to Sappho?"

She stopped. How could she tell Arete what she had learned on the mountain this morning? How could she describe the two women she now called family?

"I am glad to see you, Arete. I have missed you, too. But no, I have another family now." She looked down at the hole her big toe was digging in the soft earth. "There are three of us," she said. "Maia is old and wise. She knows things I could not imagine anyone knowing. Kissa is a child still, but wise in her way. She speaks without words. She cannot hear, but she makes music with her body. She has rhythm in her heart. They are my family, Arete. I am more at home with them than I have been with anyone. My life is there now."

The night air was beginning to make them shiver. They turned to retrace their steps. Arete's voice, when she finally spoke, was low and plaintive.

"Niki is gone, and the boy is so different. He doesn't seem to need me. He sits and builds things or else goes with his father to the mess hall. Now with the old woman gone...." Arete's voice broke. "Oh, Lykaina, I am so lonely without you. I had so hoped you would come back to stay. It doesn't matter what my husband says. He will be gone soon anyway. Things could be like they were."

Lykaina put her arm around Arete's shoulder.

"I could ask you to come with me, but I know you won't leave here. Perhaps it's time you did what other Spartan women do—take this young girl your husband has brought you and teach her love, teach her the ways of Spartan womanhood. She can be your companion and after her, another one."

Arete leaned her head against Lykaina's arm as they climbed the stairs back to the house. Inside, she laid the baby onto a mat and turned to face Lykaina.

"You're right. I cannot leave my babies, even if they are to be taken from me. I cannot leave here. And you cannot stay, I know that." She reached out both her arms. "Come, Lykaina, for old times' sake, spend one last night with me. Let me taste you once more before you go your way, let me remember you with love."

Lykaina eased into her arms. There was too much parting in her life. Too many people she loved whose worlds were not her own. Too much loss.

She held Arete to her, her thoughts still swirling through her mind. The old woman's dying had made her feel the need to see the people of her early life. She had been looking for pieces of her past, pieces of her self that had started there in the mountains. But even when Fate cuts the thread, she knew that those who had been part of her before continued to rest inside her. The pieces she was leaving in these hills were matched by the pieces that remained in her. With each loss there was a gain, something inside her that remained connected to those she left behind.

"I will always carry you with me," she whispered, as they made their way to the inner room.

Chapter 13.
The beginning again

The waxing moon, still visible in the mid-morning sky, hovered over the Gulf of Hieras. It had been a long journey back. Winter seas and high winds had kept all ships safe in the harbor at Corinth, and spring had seemed forever in coming. The first boat to leave the Peloponnesian shores had meandered from island to island, trading wine for grain, grain for oil, oil for mastic. Now at last on the path from Mytilene to home, Lykaina brushed past brambles whose pale pink petals had already turned into hard green berries. At the familiar clearing, she stopped and peered through the dense green foliage, trying to catch a glimpse of the loom or the lean-to. Too thick for sight, she thought, pulling her aulos from her belt, but not for sound. She sent a covey of notes to penetrate every corner of the dark forest. And one grand one for you, Hecate, guardian of wayfarers, she prayed, as a single long wail reached toward the pale waiting moon.

Lykaina headed down the path and found Kissa waiting for her at the crossing where the rough track led up to the goat pasture. Kissa was as tall as Lykaina now, and small round breasts pushed at her tunic. She threw her arms around Lykaina, babbles of joy falling from her lips. At the edge of the clearing, Maia stood with warm and welcoming eyes in her leathery face. She folded Lykaina to her breast.

"You have returned."

"I have returned. This is my hearth."

Kissa touched Lykaina's arm. Lykaina turned and watched a dance unfold. Kissa's body, no longer the body of a child, told a story with a new womanly grace. She created a full moon in a sky full of stars; below it, warm spring breezes ruffled the gulf waters. She made a great shadow cross the moon's path and turn the golden circle dark. Then an offering. But what was the offering? puzzled Lykaina. Again and again Kissa cupped her hands beneath her vulva and then raised her arms toward the now fading crescent.

"Moondew." Maia's arm was still firm around Lykaina's waist. "She shed her first blood just as the earth's great shadow passed over the last winter moon. It meant good fortune. We knew you were coming home."

Lykaina looked from Maia to Kissa. "We were all born out of time," she whispered, "but we can have our own hearth."

She looked around the clearing. A mud-brick beehive squatted where the lean-to had once stood. A new loom made of tall saplings and strung with bright red warp threads waited for the shuttle. Down at the shore, the coracle lay half-beached, its stern bobbing in the water. Everything seemed in its place, as if waiting for her.

But no. Farther along the shore a second boat bobbed. Two broad-hipped women, carrying between them a basket filled with fish, walked toward the hearth. Lykaina looked at Maia.

"They have been waiting for your return. They came in their boat under the last full moon. They have poems they want you to hear."

The two women set their basket next to the firepit and folded their muscled arms across full breasts. Their brown faces, framed in long fat braids, set them off as family. The one with gray-streaked braids spoke, her nasal twang strange, but her words recognizable.

"We have crossed the seas from our native Crete," she said slowly and carefully, "to hear the song of the other Sappho. We learned of you one day when we were singing and mending our nets on the quay of Heraklion. A woman majestic as a whale with black skin and gold in her hair heard us. Her speech was like music, but we did not understand her words. A woman like her told us that we must seek you out and learn from you. I am Phillipa, and this is my daughter Ariadne."

The hearth expands, thought Lykaina. Aloud she said, "Well you have come, my sisters. I will be pleased to listen to your song."

Maia poked the coals in the firepit.

"We will celebrate your return with food first and then with poetry."

Green spring marched into brown summer. Now four of them performed at fairs and weddings. Sometimes the Cretan women sang short love couplets that perhaps likened the netting of a cuttlefish to the ensnaring of a loved one. Other times they sang long narratives about journeys by sea of long-ago heroines. Their voices echoed each other. Phillipa's line would be repeated by Ariadne, Ariadne's by Phillipa. Each had a small lyre whose strings were given voice by a tightly strung bow.

Just before the moon mysteries at Sigri, another woman found her way into the camp. This one was stocky and fair-haired; her features bore a marked resemblance to Kissa's. She was Thracian, she told them, and her father had sold her into the kitchen of a household in Mytilene. There she had heard talk of the woman in the woods whose song was supreme. She had slipped out of the house every night to go to the waterfront and rent her body to sailors until she had earned enough to buy her freedom. Then she had taken her Thracian cymbals and searched until she had found the beehive hut.

When the slopes of Mount Olympos started to take on the bright colors that heralded summer's end, two sisters arrived from a farming village on the other side of Lesbos. They had heard Lykaina at a festival. Since their marrying age had been approaching without any hope of dowries from their family's scraggly fields, they had persuaded their father to let them journey to the city in search of work. They had come directly to Lykaina's hearth instead.

Shortly before the first winter rain, a young woman from Lemnos joined them. She, too, had been of marrying age but, unlike the sisters, she had an adequate dowry provided for her by her father. He had, in fact, already selected the groom, a handsome young man with a honeyed tongue who did not believe that the art of poetry should be sullied by the voice of a woman. She had taken a silver cup from her dowry to pay her passage to Lesbos and there inquired after the woman in the hills whose voice was near equal to the great Sappho's.

One by one the women joined the hearth, each bringing with her a gift of song struggling to shape itself freely. Each time the hearth expanded, a new hut sprang up in the trees. By day, the women fished or foraged or turned milk into cheese; at night, the firelight burned on singing faces, the dark woods echoed with fledgling poems. It was not an easy winter. Cold rains often prevented the boats from leaving the shore; snow made the paths slippery and grazing hard to find. But once every mooncycle a donkey loaded with cheeses and weavings was led out of the clearing bound for the market in Mytilene. And whenever the cold was too penetrating, a dance pumped warm blood into numb fingers and toes.

Lykaina's market turn came just when the trees were promising new buds. She and Kissa and two loaded donkeys set off up the trail before daybreak. Surrounded once again by the bright colors and tantalizing smells of the agora, Lykaina breathed deeply and sighed. She loved Mytilene. She loved the women with their graceful bearings, the men gathered in groups to practice the fine art of conversation, the children rolling hoops and throwing balls. She left Kissa and the donkey loaded with Maia's weavings on the square with other weavers and made her way toward the row of cheese vendors where she found a space next to a woman presiding over a pyramid of large yellow cheeses. An infant fretted on the woman's hip, a toddler kept trying to reach the topmost cheese of the pyramid. Lykaina hung her balance scale from the donkey's harness and began to call out her wares. A young man asked her about the bag of soft white cheese that hung from the donkey's saddle.

"It's from my cleverest nanny," she told him, "the one that always finds the sweetest clover. I was saving it for a special customer, but for you...."

Her eye caught sight of a pair of women strolling arm in arm through the agora. One was very young, her exquisitely formed face turning one direction and then another to take in the sights of the marketplace. The other woman was short and dark and—Sappho! Lykaina watched the two women glide through her range of vision and lose themselves in the crowd. She gave the man his change and mechanically turned to her next customer. The sun had rotated through many seasons since she had last seen Sappho. Yet whenever a perfectly formed phrase came to her, one that expressed exactly the thought required with the grace and beauty of a fresh-blooming rose, then an image of Sappho would spread like a transparent veil over her mind, letting her know that such a phrase had been shaped in part by the woman who had been her whole life for that brief interlude.

The sun was almost at its zenith when she sold her last cheese and began to pack up the donkey. Next to her the woman's husband, returned from the wine shop, berated his wife for not taking in enough money. The infant howled on her hip, the toddler clung to her knees sniveling. Lykaina left the quarreling family and threaded her way through the crowd in search of Kissa. As she entered the weavers' area, she felt a touch on her arm.

"Wait."

One word, perfectly shaped, golden in tone. Lykaina turned and looked down at the diminutive Sappho. The dark face was as arresting as the day she had first seen it. A few more wrinkles at the edge of the black eyes, perhaps, and a single strand of gray that seemed to have eluded the hairdresser's dyes. But it was Sappho, alive and brilliant as the evening star that makes all the others seem lusterless. The young woman who had been hanging on her arm earlier was nowhere in sight.

"Will you walk with me?" Sappho was saying. "Will you say a few words to me? I saw you with your cheeses, and I knew I could not let the morning pass without speaking. Have you time?"

Sappho's hand rested on Lykaina's forearm. Lykaina clasped it with her own and looked into Sappho's eyes.

"I saw you before from a distance. Let me find Kissa. Then we can talk."

Holding Sappho's hand, Lykaina opened a path for them through the crowd. They came upon Kissa standing patiently beside her donkey, the weavings all sold. Sappho embraced her and kissed both her cheeks.

"She is a young woman now," Sappho exclaimed, holding her at arms' length and looking at her. "Clearly she thrives in her life with you in the woods."

"I have come to love her like a daughter," responded Lykaina. "She means more to me now than anyone."

The three women made their way out of the crowded marketplace and down the stone steps to the bridge that joined the two parts of the city. Sappho stopped and stood at the rail. Lykaina and Kissa came to stand beside her. Lykaina remembered the first time she had looked out at the boats in this harbor—her first visit with Sappho when every word that fell from Sappho's lips had seemed golden. The sound of her voice still fell on her ears like sweet wine into a crystal glass.

"In my kitchen," Sappho was saying, "they tell of a wonderful poet who has gathered around her others like her—women of the mountains and women of the sea. They never speak when they know that I am listening, but I have stood silently outside the door sometimes. They say she sings about people like themselves. They especially like the song about the nursemaid's daughter who rides a flying Amazon horse into the battlefields of Troy."

Lykaina smiled at the thought of Sappho eavesdropping on her kitchen slaves. "It is a poem that always seems to reach the ears," she said, pleased that her song, like a pebble dropped in still waters, sent its message outward in ever-widening circles.

"I would like to come and visit you," said Sappho. "I would like to see you teaching others as I taught you. Will you permit me?"

By now they had left the bridge and were climbing the street that led to Sappho's house. The streambed running beside the steps was full of clear rushing water; the flowers of the oleanders beside it were still furled in their green buds. Lykaina tried to imagine Sappho at her hearthfire. There were no finely carved chairs with soft cushions, no mosaic floors. And the poems that she and the others sang were not the carefully wrought gemstones that brought praise in Sappho's house—they were larger and more robust, they told of adventures in which the heroines might be slaves or peasants, their images might be oxen drawing a silver plow or a golden net drawing in thousands of fishes.

"You are always welcome at my hearth," she replied. "We will be honored by your visit. We lead a simple life, though. My home is not like yours."

They were standing in front of Sappho's red door.

"Do you think I care only for luxury?" asked Sappho. "The pain of losing you still lingers in my heart. Only the thought that you are happier now makes your going away bearable. But I must come and see for myself. And I must hear your new poetry. If what I taught you here is still part of it, then I will be happy. If it is better than what you sang for me, then I can ask for no more. I will come tomorrow evening."

Sappho embraced her and disappeared into the house. Lykaina stood for a moment, savoring the touch of Sappho's kiss on her cheek. Then she held out her hand to the waiting Kissa, and together they ran up the street.

After the others had gone to bed, Lykaina approached the beehive hut. Standing outside, she admired the clean cut of the gray mud bricks, how each row became smaller as the walls curved into the roof. Maia and Kissa built the hut just after Kissa's first moonblood, when they had known that Lykaina was coming home. After she had arrived, the three of them built the second hut, round like the beehive but made of reeds from the shore and topped with a straw thatch. The other huts were built one by one as the other women arrived.

Lykaina ducked her head and stepped under the carved lintel, wondering how Maia would react to news of Sappho's visit. Inside, the hut was lit only by the red glow of coals in the three-legged brazier set in the middle of the room. Maia was seated on a low stool, sorting yarn. Lykaina sat down cross-legged on the hard-packed mud floor and looked across the fire. Maia's weathered face was fierce as always, but the piercing look of her black eyes was also soft. Lykaina drew the rich fragrance of the thyme-fed fire into her nostrils. Just as she was about to open her mouth, Maia spoke.

"When is she coming?"

As long as Lykaina had known Maia, she still found her foreknowledge of things to come unsettling.

"Tomorrow," she replied, "in the evening, after dinner. She wants to listen to the poetry."

The fire hissed. Maia stood up and tucked the yarn into a basket.

"And your mind has wandered into the mists." She held out her hand. "Come. Let us look into the night air and see whether her coming marks the beginning of good or bad things for you."

Lykaina trailed her out of the hut. The almost-full moon was blanketed by a bank of clouds. The gulf was dark and forbidding. They started up the trail that led to the waterfall and the cache where Sappho's letter still lay hidden. As they turned off onto the narrow trail that led to the sanctuary, a whoosh of night air close by her left shoulder told her that an owl had fluttered by. Maia stopped, listening to hear where the bird had landed.

"The first sign," she said, "and a good one."

They entered the sanctuary. Maia built a fire in front of the altar. As it started to burn, she placed a handful of laurel leaves onto it.

"Breathe deeply," she said, taking both of Lykaina's hands into her own. "Breathe deeply and look carefully at what you see."

Lykaina stood still, her eyes closed, and breathed in the laurel-scented smoke. The clouds of the night sky seemed to have filled the inside of her head as well. She felt as if a storm were rising inside her. Maia, still holding her hands, began to speak in a low monotone.

"In the springtime, when the Great Mother sends thunder to move the heavens, everything sprouts and grows. The farmer who pushes the wooden plow through the black earth does not think of the harvest. The earth, torn apart by the blade of the plow, does not complain, knowing that out of the furrows plants will grow, and the Great Mother will heal the rending. What belongs to us cannot be lost, even if we throw it away."

As Maia spoke, the clouds inside Lykaina's head began to lift, revealing a lone mountain rising into the heavens.

"Each evening," Maia continued, "when darkness falls, the light pulls back, waiting for another day. However high a mountain rises, yearning to reach the heavens, the heaven is always beyond it, the mountain is always alone. When the time comes to turn back from a path you have chosen, the light that makes the way clear is inside you. Your feet are cautious, feeling to make sure there are no stones in your pathway. But even the bird that tries to fly before it is fledged and falls to the earth can learn to fly if its mother does not abandon it."

Lykaina approached the mountain and saw the stone well of Sappho's garden. Its gray stones were beginning to take on a pinkish tint of the sunrise.

"The wellspring of the spirit," Maia continued, "is inside you. Wherever the path takes you, however much the mountain changes, the source remains the same. If the rope is long enough, you can draw up the water and drink. The Great Mother replenishes."

Lykaina could hear a thundering coming from inside the well. She peered over the edge and looked down. Far below she saw water churning, splashing great waves against the inner walls of the well. Leaning farther over, she saw it was not waves of water but waves of dust kicked up by a band of stampeding horses, their eyes rolled back in fear, white sweat flecking their flanks. Then she was running with them, letting the wind comb her mane, feeling the solid ground under her hooves. The lead mare—black with gray mane and gray tail, a green stripe down her back—turned the pack, lifting her feet high in a graceful canter, arching her neck to catch the first rays of the morning sun.

All movement stopped. There, where the plain met the mountain, a small horse stood still, the gold of the sun reflected in its shining coat. The black mare left the others and approached it gingerly. Two noses reached out to touch. Far away, Lykaina could hear thunder rumbling in the mountain. A cool summer rain had begun to fall, washing the dust from her back, cooling the sweat on her flanks. Maia's voice continued its drone in her ear.

"When thunder and rain end a summer's drought, the air is cleared, the plants renewed. New shoots push up. All obstacles to growth are washed away. The goddess inside each blade of grass rises to meet herself."

Lykaina opened her eyes. The strong smoke still hung in the air, but the last coal had turned to gray ash. Maia's face was stern, but her eyes were warm. Lykaina let herself be pulled forward into Maia's strong embrace. Maia held her tightly as the last clap of thunder rolled away, the soft rain still washing the inside of Lykaina's head. The two horses nuzzled each other's necks. Then, their heads raised high, each pranced backward a few steps. Moisture glistening on their flanks, they turned and cantered in opposite directions.

Still holding hands, Maia and Lykaina left the sanctuary. At the beehive hut, they embraced. Lykaina turned away and hurried to her own hut. In the darkness, she slipped in beside the sleeping Kissa.

Kissa was the first to see her. They were all sitting at the blazing hearth, eating a cuttlefish stew and listening to the Cretan women sing to the accompaniment of their tiny bow-drawn lyres. Kissa slipped away unnoticed while the others listened to the tale of Scylla, daughter of Hecate, kept prisoner by her father in a tower. After her father's city was sacked, the mother Phillipa sang, Scylla jumped into the sea. Her father's soul, the daughter Ariadne sang back, swooped down in the shape of an eagle.

○

Suddenly the song stopped. Sappho, her dark curls held in place by a crown of violets, stood at the edge of the circle with Kissa. Although Lykaina had forewarned them, the women were embarrassed and speechless in Sappho's presence. Kissa dipped a portion of the stew into a bowl and held it out to Sappho. Lykaina guided her to the chair she had spent the morning carving.

"Sappho, whose poetry has delighted you all," she said, "honors us with a visit. She wishes to hear our poems. We must welcome her to our hearth."

The women looked at one another apprehensively.

"Word has reached the city of the songs in the woods," said Sappho. "You are kind to accept me into your circle."

Her flutelike voice made the women relax. Sappho held the bowl of stew with both hands on her lap and smiled at the Cretan women.

"I would be grateful if you would continue your song about Scylla. What happened after her father's soul attacked her?"

The two women picked up their lyres and began to play again, tentatively at first, then with more vigor. Small bells attached to their bows accented the music with silver rhythms.

"She became a great purple cuttlefish," Phillipa sang, "a cuttlefish with the whimper of a newborn pup."

"From her great rock in the straits she seizes sailors from their ships," sang back Ariadne. "Her twelve tentacles catch them, her six heads crush their bones."

By the time the song had ended, Sappho seemed to be part of the circle. One by one, the others gave her the gift of their song. When everyone had sung, Sappho turned to Lykaina.

"You have gathered around you poets whose words reach into human hearts, whose voices are strong." She turned to the women. "It is clear that you sing for the joy of singing, that your poetry rises out of a place that cannot be silenced. Your songs have already touched many people. I am grateful that you have allowed my ears to hear."

The women kept their eyes lowered but let the corners of their mouths quiver into modest smiles. Sappho turned back to Lykaina.

"And your song, my Lykaina," she said, "where have the muses taken your song?"

Lykaina looked out over the radiant waters of the gulf. The full moon hung high in the sky. She stood up and put her aulos to her lips. As she played she moved, as if following the notes toward the shore. The music rose on the late-night breeze and floated out over the water. From the mountains on the far shore, echoes returned to join with new sounds. She played for a long time, lost in the music yet still aware that the other women had left the two of them alone, that Sappho was standing a few steps behind her. She broke off playing and sang.

The moon dropped her face into a crystal fountain
where a wild dove, washing her feathers, put it onto her wings.

Lykaina let the wild dove soar with the music. She sent her circling around the mountain and into a dark ravine, over the waters of the wide blue sea, and along the rocks of the shore. In a series of falling notes, she brought her to rest at last on the branch of an alder where, ruffling her moon-beamed feathers, the wild dove sang between heaven and earth.

Her words still hanging in the night air, she began to walk along the shore. Sappho kept pace with her. Small waves lapped the rocks. The horned owl that usually hooted outside Maia's hut seemed to be moving from tree to tree in the woods behind them. Sappho touched Lykaina's arm lightly.

"You have come into your own, Lykaina. You have taken what you brought to me and what I gave you, and you have gone beyond. You are a poet without peer."

Lykaina let her hand slip into Sappho's.

"Each time a phrase comes out perfectly," she said softly, "I think of you. Each time a new image rises to meet a thought, I feel it coming from a place inside me where you still are."

"Where I still long to be more than a memory."

Close by them a fish flashed silver out of the water, caught the moon's rays, and disappeared with a quiet splash.

"We live in two worlds," Lykaina said slowly and evenly, "two worlds that cannot touch one another. You can visit mine, and I can visit yours, but we cannot cross each other's thresholds without putting on the garb of a stranger. There is no place for our love to blossom, no common ground. The rain that refreshes your world is only a cloud in mine. The sun that warms my earth is only a reflection in yours."

Sappho squeezed her hand. They stopped walking. The moon spread a broad reflection on the water in front of them. A lone sea mew glided along the moonpath, its low cry piercing the night air. It settled onto the waves and was joined there by another.

"Perhaps one day," said Sappho, her arm encircling Lykaina's waist, "when we are as old and as wise as your Maia, we will find ourselves in another world, different from either of the ones we live in now. Perhaps then our love will blossom fully. And each of us could bring into this new world only those things that would fit. Nothing else would matter."

They watched the two sea mews lift their wings and fly away into the darkness.

"When we are as old and as wise as Maia," responded Lykaina, "it

O

may not matter that our worlds are different."

There seemed no more words to speak. The two women stood together, each reluctant to let go of the other. Eventually the full moon paled as streaks of dawn began to rake the eastern sky. They turned and walked in silence back to the camp. Maia was already hovered over her fire, brewing her nettle tea. Sappho let go of Lykaina and squatted beside the fire, her gown trailing in the dirt.

"It is your hand that has guided her to greatness," she said, her fingers touching Maia's shoulder.

Maia lifted her face and looked into Sappho's eyes.

"The greatness was within her. She has looked to others, but the spirit inside her has been her guide."

Sappho leaned over and kissed Maia's weathered cheek. Then she rose and hurried down to the shore where a small ferryboat waited. Lykaina caught her as she passed and held her tightly.

"Our paths diverge. May they cross again."

They both let go. Lykaina watched until the boat had carried Sappho out of sight. The bleating of goats above her told her that Kissa was already on her way to the upper pasture. She tightened her belt around her aulos and ran to catch up.

Notes

The epigraph and the poems on pages 2, 110, and 159 are Mary Barnard's translations of Sappho's poetry; the poems on pages 109, 142-3, and 189 are Willis Barnstone's translations. Fragments of Sappho's poetry that are embedded in conversations throughout the novel are my own renderings of the literal translations found in *Sappho of Lesbos* by Arthur Weigall and *Songs of Sappho* by Marion Miller and David Robinson.

The remaining poems are my translations and transformations of modern Greek folksongs. The play fragment that appears in Chapter 10 is my translation of a scene from one of Andonis Mollas' modern Greek shadow plays. I inject modern Greek folklore into a novel about ancient Greece because, in the realm of oral literature at least, time moves slowly. The germ of this novel, in fact, was watered by my recognition of images found in modern Greek folksong that are markedly similar to some of those found in Sappho's poetry.

My interpretations of Greek myth, ritual, Great Goddess lore, and oral poetry were greatly influenced by Barbara Walker's *The Woman's Encyclopedia of Myths and Secrets* and *The Woman's Dictionary of Symbols and Sacred Objects*; Monica Sjöö and Barbara Mor's *The Great Cosmic Mother*; Buffie Johnson's *Lady of the Beasts*; Margaret Alexiou's *The Ritual Lament in Greek Tradition*; Robert Graves' *The Greek Myths*; Walter Burkert's *Greek Religion*; J. C. Lawson's *Modern Greek Folklore and Ancient Greek Religion*; and Albert Lord's *Singer of Tales*.

Other titles from Firebrand Books include:

The Big Mama Stories by Shay Youngblood/$8.95

A Burst Of Light, Essays by Audre Lorde/$7.95

Diamonds Are A Dyke's Best Friend by Yvonne Zipter/$9.95

Dykes To Watch Out For, Cartoons by Alison Bechdel/$6.95

Eye Of A Hurricane, stories by Ruthann Robson/$8.95

The Fires Of Bride, A Novel by Ellen Galford/$8.95

A Gathering Of Spirit, A Collection by North American Indian Women edited by Beth Brant *(Degonwadonti)*/$9.95

Getting Home Alive by Aurora Levins Morales and Rosario Morales/$8.95

Good Enough To Eat, A Novel by Lesléa Newman/$8.95

Humid Pitch, Narrative Poetry by Cheryl Clarke/$8.95

Jonestown & Other Madness, Poetry by Pat Parker/$5.95

The Land Of Look Behind, Prose and Poetry by Michelle Cliff/$6.95

A Letter To Harvey Milk, Short Stories by Lesléa Newman/$8.95

Letting In The Night, A Novel by Joan Lindau/$8.95

Living As A Lesbian, Poetry by Cheryl Clarke/$6.95

Making It, A Woman's Guide to Sex in the Age of AIDS by Cindy Patton and Janis Kelly/$3.95

Metamorphosis, Reflections On Recovery, by Judith McDaniel/$7.95

Mohawk Trail by Beth Brant *(Degonwadonti)*/$6.95

Moll Cutpurse, A Novel by Ellen Galford/$7.95

More Dykes To Watch Out For, Cartoons by Alison Bechdel/$7.95

The Monarchs Are Flying, A Novel by Marion Foster/$8.95

My Mama's Dead Squirrel, Lesbian Essays on Southern Culture by Mab Segrest/$8.95

Politics Of The Heart, A Lesbian Parenting Anthology edited by Sandra Pollack and Jeanne Vaughn/$11.95

Presenting. . .Sister NoBlues by Hattie Gossett/$8.95

A Restricted Country by Joan Nestle/$8.95

Sanctuary, A Journey by Judith McDaniel/$7.95

Sans Souci, And Other Stories by Dionne Brand/$8.95

Shoulders, A Novel by Georgia Cotrell/$8.95

The Sun Is Not Merciful, Short Stories by Anna Lee Walters/$7.95

Tender Warriors, A Novel by Rachel Guido deVries/$7.95

This Is About Incest by Margaret Randall/$7.95

The Threshing Floor, Short Stories by Barbara Burford/$7.95

Trash, Stories by Dorothy Allison/$8.95

The Women Who Hate Me, Poetry by Dorothy Allison/$5.95

Words To The Wise, A Writer's Guide to Feminist and Lesbian Periodicals & Publishers by Andrea Fleck Clardy/$3.95

Yours In Struggle, Three Feminist Perspectives on Anti-Semitism and Racism by Elly Bulkin, Minnie Bruce Pratt, and Barbara Smith/$8.95

You can buy Firebrand titles at your bookstore, or order them directly from the publisher (141 The Commons, Ithaca, New York 14850, 607-272-0000).

Please include $1.75 shipping for the first book and $.50 for each additional book.

A free catalog is available on request.